THERESA HOWES lives in London, and has a background as an actor. Her work has been long-listed for the Mslexia Novel Award, the Bath Novel Award, The Caledonia Novel Award, The Lucy Cavendish College Prize, and the BBC National Short Story Award.

The Secrets We Keep

THERESA HOWES

ONE PLACE. MANY STORIES

HQ
An imprint of HarperCollins*Publishers* Ltd
1 London Bridge Street
London SE1 9GF

www.harpercollins.co.uk

Harper Ireland
Macken House, 39/40 Mayor Street Upper, Dublin 1
D01 C9W8

This paperback edition 2022

2

First published in Great Britain by
HQ, an imprint of HarperCollins*Publishers* Ltd 2022

Copyright © Theresa Howes 2022

Theresa Howes asserts the moral right to be
identified as the author of this work.
A catalogue record for this book is
available from the British Library.

ISBN: 9780008547882

Printed and bound in the UK using 100% Renewable Electricity
by CPI Group (UK) Ltd, Croydon, CR0 4YY

To Mum and Dad
for always being there.

Chapter 1

June 1944

It would only take the crack of a twig to give Marguerite away as she crept through the park in the dead of night. Even the unexpected crunch of leaves beneath her feet would be enough to reveal her position, but still she continued, bravely placing one foot in front of the other as she ventured into the unknown darkness.

The Allied air raids had continued along the Cote d'Azur until the early hours, leaving the night thick with the smell of cordite and distant fires. The bombs, scattered with abandon by the RAF Lancasters, had turned over the beaches and destroyed homes, as if the people weren't suffering enough under the German Occupation.

She'd waited for the all-clear before slipping out, cycling through the least trodden streets in the quietest part of the town, clinging to her breath as if the release of it would somehow betray her. It was long after curfew and she'd taken a risk, keeping her head down while she locked her bicycle to a lamp post, her feet brisk as she slipped through a gap in the fence and made her way to the remotest corner of the park. Once a destination for lovers' trysts it was now a place of quiet abandon. Since the

Occupation, not even the greatest passion was worth the danger of being caught out after curfew by a German patrol.

Now, Marguerite waited at the appointed place, the pine cones giving way under her shoes like the moulding carcasses of rats as she shuffled from foot to foot, trying to shake off the cold and the fear, a shadow among the shadows in her black mackintosh, her hair shrouded in a crow-black scarf. With her head down and her eyes lowered she could have been anyone of any age, her war-starved figure giving away a girlishness as much as it could have indicated an old woman.

The person she was there to meet wouldn't try to recognise her. In this case, it would be the opposite. This was how things went. When anonymity could be the key to survival, it was too dangerous even to exchange glances. A brown envelope, passing from one gloved hand to another, was all that was needed. Under these circumstances, there'd be no mistaking anyone or their purpose when that was what they were there for. At this time of night, and in this occupied land, who else would be brave enough to venture out and with what intent?

In the event of a bombing raid, it was a known rule that a pre-arranged meeting would be rescheduled to take place exactly one hour after the all-clear sounded. And so here she was, waiting. She'd gambled that the enemy patrols wouldn't be out so soon after a raid. For all their bluster, the Germans were cowards when it came to facing the threat of Allied bombs. This was what she told herself as she listened for footsteps breaking the silence in a way that wouldn't be noticed by anyone apart from those who were alert to them.

But this time she'd made the wrong guess. Suddenly, a beam of light swept the ground in front of her, barely missing the corner where she hid, the quiet broken by the bark of salivating Alsatians, their throats constrained as they pulled at the lead.

Marguerite snatched a breath. Somewhere to the right, she saw a tall shadow and heard the slip of a shoe unbalanced by the unexpected angle of a sharp stone. At the same moment, a burst of rough German voices demanded to know who was there. It was the dogs, smelling her fear, that had alerted them.

She held herself rigid against a tree, defying the swaying arc of light from their torch as it swung across the low growing shrubs and the empty flower beds. Surely the soldiers wouldn't risk their pristine uniforms climbing through the overgrowth of thorns or dirty their boots among the decay of last year's leaves? Still the dogs barked, the sound sharp and insistent as they stood on their hind legs, straining at the lead and refusing to give up.

The tall shadow moved closer, black-coated and stealthy in the darkness. Whoever it was, it wasn't her contact, whose small silhouette always appeared in the shape of a woman. This was unmistakably a man.

There it went again, the glare of the searchlight, getting nearer with each sweep. Marguerite swallowed her fear, feeling the soft crack of the envelope tucked in the waistband of her skirt. If they took one more step, she'd no longer be in shadow. She'd no longer be able to pretend she was part of the undergrowth.

The soldiers were so close now she could smell their cheap hair oil. She could pick out the sound of the dogs' claws scratching the earth to gain traction. It would only be a matter of seconds before one of the animals caught the movement of her lips, the rare blink of her eyelids.

And in that passing second, as the German voices shouted, the man in the black coat stepped in front of her, blocking her from the sight of the soldiers. He was a good head and shoulders taller, his body looming large as he tried to hide her. His gesture could have been an assault, but Marguerite had no choice but to trust him.

'Kiss me.'

Instantly, she felt the dizzying press of his lips against hers, the rigid form of his lean body creating a barricade between her and the approaching soldiers as he wrapped himself around her. All at once the dogs were silent, the tread of the soldiers' boots vanished as the world spun, and all she could hear was the rapid beating of her own heart, all she could feel was the heat of the stranger's body as his passion overwhelmed her.

But there was no denying the presence of the three soldiers or their jeers as they enjoyed the spectacle. Eventually, the stranger stepped back and looked over his shoulder at the uniformed men standing only a few steps away, their torch focused on Marguerite's face as she gasped for breath.

Faced with the aggressors, the stranger coolly took out a hand-kerchief and wiped Marguerite's red lipstick from his mouth before pushing it back into his pocket, never once letting go of her.

'What are you doing out after curfew?'

The smallest of the soldiers barked the question, his diminutive stature inspiring his vitriol. The German army were so desperate for soldiers these days that even the feeblest seemed to pass muster.

The stranger pulled Marguerite closer into his body. 'Isn't it obvious what we're doing?'

The soldier laughed, skimming his boots along the ground. 'You know I should arrest you for this?'

'For what? For making love to a beautiful woman? When did that become a crime?'

The soldier looked Marguerite up and down in a way that made her skin crawl, but it could have been worse. He could have insisted on searching her.

'Is there anything else we can help you with?'

He was pushing his luck with the soldiers, but after the way he'd come to her rescue, she'd forgive him anything.

The soldier considered Marguerite as if she were a carcass in a butcher's window. 'I'll let you off this time. Go home to bed. You're making the rest of us jealous.'

Before Marguerite could promise to obey them, the soldiers disappeared. The black-coated stranger, who she now thought of as her saviour, released his grip, the tension in his body finally easing as they found themselves alone.

4

'Are you alright?'

Even in the blackout, she could see the startling blue of his eyes, the thick sweep of hair beneath his fedora.

'Thank you for coming to my rescue.'

'I think we rescued each other.'

The night air felt colder as he stepped away from her, creating a respectable distance between them. Suddenly, he was the polite stranger he was meant to be and not a passionate lover at all.

'Given the circumstances, it's probably best we don't introduce ourselves.'

She nodded, pushing down the disappointment that he didn't want to know more about her, that he could kiss her with such intensity and pretend it had never happened.

'It's not safe for you to be out alone. Will you let me walk you home?'

They left the park, crossing the road to where Marguerite had chained her bicycle to a lamp post.

'I'll be fine from here.'

He'd never tell her what he was doing in the park at such an hour and she knew better than to ask. He could be anyone from anywhere, and not knowing who he was had to be unimportant. They'd saved each other when it mattered and that was all there was.

He looked left and right, listening for the sounds of soldiers in the blackout, but the street was deserted. 'Are you sure?'

She nodded, trying to show she was more certain than she felt.

He lifted his hat and said goodnight, his eyes lingering on her for longer than was necessary as she climbed onto her bicycle and pushed down hard on the pedal.

Gathering speed, she continued along the street, frustrated that her mission had been thwarted, wondering if the stranger was still there and not daring to look back, not daring to betray her desperate need to know if he was still watching her.

Chapter 2

Marguerite was leaning her bicycle against the stone wall of the old farmhouse when Simone appeared at the front door, her eyes wide in the moonlight.

'Is everything alright? You've been gone so long.'

'I wasn't able to complete the handover. I was almost caught by a German patrol.'

'Were you followed?'

Marguerite pressed her finger to her lips, urging silence as she ushered Simone inside. Although their nearest neighbours were five hundred metres down the lane, it didn't do to discuss these matters where there was the slightest chance someone could overhear. Even in this isolated place, uncertainty had led to denunciations over the smallest things; the keeping of hens, the perceived possession of an abundance of fruit on the apple trees.

It was a relief to be in the cool dark embrace of the old farmhouse. Marguerite took her shoes off at the door, instantly soothed by the chill of the stone flags beneath her feet. The house had stood for over two hundred years, giving it an atmosphere of solidity and steadfastness that always reassured her. For a decade, it had been her refuge and a place of inspiration for her paintings.

Over time, her soul had become as entwined with it as the wild rosemary that grew in clumps in every dry corner of the garden.

She closed the door quietly and gave Simone a hug, reassuring her that she hadn't been followed.

'You look tired.'

'I couldn't go to bed until I knew you were safe.'

The continual strain of the war had added years to Simone's beautiful face. Her hair was now more grey than black, her eyes sunken behind her broad cheekbones, and despite the freshness of the Mediterranean air, there was a pallor to her complexion, brought on by enforced hunger and her constantly troubled soul.

They were eighteen years old when they first met. Marguerite had been a student at the Slade School of Art and Simone had been a nanny to the children of one of her tutors. Soon they were inseparable, gadding about London during the 1920s – Simone with her dark-eyed beauty and Marguerite, much fairer, and a good head and shoulders taller than her friend. They were like chalk and cheese as the English would say, and yet for all their differences, theirs was a friendship built on a meeting of hearts and minds, on the habit of shared laughter and trust.

Simone opened the door to the sitting room that led off from the kitchen, indicating the shadow of a sleeping body on the sofa.

'Jeanne is still here. She fell asleep hours ago and I didn't have the heart to wake her. She's exhausted. It breaks my heart, knowing the baby is growing inside her and we can't get the right foods to nourish her.'

Jeanne was the daughter of Simone's friend, Nicole. Her husband, Paul, had been taken to a forced labour camp in Germany, leaving Jeanne alone during her pregnancy, although with Simone, Marguerite and Nicole looking after her, Jeanne was never truly alone.

Simone rearranged the blanket where it had slipped from Jeanne's body and closed the door quietly behind her. Returning to the kitchen, she retrieved the last of the daily bread ration from the larder and handed it to Marguerite, encouraging her to eat.

'There's a new padlock on your studio door. The key is hidden in the false drawer in the dresser. You'll need to use the handle of a coffee spoon to prise it open. It should only be a temporary measure.'

Marguerite broke the bread in two and handed half of it back. She couldn't eat when Simone was starving. 'There was no need to go to so much trouble. There's nothing in there anyone would want to steal.'

Marguerite's art studio was in the old timber barn that stood to the right of the house. These days, it was the only place she could escape the war. When she stepped inside and closed the door, nothing else in the world existed.

Simone's eyes betrayed something was wrong. Marguerite grabbed a coffee spoon from beside the sink and used it to lever open the false drawer inside the dresser. Once she'd retrieved the key, she marched to her studio in her bare feet.

Simone ran after her, whispering through a mouthful of bread. 'It's nothing to worry about. It'll only be for a short time. Nobody will find out.'

It was an old padlock and it was a minute before Marguerite was able to negotiate the key in the rusty hole.

'Don't open the door too widely, Marguerite.'

Marguerite swallowed the last of her bread and stepped inside, pulling open the blinds that covered the windows at one end of the building and throwing a bar of moonlight across the room.

Simone followed, reclosing the blinds, but not before Marguerite spotted a rough blanket that had been used to cover something in one corner. Marguerite cursed as she pulled the blanket, revealing what was hidden beneath it.

'Is this Armand's doing?'

'I'm sorry, Marguerite. I didn't give him permission to do this. He promised they'll be gone by tomorrow morning. He needed somewhere to hide them quickly. There was a tip-off that the garage where they were being stored was about to be searched.'

Marguerite stared at the cache of guns, the pile of ammunition that had been hidden beneath the blanket.

'Where did he get them?'

'From the Italian soldiers. Some of the guns were abandoned in the streets when they retreated from the advancing German army last September, others were offered to anyone who would take them.'

'And they knew to offer them to Armand?'

Simone and Armand had been lovers for years, but it was a mystery to Marguerite why Simone allowed him to come and go as he pleased. He owned a popular bar in town, but that was only the half of it. His other activities were known and not known, his associates suspected by some and not others. During these dangerous times, most people chose not to know more than was good for them and few were brave enough to act in a way that would eventually lead to their name being carved on a stone monument.

'I'm sorry, Marguerite. I know you can't risk any unwanted attention, but Armand knows nothing of that; being occupied by a foreign army sits heavily with him. The liberation can't be far away now. He's determined to keep the weapons safe so the rebel fighters can be armed to help the Allies when they finally advance.'

Armand had been turned down for active service because of the tuberculosis he'd suffered as a child which had left him with a weak chest. He'd even been rejected by the Germans when they'd rounded up the men of working age for their forced labour camps. With his beloved country under occupation, he was determined to wage war against the enemy on his own terms.

As her eyes grew accustomed to the dark, Marguerite began to spot other blankets in the far corners of the studio which had been used to hide more piles of guns and ammunition. The sight of the weapons in her sanctuary was more than she could stand, but none of this was Simone's fault. It was all Armand's doing.

9

'Tell him to get rid of them as soon as he can. I have work to do. I want my studio back. I can't paint with the blinds drawn.'

'What's going on? Your voices are loud enough to wake the town.'

Jeanne had wandered over from the house and was standing in the doorway of Marguerite's studio, her body sagging with exhaustion as she cradled the smooth round of her stomach.

Marguerite lowered her voice to a soothing whisper. 'It's nothing. I'm sorry we woke you. Why don't you go upstairs and sleep in my bed? I'll take the sofa.'

Jeanne yawned, her eyes narrowing on the blankets covering the cache of guns and ammunition. 'Is this Armand's work again?'

Simone brushed off the question with a shrug. 'You shouldn't stand around in the cold, Jeanne. Go back to the house and take the offer of Marguerite's bed before she changes her mind.'

Once Jeanne had gone, Simone tugged at the edges of the blinds, making sure nothing out of the ordinary could be seen from the outside.

'Everything will be gone by tomorrow. Or the day after. I promise.'

Chapter 3

Marguerite was unlocking her studio the next morning when Biquet appeared with a summons to report to the local mayor. The young boy waited while she read it; his hands pushed into the pockets of his ragged trousers, his fingers jangling the few coins that rested there.

She looked up from the note, her heart almost breaking at the sight of his pale face. 'Have you had breakfast, Biquet? There's a little bean casserole, if you'd like some.'

The casserole had been set aside for today's main meal, but she couldn't stand to think of Biquet going hungry.

'No thank you, Madame. Maman says I mustn't take food from anyone's mouth.'

She ruffled his hair and pushed a few centimes into his hand. 'Then off you go. Don't be late for school.'

At the age of twelve, all Biquet's thoughts of school had been left far behind. Since his father had been killed in action fighting for the French First Army, he saw it as his duty to take care of his mother. Sweet-natured and eager to please, if anything needed doing, Biquet was the boy to call upon.

'Will you be coming back for your lesson later?'

Biquet stood up a little straighter, a smile breaking out all over his face. 'Yes please, Madame.'

For the last two years, Biquet had helped Marguerite around the studio in exchange for art lessons. She had no need of an assistant and his help had little bearing on anything, but he was the most promising of all her students and she refused to let his inability to pay stand in the way of his education and his ambition.

Simone waited until Biquet had gone; her arms folded against uncertainty as she stood on the doorstep watching Marguerite climb onto her bicycle. 'Why does the mayor want to see you?'

These days, it was too complex a question to even consider. 'I'll let you know when I find out.'

'Stay safe, Marguerite. Don't take any risks.'

Marguerite nodded, the unspoken pact already sealed between them. 'Make sure Jeanne has something to eat when she wakes up. I left some dry crackers on the bedside table in case she's feeling unwell. Tell her to nibble one before she tries to move.'

Jeanne's morning sickness had carried on much longer into her pregnancy than would usually be expected. Marguerite put it down to the exceptional circumstances they were forced to live under. Until the Cote d'Azur was liberated, all they could do was take care of each other as best they could. Their survival was the one true victory they were determined to win over their oppressors.

It was mid-morning by the time Marguerite reached the outskirts of the town. These days, the streets were deserted. Before the war, everyone would have been out walking their dogs, but the lack of food meant most could no longer keep a pet and no one had the energy for exercise. People still nodded when their paths crossed, but the gesture barely covered the fear and suspicion behind their eyes and the gnawing hunger that was eating everyone alive.

At one time, the streets and the promenades had been full of colour and life, the hotels brimming with foreign visitors. Wealthy Americans and the British aristocracy had come for the sunshine, the wine and the food and stayed for love, while the writers and the artists had been drawn by the light, only to be dazzled by the freedom and the liberality. In those days, you couldn't walk down the street without seeing a film star or a maharaja, or the disgraced mistress of a crown prince.

The summer of 1939 had been the most spectacular of all. Every night, there'd been fireworks and balls, open-air concerts and parties, the strings of lights glowing along the Croisette each evening at dusk throwing their gaze on the beautiful women dressed in Chanel and Schiaparelli. Everyone had lived as if the gaiety would last forever. No one had thought war would come. It was unthinkable that such a thing could happen in paradise. Everyone had believed that the Maginot line, built after the Great War to thwart another German advance, would be enough to prevent an invasion. It hadn't crossed anyone's mind that the Germans would simply go round it.

Now, many of the shops were shuttered and sandbagged, and the romantic spirit of the grand hotels had been trodden underfoot by the heavy assault of the occupying army's boots, the glitter and the glamour of the high life, the comfort and assurance of any reasonable life at all, rubbed into the dust.

The arrival of the Third Reich had been a lesson in how quickly things could change in wartime. Only last September, Marguerite had stood at a high point on the grey limestone hills with Simone, the air brittle with the scent of pine and eucalyptus, as they watched the Italian troops begin their disorderly exit from the town, the black cockerel feathers in their hats making them ridiculous as they fled. They'd been the enemy occupiers for almost a year, but as soon as Mussolini signed an armistice with the Allies, the farmers' boys from across the border who'd been made to swap spades for guns, had dropped their weapons and returned to their mamas, and it was some of those guns that were now hidden in Marguerite's studio.

Within a day of the Italian departure, the German tanks had rolled in, the goose-stepping of advancing soldiers sending an earthquake through the quiet streets, their cold eyes peering out from beneath their metal helmets, assessing what kind of place it was they'd conquered.

From that moment, the region was subjected to a much harsher occupation, as the swagger of the Italian soldiers, who'd treated being stationed on the French Riviera as a holiday, was replaced by the stiff formality and iron-lawed scrutiny of the Third Reich, the swastika stamping its black mark of terror on every street and on every public building.

Now, as Marguerite entered the main square, she spotted a couple of German soldiers enjoying a cigarette beside the fountain. With everyone reduced to smoking parched vine leaves and dried eucalyptus, the smell of their foreign tobacco was a reminder of the otherness of the outside force that had been imposed on the town. Their grey-green uniforms were sharp and crisp in contrast to the shabby state of her own clothes; her culottes which were once a snug fit, were now pulled in tightly around her waist with an old leather belt to stop them falling down.

She focused on steering her bicycle as they nodded a formal hello, giving only the merest response in return, not daring to look up, or over her shoulder as she stopped to lock up her bicycle and contemplated the ornate stone building that accommodated the mayor's office.

Its atmosphere of formality sent a chill through her. Until the war, it had been a place nobody had any reason to fear. The rules the office enforced were no more than minor irritants, dictating what colour you were allowed to paint your window shutters, how much eau de vie you could get away with producing in your private still without too many pairs of eyes rolling. Now, each day the mayor was obliged to impose ever more stringent laws.

She entered the building and smiled at old Emile who'd occupied the front desk and been the mayor's assistant for as long as anyone could remember. In this hard living country, retirement wasn't something that was recognised unless infirmity left no choice in the matter. The people here were as rugged as the hills that surrounded them, as formidable as the Mediterranean Sea that beat relentlessly against the harbour walls.

He looked up from his ledger, the twitch of his white moustache betraying his recognition. 'Madame, the mayor is expecting you. Go straight in.'

It was with respect to her age that he called her Madame rather than Mademoiselle. To most people, it was unaccountable how Marguerite, now almost forty, could have failed to find herself a husband.

She expected to see the familiar soft-moulded face of Pierre Jupin sitting behind the mayor's desk, just as he'd always done, and to suddenly be confronted with someone different caused her to hesitate at the door.

Yves Musel snatched a look at his watch and signalled for her to sit down, his lean figure fighting against the slumping nature of the old leather chair that over the years had taken on the shape of the previous occupant.

'Thank you for coming to see me so promptly.'

He opened an official-looking brown folder in front of him, his movements slow and unflustered as if he were about to announce the winner of a prize and wanted to prolong the anticipation.

'Where's Monsieur Jupin today? Is he taking a little holiday?'

The directness of Musel's gaze as he looked up from the file made her skin prick.

'Jupin didn't feel able to carry on as mayor any longer. He wasn't coping with the extra paperwork now we're directly under the rule of the Third Reich.'

'I see. Poor man.'

'Nobody objected when I offered to take over.'

He said it in such a way that she wasn't surprised nobody had objected. She wondered what everyone else in the town thought of him usurping Jupin's position. In this place, everyone knew everyone's business and there wasn't a single person who wouldn't have a view on it.

'They'll miss you at the bank.'

'Any fool can count money. My talents are better employed here.'

Her spine stiffened at the change in his tone. She knew Yves well and considered both him and his wife, Celeste, to be friends. She'd been visiting their house every Saturday afternoon for the last three years to give drawing lessons to their daughters, Nancy and Alyce. Such things had to count for something.

There was nothing to worry about. His formality went with the job. It was merely something to be taken on and off, like a uniform at the beginning and end of each day. He was assuming this manner to protect the interests of the town against the occupying enemy. That's all it was. This is what she told herself. If only she could believe it.

Musel had already turned his attention back to the file. 'You understand it's my job to go through all the records, to familiarise myself with anything that might be out of the ordinary?'

She nodded, her fingers closing on her palms to hide the sweat that had suddenly erupted in the creases of her skin. 'I'm sure Monsieur Jupin kept everything in order.'

Musel leaned forward on his elbows, a slight dent deepening between his eyebrows as he examined her face. 'How long have you been living in this town, Madame?'

Each Saturday, after she'd finished Nancy and Alyce's lesson, Marguerite took a glass of wine with Yves and Celeste. Yves was such a jovial host, always making her welcome and always with an amusing story to tell. Now, the eyes that sparkled as he shared a joke were narrowed on her face, cold and grey as tumbled stones.

Marguerite forced herself to meet his gaze. Now wasn't the time to show uncertainty. 'Since the summer of 1934.'

'May I see your identity card?'

She reached into her bag and handed it to him. 'Everything is in order, as you can see.'

He compared the information on her identity card to that in the file before handing it back to her. 'You were living in Paris before you came to live here in the south?'

'As you know, Simone inherited her grandmother's house just outside the town. I was finding it too expensive to live in Paris on the little money I was making as an artist, and so she invited me to live with her here.'

He sniffed, visibly uncomfortable at the thought of two women living together and what the circumstances of that might be, even though it was no secret that Simone and Armand had been lovers for many years.

Musel leaned back in Jupin's old chair and considered her as if she were a stranger, as if every Saturday afternoon for the past three years hadn't occurred.

'Who do you sell your little paintings to now the foreign visitors no longer come?'

'Monsieur Boucher displays some of my work in his local gallery, but there are few buyers since the war. I live mainly by teaching and from private commissions, although these are rare now and art materials are hard to come by.'

'Your work isn't original enough. That's where your trouble lies. You need to find your own style.'

Where had his sudden criticism come from when he'd always championed her work?

'The last painting I saw of yours reminded me of that English woman artist.' He clicked his fingers as if to summon a name from the back of his memory. 'The one with the more successful brother.'

Gwen John was Welsh, but it didn't seem the appropriate time to correct him. 'I find most people like to have a picture of a soothing landscape or an interior hanging on their walls, even if it's been painted by an unknown.'

'Nobody in France wants to be reminded of the English anymore. They could have stopped the German invasion. They won't be forgiven for holding back their air power when we needed it and the way they retreated from Dunkirk was a disgrace. It's their fault we suffer now.'

Marguerite said nothing, knowing it wouldn't have been as simple as that. In wartime, nothing ever was.

When she didn't answer, he considered her more closely. 'Things must be hard for you.'

He must know how difficult things were for her. They were difficult for everyone.

'Simone still has her salary. She's a senior teacher at the local school now. We grow as much as we can on the small plot of land that came with her grandmother's house. We survive because we have to, just like everybody else.'

Musel remained silent while he turned over the papers in front of him. It was only when she caught sight of the heading that she realised the file was dedicated solely to her.

'The identity card you've just shown me matches the information we have in our files.'

'Then everything's in order.'

'This is the identity card you presented to Monsieur Jupin when you registered with the authorities at the outbreak of war?'

'Of course; I have only the one.'

Musel leaned back in the chair and folded his arms as if he were considering an insurmountable problem.

'Under the new rules, I'm required to do a routine audit of our records. When I checked the details we held on your identity card with the authorities in Paris, I discovered that Marguerite Segal, the woman it refers to, died in a fire in an apartment block in the city in 1932.'

'It's not possible. There must have been a mistake.'

'Death certificates don't lie. She's buried in the cemetery of Père Lachaise. Her date of birth is the same as appears on your file.'

'It must be a coincidence. Someone must have confused the records.'

18

'Perhaps, but if I'm forced to explain it to an official of the Third Reich, I don't know what I'll say.'

Musel's tone was matter of fact, his eyes searching her expression as she fought to control her reaction.

'It's an administrative error. It's as simple as that. The mistake isn't of your doing, or mine. Perhaps we should ask Monsieur Jupin for advice. He . . . '

'Monsieur Jupin died three days ago.'

This was a shock to Marguerite. With the local newspaper shut down by the Third Reich, everyone relied on word of mouth for news and nobody had mentioned it.

'I didn't know he'd been ill.'

'His wife found him hanging from the black pine tree at the bottom of their garden.'

He broke the news as if poor Monsieur Jupin had been a stranger rather than the previous mayor and a life-long friend of his father's.

'I see.'

But in truth, Marguerite saw nothing at all. The only thing in front of her was Musel's lean face, his eyes concentrated on hers.

'We know he was worried about any mistakes that might be discovered in his paperwork. It's the only explanation for his suicide.'

'The poor man must have been under a great strain to have resorted to such a desperate measure.'

Musel turned his attention back to the file. 'When I checked, there was no record of you. I could only find this other Marguerite Segal. If you really exist, it must be there somewhere. It can't simply have disappeared. Where did your mother register your birth?'

'I don't know. She died when I was fifteen so it's not as if I can ask her. Perhaps the error lay with her, but I suppose we'll never know.'

Her instinct told her to run from Musel's scrutiny, but if she gave away any hint of her fear, she'd be lost.

It was a long time before Musel replied, as if he were working something out in his mind, unsettling her with his direct gaze.

'I'll have to keep the investigation open, Madame. There's nothing else for it. If anyone asks, at least I can tell them I'm still looking into the matter. That way, I can't be accused of protecting you.'

He was no longer the friend she'd once known, the jovial family man who'd welcomed her into his home and encouraged his daughters to learn from her. He was a stranger in a new and uncomfortable world and he no longer trusted her.

She gave him a cool look. She'd become skilled at deflection. There was no reason why this skill shouldn't stand her in good stead now.

'Where does that leave me?'

He gestured towards the door, dismissing her from his presence. 'Only you, Marguerite, if that's who you really are, know the answer to that question.'

Chapter 4

It took little more than five minutes for Marguerite to realise she was being followed after she left the mayor's office. At first, she thought it was her imagination. Her nerves had been so shaken by the interview with Musel that she feared everyone knew the truth about her, but it couldn't be the case. She'd always been careful, living quietly and going out of her way to avoid making enemies.

She didn't think Musel was an enemy, but how could she be sure? He suddenly appeared a changed man in his new office. Perhaps he was only trying to protect the people of the town and his family, but at what cost, and who was he prepared to sacrifice in the process? He'd made it clear that if it came to it, she'd be left to her own fate. He wouldn't stand up for her in the face of enemy scrutiny.

She kept her head down as she cycled, trying to shake off whoever was following her, taking the quietest streets through the town where she was least likely to run into any soldiers. During her trips to buy food, she'd worked out the main routes of the German patrol, noting the places where they made their presence felt through the sound of their rough laughter and the ring of their stiff leather boots on the paving stones. She knew the bars and cafés where they liked to linger over an Armagnac. Armand's establishment was a particular favourite, just as it had been with the Italian soldiers before. Armand might be secretly waging war against the enemy occupiers but he was still happy to take their money.

Marguerite kept up a steady pace as she left the town behind her, the dust thrown up by the irascible breeze mingling with the scent of the umbrella pines that lined the route and the wild thyme growing like havoc along the roadside. She was half a kilometre onto the open road and the woman on the bicycle who'd pulled out from the side street as she'd left the mayor's office was still behind her. She'd followed her through the maze of streets in the town as Marguerite doubled back on herself to throw her off, and she was still with her now on the long straight road that led hardly anywhere but to the overgrown lane and the isolated farmhouse where she and Simone lived.

Despite Marguerite's efforts, the woman kept up with her, wheel turn for wheel turn. She tried steering to the far edge of the road to let her pass, but still she dogged her heels. On and on they went, with Marguerite unable to outpace her, while the follower made no effort to overtake. Breathless now, Marguerite risked a glance over her shoulder. It was just long enough for the woman to catch her eye.

'Stop, please.'

The woman shouted the instruction in English. When Marguerite failed to respond, she increased her pace and swerved into her back wheel, deliberately knocking her off her bicycle. By the time Marguerite had recovered, the woman had dismounted from her own bicycle and was standing beside her.

'Are you alright? Why didn't you stop when I asked you to?'

Her voice was pure Home Counties. Her ample vowel sounds rounded to perfection, although her grey skirt and cotton pin-tuck blouse looked decidedly French, as did her chestnut hair, pinned in a pleat to the back of her head.

Marguerite examined the damaged bicycle. 'Have you any idea how impossible it is to replace back wheels these days?'

'Forgive me, but I need to talk to you.'

'I don't talk to strangers,' Marguerite snapped, made furious by the damage to her bicycle.

'Then allow me to introduce myself.'

The woman held out her hand, which Marguerite ignored. Shaking hands wasn't exactly a French custom. Realising her mistake, the woman promptly lowered it.

'You can call me Violet. There; now we're no longer strangers.'

'You realise you're in enemy territory.'

Violet looked nervously around her. 'All I ask is for two minutes of your time.'

They stepped off the road to avoid any traffic that might pass and onto a narrow dirt track where the shadows of the umbrella pines put them out of sight. Marguerite propped her bicycle against the remains of a crumbling stone wall and rubbed the dirt from her grazed palms.

'What is it you want?'

'You've probably gathered by now that I'm not here to take in the scenery, lovely though it is.'

Marguerite had been anticipating this moment since the German invasion. Her eyes darted to the end of the dirt track, worried that someone might see them. 'Then you're missing out on some great pleasures.' She took her bicycle by the handlebars, testing the back wheel on the ground to see if it was safe enough to ride.

Violet placed a hand on Marguerite's arm to draw her attention. Her fingers were icy to the touch, despite the heat of the day. She couldn't have been more than twenty. Her voice shook as she spoke and there was a fine mist of perspiration on her upper lip. Marguerite couldn't tell which of them was more nervous.

'How did you know where to find me?'

'I couldn't say.'

'Can you tell me anything? I need to know I can trust you.'

'You left England ten years ago and nobody there has seen you since. Now, here you are, thinner than before and with shorter hair from what I've seen in old photographs, but most definitely here. You're living under a different name, but you're the same person. The one I've been asked to contact.'

'Who sent you to find me?'

'I can't tell you that, either.' Violet paused, as if she were censoring the words in her mind before she released them. 'It was someone in the British government, from one of Mr Churchill's secret intelligence departments.'

Marguerite had heard rumours of British agents being inserted into France as early as 1940 to support local resistance fighters. Living as quietly as she did, she'd never expected to come face to face with one herself, but if Violet wanted her help, she couldn't refuse – not while there was a war to be won. Sometimes, duty had to be put before personal safety.

'They've known about me all this time?'

'Why else do you think Monsieur Jupin turned a blind eye when you registered with the authorities here under a false name? You trusted yourself to his incompetence. We relied on his secret determination to arm France against an approaching enemy.'

'Do you know why he took his own life?'

'Sometimes, courage runs out.'

'And Yves Musel?'

Violet shrugged. 'Do you go to church?'

'No.'

'There's a local priest. His name is Father Etienne Valade. He's keeping close company with a number of high-ranking German officers – in particular, Otto Schmidt. We want you to get to know the priest. Find out whose side he's on and whether you can trust him.

'The Allied invasion is imminent. We know from experience that the Third Reich destroys all incriminating files before they retreat from the places they've occupied. Schmidt and his associates are responsible for the rounding up and the transportation of all the Jewish people who took refuge here when the Cote d'Azur was under Italian rule. As you know, Mussolini made it a haven for anyone under threat of being sent to the prison camps, but all that changed when the Germans took over the Occupation.

'If Father Etienne Valade is a friend of Schmidt as we suspect, convince him to help you gain access to his files. If you can photograph them, they can be used as evidence of war crimes against Schmidt and the rest of his associates. It will also help us to trace those he sent to their deaths.'

'I'm not a Catholic. Why would the priest want to know me?'

'Before the war, his brother ran a contemporary art gallery in Paris. It was a family business and Father Etienne was closely involved with it. Use your shared professional background in the art world to befriend him. Win his trust. Work out whose side he's on. If he's on the side of the enemy, win him over to us. His close association with Schmidt makes him best placed to gain access to the information we need without raising suspicion. It's vital we get the information from those files before they're destroyed if Schmidt and the rest are to be punished for the atrocities they've committed.'

'And if the priest turns out to be an enemy collaborator and has me arrested, what then?'

'Then you must make sure you can't be traced back to us.'

It was too much to take in. Marguerite's head was spinning. 'If I get the information, where do I send it?'

'Someone will contact you. They'll be watching and waiting.'

Violet reached into her shoulder bag and pulled out a leather purse which she thrust into Marguerite's hand. Inside was a silver filigree locket the size of Marguerite's thumb.

'It's a camera. Wear it around your neck always. Use it to photograph the documents.'

The purse also contained a pistol. Violet looked away when Marguerite spotted it, as if even a passing glance at it could be deadly.

'It's to be used at your discretion, but only as a desperate measure, obviously.'

The sight of the pistol was just as alarming to Marguerite as it was to Violet. Suddenly the danger was all too real.

'I don't know how to do any of this. I have no training. I'm just an artist.'

'You've been living under a false identity in this town for a decade. No agent could have a more convincing cover. Your life here is built on subterfuge; use it to your advantage.'

Marguerite watched as Violet pushed her bicycle along the dirt track, breathing in the scent of the pine trees and the Mediterranean Sea carried on the breeze. All at once she was a young woman out to enjoy an hour or two of fresh air and exercise as if she didn't have a care in the world.

Once she was back on the road, Violet climbed onto her bicycle and set off, mouthing *good luck* over her shoulder to Marguerite as she leaned over the handlebars and began pedalling at full speed before disappearing into the soft light of the distant hills.

Afterwards, it was all Marguerite could do not to think that Violet had been a figment of her imagination, but the weight of the gun in her bag told a different story. She should have known that one day her true identity would catch up with her, that the jeopardy she'd left behind in England would manifest itself in a different guise.

At least now, she'd been given the opportunity to do something worthwhile for both Britain and France. If she could play her part in ensuring justice was served on behalf of some of those who'd suffered under the Third Reich, then her life would finally count for something. She'd no longer be the woman who simply ran away. It was time to step out of one set of shadows and into another. It was time to join the fight. If nothing else, her experience of living a lie should stand her in good stead for whatever came next.

Chapter 5

Thanks to the buckled back wheel, Marguerite was forced to push her bicycle the rest of the way home. The walk gave her time to consider the exchange with Violet.

How was she supposed to befriend the priest when they had little in common? She knew nothing of the Catholic Church or of his life, and a man of his calling would have no interest in her as a woman. It would have to come down to art, as Violet had suggested. There could be nothing else between them. But how could she expect a man like Father Etienne Valade, bound by sacred vows, to see the emotion that lay buried in even the most domestic and commercial of her paintings? Each one, she'd come to realise, was a study in loneliness and this was something a man committed to a life of celibacy could never relate to.

And who was it that had alerted British Intelligence to her existence? Simone was the only person who knew Marguerite's real name and the circumstances that had led to her disappearance from England all those years ago, but she wouldn't have been the one to betray her. Marguerite trusted her with her life. Yet somehow they'd found out where she was; it seemed they'd probably known all along.

Simone was leaning out the bedroom window watching for Marguerite's return when she arrived back at the house. She called out as Marguerite pushed her bicycle up the garden path, the buckled back wheel making it impossible to keep a straight line.

'What happened to your bicycle?'

Marguerite held up her hands to show her grazed palms. 'I was forced off the road. The collision sent me flying. Is Jeanne still here?'

'She left not long ago. She said to thank you for the crackers.'

It was time to warn Simone of the danger Marguerite was putting them in. It wasn't only the instruction from Violet she needed to be aware of, but Musel's investigation into her identity. It wasn't just her life that would be under threat, but by association, Simone's too.

Simone took a moment to consider the situation after Marguerite sat her down at the kitchen table and told her everything. 'We should have guessed something like this would happen. The only surprise is that it's taken them this long to approach you.'

'They've been biding their time, waiting until I was most useful to them.'

Despite the propaganda, everyone knew the war was going badly for the Germans. They'd exhausted themselves against the Soviets in the East and been forced to retreat from North Africa. More recently, the Allies had moved into the south of Italy and were advancing through the country.

Simone sighed, drumming her fingers on the old wooden table. 'And all the while, France still remains in abeyance, much to our great shame.'

'Not for long. The information I've been asked to find suggests the Allies are working towards liberating us. It's only a matter of time before it's all over.'

'One day, the people of France will thank you for risking your life for us, Marguerite.'

'France offered me a haven when I most needed it. This is the least I can do to repay the kindness.'

'When this is all over, will the British respect your false identity? The last thing you want is them splashing your name in the English papers. Lance won't remain in prison forever. He's bound to come looking for you when he's eventually released. He's not a man to be crossed and he's still your husband. If he catches up with you, you'll have some explaining to do.'

'I can't worry about that now when we're facing more immediate dangers.'

Simone reached for Marguerite's hand and gave it a squeeze. 'Whatever happens, I'll always be here for you.'

Marguerite was glad of the reassurance, but it only went so far. 'Let's keep this between us. Don't mention it to Armand.'

Simone laughed. 'We won't tell him until we want the whole town to know.'

Chapter 6

The fear that sparked the air like electricity during the day transformed under the cover of darkness into a strange energy that spat and crackled in the hearts of those who couldn't sleep. Marguerite lay in bed, curled up against the small hours, listening to the whisper and creak of the familiar night-time sounds: the rafters of the farmhouse shifting like an old man moving from foot to foot, the flip and swoop of bats, and the hollow call of wolves carried on the breeze as the air rubbed its hands together for warmth.

And yet that night there was a different sound. At first she thought she'd imagined it, that in her mind, she'd drifted back to her old studio in Bloomsbury, that what she was hearing was the rattle and bang of the London life outside her window. A drunk in Gower Street tripping over a kerb and cursing its existence, the slamming of a front door by a disgruntled lover determined never to return. But as she stared into the darkness, she knew it was none of these things. Someone was knocking on the front door.

The blood froze in her veins as the memory of the meeting with Yves Musel came back to her. She wanted to believe the knocking was just a dream in which the tall stranger in the black coat had returned to kiss her again, but Simone was moving around in her room next door and Marguerite couldn't have imagined it if it had disturbed her too.

She listened to her friend's slippered feet padding their way downstairs, the sustained creak of the front door as it slowly opened. Marguerite held her breath, not knowing what was coming next. Soon, sharp whispers infiltrated the house, Simone's irritated tone clearly audible above the quiet murmurings of a male voice. Armand. Marguerite recognised the sound of his pleading.

Assuming he'd come to collect the Italian guns, she crept downstairs, determined to warn him off any future action that would put them in danger unless he'd discussed it with them first. The man was reckless beyond measure and she couldn't take any more risks.

Simone and Armand were sitting in candlelight around the kitchen table, the shadows flickering in the half-light revealing not two people, but three.

Armand rose to his feet as soon as Marguerite entered. 'Forgive me for disturbing you at this hour, but it's an emergency.'

Everything to Armand was an emergency, from the change in the weather to the roughness of last year's wine. Marguerite had never understood Simone's loyalty to him and assumed their intimacy was more to do with habit than attraction. He'd been inviting himself into her bed for years and she never seemed to refuse him. Sometimes she'd go for weeks without seeing him or hearing from him. Other times, they couldn't get rid of him, his unique odour of sweat and sour wine filling every room in the house, while Simone fed him the best food they had, and washed and darned his clothes.

'What kind of emergency is it that it couldn't wait until morning?'

Before he could answer, Simone placed a hot drink in front of the third person at the table. 'This is Miss Dorothy Nicholls, the renowned English novelist.'

The woman looked up from beneath her broad-brimmed hat. Marguerite recognised her instantly. Dorothy Nicholls was one of the new wave of Modernist writers who'd made a great splash in the literary world during the last twenty years, and was known for her radical prose style and for putting the female experience at the forefront of her work. The explicit nature of her stories and her unconventional private life divided both readers and critics alike. It was impossible for Marguerite to comprehend that such a notorious woman was sitting at their kitchen table.

'Why are you still in France? Don't you know how dangerous it is for you to be in enemy-occupied territory?'

Most of the English had returned home in the summer of 1940, just as France was on the verge of announcing an armistice with Germany. It was rumoured that a number in the south had chosen to stay, that they'd retreated from the coast and were living quietly in modest villas in the hills. Among them were known to be at least two of the king's previous mistresses. None of them were ever seen on the streets and it was a mystery to Marguerite how they survived.

Dorothy took off her hat and ran her fingers through her unruly crop of grey curls. 'Why would I choose to live in a damp flat in England, when for the same money, I can live in a villa in the lavender-scented hills of Provence?'

She must have been sixty, but held herself with the poise of a woman half her age. With her blunt stature, dark eyes and red lipstick, she could easily pass as French on a busy street.

Armand returned to his seat next to Dorothy. 'Miss Nicholls has been living quietly here in the south since before the war. She's been perfectly fine until now. The Italians had no interest in her, but the Germans are a different matter.'

Aside from her controversial work, being an Englishwoman in enemy-occupied territory made Dorothy an illegal alien. If she was found, she'd be imprisoned and whoever was caught hiding her would be shot. As the war progressed, restrictions had grown ever tighter. English churches had been closed, libraries ransacked and books burned in an attempt to remove all traces of English culture from France.

The situation had become even more dangerous since the German Occupation. As Violet had reminded Marguerite when she instructed her on her mission, many of the persecuted who'd fled to the Cote d'Azur from the rest of occupied France and Europe had been rounded up by the Gestapo and taken away, their fates unknown. Jewish refugees, artists and writers, and free thinkers of all kinds had disappeared overnight. In this once liberal place, there was now little hope for anyone who came under Hitler's disapproval. It was a terrifying lesson in how radically things could change in wartime.

Dorothy shrugged off her muskrat coat, encouraging it to tumble over the back of the chair like a restless cat.

'The Italians always appreciated my liberalism. Not so the Germans, alas. They've been burning my books in Berlin for years. I'd always seen it as a badge of honour until now.'

Armand slurped his drink before scowling at it. The roasted chicory they were reduced to drinking was no substitute for coffee.

'The Germans consider novels about female desire to be degenerate. Nor do they like sentences without punctuation.'

Dorothy pulled a crumpled letter from her pocket, her hand trembling as she unfolded it.

'I thought I was among friends here, but I was mistaken. Some bastard has threatened to denounce me to the Boche unless I pay them ten thousand francs. It's the going rate for condemning someone now, apparently.'

Armand snatched the paper and waved it above his head. 'A blackmailer with a black heart. None of us like the British, but few of us would stoop to this.'

Dorothy sniffed, visibly riled by Armand's criticism. 'How much money do they think a writer like me earns? I've barely scraped a living since the war started.' She snatched the letter back and screwed it up. 'Damn Edith for leaving me. This wouldn't have happened if she'd been here. She'd have known exactly how to sort this mess out.'

Simone threw Marguerite a cautious look before turning to Armand. 'What do you want us to do?'

'She needs to return to England. Hide her until we can arrange to get her across France and over the border to Spain.'

'How about the threat from the blackmailer?'

Armand shrugged off Simone's question as if the blackmailer were nothing but a minor inconvenience, which compared to the task of getting Dorothy safely back to England was probably true.

'If they can't find her, they'll give up. There's no point denouncing someone who can't be found. There's no reward in that. They're probably already sharpening their teeth on their next victim.'

Dorothy squeezed the ball of paper in her fist until she couldn't make it any smaller. 'I don't want to cause you any trouble. I just need to get back to my little flat in Chelsea. It's the only place I'll feel safe. That's if the Boche hasn't bombed it to pieces.'

She must have left home in a hurry because she was travelling light, with only a carpet bag and a portable typewriter. Marguerite's heart went out to her, understanding the fear that threat brought, how it made you want to run away and never look back.

'We'll do what we can.'

Already Simone was out of the chair and making plans. 'We'll hide you in the cellar. There's no natural light and it's always either too hot or too cold. Do you think you can stand it?'

Dorothy got to her feet, pulling her fur coat around her shoulders as if it were the only defence she had against the world, which it probably was.

'I couldn't ask for anything better. The lack of distraction will give me the perfect conditions to write my next novel.'

As Simone led Dorothy to the cellar, Marguerite hung back to speak to Armand.

'This is two dangers you've brought to our door in the last few days. No more, Armand.'

He shrugged, his face tense and prematurely aged by the strain of life under the Occupation, his thickset frame permanently stooped from trying to make himself invisible.

'Simone told me what happened in the park. Jeanne will act as a courier from now on. We can't risk you being caught. Your skills aren't so easy to replace.'

'Don't be ridiculous. We can't put Jeanne in danger. She has the baby to consider.'

Armand shrugged. 'It's all arranged.'

He retrieved a clutch of identity cards from his wallet. 'These need the letter J removing and the names need to sound more French. Jeanne will collect them tomorrow afternoon. You can pass on the papers you failed to deliver the other night at the same time. She'll take care of it.'

Marguerite slipped the identity cards into her dressing-gown pocket. There was no point arguing over Jeanne now. She'd talk her out of it herself. 'We'll have to be more careful now we have Dorothy.'

'She came to me for help. What could I do?'

'Fine, but if you want me to alter the identity cards, I'll need my studio back. You need to remove the Italian guns and ammunition. Today.'

Armand raised his hands, stepping back from her insistence. 'Of course. Trust me.' He gave her a smile, his charm, once used to seduce every woman he met, now employed as an assault weapon to help him to win his personal war against the enemy. 'What I do, I do for France, which means I do it for all of us.'

Once Armand had gone, Marguerite slipped on an old overcoat and crept out of the house. Her head was still buzzing with the memory of the conversation she'd had with Violet. The sun hadn't yet risen and the air was sharp with the night-time damp that made her shiver as she unlocked the door to her studio and stepped inside. It was the only place she could think clearly. She needed to figure out what to do and she didn't have long to do it.

Tugging open the first of the blinds, she noticed something propped up against the far wall, its angular frame throwing tangential shadows across the stone floor in the moonlight. A bicycle. It wasn't hers or Simone's. They kept their bicycles in the outhouse at the bottom of the garden. This one was almost new and had hardly been ridden, the tread on the tyres barely worn. When she looked closely, she realised it was Violet's, with its pristine brown leather saddle and freshly painted frame. The scratch on the front mudguard showed exactly the point where it had been ridden into Marguerite's back wheel.

How it came to be there was a mystery. She cast her eyes around the studio, expecting to see Violet loitering in the shadows or hiding behind a stack of canvases, but there was no sign of her. Marguerite's stomach turned over at the thought that the cache of guns and ammunition, still hidden under blankets in the far corners of the room, might have been discovered – that whoever had delivered the bicycle had seen Armand bring Dorothy to their door and leave without her.

'Is anyone there?'

Nothing came back, only the echo of Marguerite's own voice, tense in the cool blue light of the moon. She drew in a breath, sniffing the air for intruders as if she had the animal perception to sense them, but there was only the usual comforting smell of oil paint and turpentine, damp clay and new wood.

The bicycle hadn't been there the previous evening and the studio had been locked ever since, the key to the padlock hidden in the false drawer in the kitchen dresser. And yet nothing in the studio had been disturbed. The lock was still intact and there was no sign of a break-in. If Violet had let herself in undetected and left the bicycle to replace Marguerite's because of the damage she'd inflicted on it, then she'd underestimated her. She was more capable than Marguerite had given her credit for. If these were the kind of people she was dealing with, she'd have to work just as cleverly. Despite the mystery of it, she was grateful for the replacement bicycle. A new set of wheels might just make life a little easier.

Chapter 7

When Marguerite got up the next morning, it was as if the events of the previous night had never happened. The cups that had been left on the kitchen table had been washed and put away, the chairs neatly pushed back into their usual places, and the smell of the burning candle had drifted out through the open window.

Simone came bustling in, ready to set off for work. 'If you're looking for the old oil lamp, it's in the cellar along with a couple of spare blankets and cushions. Our guest has food and water to last the day. I've suggested she waits until nightfall before coming out for air and exercise. We can't risk anyone seeing her in the daylight.'

The entrance to the cellar was hidden behind a door under the stairs. When Marguerite investigated, she found Simone had filled the cupboard with half-empty tins of household paint, broken chairs and rusty gardening tools, giving the place an air of neglect and untidiness that suggested no one had been near it for some time other than to pile in unwanted items.

The key to her studio was back on its usual hook beside the kitchen door and the rusty padlock had disappeared. In the studio, everything was as it should be, with the blinds thrown open to the cool morning light. Armand had been as good as his word. After

Marguerite had returned to bed, the guns and the ammunition had been removed and in such a quiet and orderly manner that she hadn't even been aware of it.

Despite her protestations, Biquet had insisted on missing school that day to help her in the studio. He sat at the bench cleaning her paintbrushes while Marguerite settled to work, using lactic acid to bleach the official blue Waterman ink on the identity cards so she could change the Jewish names. So far, the German authorities hadn't realised that such a trick was possible, that thanks to it, hundreds of persecuted people were able to live under the camouflage of assumed identities.

She'd just set the first identity card to dry when she heard someone outside the house, the crunch of feet on the gravel path indicating they were approaching the studio with a determined pace.

Biquet climbed down from his stool, his little body braced for action. 'Madame, there's someone coming.'

Marguerite's heart leapt into her throat. She quickly hid the identity cards behind the nearest framed canvas, hoping that whoever had decided to visit hadn't come to search the place.

The door flew open and suddenly Dorothy was standing before them, smiling as if it were the first day of a holiday and looking relaxed in an over-sized man's sweater and Oxford bags.

'Good morning. Lovely day, isn't it?' Her jaw dropped when she saw Biquet. 'You didn't tell me there was a boy.'

Marguerite grabbed Dorothy's arm and pulled her inside, closing the studio door behind them. 'How did you get out of the cellar?'

'I gave the hatch a bit of a heave-ho with my right shoulder and up it came, sweet as a nut.' She took a moment to straighten her sweater where Marguerite's rough treatment had upset it. 'I'm afraid I've knocked over some paint. I had no idea the pots had been placed on top of it. What a clever thing you are to think of it.'

A rush of anger flooded Marguerite's veins. 'It wasn't my idea. It was Simone's. You'd better get back inside before someone sees

39

you. I'll tidy up the mess.'

Dorothy's face crumpled. 'But I want some air. There's no one around here for miles, surely? You can't expect me to stay in the cellar on a beautiful day like this.'

The sky was cobalt blue. The rock roses were in flower and the butterflies hovered on the warm breeze, but Marguerite couldn't allow Dorothy to be seduced by it.

'If anyone sees you, we'll all be in danger, not only yourself.'

Biquet took Dorothy's hand and led her to the door. 'You should do as she says, Madame. If anyone finds you here, it is Marguerite who will be shot, not you.'

Dorothy started to make her way back to the house, covering her face with her hand. 'You're going to hate me now; I know it.'

'Not at all, it's just . . . '

The sentence died on Marguerite's lips as she entered the house and realised it wasn't her escape from the cellar that Dorothy was worried about, but the paint that had been spilled over the Indian rug from the cans Simone had piled above the hatch to hide it.

'I'm truly sorry. I realised there'd been a calamity as soon as I clambered out of the cellar, but it was too late by then.' She gave Marguerite an uncertain look. 'Armand told me you're an artist. I trust you know how to remove paint stains?'

It was more than just a stain. It was a sea of glossy daffodil-yellow paint, running here and there in streaks, channelling between the ridges and bumps of the ancient rug. Marguerite didn't know whether to rage against Dorothy or crawl onto the sofa and cry. Knowing neither of these actions would be helpful, she bustled Dorothy back into the cellar and closed the door on her descending figure.

'Please stay out of sight. We'll arrange for you to come up for some air when it's dark.'

* * *

Biquet was on his knees in the front garden, trying to scrub the paint out of the rug when Simone returned home for lunch. She cried when she saw the damage. The rug had belonged to her grandmother and was a great favourite. Its age and condition did nothing to diminish the emotional value she attached to it.

Biquet threw his arms around her. 'Don't worry, Madame. I'm removing the paint for you. When I've finished, it will be as good as new.'

Simone hugged him back, her eyes raised to Marguerite, questioning. 'How did it happen?'

'Dorothy took it upon herself to leave the cellar.'

Biquet pulled away from Simone's embrace and returned to scrubbing the rug. 'Now I understand why they say the English are mad.'

Simone's eyes widened with disbelief. 'Biquet was here when Dorothy came out of the cellar?'

'I won't say a word, Madame.'

He put aside the scrubbing brush and began picking at the rug, trying to loosen the paint from the pile with his fingernails, but no amount of encouragement would lift it.

'You're a good boy, Biquet.' Simone ruffled his hair before turning to Marguerite. 'I knew Dorothy would cause us trouble. I told Armand I didn't want her here, but he swore there was nowhere else for her to go.'

'She's scared. It's bound to make her restless. Who knows what's going on inside her head? I don't envy her novelist's imagination.'

Simone shrugged, already resigned to the situation. 'There's been no word from Armand today. I suppose we'll just have to be patient. There's no saying how long it'll be until she can be moved.'

She dug into her satchel and pulled out a dozen sheets of plain paper. 'I begged this from the headmaster's secretary at school. If we can keep Dorothy occupied with writing a new novel, she might stay out of trouble.'

41

Marguerite had just handed Dorothy the stash of paper and closed the cellar door when Jeanne arrived, struggling up the garden path in the midday heat, her feet splayed in ill-fitting sabots. Her mother, Nicole, was trailing behind, her face troubled as she muttered under her breath.

Jeanne threw her arms around Simone, whose loving nature she claimed as a haven. Only Marguerite was allowed a glimpse of the grief Simone suffered at witnessing her beloved France laid to ruin by enemy invaders. To everyone else, she was a tower of strength and wisdom.

The joy of seeing Jeanne was compromised by Armand's news that she was to act as a courier in place of Marguerite. Simone raised it as soon as they sat down.

'We can't let you do it, Jeanne. Not with a baby on the way.'

Nicole rolled her eyes. 'I've been telling her this all morning. Perhaps you can talk sense into her.'

'Of course I can do it. The baby isn't due for months.'

Marguerite exchanged a glance with Simone, their minds registering the same thoughts. 'It's too dangerous, my love. We can't risk anything happening to you or the baby. We'd never forgive ourselves.'

Nicole nodded. 'And neither would I. I've told you a hundred times that I'm against you getting involved in any resistance activity.'

'The baby is the perfect cover. Nobody would suspect a pregnant woman of taking risks.'

Jeanne's face was red from too much heat and she was perspiring heavily. Simone handed her a glass of water. 'How did you get Armand to agree to it?'

'He took a bit of convincing when I offered to help, but he eventually saw the sense in it.'

Marguerite understood what it meant to take a risk, just as she knew the fear that went with it, fierce enough to set your heart racing until you thought it would burst. She'd been hiding for much of her adult life, but Jeanne was hardly more than a child. Her hopes and dreams were still intact despite the daily humiliation of war. She had her whole life ahead of her and now she had a baby to think of.

'I'm sorry, Jeanne. It's too dangerous. I can't let you do it.'

Jeanne stamped her foot, just as a child would. 'It's not for you to decide, Marguerite. There are people waiting for those papers. They're desperate. Their lives depend on it. They're expecting to receive them this afternoon. We can't simply say no, it's too dangerous, because that's what we feel like doing.'

'But what if you're caught? How will we ever forgive ourselves?'

'I won't be. I'm too clever.'

Nicole sighed, rubbing fiercely at her eyes to banish the tears. 'I'm sorry, Jeanne. Marguerite's right. We can't let you do it. You're too dear to us.'

'You don't have a say in it, Maman. I'm going to do it.'

The four of them sat in silence, considering each other's arguments across the kitchen table until Biquet appeared at the door, his fingers yellowed with paint.

'I'll go with her, Mesdames, to make sure she comes to no harm.'

Jeanne beckoned him over and kissed the top of his head. 'Bless you, Biquet.'

Simone sighed; her arguments were futile against Jeanne's determination. 'Has Armand explained what's required?'

'I walk through the town square every afternoon after I've finished working at the café. People are used to seeing me; they stop and talk to me. It'll be the easiest thing in the world to hand over documents as we pass the time of day.'

Simone looked to Marguerite and Nicole for reassurance. 'Perhaps she could do it once or twice, no more than that. I'd do it myself, but it would look suspicious when I'm supposed to be at school.'

Jeanne was determined to do this. Marguerite could see it in her eyes, in the set of her jaw. 'You promise not to go out after curfew or do anything out of the ordinary?'

43

'I promise.' Jeanne ran her hand over the gentle curve of her stomach. 'I'm doing it for this little one. I won't put my baby in danger. They have a right to grow up in a free France and I'm prepared to fight for them to do just that.'

Nicole sighed, defeated by her daughter's arguments and her determination to play her part in winning the war. 'You know how I feel, Jeanne, but I can't stop you doing it.'

Marguerite walked calmly out of the kitchen and beckoned Jeanne to follow. 'Come to my studio. I'll give you the papers.'

Chapter 8

That night after dark, Marguerite and Simone invited Dorothy out of the cellar. Together they walked the land surrounding the house, their only light coming from the fireflies that twitched and flickered against the black sky; the wide sweep of the cypresses and the old-men shapes of the olive trees casting strange figures in the night and throwing disapproving glances at their audacity, reminding them it was dangerous to be out after the curfew, even if you stayed on your own patch of land.

When Marguerite first saw the garden, she'd thought it a paradise. Now, with most of the local produce being redirected to Germany, they increasingly relied on it to keep them fed. Despite its outward promise, the coastal climate and the poor soil made cultivating anything beyond squash, lettuce and swede a challenging and often unrewarding task for all their backbreaking efforts.

Last spring, Marguerite had tempted a swarm of bees into a disused hive beside the oleander. For months she'd lived in hope that there'd eventually be some honey, but the bees weren't inclined to stay or else they were charmed away by a scheming neighbour. She'd cried for a whole day when she realised they'd gone, the desperate hope of a taste of sweetness in an increasingly bitter world dashed.

Tonight, they talked in whispers while Dorothy stretched her legs around the garden, surprising them by turning cartwheels one after another like a rolling firework bursting into the night while suppressing the bubbles of laughter that seemed a reckless response to her fear.

Simone gasped at the sight of her sturdy body tumbling along the length of the narrow path that ran between the vegetable beds as time and again she took her bodyweight on her hands, her short legs flying through the air with abandon as if she were fifty years younger.

'How do you do that?'

Dorothy paused to catch her breath, brushing the dust and the tiny pointed stones from the fleshy pads of her palms, her mouth a white smile of teeth.

'When I was eighteen, I fell in love with a Russian trapeze artist named Sophia and followed the circus. After a while they allowed me to join the act. For the next two years I was part of the acrobat team.'

Simone grinned at Marguerite as if to say it couldn't possibly be true. Dorothy caught the look, and to prove she wasn't lying, did a back flip on the spot, her legs flying through the air with the swiftness of a firefly.

'There must be some trick to it.'

'I trained for ten hours a day, every day for the two years I was with them. I was never the best in the team, but I was young and I was strong and supple. Those years gave me a physical confidence that most Englishwomen can only dream of. That's all gone now, of course; age and too many hours spent hunched over a typewriter has seen to that, but I still do a few cartwheels and back flips every day, just to stay strong.'

Simone's eyes gleamed in the darkness, hungry for more details. 'Why did you leave the circus?'

'Sophia decided to marry Gregory, the lion tamer. She didn't love him, but that's the way of things in the circus. However much I tried to prove my devotion, I'd always be an outsider. If I'm honest, I was growing restless of it all by then and was ready for a change. I was longing to return to England, to sit for hours beside a coal fire and read Dickens. I may be a vagabond by nature, but I still need my home comforts. Even so, Sophia's rejection broke my heart.'

Marguerite pictured the circus in her mind, the Russian trapeze artist and the lion tamer, with Dorothy at the centre of the exotic love triangle.

'It's such a romantic story, but I don't believe a word of it.'

Dorothy laughed, refusing to deny or admit anything as they continued their stroll around the garden in a more sedate manner. If nothing else, Dorothy's story had proven a distraction from worrying about Jeanne. Earlier that evening, Biquet had run across town to let them know the identity cards had been successfully handed over, but it didn't mean Jeanne would escape the attention of the German soldiers next time or the time after that.

Seeing she was lost in her thoughts, Dorothy clicked her fingers in front of Marguerite's face. 'Penny for them?'

'It's nothing.'

It felt strange to be speaking English again after so many years. At first Marguerite strained to find the words, building the sentences almost like a beginner, until slowly the rhythms and the cadences of the language came back to her, so different to French in every way and yet ultimately as familiar as a long-forgotten friend who suddenly appears one day and you find you're able to pick up with them quite naturally, as if the time you'd spent apart had never been. It was only now, talking to Dorothy that she realised how much she'd missed it and acknowledged how far her life had come since those lost days in England and the person she used to be.

And with the thought, came the longing to return, to walk the busy London streets and the windswept country lanes of her childhood, to return to the person she once was, but while there was a risk of Lance finding her, she knew it could never be.

While he lived, she would always be Marguerite. Her cover was secure, just as long as Yves Musel or anyone in the Third Reich didn't dig too deeply into her past. If she was to fulfil her duty to Britain and France, she had to put all other worries aside and concentrate on completing her mission for Violet. To achieve this, she first had to find a way of getting to know Father Etienne Valade.

Chapter 9

To engineer a meeting with the priest, Marguerite had to lay a trap for him and she decided the best way to do this was to hold an exhibition of her work. If Father Etienne had been involved in the running of his brother's art gallery in Paris before the war, as Violet had said, then perhaps this would catch his attention. Exhibitions were unheard of these days and his curiosity might be enough to draw him in. If nothing else it would offer a little entertainment to the people of the town.

Monsieur Boucher, who owned the small art gallery on the Rue d'école, was delighted when Marguerite approached him with the idea, even though there was no money to be made.

'It's a wonderful suggestion, Madame. Let's make it a celebration. It'll remind everyone of old times.'

Like many other people in the town, Monsieur Boucher had aged a decade in the years since France had signed the armistice with Germany. His habit of making quick-fingered gestures when he spoke had stilled, and the spark that lit his eyes whenever he saw a painting that delighted him had dimmed to a flickering glow like a candle burning in its last pool of wax. These days, he only had the energy to open the gallery one or two days a week, but the prospect of having new work to exhibit seemed to inspire fresh life in him.

Before the war, Marguerite's landscapes had sold well to foreign visitors and been praised for the way they captured the mood of the weather and the atmosphere. Now that replicating images of the area was banned, she could no longer paint them, even if there'd been a market for them.

Alone in her studio, she considered her unsold pictures, holding each one in turn up to the light and judging its merits, asking herself whether it was worthy of a place on the walls of Monsieur Boucher's gallery. Most of them were still lifes – studies of wild-flowers, or silk scarves artfully arranged on sofas or the backs of chairs, and any number of domestic scenes involving china plates and coffee cups reminiscent of the works of Vanessa Bell and, as Musel had pointed out, Gwen John. With an increasing shortage of materials, she'd painted less with each passing year of the war, but on the other hand, little had been sold. These days few people had the money or the spirit to buy anything beyond necessities.

Despite a lifetime of commitment to her art, she'd failed to develop her own unique style. After leaving the Slade, she'd mimicked the work of more successful artists in order to survive. Even now, her paintings always contained a hint of someone else, serving as a cover for her true self in the same way as her assumed name.

The suppression of her creativity was all part of her battle to remain unnoticed, but there was nothing to regret. Every decision she'd ever made had been determined by her compulsion to paint. Every subterfuge and deflection had been for her art, whether it could be easily attributed to her or not, because the time she spent with a brush or a pencil in her hand was the only time she felt at peace.

Simone only found out about the exhibition after she wandered into Marguerite's studio and saw the posters she was making to advertise it.

'Are you sure this is the best way to catch your man, Marguerite? Nobody is in a position to buy your pictures and I worry that you might draw too much attention to yourself.'

'It's quicker and simpler than taking up the Catholic faith.'

'They say all Nazis are Catholics. I wonder if it's the same the other way round.'

They only then noticed Biquet sitting on the garden wall, kicking his heels against the old stone and sending the moss flying. He hadn't said he'd be coming to help her today, and Marguerite's stomach clenched, dreading that he might have come with another summons from Musel. She forced herself to smile. She couldn't bear to think he might guess she wasn't pleased to see him.

'Do you have something for me, Biquet?'

He held out his hands, still stained with yellow paint, his eyes glinting. 'Only these, Madame. Monsieur Boucher told me about your exhibition and I guessed you'd need my help.'

Her heart melted at the hope in his eyes, the expectation he had of a better life to come, if only he tried harder to please everyone.

'Well, Monsieur Boucher was right. I do have a job for you.'

She went to the outhouse at the bottom of the garden and returned with her old bicycle. It had taken a whole evening, but she'd managed to straighten the bent spokes and realign the back wheel so it was safe to ride.

'I want you to go around the town and tell everyone about my exhibition. You'll need this. I assume you know how to ride it.'

Biquet's face lit up as she handed him the bicycle, a thing so precious that these days, it was beyond all means.

'I'll bring it back safely, Madame.'

'It's yours to keep, Biquet. Just make sure you do a good job for me.'

Grateful for the bicycle, Biquet cycled all over town, putting up the posters advertising the exhibition, and encouraging everyone he saw to come, insisting there was no obligation to buy, just as Marguerite had instructed. When they asked why she was doing it, he said it was for a little entertainment, that was all. And there was no reason for people not to believe him.

* * *

Simone raised the subject of the exhibition again later that night as they walked Dorothy around the garden. They'd expected Armand to have moved her by now, but there'd been no word from him.

Dorothy had settled into her subterranean life like a nocturnal animal retreating to its burrow, but she was beginning to look pale and the energy generated by her initial fear was fading. It was the drawn-out hunger and the uncertainty that did it. No one could be expected to stay well for long confined to a dingy cellar with no windows or fresh air, and they were all counting the days until she could make her escape.

Her eyes lit up like glow worms when she heard there was to be an exhibition. 'I'll come and support you. I have a knack for talking doughty old matrons into parting with their money. I'm guaranteed to shift a few paintings for you.' She clapped her hands, recalling past pleasures. 'I haven't been to a party since Willy Maugham's last bash at La Mauresque on Cap Ferrat. That was before he fled France, of course, coward that he is. It wouldn't surprise me if he was holed up somewhere exotic by now, growing fat on cigars and brandy and earning his crust as a spy.'

Spy. The very mention of the word sounded like a hiss as it escaped from Dorothy's lips, or maybe it was the way she whispered it, just as the meaning of it warranted. However it sounded, Marguerite felt as if she'd been called out. She'd never thought of herself in those terms before, but wasn't that exactly what she was meant to be?

Simone gave Dorothy's arm a squeeze. 'Much as we'd love to have you there, we can't risk you being seen in public.'

'It'll only be a few friendly locals, surely? They won't know me from Adam. I'll assume a mysterious demeanour. I'll even throw in a few Russian words to put them off the scent. I bet a pound to a penny I could pass myself off as a White Russian spy.'

This idea wasn't as mad as it seemed. Rumour had it that the Gestapo was employing White Russians to roam the streets and root out any remaining Jewish people, identifying them by their physiognomy. It wasn't only fake identity cards that were required to keep people safe. You also needed to keep your head down and rely on a good dose of luck if you were to survive.

'I'm sorry, Dorothy. It's too much of a risk. Posters have gone up all over town. Anyone could turn up and these days, you can't be sure whose side anyone is on.'

Marguerite hoped Simone was right. She didn't care who else was there as long as it brought her to the attention of Father Etienne Valade.

Chapter 10

Marguerite had no idea what Father Etienne Valade looked like. Men of his type made themselves invisible in their black cloth, ensuring only their role was evident and not the person behind it. Now, she was relying on his soutane and his behaviour in the gallery to give him away.

Most people visiting an exhibition strolled absently around the space, their attention focused on the other visitors rather than on the paintings. Experience had taught her that those who truly lived for art behaved differently. When something caught their eye, it was as if nothing else in the room existed. They'd stand in front of a picture for twenty minutes without blinking. They could be barged by a dozen casual browsers and not notice. This was the reaction she was counting on from the priest. If she could get him to notice her art, then he'd seek her out and the rest would follow. Her plan relied on her work being up to his scrutiny, on him seeing beyond the domestic imagery and her imitation of others to the deeper emotional message buried within it. If he didn't see that, she was lost.

Yves Musel was one of the first to arrive at the exhibition. Marguerite spotted him as he walked through the door with his wife, Celeste; his two daughters trailing behind like excited ducklings let out on the big pond for the first time.

At sixteen, Nancy was the image of her mother, tall and slim with a billow of blonde hair that refused to be confined whichever way it was pinned, her complexion as pale as the early morning midwinter sun. Having taught her since she was twelve, Marguerite still thought of her as a child, but seeing her outside the confines of her home, she realised for the first time how she'd developed the capacity to make heads turn. She was moving from girlhood to womanhood and the shine in her eyes, the tantalising flick of her head, told Marguerite she was beginning to discover the power her striking looks granted.

Alyce on the other hand, was still at that tender stage of childhood where everything is possible and little understood, the moment when dreams are real and nothing is unattainable, and it was all Marguerite could do not to run across the room and embrace her for it.

Instead, she wandered over to them, a hostess's smile firmly fixed in place. She didn't know if Musel was there to support her as a friend or to see what company she was keeping. She had no idea what conclusions he'd drawn from the questions surrounding her identity or what he thought might be the reason behind it. The only thing he'd made clear was that he wasn't prepared to protect her if she came under the scrutiny of the Third Reich. She couldn't blame him. These days, it was every man for himself. Lately, he'd begun entertaining some of the high-ranking German officers in his home. Given his position as mayor, nobody had openly questioned his intentions, but it didn't stop people murmuring behind closed doors. Armand in particular had been vocal about it, but given that he welcomed the enemy into his bar every night, he wasn't in a position to criticise.

Musel took a glass of wine from Biquet, who'd offered his services as a waiter for the evening, and raised it to Marguerite.

'Congratulations on a splendid event, Madame. Only you would think of putting on an exhibition at such a time and it was exactly what the town needed.'

Once again, he was the family man who greeted her at his home every Saturday afternoon rather than the stern figure who sat behind the mayor's desk, although now she'd seen that side of his nature, she'd never forget it. For her own safety, she had to assume he'd gone over to the side of the enemy and behave accordingly.

He peered at a small watercolour study of hyacinths, the bold blue flowers striking against the grey and white tones of the earthenware jug. 'Such cleverness, Marguerite. You can almost smell the scent of the flowers.'

Alyce stood up on her toes to get a better view of it. 'I love it, Daddy. Can we buy it?'

He winked at Marguerite. 'Perhaps. Let's look at the other pictures first.'

Tonight he was jovial, throwing out praise, while Celeste clung to his side, her lips stretched tightly over her teeth as she scanned the room. Marguerite touched her gently on the arm to get her attention.

'Thank you for coming.'

Celeste's expression didn't change as she turned to Marguerite, her focus shifting from the general to the particular.

'Nancy and Alyce wouldn't have missed it for anything. They've grown so fond of you over the years, and we like to do what we can to support local artists.'

Marguerite suppressed her irritation at Celeste's condescending tone. She wasn't the first wife to have her head turned by her husband's sudden rise in his social standing. She'd never shown any interest in art and it surprised Marguerite that she continued to indulge Nancy's and Alyce's desire for lessons when she paid so little attention to what they were taught.

The small gallery started to fill up as more people arrived. Marguerite was still talking to Celeste when she realised a priest had entered, his tall figure all the more striking for being dressed in black. It was the way he moved through the crowd, lithe as a cat that first caught her eye even though he had his back to her. Beyond this, it was his stillness as he stood in front of her watercolour study of Simone's favourite armchair that transfixed her.

It wasn't until Biquet offered him a glass of wine, drawing his attention from the painting, that she saw his face. Instantly, her heart began to pound. She'd seen him before. She'd know him anywhere – the man in black, a head and shoulders in height above her in his fedora. He was the man who'd kissed her in the park. She could still feel the heat of his embrace, the sensation of his lips pressed against hers.

It had to be Father Etienne Valade. The German soldiers who caught them together must have known he was a collaborator; otherwise, they'd have both been arrested. The kiss was probably nothing but a performance, a way of taking advantage of her, or to hide from her the fact that he was on the side of the enemy. Whatever his motivation, it had felt genuine at the time. Now she realised she'd been a fool to be taken in by him. If she was going to convince him to help her gain access to Otto Schmidt's files without him betraying her, she'd have to keep her wits about her.

Still, he was the only one looking at the paintings the way they were meant to be looked at, taking each one in, just as you'd take in a breath, and holding it as you'd hold a thought. He either understood them or he was very good at pretending.

She couldn't take her eyes off him as he moved about the room, considering first one picture and then another, projecting a sense of tranquillity and concentration that set him apart from the bustle that went on all around.

Jeanne, who'd spent the day at the gallery helping Marguerite to hang the pictures, must have noticed her unease, because she suddenly appeared at her side.

'Are you alright? You've gone very pale.'

'I'm fine. Sit down and take the weight off your feet. You're exhausted.'

The gallery had suddenly grown hot and Jeanne was perspiring. Marguerite asked Biquet to fetch her a glass of water and made her comfortable in a nearby chair before she turned her attention back to the priest.

Should she approach him, with the eyes of everyone on her? Would she give herself away and would he remember her? There was something in his manner that made her hesitate, a look of intelligence behind his eyes that suggested he'd see right through her. Whatever happened, she must never forget his subterfuge in the park.

Before she could work out what to do, three German officers entered the gallery, their leather boots polished to the same high shine as their laughing faces, their uniforms immaculate in contrast to the shabby Sunday best worn by the rest of the guests.

The atmosphere changed before they'd even removed their caps, the relaxed flow of a dozen conversations falling into silence as everyone turned to look at the unwelcome intruders. The youngest one among them, who was no more than seventeen and too fair to yet have the need of a razor, scanned the room until he spotted the priest and rushed to his side.

Marguerite watched as they talked, the priest now quietly leading him around the gallery, pointing out particular features in one painting and then another. After a few minutes the other two officers joined them, nodding at the priest's every word. Each time they moved, the crowd parted to allow them through, turning their backs so as not to meet their eyes.

Soon, a fourth officer appeared. This one was much older, with dark greased hair, his uniform taut around his wide girth. The younger officers greeted him with a deference that suggested he was their superior before they turned their attention back to the priest, who nodded at the older officer to acknowledge him.

'You're here to advise us on a bargain that will one day make us rich, eh, Father?' The superior officer's eyes scanned the walls of the gallery. 'At least there's none of that degenerate rubbish here. No doubt the Fuhrer would approve. Don't you think so, Father?'

Marguerite failed to catch the priest's reply, distracted by the cold touch of Celeste's fingers on the back of her hand as she leaned over and whispered.

'That's Otto Schmidt. If you're nice to him, he might buy one of your paintings.'

So that was Otto Schmidt, the man responsible for the deportation of so many innocent people to the prison camps. Marguerite tried not to let her contempt show on her face. She'd gather the evidence to see him punished if it was the last thing she did.

The arrival of yet another German uniform was too much for the other guests. In every corner of the room, the cheap wine handed out by Biquet was being gulped down, the half-empty glasses abandoned as people began to leave.

Marguerite knocked back the last dregs of her wine, furious at the intrusion of the officers. Her guests had come to relive a little of their former life and enjoy an evening without the constant threat of being watched, but now it was spoiled. It had only taken the sight of the German uniforms to break the pretence that she'd gone to so much effort to conjure.

Soon only a few guests lingered; among them was Yves Musel, who now caught the attention of the officers and beckoned Biquet to bring over another tray of drinks.

'Gentlemen, have a glass of wine. It's a little young, but it'll give you a taste of our local grapes.'

Whether the priest noticed the place emptying or not was unclear because he still only appeared to have eyes for Marguerite's paintings. After a while, he spoke to Simone, who was collecting the abandoned glasses from around the gallery. He must have asked her to point out the artist, because Marguerite suddenly felt the heat of his gaze.

His expression didn't change when he caught her eye, but he must have recognised her from the park. It was impossible that he hadn't.

Her fingers gripped the stem of her empty glass as he approached and introduced himself, her heart beating wildly against her chest. She'd done it; she'd reeled him in. The tall man all in black with eyes of blue ice and an expression that gave nothing away was Father Etienne Valade.

Marguerite stayed silent, her skin pricking as he stood close to her, not knowing if they should act like strangers or the intimates they'd once been.

'Congratulations on the exhibition, Madame.'

'Thank you.'

He was giving her no clues as to how she should be with him. She stared at her empty wine glass, longing for a refill. His polite manner was too convincing to be trusted. He was a priest. How could the man who'd kissed her so vehemently be a priest? And what had he been doing in the park in the dead of night?

'Your work is very interesting.'

'Thank you.'

She didn't know if she was addressing the man or the cloth he was hiding behind. It was a cunning subterfuge, but it also struck her as cowardly. Growing up, her life and education had been Bohemian, unconventional. No variety of religion had ever been offered to her and it had never crossed her mind to reach out for it. Art had been the only god she'd ever needed, the practice of it, her only act of worship. How could she now be expected to converse with a priest, with this man above all others?

He continued to examine the work on the walls, commenting on the sense of light she'd achieved in a watercolour study of a sprig of mimosa in a blue jug. She expected him to be condescending about her painting, as many men were, but he wasn't. Violet had been right. Few people understood art the way he appeared to.

'There's no price on this painting.' He turned to her as if it were an affront. 'How much is it?'

There'd been no thought of pricing the pieces in the exhibition. She hadn't expected to sell anything and it wasn't the point of it. Before she could explain this, he looked over his shoulder and summoned the first young officer, nodding to the watercolour.

'Hans, I advise you to buy this one.'

The priest looked at her again, his eyes urgent, demanding a reply. 'Hans would like to buy your painting. How much is it?'

Marguerite thought quickly, recalling how much she'd sold her last landscape for before the war, and wanting to put him off buying it, she doubled it.

Hans pulled out his wallet without flinching, his fingers flipping over the notes as he silently counted the multiples of tens and twenties, thrusting them at her without meeting her eye. She was appalled at the thought of taking his money, which was madness considering how they were nearly starving.

She pointed to the gallery owner, stationed behind his counter, the mahogany drawer that held the takings sadly empty. 'Monsieur Boucher is looking after the sales.'

By now, everyone else had left. Only Simone, Jeanne, Biquet and the priest remained. No one had approached her to say goodbye on their way out. Even Musel had offered nothing more than a discreet wave as he ushered Celeste and his daughters through the door.

While Monsieur Boucher wrote out a receipt, Marguerite removed the painting from the wall. Ordinarily she'd have wrapped it in fine paper and tied it with a ribbon, presenting it as an exquisite gift, but with such things no longer available, she simply handed it to the young officer.

Jeanne watched the transaction with her arms folded, her fierce stare sending the message that she wasn't afraid to scold him if he showed any disrespect.

Hans, so pleased with his purchase, seemed oblivious to the fact that he wasn't welcome, that his money wasn't wanted, or else he didn't care as he shoved the painting under his arm and slammed the gallery door behind him on his way out. After all, in his eyes, he was the conqueror and everything was his for the taking.

And still the priest lingered, his eyes moving from one picture to another in a way that was almost predatory. He didn't seem to have noticed that everyone else had gone. Marguerite coughed to draw his attention. Now she had him pinned, she wanted him to leave.

He stirred at the sound, as if she'd wrenched him from a faraway place. He turned to look at her, not even smiling as he met her eye.

'Your work is remarkable.'

She was used to praise, just as she was used to indifference, but this was something else: an opinion delivered in a way that was almost matter of fact. Unlike most men, he hadn't set out to flatter or patronise her. He'd simply stated his belief. Before she could think of anything to say, he swept out of the gallery, whispering something under his breath which she failed to catch and which she was too flustered to ask him to repeat.

Jeanne murmured *good riddance* behind his back while Simone put down the tray of wine glasses and checked the street to make sure the German officers had gone.

'How could you let that Hun buy the picture of my grandmother's blue jug? I can't stand to think of it hanging on his wall.'

Biquet grabbed a half-empty wine glass from the tray and knocked back its contents. 'Would you like me to steal it back for you, Madame?'

Marguerite moved a second glass out of his reach. 'I don't think that would be a good idea, Biquet.' She turned to Simone. 'How did you expect me to refuse him?'

'I don't know, but by taking money from the enemy you make yourself beholden to them.'

'It would have been too dangerous to refuse him.'

Having deducted his agreed commission, Monsieur Boucher offered Marguerite the money for the picture. Once again she stared at it, unwilling to take it despite the things it could buy: a couple of hens to supply them with a few eggs, the first decent cut of meat they'd tasted in months.

'Please, Monsieur, keep it all for yourself. Treat you and your wife to something nice with it.'

He lowered his eyes, reluctant to take the money. 'It wouldn't be right, Madame.'

'Think of your wife, Monsieur. A few good meals might bring back some of her strength.'

Madame Boucher hadn't fully recovered from a bout of tuberculosis the previous winter. Each time Marguerite saw her, she appeared thinner, her shoulders stooped a little further over her walking stick.

'You're very kind, Madame. Then you'll allow me to continue to display your unsold pictures. I'll contact you if there's any further interest.'

As they prepared to leave, Simone whispered to Marguerite, 'Was that the priest I saw you talking to?'

Marguerite nodded. 'It's the same man who came to my rescue in the park. I can't work out if it's a coincidence or not.'

'Madame Damas from the bakery saw him recommending your paintings to the German officers. She told me he lives in one of the villas that were requisitioned by the Germans.'

'Is that a fact, or local gossip?'

'Be careful, Marguerite. He might be a good kisser, but he's also a known collaborator. People don't forgive that sort of thing. If you associate with him, you risk getting on the wrong side of everyone in the town.'

Marguerite knew the risk she was taking. Day and night she tried to work out how to fulfil her duty to Britain and France while keeping everyone safe. Violet had already warned her that the priest might be an enemy collaborator. It was the reason she'd been ordered to befriend him, but it was a dangerous game, and now she had a sense of the kind of man he was, she had no idea what to do next.

The four of them had just left the gallery when they heard the sound of German voices coming from the house on the corner of the deserted street. Jeanne gripped Biquet's shoulders, her eyes widening with the fear of what was coming next.

'Isn't that Dr Goldman's house?'

Simone nodded, although they weren't supposed to call him 'Doctor' anymore, because the Third Reich refused to let him practise.

Suddenly, there was the sound of gunshot from an upstairs room. A moment later, Madame Goldman was dragged from the house by two German soldiers and thrown into the back of a truck, blood pouring from the gash on her head where she'd been struck.

Marguerite ran towards them, her rage extinguishing all sense of danger as she screamed, 'How dare you!'

Simone went after her and grabbed her around the waist, using the full force of her weight to pull her to the ground and hold her down.

'Don't, Marguerite or you'll be next.'

Jeanne turned Biquet's face away from the scene as a third soldier carried Dr Goldman's body out of the house and threw it into the back of the truck where it landed in a slump next to his sobbing wife.

'Let go of me.'

Marguerite kicked and struggled to break free of Simone's clutches, but Simone was stronger and more determined.

'I won't let you run towards your death, Marguerite.'

It was all over in a matter of seconds and the truck disappeared with its victims as quickly as it had arrived. Murder had taken place, swiftly and efficiently in the quiet street, and nobody would be held to account for it.

The four of them stayed where they were, unable to take in

the terrible crime they'd witnessed until Marguerite clambered to her feet, exhausted from her fight with Simone.

'You should have let me intervene.'

'They'd have shot you too, Marguerite. You're no use to the cause if you're dead.'

Jeanne hugged Biquet as if both their lives depended on it. 'I thought the Goldmans had left the town months ago when the round-ups first started.'

Simone brushed the dirt from her dress, her fingers worrying at the tear where Marguerite had tried to fight her off. 'Someone must have known differently and been prepared to denounce them for the price of a square meal.' She studied Jeanne's face. 'Are you alright? Take deep breaths. Try not to get upset. You have to think of the baby.'

'I'm fine. The baby's fine.'

Shamed by what had happened, Marguerite couldn't bear to look at anyone. Jeanne placed her hand on Biquet's head to comfort him as he sobbed quietly against her arm.

'I'll take Biquet home. His mother needs to know what's happened.'

After saying goodbye, Simone and Marguerite continued on their way in silence, too stunned by the events to express their emotions. It was only when they reached the bottom of the lane that led to the house that Simone started to cry. Marguerite held her as she let the worst of it out.

'Don't blame me for holding you back, Marguerite. I was only trying to protect you.'

Without Simone's intervention, Marguerite's body would now be slumped in the back of the truck alongside Dr Goldman.

'I'm too hot-headed. You always tell me so.'

'I know there's a war to be won, but I won't have you dying in the street like a dog.'

They clung to each other in the darkness, unable to discuss what they'd witnessed, or to judge whether their failure to intervene on behalf of the Goldmans had been shameful or wise.

Chapter 11

Father Etienne Valade appeared in Marguerite's dreams that night. The cold light of his eyes bored into her like chips of ice, clear and sharp as they examined her soul, her troubled mind confusing them with the eyes of the soldiers she'd witnessed dragging Dr Goldman's body from his house.

Distressed by her nightmare, she lay awake mourning the countless victims that had fallen prey to the Third Reich for simply daring to exist. She thought of the art that had been forcibly removed from the galleries and the homes of private collectors under Hitler's instruction. By fraternising with the enemy, was the priest condoning the cleansing of the art world to suit the uninformed taste of one ignorant dictator?

Those degenerate artists who'd so far managed to stay alive had fled their homes and were now living in fear or in hiding, just as Dorothy was, just as Dr Goldman and his wife had been forced to do until they were denounced. A whole generation of free thinking and diversity had been lost and it couldn't be allowed to continue.

The concentrated look she'd seen on the priest's face as he'd studied her work remained at the front of her mind like a fly buzzing around her head that couldn't be swatted. Every time she closed her eyes, there he was, tormenting her with those parting words he'd whispered that she'd failed to catch. And he was still with her the next morning as she dug over the sun-baked soil in the garden, preparing the bed for a second crop of lettuces.

'No rest for the wicked, I see.'

Marguerite jumped at the sound of the familiar voice. Dorothy had crept out of the cellar again and was strolling around the garden as if she hadn't a care in the world. She held up her hands when she saw the horror on Marguerite's face.

'I know I shouldn't be out; you don't have to tell me.'

A bird landed on a rustling branch. Marguerite glanced at it, feeling its eyes on her. 'I know it's difficult for you, but . . . '

'I didn't finish telling you what happened to Gregory.'

Anyone could arrive without warning and the pitch of Dorothy's voice carried far and wide on the morning breeze.

'Please go back inside. You're putting us all at risk.'

'Mauled, he was, by one of his own lions. It turned on him without warning during one of the shows. The whole crowd witnessed it, but there was nothing anyone could do but watch. If anyone had attempted to intervene, he'd have killed them too. Do you understand what I'm saying?'

Marguerite nodded, forcing her trowel into the unyielding soil.

'Instead, they bided their time, waiting until the lion was least expecting them, then they finished him off and made sure he never killed anyone again.'

'But it was too late for Gregory.'

'Gregory's death was avenged. He couldn't have asked for any more than that.'

Marguerite looked up, shielding her eyes from the sun, but Dorothy was already on her way back to the house. She must have overheard their conversation the night before and felt the weight of their sorrow through the stone floor that divided the kitchen from the cellar. Out of sight, but never out of hearing, it seemed Dorothy was destined to know all their secrets.

* * *

It was late in the afternoon and Marguerite was in her studio with Biquet. It was the day for his regular lesson and she'd set him the task of drawing a perfect circle with nothing but a fine pencil and his free hand. He was still shaken from witnessing the brutality inflicted on the Goldmans and she hoped the task would take his mind off it, even if only for a few minutes.

At first she thought she'd imagined the sound of the bicycle tearing up the loose stones in the lane that ran along the front of the house, until she heard the squeak of the metal gate and the following crunch of boots on the path, the rusty hinge and the rough gravel primed to alert them to anyone approaching the house.

Biquet looked up, his pencil twitching in his fingers. 'Someone's coming, Madame.'

She placed her hand on his arm to calm him. 'It's alright. We're not doing anything wrong.'

Thankfully, Dorothy's typewriter had fallen silent after a fervent outpouring earlier in the day. Having realised how the sound carried, they'd hung a large bell on a rope by the front door for visitors to ring, so she'd have a warning that someone was about to enter and know to stay quiet.

Marguerite waited until the bell had been rung. Peeping through the window, she saw the priest standing on the doorstep. She'd been ordered to befriend him and now here he was. She shouted hello, trying to make herself sound as if she were surprised to see him, hoping he wouldn't guess how much she'd been thinking about him since they first met.

'Madame, please excuse the intrusion. I was passing and wondered if it would be possible to look at more of your work.'

'Of course.'

He wiped his feet before he entered, as if her studio were a holy site, and took a deep breath, filling himself up with the smell of it like a traveller returning home after a long absence.

'This is Biquet. He's one of my students.'

The priest smiled. 'I'm delighted to meet you, Biquet.'

Biquet climbed off his stool and stood to attention. 'I'm not only one of Madame's students, Monsieur. I'm also her assistant.'

Marguerite ruffled his hair. 'Off you go now, Biquet. Your mother will be expecting you.'

He gathered up the drawing he'd been working on and pushed it into his pocket. 'I'll finish this at home, Madame, and bring it to show you next time.'

As soon as Biquet had gone, the priest began to explore the studio, nodding knowingly at the completed canvases stacked against the walls, the unfinished pieces on the easels. She followed his gaze as his eyes ranged over the wooden models of the human form she'd had since her days at the Slade, her jars of brushes and boxes of charcoal, her pencils and pens and watercolours, the cheap plaster statue of a cherub she'd bought in the street market in Arles.

Laid out in front of him was the history of her art and the inspiration for her future work, and in between was the place where she was now, stifled by her newfound struggle and the mission she had to risk revealing to him. 'I knew it. As soon as I saw your work in the gallery, I knew it was only scratching the surface. There's so much more to these domestic paintings than what most people see in them.'

His eyes searched her face, as if he were hunting out her darkest secret. It wasn't a priest now who stood before her, but the man who'd kissed her passionately in the park, his whole body alive with the excitement of what he'd just discovered. His eyes, those chips of blue ice, not only had the power to chill, but also to burn.

It was a warm day and he'd undone his soutane. Now, as he stood before her, she saw the lean figure he kept hidden behind the black cloth. The soft cotton of his white shirt, damp with perspiration, clung to his chest as it heaved with the exhilaration of discovering the hidden soul in her paintings.

Still he didn't mention their meeting in the park, or the kiss that had not only saved her from being arrested, but brought a part of her to life she never knew existed. Despite the deep connection that was beginning to bond them through her art, it was as if it had never happened.

She waited in silence while he examined everything in her studio again, his nose pushed up so close to the works he must have been able to smell the paint and the canvas beneath. His behaviour was respectful but intimate, as if he were examining every part of her body. She might as well have been naked in front of him. The thought of it made her shudder. He must have noticed her reaction because he suddenly turned to face her.

'Forgive me; I don't mean to invade your privacy. It's just that I find your work enormously interesting.' He picked up a watercolour study of the limestone hills that rose up behind the house, backed by the lilac sky. 'Why didn't you put this in your exhibition?'

'We're not allowed to reproduce images of the landscape since the Occupation. I painted it before the war, but I couldn't risk arrest by allowing it to be seen in public.'

'Of course. I should have realised.' He was still holding the painting, reluctant to put it down. 'Will you allow me to buy it?'

She thought of the German officers he associated with, how they'd look at this outlawed work and insist on destroying it if she let him have it.

'There's no need.'

'It's not an act of charity. I want to send it to my mother. Her apartment in Paris was bombed in 1940. She spent her life collecting lovely things: paintings and silver, delicate pieces of china. All of it was destroyed. I'd like her to have this. She needs beauty restoring to her life. It's the only thing that gives us hope for a better future. This painting will make her happy.'

She mentioned the price, doubling what she'd normally expect to get for such a piece to put him off, but he shook his head.

'That's not enough.'

Without giving her time to argue, he pulled a pile of notes from his pocket and placed them on her work bench, sliding them discreetly under a china saucer. Despite his good intention, something about the gesture made her feel cheap, as if he'd taken something away from her rather than acknowledging something for its value.

'You seem to know a lot about the value of art, Father.'

'You don't have to be so formal. Please call me Etienne.'

Had she broken a religious rule by calling him Father? 'So how do you know so much about art, *Etienne*?'

He looked down at his feet, trying to hide his smile. 'You don't have to say it quite like that.'

Was he ever going to mention the kiss?

She studied him as he talked. How old was he? Somewhere around forty. The fine lines that gathered around his eyes when he smiled hinted at a warm nature, the first signs of grey in his hair a testament to the decades he'd lived, the worries he'd nurtured.

'My father owned a gallery in Paris specialising in contemporary art. He gave his whole life to it, which meant it became my life too. When he died, my brother Thierry carried on the business. Despite my calling to the priesthood, I remained closely involved with it.'

'And so a priest can also be an art curator.'

'A man can have more than one passion. I see no distinction between a love of art and a love of God. One is simply a representation of the other. Anyone who can create beauty from nothing deserves admiration.'

For a moment, Etienne wasn't a priest. He was simply a man who loved art, and she had to remind herself why she'd been instructed to get to know him. What had he been doing in the park that night and why was he avoiding mentioning what had happened there between them? And if he wasn't a collaborator, why hadn't the soldiers arrested them? Surely it wasn't simply the

71

kiss that had saved them. As the thought of revealing her mission to him came back to her, her heart dipped and she was pulled back to the present and all its uncertainty.

It was impossible to think clearly in his presence. She wanted him to leave now, but still he lingered, exploring deeper into the corners of her studio as if he were unable to tear himself away.

He didn't seem to realise he was trespassing on her soul. Yet, by being in this place, she sensed that he too had left the war behind, and for those few precious moments, nothing else existed but the two of them, connected as they were by Marguerite's artistic gift and his appreciation of it.

More minutes passed. She was desperate now for him to leave, worried that Dorothy might think the coast was clear and start tapping away at her typewriter. They'd agreed to ring the bell at the door to signal the all-clear, but she didn't trust Dorothy to rely on it when the muse was upon her. And there was always the possibility that she might suddenly burst into a Russian folk song or emerge from the cellar demanding a blast of air.

Still he lingered over one particular painting, the one Musel had said reminded him of Gwen John. 'Has the war changed the way you see the world?'

If he'd witnessed the brutality served on the Goldmans first-hand, he'd have realised the naivety of his question.

'I have to paint what people will buy.'

'At the expense of hiding who you really are?'

'Yes, even at the cost of denying my true expression.'

'Then you do your talent a great disservice.'

No one had ever seen what he recognised in her work, the style and ambition she fought to constrain. Despite all the years they were married, not even Lance had understood her work like this.

'Art materials are hard to come by; I can't risk wasting them on paintings people won't buy.'

'I think you underestimate what you're truly capable of.'

Just when she thought he'd never go, he picked up his landscape painting, indicating his intention to leave before changing his mind, his eyes drawn once more to the plaster cherub, comparing it to the watercolour study she'd made of it.

'How did you manage to put so much grief into its expression?'

'I didn't realise I had until you just pointed it out.'

If he could read her work so deeply, then he'd know everything about her. The idea would have scared her if she hadn't been so surprised by it.

He seemed taken aback by her response, as if he'd trodden on unsettled ground. 'Perhaps it's just that those of us who have suffered choose to see grief everywhere.'

She could see it now when she looked at him, the emptiness behind the eyes. It wasn't there in the face of the priest, but it was there in the face of the man. To ask him about it now would have been too personal.

She inched towards the door, hinting that it was time for him to go. If Simone came home from work, hopefully she'd see his bicycle and know to be cautious. She'd curse her for bringing a German collaborator to their home, but what could Marguerite do? It wasn't as if she'd invited him.

Finally he began to leave. 'Our paths will cross again soon, perhaps.'

'I'm not one for going to church.'

There it was again, the smile he tried so hard to hide.

'I wasn't asking you to come to my church, although there are some beautiful frescoes in the crypt. You're welcome to look at them. My door is always open.'

She watched him leave, the painting he'd bought from her pressed against his heart as if it were something precious. It was only after he'd gone that she realised she hadn't had the presence of mind to offer to wrap it in brown paper or a piece of cloth to protect it.

For all his apparent charm and for all her uncertainty over where his loyalties lay, she had to see him again. It wasn't that he'd turned her head with his understanding of her work. She was only doing what she'd been instructed to do. She wasn't doing it for herself and she wasn't driven by the passion he'd ignited in her; she was doing it for France.

Chapter 12

The stone church was set back from the square at an uncertain angle, as if it were nervous of intruding and unsure whether it should be there at all. In reality, it had been in existence since before the square itself. Here, in the oldest part of the town, it was the most ancient building, erected even before the narrow streets that now led to it. Everything else on this little outcrop of a hill had grown up around it, the old houses constructed at a discreet distance, too fearful of its holiness to risk nudging up against it. Its bell tower, a landmark for miles around and perfectly positioned for looking out to sea, had dominated the skyline since before memory, before history. If it hadn't been a house of God, it could easily have been a fortress.

The area was on the wrong side of town and had long fallen out of fashion. It was the churches on the grander boulevards that now attracted the bigger congregations with their marble and mahogany interiors and stained-glass windows, and yet still this unassuming building endured as place of worship, steadfast behind its plain walls. As Marguerite stepped inside, feeling the cool embrace of the stone chilled air, she realised that this must largely have been down to the efforts of Etienne.

It was as if the mention of his name inside her head had the power to summon him, because suddenly there he was, standing at the altar celebrating Mass. She crept into a pew at the back, not wanting to cause a disturbance in a place that appeared almost empty but for the echoes of Etienne's voice.

After the brightness of the new day, it took a minute for her eyes to adjust to the low light, until slowly out of the darkness, figures emerged on the pews in front of her: a hefty figure here, his shoulders hunched against the cold, another figure there, his head bowed, the angle of it giving away his deep concentration. A cluster of three in one corner, their backs upright as if they were sitting to attention.

The one thing they all had in common were their German uniforms. There were no local people here, only enemy soldiers. Marguerite went cold at the realisation. She remembered how people had left her exhibition when Etienne arrived. It wasn't only the German soldiers they were avoiding. It was Etienne too. They didn't come to his church for the same reason that they didn't want to associate with him at the gallery. No one wanted to worship in the company of the enemy and no one wanted to take religious instruction from a priest who welcomed them.

In spite of what Violet had said, Marguerite hadn't expected him to have this amount of complicity with the enemy. It explained why she'd been told to target him as part of her mission. The cold air, mixed with the smell of incense, suddenly made her feel ill, but if she got up to go, it would be too obvious. It wouldn't only be her decision to leave that would put her under scrutiny, but the reason she'd come here in the first place. She had to sit and wait it out, no matter how long it took.

Etienne must have spotted her from his place at the altar. As soon as the ceremony was over, he began to make his way to her. He'd only taken a few steps when he was intercepted by the group of three German officers who'd been sitting together in the corner.

The loudest officer in the group patted him on the back,

drawing him into a jovial conversation as if he were an old friend. Her stomach turned over when she realised it was Otto Schmidt. She also recognised Hans, the young officer who'd bought her painting of the mimosa in the blue jug. Marguerite stayed where she was, not wanting to draw attention to herself. If she left now, Etienne would know she'd run away and want to know why.

While she waited, a young girl of about sixteen appeared from a side door and crept around the church, moving slowly from pillar to pillar as if she didn't want to be seen. Whisper thin and with milk-white skin, she could have been a ghost. Her blonde hair, thickened by its natural curl, was the only aspect of her that was of any substance beyond her beauty, which was striking enough to stop anyone in their tracks, man or woman.

Etienne must have noticed her hovering out of the corner of one eye, because he suddenly broke off his conversation and went over to her. Marguerite strained to hear what he was saying as he took her hand and gently stroked it, but his voice was too low to be audible even in this echo chamber of a building.

Schmidt leered at the girl, the snide angle of his lips shifting as he whispered something to the other two officers who sniggered. Her innocence was already a victim of their cruel minds even if she was too innocent to realise it.

After a moment, an older woman in a neat floral tea dress appeared at the girl's side and gently took her arm. She apologised to Etienne for the interruption before spiriting the girl away, her low voice scolding her in a sing-song rhythm that was really no admonishment at all.

The distraction was enough to break up the group and the soldiers finally began to leave. Marguerite stayed where she was, head bowed and hands clasped in mock prayer so they wouldn't notice her on their way out.

The door had barely closed behind them when Etienne approached her, taking off his ceremonial robes as he drew nearer. It surprised her to see that even in church he wore a simple white shirt, the cotton fabric taut across his broad shoulders and the lean muscles of his chest. Dressed like this, he could have been any man on the street, but not just any man because it could only ever be Etienne. It was only their fourth meeting, but already she'd recognise him in a crowd.

This time, he didn't bother to hide his smile as he slipped into the pew beside her, his arm brushing against her as he leaned over and whispered, 'I'm glad you came. I didn't know if you would.'

The touch of his warm body caused something inside her stomach to clench and all at once she was back in the park with his arms wrapped around her.

'You promised to show me some frescoes.'

'Come with me.'

He led her to the back of the church, down a set of stone steps and through a labyrinth of ancient passages to the crypt. As they walked, she asked him about the girl she'd seen.

'That was Catherine. She's my brother Thierry's child. She's staying at the presbytery. We thought it would be safer for her here than in Paris.'

'Is the woman your brother's wife?'

'No, the woman you saw is Madame Mercier.'

'She's your housekeeper?'

He seemed embarrassed by the notion although it wasn't uncommon for members of a congregation to pay someone to take care of the domestic work in a presbytery, leaving their priest free to concentrate on higher matters.

'In a manner of speaking, although her main duty is to take care of Catherine while her mother remains in Paris.'

'Is your brother still running the family art gallery?'

She'd heard about the art scandal that was happening under German rule. Many dealers were buying and selling degenerate art for unreasonably low prices, swindling both the artists and the art collectors. She wanted to know if Etienne's brother was caught up in it, whether Etienne himself was also involved.

There was no natural light in the deep cavern of the church and nothing to connect them but their voices and the soft touch of Etienne's hand as he continued to lead her deeper into the mystery of the ancient building.

'So many questions.'

She faltered, disoriented by the place in which she found herself. 'I'm sorry. It's none of my business.'

They were silent while he lit a candle. Together they watched the bright spark of the flame begin to bud in the small space where they stood.

'Look, Marguerite. Can you see?'

He held the candle in front of her, guiding its light to show up the frescoes, the shapes and dips of the paint bedded into the ancient plaster by previous hands. Hidden away for centuries, the faces on the figures remained bright and full of hope, the flowers they clutched as fresh as if they'd just been picked from a midsummer meadow. She'd never seen anything so vital, so secret.

'Can I touch it?'

He reached for her hand, tracing her fingers along the outline of the young woman, following the contours of the flowers in her hair, down the long line of her neck and shoulders and the length of her body. Marguerite felt a chill run through her, as if the fingers were tracing the curves of her own body, touching her in a way she longed to be touched. She remained silent, not wanting to break the mood as she admired the images painted by unknown artists whose lives she could only imagine.

All too soon the minutes passed and the small nub of candle began to give up the last of its flame. Seeing she'd begun to shiver, Etienne placed his arm around her.

'You're cold. We should go.'

'I wish we could stay here forever.'

Her voice sounded strange, even to her own ears, and more vulnerable than she'd ever want to admit. It was the deadening effect of the stone that did it, the weight of so much history closing in around her.

'It's time to go, Marguerite. It's only special if we're left wanting more of it.'

The mood was broken as they retraced their steps back into the light, the intimacy they'd shared in the ancient space gone as surely as he closed the door on the crypt. His manner was more formal as he let go of her hand and stood apart from her, just as he'd done in the park once the threat of the soldiers had passed.

Suddenly the day felt much colder. She cleared her throat, embarrassed by the vulnerability she'd revealed to him. 'Thank you for showing me the frescoes.'

'Would you like me to show you around the rest of the church? We have a number of interesting paintings. One was once reputed to be by Rubens, but it turns out it's a copy made by any number of his assistants. It's worth seeing, nevertheless.'

'If it's only a copy, it would explain why your German friends haven't taken it for themselves.'

The words were out of her mouth before she could stop them. Thinking about his family's art gallery in Paris had unsettled her, that and the fact that Catherine had been removed from Paris for her own safety only to be forced to endure the attention of the German soldiers in Etienne's church. Didn't he realise what he was doing? What the monsters he was associating with were guilty of?

He looked as if she'd struck him. 'They're not my friends, Marguerite. If the German soldiers choose to come to my church, it's not my place to turn them away.'

'But they're our enemy.'

'They're men. Some of them are no more than children. They're scared. They want their mothers.'

She thought of Otto Schmidt, of his loud voice and his swagger, his overfed belly when the French nation was starving.

'Not all of them, Etienne. Some of them are killers.'

'If I can offer them religious instruction, perhaps they'll become better men. Doing good deeds in war sets us apart from those who seek only to kill.'

'You think you can change these murderers? That you can save their souls?'

'We're at war, Marguerite. We're faced with impossible choices every day. I want to be able to look back on these dark days and know I did my best, that I did more good than harm.'

His words struck her as arrogant. This was why the people of the town refused to attend his church, why they called him a collaborator.

'This is a house of God, Marguerite. It's not my place to turn anyone away.'

'Do you forgive them for what they do?'

'It's not for me to forgive.'

It felt good to see the confusion in his eyes after the way he'd kissed her in the park, after he'd put his arm around her in the crypt and whispered to her in a way he shouldn't.

'How can you be friends with such men?'

There was no room for compassion for the enemy at such times. How could she trust him to help her fulfil her mission when he spoke like this?

'I'm sorry I've offended you. It wasn't my intention. You must excuse me.'

He walked away, his footsteps fading as he retreated to the sacristy. Realising her blunder, she called after him, but he didn't look back and he didn't say goodbye.

The door echoed to a close and suddenly she was alone in the church. All around, the plaster idols looked down on her, their accusing eyes silently begging to know what she'd been thinking. But she hadn't been thinking anything; she'd simply wanted to understand how a man of such sensitivity and intelligence could entertain men who were guilty of such brutality, and in wanting to know this, all sense of her mission for Violet had been forgotten.

* * *

81

As Marguerite stepped out of the church, she spotted an old woman on her hands and knees in the square. Her long grey hair and baggy clothes had been pulled in all directions where she must have been dragged by the group of German soldiers who were standing over her, taunting her over her age and her shabbiness.

Marguerite ran towards them, shouting at them to stop while everyone else in the square, the young mothers and the old men taking the morning air, looked the other way and pretended not to see what was happening.

'Leave her alone.'

She recognised the tallest of the soldiers from the church. He'd been sitting alone somewhere off to one side and had marched out as soon as Mass had ended, his boots heavy on the ancient terracotta tiles.

'You'll stay out of this, Madame, if you know what's good for you.'

He stood with his legs astride, hands on hips, his fingers glancing the barrel of the pistol in his belt as if to bolster his sense of power.

'Marguerite, let me deal with this.'

She hadn't realised Etienne was there until she heard his voice behind her. She watched as he crossed the square with great strides and helped the old woman to her feet, brushing the dust from her skirt and picking up her string bag which one of the soldiers had ripped from her hand.

'Come into the church and rest for a while, Madame. I'll find you something to eat.'

He acted as if the soldiers weren't there, treating the old woman with respect and restoring her dignity with his soothing words. Once she was calmer, he turned to the soldiers, his expression full of disappointment.

'Shame on you.'

His words were enough to shift the burden of the old woman's humiliation onto the young men's shoulders, and they sloped off to the far corner of the square, where they lit a cigarette beneath the shelter of the lime trees and stared at their boots.

Before he entered the church, Etienne caught Marguerite's eye. 'I'm sorry you had to witness that, Madame.'

What did he think her life was like if he expected her to have been shocked by such a scene? Did he think she was immune to such sights? Didn't he understand the effect the German occupiers were having on the lives of everyone? And if he knew of their atrocities, why had he befriended them?

Chapter 13

'Are you alright? You've been gone for hours.'

Simone was sitting at the kitchen table with Jeanne, her eyes narrow with anxiety. These days, she worried every time Marguerite left the house, but the war wouldn't be won if everyone stayed at home.

'I went to visit Etienne's church.'

She told them about Catherine; about how distracted she'd appeared at the end of Mass, wandering about like the ghost of a lost child, and how Etienne seemed to know just how to comfort her.

Jeanne placed her swollen feet on Simone's lap and leaned back in the chair, considering Marguerite's story. 'Etienne claimed she was his niece, you say?'

'I could see the family resemblance in their height and their good looks.'

Simone frowned at the mention of Etienne's good looks. 'Did you hear her call him uncle?'

'No, she didn't speak at all.'

'So how do you know she's his niece and not his daughter?'

Marguerite laughed at the absurdity of the question. 'Because he's a priest.'

'He's also a collaborator and a red-blooded man. Remember how he kissed you in the park. Was that the innocent kiss of a priest?'

She still hadn't worked out what he'd been doing in the park, how he'd managed to stop them being arrested.

Marguerite was saved from answering by Dorothy's knock on the cellar door, the regular three taps indicating she wanted to come up for air.

'Forgive me for interrupting, but I couldn't help overhearing the conversation and wanted to throw in my penny's worth.'

Marguerite closed the window shutters so no one would see her if they happened to approach the house. 'What do you think, Dorothy? Should I trust this priest?'

There'd definitely been something odd about the situation in the church and Etienne had been evasive when she'd asked about his family. She needed to be more certain she could trust him before she risked asking for his help in obtaining the documents incriminating Otto Schmidt for war crimes.

Jeanne paddled her feet, encouraging Simone to massage them. 'There's more to this priest than meets the eye.'

Dorothy took a seat at the table, resting her chin on the palm of her hand as she considered Jeanne's comment.

'Trust can be an elusive creature. It can be hard to grasp and once it slips away, it's gone for good.'

'Do you think I should believe what he tells me?'

Dorothy mulled over Marguerite's question. 'You need to get to know him better. If he's a bad 'un, he'll soon reveal himself.'

That was all well and good, but after their heated discussion in the church, he probably wouldn't talk to her again. How could she have made such a blunder when it had been going so well?

'I went to see Monsieur Boucher on the way home.'

Simone looked up from Jeanne's feet and frowned at Marguerite's comment. 'You're changing the subject.'

'Yes, I am. He's sold another three paintings. It means we can buy extra food and candles.' Now there were no light bulbs to be had, candles had become a necessity.

Simone stared at the money as Marguerite placed it on the table between them. 'The paintings were bought by the Germans, I suppose. You know what that makes you in the eyes of everybody in the town?'

It had come as a shock when Monsieur Boucher told her that Hans and two other officers had returned to buy further paintings, and that they'd done it at the suggestion of Etienne.

'The sale was through the gallery, so there's no direct connection to me.'

Dorothy raised her hand as if enlightenment had suddenly struck. 'There we have it. The priest is either doing you a favour out of the goodness of his heart or he wants you beholden to him.'

Simone placed Jeanne's feet on the floor and got up from the table. 'Do what you like with the money, but don't expect me to eat any food you buy with it. I'd choke on it before I could bring myself to swallow it.'

They all had to do what they could to survive, but was this consequence of following Violet's orders a step too far? Marguerite's throat constricted at the thought of being considered a collaborator by the people of the town and what the consequences of that might be. She pushed the money across the table to Jeanne.

'Please take it. Buy yourself some extra food or get something for the baby.'

It was then Marguerite noticed an envelope had been pushed under the front door. She picked it up, not recognising the handwriting. Her blood ran cold as she tore it open, dreading what was inside.

Marguerite,

Stay away from that Nazi collaborator Etienne Valade. This is the only warning you'll get. If you disobey, the punishment will be worse than anything the Germans would do to you.

Jeanne's face turned pale as Marguerite passed it around the table for them all to read. 'Someone must have approached the house while we were talking. Do you think they overheard us?'

Marguerite shrugged, fear making her cautious. 'You'd better sleep here tonight. We don't know who might be waiting outside.'

Unsettled by the thought of being seen, Dorothy slipped back to the cellar. Simone closed the hatch after her, covering it with the accumulated junk.

'That's the thing you need to understand, Marguerite; however careful you are, there's always someone better at keeping themselves out of sight. And they're watching you, even when you think they're not. If you insist on seeing this priest, it will only bring more trouble to our door.'

How tiny a transgression it had seemed, visiting the church to see the frescoes, and yet watchful eyes had found her out and were prepared to judge her without knowing the reason behind it.

She turned the letter over in her hand, recalling what had happened during her visit to the church. By challenging Etienne for welcoming the enemy, she'd failed to gain his trust, which meant she'd failed in her duty to France. This was the truth they should be berating her for, not for associating with a collaborator. She must learn to keep a cooler head.

Reluctant to waste a precious match on burning the note, she tore the paper into fine shreds until there was nothing left of the venomous words, only abstract marks on the tiny strips, which she took outside and sprinkled on the upturned soil for the oncoming rain to disintegrate and the snails to chew on. By morning, there'd be little left of it but the bad memory of its bitterness and the unseen mark it had scored on her heart.

Chapter 14

That night the smallest sounds caused Marguerite alarm every time she closed her eyes. The soughing of the trees as a cool mist of rain imposed itself on the warm summer night. The rustling of the long grass at the edge of the lane where the old man from the nearest house checked the traps he'd set for the wild rabbits. When she concentrated she could identify every disturbance, but still she wasn't reassured as hour by hour she learned to live her life on the precipice of fear.

Having had such little rest, she was listless and thick-headed when Armand arrived the next morning.

Simone smiled as she greeted him, running her fingers through her hair and smoothing down her dress to make the best of herself.

'Armand. We haven't seen you for so long.'

He threw himself down into a chair, looking as if he hadn't slept, the dark shadows beneath his eyes making him appear moody, sullen.

'The bar is busier than ever. Those Germans know how to drink.'

He picked up one of Marguerite's pencils from the table and started tapping it rapidly against his knee. 'On top of the extra work, there's the other business to attend to.' He nodded to the floor, indicating Dorothy in the cellar.

'How soon will you be moving her?' Simone lowered her voice. 'It's not safe for her to stay in one place for too long.'

Armand shrugged, visibly irritated by what he considered a defeat. 'I can't find anyone to take her. People are too nervous of the Germans. They're not like the Italians. They're too sharp-eyed and prosperous enough not to be tempted by a bribe.'

He turned to Marguerite, jabbing the pencil in the air. 'She's not helping. Everyone in the town is talking about her selling herself to the Germans.'

'I haven't sold myself. They bought some of my paintings. It's no different to you taking money from them in your bar.'

'You're a woman. Selling your art and selling yourself. It's the same thing.'

'It's not the same thing at all.' Marguerite snatched her pencil from his fist before he snapped it in two. 'Anyway, you can think what you like.'

He squinted at her from beneath heavy eyelids. 'Have you heard what happened to the priest?'

Marguerite tried not to react. 'No. What priest?'

'The one who denounced Dr Goldman and his wife.'

Her stomach turned over. Surely Etienne wasn't capable of such a thing?

'What was his name?'

'He told the Gestapo where they were hiding in exchange for a hefty donation to his church. Twenty years the good doctor had delivered the babies in this town and healed the sick, but it didn't stop the Germans shooting him in cold blood.'

'Who was it, Armand? Who denounced them?'

Armand threw Marguerite an irritated look. 'I told you. It was the priest. We shot him in the stomach and left him to die in a ditch like a dog. Let's see if that gets him into Heaven.'

Simone grabbed Armand's jaw to get his attention. 'We know it was a priest, but which one? What was his name?'

'What does it matter? Priests are all the same.'

Simone gave his cheek a sharp slap. 'We need his name, Armand.'

'I bet you do.'

Marguerite looked him in the eye. 'Stop playing games, Armand. Tell me his name.'

'Father Pierre Giraud. That was his name. Does it ring any bells with you?'

She shook her head, not wanting to give away any signs of her relief.

'We stripped him of his clothes, whipped him and dragged him through the streets before we shot him.'

'Then your brutality is no better than the Germans.'

'True. And I tell you this as a warning, Marguerite.'

'What warning's that?'

'Stay away from that German-loving priest. You're not even a Catholic. You've haven't stepped inside a church in all the years you've lived here. I won't have you risking our work with your vile associations. You're putting everyone in danger. I trusted you. I brought Dorothy here because I thought she'd be safe.'

'You brought her here because we speak English and because you knew Simone wouldn't be able to refuse you. You don't think of the danger you've put us in with your reckless actions.'

Simone placed a steadying hand on Marguerite's shoulder. 'Don't make matters worse than they already are.'

Marguerite gave Armand a cool look. 'See, she's scared of you. That's not love in her eyes, that's fear.'

'Please stop shouting at each other.'

They'd been so busy arguing, they hadn't noticed Jeanne slip into the kitchen. She helped herself to a glass of water and leaned against the dresser as if to anchor her body against a spinning world. 'It's impossible to rest when you're all making so much noise.'

'I'm sorry, my love.' Simone gave her a hug, apologising for the disturbance before turning her attention back to Armand. 'Have you brought us any food?'

Since keeping Dorothy in hiding, it had become a battle to

keep the three of them fed on the rations meant for two people. Rations that had been reduced so much during the course of the war, that they were barely enough to keep one person from starving. Now, food was what they thought of most of the time, the emptiness in their stomachs the thing that kept them awake at night and determined almost every waking activity.

Armand shrugged. 'Getting extra food isn't as easy as all that.'

It was another promise he'd failed to keep. Before he could offer more false hope, they heard the sound of knocking from the cellar. Simone opened the door under the stairs where Dorothy was crouched among the rusty gardening tools, having negotiated her way out of the hatch with her carpet bag clutched to her chest.

'I'm sorry I've been such an awful nuisance. I never meant to bring you all this trouble. I'll get off now. I've packed my bag. I'll make my own way to the border.'

Marguerite grabbed Dorothy's arm. 'You can't leave. It's not safe and you'll never find your way alone.'

'I'll ask directions. I refuse to be the bore who stays too long at the party.'

Armand threw his hands in the air. 'What am I supposed to do about this?'

Simone encouraged Dorothy into a chair and wrestled her carpet bag from her. 'You can't go anywhere on your own, Dorothy. Your French is terrible.'

'Then I'll charm someone into escorting me. Cartwheels and back flips aren't my only talents you know.' She sighed, her body slumping with the depth of her tormented mood. 'If Edith hadn't left me, none of this would have happened. It was too cruel of her to go when she knew how much I depended on her.'

It was only now, in the unforgiving light of day that Marguerite realised how thin Dorothy was, how her skin had become as white as porcelain from a lack of sun and constant fear. The sight of her vulnerability made Marguerite want to cry. 'Wait a bit longer, for my sake.'

'It's too good of you, but I couldn't possibly.' Dorothy rose from the chair with a forced brightness that fooled no one. 'I'd better get going while there's plenty of daylight. Toodle-oo and thanks for everything.' Sniffing back a tear, she picked up her carpet bag and glanced over her shoulder towards the cellar. 'You don't mind if I leave my typewriter, do you? Not sure I'd manage to carry it all the way back to Blighty.' She tapped her bag. 'The novel's in here, safe and sound, so there's no need to worry on that score.'

Simone locked her arms around her and pinned her to the chair, laughing as she did it, as if to mock the danger they were in. 'I'm not letting you go. You'll stay as long as necessary. We won't abandon you and we won't pass you into anyone else's care until we're sure it's safe.'

Armand rubbed his fingers through his four-day growth of beard. 'Listen to what Simone says. For once, she talks sense. We're in this together. If one of us is betrayed, then we all are.'

Marguerite was all out of patience with his petulance. 'What did you come here for, Armand, if not to help?'

He shot to his feet, needled by her tone, and stepped towards her, pushing his face close up to hers and clenching his fists. 'Be careful, Marguerite. For all your years of living here, you're still an outsider, a stranger. When it comes down to it, we don't know who you are.'

'And who are you, beyond a man growing rich from selling foreign beer and Armagnac to the enemy?'

'You've gone too far, Marguerite. Don't think we'd put up with you if you weren't necessary to us.'

He retrieved three identity cards from inside his jacket. 'These need the letter J removing from them and the names changing to something French. Do them straight away. There's a rumour the Gestapo are planning to round up another family this evening. Now they're close to losing the war, they're increasing their searches and are more brutal than ever.'

He glanced at Jeanne who was still leaning against the dresser, sipping water. 'She can do the handover this afternoon.'

'It's too dangerous. I won't have Jeanne taking any more risks.'

Jeanne brushed off Simone's comment. 'Of course I'll do it.'

Armand nodded, chastened by Simone's words and Jeanne's bravery. 'The handover will be at the same time and place as before. This will be the last time, I promise.'

Marguerite slipped the identity cards into her pocket. 'I'm running out of lactic acid. It's the only thing that will remove the official ink. Can you get me some more?'

'I'll see what I can do.'

Still full of bluster, Armand stormed out of the house, slamming the door behind him and determined as always to have the final word.

Simone waited until the sound of his footsteps on the gravel had silenced and he'd banged the gate before she spoke. 'You shouldn't say such things to him, Marguerite. You know it makes him angry. He hates being servile to the Germans. It's humiliating for him to have to allow them to drink in his bar.'

'Accusing me of fraternising with the enemy makes him a hypocrite.'

'The alternative is to tell him the truth, and we can't risk that, can we?'

Marguerite sighed. Simone was right, as always. 'You deserve to be loved by someone better. Why do you put up with him?'

'Because there's no one else. The best of our men have been slaughtered or taken prisoner, in case you hadn't noticed.'

They'd been so busy arguing over Armand that they'd forgotten about Dorothy until she suddenly piped up.

'I suppose I'd better toddle off back to my lair before there are any more unexpected visitors.' She paused on her way to the cellar and turned back to face them, a stray tear escaping from the corner of one eye. 'I'll be forever grateful to you for what you've done for me. I'll make it up to you both; you have my word, if not in this life, then in the next.'

Chapter 15

It was late the following day. Marguerite and Biquet had been working in her studio all afternoon, changing the names on another batch of identity cards when they heard a car pull up in front of the house. She looked out of the window, angling herself so she couldn't be seen; a surge of panic running through her veins as four German officers climbed out of a black Citroën.

'Biquet, run away. Use the back door. Go quickly.'

Someone must have betrayed her. She thought of the vile letter that had been pushed under the door after she'd been seen entering Etienne's church. People didn't forget such things, nor did they forgive. She slipped the identity cards between the pages of an old sketchbook and locked it in a drawer. If they searched the studio, they'd inevitably find them, but there was no time to put them anywhere else.

The soldiers made their way to the house and rang the bell. Marguerite didn't respond, buying Biquet time to slip out through the garden and disappear into the woods beyond. If she didn't answer at all, how long would it be before they started nosing around, prying into hidden corners? If they spotted her, she'd have to pretend she'd been too absorbed in her work to hear them.

She turned to one of her sketchbooks and began to draw the

plaster cherub, making it appear as if she were in the middle of something that needed concentration, risking another glance out of the window just as a second black Citroën pulled up and Otto Schmidt climbed out of it.

Soon his fist was banging on her studio door. When his face appeared at the window, she tried to appear distracted, as if she'd been too focused on her work to hear his knock. Forcing herself to catch his eye, she rose from her work bench and unlocked the door, hiding the contempt she felt every time she saw him.

He clicked his heels, drawing her eye to the pristine leather of his boots, polished to a high shine. This was why there was no leather for shoes, why people were reduced to wearing wooden sabots. The Germans had taken it all, just as they'd taken their animals and their food, their produce and their self-respect.

'Forgive the intrusion, Madame, but I saw the watercolour of the mimosa in the blue jug you sold to Hans and I want to see more of your work.'

'Monsieur Boucher still has some of my paintings on display in his gallery.'

'We visited there too, but I want to see *all* your work.'

The emphasis on *all* carried a sinister ring. She stepped aside, letting the officers in because she had no choice. At least they weren't here to search the house, or not yet anyway.

'My studio isn't arranged for visitors. You'll have to take it as you find it.'

Thank God Armand hadn't taken it upon himself to hide any more weapons in the studio. His recent suspicion of her had achieved one thing, at least.

Schmidt grinned, clearly relishing the power his position gave him. 'Our arrival has startled you.'

She tried to seem casual, as if they hadn't given her the fright of her life. 'Don't make these young men buy anything they don't want.'

He scanned her studio, taking nothing in beyond Marguerite herself, in her bare feet and her shabby tea dress.

It was impossible to keep her eyes on all five men at once. 'Are you interested in any particular kind of art?'

Schmidt sniffed, his attention drawn by a painting of a wicker chair at an open window. 'Not women's art, that's for certain.'

His condescension didn't bother her. She didn't respect him enough for his opinion to matter. 'Then what can I help you with?'

He sat on the stool at her work bench and nodded to the four young officers. 'Wait in the car.'

Her stomach turned over. He wanted her alone. She concentrated on his face, forcing herself not to glance at the drawer where the identity cards were hidden.

He dragged her sketchbook towards him and examined the outline of the cherub, tearing the edge of the paper into fine strips. 'There must be many artists like you in the area.'

Paper was too precious to waste. She bit back her irritation. 'Perhaps; it's an inspiring place.'

'In a town like this, I'd have thought everybody knew everybody.'

'Some of us keep ourselves to ourselves.'

'You have friends here, though.'

'Of course.'

'You know the young woman who works in the café. She takes an afternoon walk through the main square, regular as clockwork. A pretty little thing she is, so full of life.'

He was talking about Jeanne. Marguerite forced herself not to react. 'I don't have time for afternoon walks.'

He drummed his fingers on the torn page of her sketchbook, his eyes fixed on her face. 'Neither do I, but once it was brought to my attention how friendly she was, how she liked to stop and chat, I decided to go and talk to her myself. You can imagine how lonely it is here for a high-ranking German officer such as myself. And so I went to the main square yesterday afternoon and watched her strolling around the fountain until she settled on a bench. She had a book under her arm, but she made no effort to read it. She seemed more interested in watching people come and go.

'But there I had it, a way of starting a conversation with her. So I sat beside her on the bench and asked her to tell me about the book she was carrying. She hesitated and stuttered and said she couldn't tell me about it because she hadn't read it.

'Yet I could see the bookmark, buried between the pages somewhere in the middle. When I pointed this out, she stuttered again. By this time, I was very interested in the book, as you can probably imagine.'

He tore another strip from the sketch. 'As she couldn't tell me anything about the book, I insisted on looking at it myself. Naturally, when I took it from her, the pages fell open at the bookmark.'

Marguerite swallowed, dreading what was coming next.

'But it wasn't a usual bookmark. Do you know what it was?'

'No.'

'It was an identity card. Can you imagine someone leaving such a thing in a book?'

Marguerite's hands were shaking. She made them into fists and pushed them behind her back. 'No.'

'There weren't only one or two, but three hidden between the pages. They appeared to belong to members of the same family and yet she said she didn't know anything about them or how they'd got there. How could someone be so foolish?'

'I don't know.'

'Can't you explain it?'

'No.'

'Nor could the young woman sitting beside me on the bench.' He clicked his fingers. 'What did I say her name was?'

'You didn't.'

He smiled, silent for a moment. 'You don't know her, of course.'

Marguerite shook her head, her eyes steady on his.

'I had to arrest her. You can understand why.'

'For carrying a book she hadn't read?'

'No, Madame. It's far more serious than that. Can't you guess?'

'No.'

'Surely you can. Why don't you have a go? What conclusions would you have drawn from such a finding?'

Marguerite's rage was rising. 'What is it you want from me?'

He forced himself off the stool and began stalking the studio, his eyes scanning every corner of the room. 'The identity cards were forgeries, but very cleverly done. It was only because they were hidden in the book that I guessed what they were.'

'The girl on the bench; what happened to her?'

'We questioned her, of course. There are things she still isn't telling us. She needs a few days to recover before we can question her again.'

His eyes flicked to her face. 'She was carrying a child, but not anymore.'

Marguerite suppressed a cry. She turned away and tidied her work bench, keeping her hands busy to stop herself flying at him.

'I'm no expert on these things, Madame, but I've been reliably informed that whoever it was who forged the identity cards was very clever, probably an artist of some kind. So now I have to make it my business to keep an eye on people like you.'

She forced herself to meet his eye. 'You've seen my work. You said yourself it's only women's art. There's no cleverness to it.'

'You're right. There's no worth in it at all.' He ripped the page from her sketchbook and tore it in half, letting the pieces fall to the floor. 'But I'll be watching you anyway.'

He walked out without saying another word, leaving Marguerite holding her breath, silencing her anger and her fear until long after he was gone.

Chapter 16

The news of Jeanne's arrest and loss of her unborn child at the hands of the Gestapo landed like a stone in their hearts. Despite enquiries through Armand's network, there was no evidence that she'd been betrayed. Her capture might genuinely have been down to ill luck, or the misfortune of having caught the watchful eye of a German soldier. It was a reminder of the risks they were taking even when they appeared to be innocently going about their daily business. Chance or the coincidence of being stopped for a random check at the wrong moment was something they couldn't protect themselves against.

Simone was too distraught to function. Unable to eat or sleep, she took herself off to bed, cursing and railing at Armand, blaming him for the brutality the Gestapo had served on her beloved Jeanne and on the beautiful unborn child who'd been murdered before they'd been allowed to live. Even if they let Jeanne go, she'd never be the same again. Life would never be the same again.

The violence they'd inflicted on Jeanne made Marguerite more determined than ever to complete her mission for Violet. The only way to avenge the murder of Jeanne's child was to make sure the evidence was gathered to convict Schmidt and his associates for their war crimes. Schmidt and all the men like him would be made to pay for the brutality and repression they'd imposed on her beloved France.

Even now, she was still tormented by her memories of the previous winter. It had been the coldest anyone had known, biting into the parts of everyday life that even the enemy hadn't managed to reach and making the cruelty and the deprivation they inflicted so much worse. The lack of fuel meant there was no heat. The lack of heat meant there was no hot food. Little food of any kind meant starvation.

She'd never forget the suffering she'd seen on the faces of the people she passed every day in the street, people who were disappearing before her eyes, not only bodily, but in spirit too. She'd never expected to see children with distended stomachs in her own town, their big eyes watching from behind the peeling shutters of their unheated homes, the snow shin-high on the ground. She'd never thought to hear of old people dying of malnutrition or of the tuberculosis that raged through the population, passed from one to another like the devil's game of tag. This was France. It was the middle of the twentieth century. Such things were unimaginable, unnecessary and they had to be stopped.

There was still no news of Jeanne when Etienne appeared at Marguerite's studio the following afternoon. After their disagreement in his church she hadn't expected him to visit again and she'd been trying to work out a way back to him for the sake of her mission.

She greeted him at the door, unsure how to begin. Seeing him dressed in a well-cut white shirt and without his soutane, she had to batten down her heart and remind herself he was a priest.

'I heard you had a visit from Otto Schmidt. I hope it wasn't too unpleasant.'

He must have spoken to Schmidt. How else would he have known this? The thought of their association made her suddenly angry.

'Did he tell you about our beloved Jeanne? How they arrested her and beat her until she lost the child she was carrying? Even now, we have no way of knowing if Jeanne is dead or alive or what they're forcing her to suffer.'

The colour drained from Etienne's face. 'I had no idea. I'm sorry. Will you allow me to pray for her?'

'Please don't. It won't make any difference. Not all of us have faith in the power of your god to defeat evil.'

She felt a sting of satisfaction as the venom in her words hit their mark. He quickly blinked away his reaction but he'd already revealed too much.

'I've brought you this.' He placed the box he was carrying on her work bench.

'What is it?'

'Take a look.'

'Whatever it is, I don't want it.' She couldn't accept his kindness, not today. Her rage was too fierce to stand it.

When she refused to look, he opened the box himself, carefully placing the objects on her work bench. Two new sketchbooks, a dozen sheets of watercolour paper, two rolls of canvas, oil paints, pencils and a block of watercolours.

Marguerite hadn't seen such treasures since before the war. She couldn't trust herself to admire them, knowing the slightest touch would make her desperate to own them.

'I can't pay for this. Take it away.'

'It's a gift. I noticed you didn't have enough materials on my last visit. I'm sure you can put them to good use.'

'I can't accept these things from you.'

'They've been lying around in the presbytery since before the Germans arrived. A friend of mine, an artist, left them behind after he came to stay. He'd be pleased to know they'd been passed on to someone who could make use of them.'

'Won't he come back for them one day and wonder where they are?'

His face fell. 'I don't know. I don't think so.'

'If people find out you've given these things to me, they'll assume they've passed through enemy hands. Do you understand?'

'No.'

'At this time, in this place, the fact that you take confession from the German soldiers, that fact that the Catholic Church, which you represent, has failed to make a stand against the Third Reich, makes you no better than the enemy in the eyes of many people here.'

'You shouldn't judge me so harshly.'

If only she'd kept the letter that had been pushed under the door after she'd been seen entering his church, instead of feeding it to the snails, she could have shown it to him. Then he'd have understood how despicable the world was determined to make her seem for the way she was feeling.

How could she make him understand that she was too vulnerable, too heartbroken to give in to his kindness? She studied him as he stared at the floor. What was it that prevented him from meeting her eye?

'I hated the way we parted after you came to see the frescoes. I never wanted to upset you. I have to accept that our views on certain matters will always be different.'

His bravery in rescuing the old woman outside his church had been remarkable. For all his association with the enemy, he wasn't afraid to stand up to them. Should she trust him enough to reveal her mission to him or should she listen to Simone's advice and steel herself against him?

'Why have you come back when you know we'll only hurt each other?'

He leaned in closer, stroking a smear of charcoal from her cheek, only stepping away when he realised the intimacy of the action.

'My mother has asked if you'll paint my portrait. Some of these materials might be useful for that. It's one of the reasons I brought them.'

'I see.'

'She adored the landscape you painted. She wrote and told me it was the first thing that had made her smile since the start of the war, and for that I'm grateful.'

Her heart gave at the loneliness in his voice. 'You must miss her very much.'

'It wasn't my choice to leave Paris. I have to go where I'm sent.'

He reached into the box and retrieved a small parcel wrapped in brown paper. 'This is also for you.'

Inside, she discovered a loaf and a small fresh cheese. She imagined the soft crumb of the bread giving under the pressure of her tongue, the crack of its crust on her lips. She turned away, not wanting him to see her reaction, but it was impossible to hide anything from him.

He rubbed at the residue of charcoal on his thumb as if it were stinging him. 'Don't cry; you'll sour the cheese.'

Her hunger wasn't only a physical obsession, but an emotional one too. She placed the food on her work bench, not daring to touch it. One taste of it and she'd want to devour it.

'I haven't seen white bread for so long. Where did you get it?'

'An anonymous benefactor leaves food at the church door. It's my duty to deliver it to where it's needed.'

'Thank you. I'll make sure it's shared.'

With a little self-restraint, even the smallest amount would go a long way over the coming days, not only for herself, but for Simone and for Dorothy. What was once considered a good meal for one before the war would now be two or three good meals for shrunken stomachs.

He smiled, knowing his kindness had won the day as Marguerite tore off a tiny corner of the bread and slipped it into her mouth.

Later, Marguerite laid out a small picnic in the cellar with the bread and cheese. Dorothy, who was half-starved and feeling too beholden to mention it, cried as much as Marguerite at the sight of it before pouncing on it like a wolf.

Simone had spent the afternoon with Nicole who was inconsolable over Jeanne's arrest and the murder of her unborn grandchild. She stared at the food for a full minute before pushing the plate away. She hadn't eaten since receiving the news about Jeanne and wasn't ready to start now.

'You're a fool if you think people won't find out about this, Marguerite. You're already suspected of being an enemy collaborator. If you start to fatten up, they'll want to know where the food's coming from.'

Dorothy ran her finger over her lips, checking for any cheese that might have escaped. 'There's more than one way to win the war. We have to do what we can to survive. The food will help to restore our strength. We can't fight without it.'

Seeing she was still hungry, Simone passed Dorothy the rest of the bread. 'I accept you have to fraternise with the priest, Marguerite, but I don't have to like it or benefit from it and I won't take a single crumb from the enemy.'

'It's not their food. It's the food they've forcibly taken from our land. It's our livestock they've stolen, our dairy produce they've snatched. It's our forced labour taking in our harvests. None of it belongs to them. We're only taking back what's ours.'

Simone made a point of looking away. 'I keep thinking about Jeanne's arrest. Why did the priest come to see you again, Marguerite? What have you told him to make him keep coming back? He saw Jeanne helping at the exhibition. He wouldn't be the first priest to have betrayed someone.'

'I don't think Etienne is to blame for what happened to Jeanne, but if he is, I'll find out and I'll make him pay for it.'

'If he betrayed Jeanne to the enemy, he'll do the same to you.'

'It's a risk I have to take.'

'Be careful, Marguerite. It won't be the first time you've fallen for a charming man and ended up having to run for your life.'

'You can't compare Etienne to Lance.'

'Did you find out anything more about that illegitimate child of his, after you saw her in his church?'

'Not yet, but there's no reason to believe Catherine isn't his niece.'

Dorothy swallowed the last of the bread, checking to make sure not a single crumb had been dropped. 'Men can be as good at subterfuge as women when they put their minds to it. It's best to remember that.' She grinned at the look of surprise on Marguerite's face. 'You think I don't know about men? The heart is a subtle and complex beast, and in wartime the stakes are high. Take heed, my love; there's danger lurking.'

Chapter 17

Marguerite leaned in close, her eyes following the soft curve of the pencil lead as her hand created a perfect arc across the blank paper. Since Jeanne's arrest, she'd put aside her domestic painting, with all its familiar truths, and turned to nature, creating a botanical study of a yew with an intense edge; each needle on each twig was a dagger, each poisonous berry a miniature unexploded bomb. It was nature, but splintered by the fractured lens of war.

She was so absorbed in her work that she didn't hear the quiet creep of the intruder as he stole into her studio, stealthy as a fox, tip-toeing up behind her, not risking the squeak of his plimsolls on the stone floor.

It was his breath she felt first, fanning the back of her neck like a bad omen blown in on an ill wind, and then the smell of him, sending her straight back to long before the war, to another life and the person she used to be.

For a second, she thought she'd imagined him, that her mind had slipped into a recurring nightmare, until everything went black and she felt the cold press of his fingers pushing against her eyeballs.

'Bet you can't guess who this is, Duckie.'

Lance. His voice was unmistakable. She stepped away from him, shaking off his once familiar touch.

'When did they let you out of prison?'

'Three months ago.'

All this time he'd been free and she hadn't known. There should be a warning about such things. 'How did you know where to find me?'

'There are posters all over town with your face on, advertising your exhibition. The old man who runs the gallery was more than happy to point me in your direction when I told him I was your devoted husband.' He tipped his head to one side, considering her. 'Why have you changed your name? I've had a devilish job tracking you down.'

'The French aren't too keen on the English these days.'

She flinched as he tried to kiss her, disguising her reaction by reaching across her work bench for a pencil. 'How did you get into France?'

'You could at least pretend to be pleased to see me. How long's it been? Ten years?'

It had been longer than that. She could have told him the exact number of days, but she wouldn't give him the satisfaction of knowing she'd counted them.

Prison hadn't changed him at all. He didn't look any different to how she remembered him, as if having been at the foremost of her mind so often he'd remained living in her present and he was just how she expected him to be. The man she'd first met when he was twenty-five was unmistakably the same man who now stood before her at forty-five. The black sweep of his hair, slicked back from his brow, had more grey in it these days and his forehead was a little higher, the creases around his eyes deeper. Laughter lines, he used to call them, because he rarely stopped laughing. And when he wasn't laughing he was grinning, because, as he'd always liked to remind her, he was a lucky boy and had a lot to smile about. That was until his luck ran out.

He was dressed in light cotton trousers and a loose jacket, cleverly put together so as not to stand out, both of no particular cut or obvious origin; his plimsolls gave the impression that he'd just stepped off a passing yacht.

He looked her up and down, raising his eyebrows at her faded dress, fraying at the seams, and her bare feet. 'I don't have to ask what kind of a war you've been having, my old duck.'

She wasn't interested in his opinion of her. She'd stopped caring about that a long time ago.

'I thought you had another five years on your sentence.'

'They need Wormwood Scrubs for the traitors and the fascists. These days, having the wrong political views is far more serious than my little misdemeanour.'

'What do you want?'

'Surely a husband is allowed to come and see his wife after all these years, especially as you left without saying goodbye.' He winked, over-emphasising the gesture like a pantomime villain. 'It's time for a nice cosy reunion, don't you think?'

'How did you know to look for me in France?'

'Call it an educated guess. Don't worry, Duckie. I'm prepared to let bygones be bygones. I don't blame you for fleeing the country after I was arrested. If it had been the other way round, I'd have abandoned you like a shot.'

He lit a cigarette and ambled around her studio, examining the canvases and her sketches, picking up objects at random – the plaster cherub, a particularly large pine cone she'd found in the hills.

'Still not doing anything original, I see.'

He sat down heavily on her stool, flicking his cigarette ash in an empty coffee cup, the pungent aroma of the tobacco mingling with the smell of turpentine.

'It's not a bad set-up you have here. It certainly beats the four walls of a prison cell.'

She ignored the jibe. 'It's just an old French barn. I had the windows put in soon after I moved here.'

'It's a long way from that tiny garret you had in London when I first met you, half-starved and with only the mice for company.'

He curled his lip, his eyes narrowing on the tip of his cigarette. 'You'd still be there, if it wasn't for me. You don't ever want to forget that.'

'Where've you been since they let you out?'

'Around and about; Switzerland mostly. All that clean mountain air has been a tonic for me.' He took a slow drag on his cigarette. 'Thanks to a spell in Geneva, my French is positively perfect.'

It wouldn't have crossed his mind to stay in England and do his bit for his country. He'd always been a survivor, always putting himself before others. She couldn't expect him to have changed his ways now, just as she couldn't expect him to have grown a different face or altered the way he walked.

'The French borders are closed. You must have had quite a job getting here.'

'Not really. Friends in high places and all that. They made sure I had the right papers. There's always a deal to be done, especially in wartime. These days, people are more desperate than ever to make a killing.' He said it as if exploitation was something to be proud of.

'It's not safe for you here. You're an Englishman, and a notorious one at that. If they catch you, you'll end up back in prison.'

He smiled, hiding his teeth, which were never his best feature. 'It's sweet of you to worry about me, but there's no need. I'm quite capable of getting myself out of any scrapes.'

'Things are different now, Lance. There's a war on, in case you hadn't noticed. You won't be able to talk yourself out of trouble so easily.' She hesitated, wondering why he'd suddenly turned up now. 'I hope you haven't come all this way just to see me.'

'As I said, Duckie, I'm here on business. Once an art dealer, always an art dealer. I have a new venture, picking up degenerate art to sell into Switzerland. The paintings are an absolute steal. It's even more profitable than my previous little scam. And it's legal too, depending on how you look at it.'

'Where are you staying?'

Lance grinned. 'I'll take that as an invitation. The thought of you keeping our bed warm is the only thing that's kept me going all these years.'

Having him here was too much of a risk. Not only to herself and her mission but also to Dorothy. If he discovered she was in hiding, he'd find a way to use it to his advantage. She had to get rid of him and make sure he didn't come back.

'You can't stay here. This is Simone's house. She wouldn't allow it.'

'Don't worry, Duckie. I've got myself a nice cosy apartment on the other side of town. You can come and live there with me. We have a lot of lost time to make up for. I'll even cut you in on my little venture, if you ask me nicely. God knows you look as if you could do with the money. You must keep it to yourself though. You can't trust anyone these days.'

'It's not possible, Lance. You're taking a big risk just by being here.'

'So are you, Duckie, but at least for me the rewards are high.'

Before Marguerite could respond, Simone came crashing into the studio, her face stricken with panic. She still had on the dress she wore for school and her smartest shoes.

'I thought I heard voices as I came up the path.'

She stopped when she saw Lance. 'What are you doing here?'

He tipped his finger against the side of his head in a mock salute. 'Simone, you haven't changed at bit.'

She stared at him, her face betraying her fury at finding him casually flicking his cigarette ash onto the floor and turning the pages of Marguerite's sketchbook.

'I didn't think you'd have the nerve to show your face.'

'I'm here to see my beloved wife. And don't bother telling me how much danger I'm in because I've already heard it.'

'I want you to go, right away.' Simone held up her hands and backed away. 'I'm leaving now. This conversation never took place. I haven't seen you. Don't come here again.'

'She's right. You can't stay here. It's too dangerous.'

'Well, if that's the way you want it.' He pulled a scrap of paper from his inside pocket and slipped it between the pages of her sketchbook. 'This is the address of the apartment where I'm staying. It belongs to an old chum who left for America before the invasion. He asked me to check on it if I ever happened to be in the area, to make sure it hadn't suffered too much damage. You can't trust the Boche to treat anywhere they've conquered with respect. I'll be expecting you.'

'Do as Simone said, Lance. This is her house. Don't come here again.'

He turned over another page of her sketchbook, running his finger along the ragged edge where Schmidt had torn it. 'Did you ever find out who betrayed me, Duckie?'

'You weren't betrayed. Your luck ran out, that's all.'

'You're wrong. Ten years of my life that betrayal cost me, not to mention the loss of a small fortune. I'll find out who did it, even if it takes until my dying day.'

The determination in his eyes made her uncomfortable. 'When are you going back to Switzerland?'

He took another look around her studio and lit a second cigarette from the fading embers of the first. 'I'm in no rush. As I said, there's business to be done.'

He was behaving as if there wasn't a war on, as if he wasn't in enemy territory. Surely he could see it for himself, feel the danger of it in the air like electricity in the midst of a thunderstorm?

She ushered him out the door, hesitating when she spotted a motorcycle parked on the grass verge. Few people had petrol these days.

'How did you come by that?'

'As I said, my old duck, I have friends in high places.' He flashed his tight-lipped smile as he wheeled the motorcycle onto the road. 'Come and see me soon, Duckie. The bed's too cold without you.'

She watched him disappear down the lane, relieved to see him finally gone. She never wanted to see him again. The way he was

111

behaving would land him in danger and she couldn't risk being associated with him. This was no longer the South of France he'd visited before the war and it was no longer a playground for the rich and the carefree.

It frightened her, knowing he was here, that he wanted her back. He was reckless and unpredictable and always had been. The fact that he'd left a neutral country to travel into occupied territory as an enemy alien proved he hadn't changed. She could only trust he'd leave when he realised how dangerous it was, that he'd have the sense not to mention their connection to anyone.

Nothing would compel her to return to her marriage. She was a different person to the one she'd been when she first met him, and she'd come too far to go back to the person she once was. Lance would never change. Now, living in such dangerous times, she had to protect herself more than ever. This wasn't simply a game of subterfuge. It was a matter of life or death.

Simone was sitting at the kitchen table when Marguerite returned to the house, her fingernails scratching the dents in the old wooden surface.

'Did you know he was coming?'

'Of course I didn't.'

'How could you welcome him after all this time? Don't you remember what he did?'

'I didn't welcome him. He's gone now.'

Simone fell silent, but for the scratching of her nails. 'Will you go back to him?'

Marguerite sank into the chair, burying her head in her hands, wishing for it all to go away. 'Of course not. His being here makes everything more dangerous.'

'Your German-loving priest – does he know about Lance?'

Marguerite grabbed Simone's hand, irritated by the sound of her fingers scratching the table. 'There's no reason for him to know about Lance. It's the safest way for everyone.'

112

Simone pulled her hand from Marguerite's grip. 'Then you'd better hope that when the priest finds out who you really are, he treats you with the same consideration.'

Chapter 18

Marguerite had carried the feather bolster from her bed all the way downstairs and into the cellar, where she'd propped it against the wall, fortifying it with half a dozen pillows and cushions from around the house. Now, under Dorothy's instruction, she was learning to shoot, aiming at a series of heart-shaped targets she'd painted on the ticking.

Simone must have heard the commotion from the garden, because she came running inside to find out what was going on. Dorothy looked up from where she was sitting cross-legged on the bed, a cushion pressed to each ear.

'Is the sound carrying far?'

The feathers from a burst pillow looked like a snowfall on the cellar floor. Marguerite kicked her way through them and placed the pistol Violet had given her carefully on the table.

'Dorothy's teaching me to shoot.'

'Was this another skill you learned in the Russian circus?'

When she failed to answer, Simone pulled the cushions from Dorothy's ears and repeated the question.

'I told you I was full of hidden mystery. Perhaps now you'll believe me.' She pointed to the bolster and the cushions piled up in the corner to represent a human form. 'Say hello to Herr Bolster the Hun. I think you'll agree he deserves to die.'

As amusing as it was, Marguerite's laughter was bitter on her tongue. She'd been determined never to use the gun, but with Jeanne's arrest and Otto Schmidt watching her, and now the unexpected appearance of Lance, it felt as if her enemies were closing in, and as there was no one to watch her back, she had to do it herself.

Dorothy must have seen the worry on her face, because she went in for another laugh. 'I'll teach you how to pick a lock with a hairpin next. It might come in handy one day.'

Back upstairs, there was a letter waiting on the doorstep. Marguerite checked the garden and the lane in case Biquet had delivered it but there was no sign of him. She hadn't seen him for a few days and she was beginning to worry. He'd missed his regular lesson and it wasn't like him to stay away from the studio for so long.

The letter was from Etienne, inviting her to his home to begin work on his portrait. The local gossip had been right. He wasn't living at the presbytery, but at the villa belonging to Gerald Mayhew, an English actor who'd lived on the coast for a decade before the war and was as famous for throwing wild parties as he was for his stage and film career. He'd been one of the last to leave in the summer of 1940, squeezing onto one of the overcrowded coal ships in the harbour with hundreds of other British civilians as they scrambled to escape France, leaving behind almost everything they owned and abandoning their homes.

Given time, it was inevitable the invaders would lay claim to them, the high-ranking officers taking the opportunity to live in luxury at the expense of the people they'd driven out. What she didn't understand was how Etienne came to be living in such a place rather than at the presbytery.

She showed the letter to Simone who frowned as she read it. 'Don't do anything foolish, Marguerite. They might have tortured Jeanne into betraying you by now. It might be a trap.'

Simone cried as she said the words. The thought of what they might be doing to their beloved Jeanne was beyond all pain and comprehension. Nicole had twice been to beg for her release, but it had had no effect. She'd been warned that any further attempt at intervention would only make matters worse. Now all they could do was wait for news.

Marguerite buried Etienne's invitation in her underwear drawer beneath her threadbare camisoles and darned stockings, the once smooth wool now bearing thick ridges at the toe from the stitching that rubbed her skin to blisters every time she wore them. That night, the thought of his words nestling among her most intimate things kept her awake. It had been a mistake to hide the note in that particular place. It was too personal, too seeing, just as Etienne had been when he explored her studio, seeing her, seeing into her soul. Then, just as now, she didn't know if she could trust him.

The next morning, Marguerite was in the cellar having breakfast with Dorothy when the bell at the front door clanged. When she went to answer it, there was no one there, but whoever it was had left another note. It couldn't have been Biquet who'd delivered it, because he wouldn't have run away so quickly.

It was another summons from Yves Musel. Her stomach turned over at the thought of what his investigations might have revealed about her, what questions she'd be forced to answer. How many more lies could she get away with telling before she tripped herself up? She didn't recognise the handwriting, which suggested poor old Emile had been replaced with someone more slapdash.

She put on her most presentable dress, now two sizes too big, buttoning a cardigan over it to hide where it gaped across her chest and left a message for Simone who was still in bed. Fear had caused them to develop a habit of always letting the other know where they were in case one of them should fail to return.

She was chaining up her bicycle in the town square when she felt a shadow looming over her. Marguerite stepped aside, assuming the stranger needed room to pass, but instead of walking by he whispered her name and signalled for her to follow.

Unshaven and in grubby clothes, she'd taken him for a vagrant; the smell of sweat from his threadbare shirt and the grime beneath his fingernails suggested he lived on the streets. He must have been about thirty and was noticeably tall, his unkempt hair tied back with a broken shoelace. She didn't recall seeing him before and she hesitated, ignoring his summons until the urgent look in his eyes made her suspect he might be a friend of Armand's, sent to escort Dorothy over the border to Spain.

She followed without speaking as he led her away from the main square and through the maze of narrow streets, past the shops that had once been the busiest part of town, to the park where the men used to gather for petanque in the shade of the umbrella pines; the same park where Etienne's kiss had saved her from the German soldiers. She stayed half a dozen steps behind for her own safety and so as not to arouse suspicion. If he made a grab for her, she'd still have the space to dodge him.

He sat on a bench in the farthest corner of the park and summoned her to join him. She took a seat, maintaining a safe distance, watching him from the corner of one eye as he spoke.

'You've been ordered to gather information from a certain individual. So far, you've made no effort to do it.'

If this man was her contact, he was nothing like she'd imagined he'd be. 'I don't know what you're talking about.'

He leaned forward and stared at the ground, shoulders hunched, his elbows digging into his meatless thighs. 'You've been given orders and you haven't carried them out.'

'I need more time.'

When Violet said someone would be watching her, Marguerite hadn't considered it might be someone local. She'd assumed the British agents were British. It seemed she'd been naive.

She'd heard about the maquisards, men who'd taken to living

rough in the hills to avoid conscription or being sent to Germany as forced labour, who devoted themselves to acts of sabotage and resistance against the occupying enemy. This explained his rugged appearance, the rancid smell of him.

'A German soldier has been shot in the Bar Blanc. Ten local boys have been arrested in retaliation for his death. They'll be executed in three days if whoever killed the soldier doesn't hand themselves in, or unless someone denounces them. Those ten innocent boys who are about to be executed would also like more time.'

The Bar Blanc was Armand's bar. Why hadn't he warned them? 'This is madness. Whoever took that soldier's life should have known there'd be reprisals.'

'The town is full of foolish men the war didn't want. Their humiliation makes them reckless.'

'What do you want me to do?'

'Ask the priest to intervene on their behalf.'

Before she could say anything else, he stood up from the bench and stalked away, disappearing through the park into the narrow backstreets. It was only then she realised what a risk he'd taken in coming to see her and she didn't even know his name.

By now, Marguerite was fifteen minutes late for her appointment with Musel. She rushed across the town to his office, bracing herself to face more scrutiny, trying to work out how to explain why her identity papers belonged to a woman who'd died in a fire in a Paris apartment block in 1932.

She stopped at the door to read the notice that had been pinned to it. It was the execution order for the ten boys. Her eyes scanned the list of innocent names. There it was, confirming her worst fears. Biquet Vollard. It explained why she hadn't seen him lately. She felt her heart plummet. He was only a child. He didn't deserve to be caught up in adult wars.

She tore the notice off the door and marched into Musel's office, waving it in her fist.

'We have to stop this. There must be something we can do.'

He looked up, blinking at her rage. 'Do you know who was responsible for killing the soldier?'

'Of course I don't.'

'Then don't waste my time.'

She sank into the chair in front of his desk. 'Surely we can negotiate, or plead? They're young boys, children.'

He stared at his hands, folded on the desk in front of him. 'Don't you think I've tried?'

Marguerite thought what their mothers must be suffering, but it was like imagining the unimaginable.

Musel prised the list from her hand. 'Was there something else you wanted, Madame?'

'You asked to see me. I received a note.'

'It wasn't from me.' The crease between his eyes deepened. 'Someone's been playing a trick on you, Marguerite.'

He picked up his pen, turning his attention to the papers in front of him as a way of dismissing her. 'I hope your journey into town hasn't been a wasted one.'

She stood up to leave, still shattered by the news of the condemned boys. 'I'll come on Saturday afternoon as usual, to give Nancy and Alyce their drawing lesson.'

Many of her students had already cancelled their lessons. Word had got out that her paintings had been selling to German officers and none of them liked the association. Everyone thought she'd encouraged their attention by having an open invitation to her exhibition. Musel was one of the few people who seemed willing to still employ her. Now, more than ever, she was relying on the generous fee he always paid.

'Nancy has grown bored of the lessons. Celeste and I both agree your instruction is wasted on her.'

'Sixteen is a difficult age. She seems distracted. Perhaps—'

'Alyce, on the other hand, shows great promise.'

'She's a model student.'

119

He nodded, cutting through anything else she might feel inclined to say. 'From now on, you'll teach only Alyce.'

'Of course, if that's what you want.'

'Celeste wanted me to dismiss you altogether. I don't have to explain why. It's only because you're such a competent artist and a good teacher that I was able to convince her to let you carry on.'

'Thank you.'

If Musel was suspicious of her, he'd want to keep an eye on her; that was probably the real reason he allowed her to continue visiting his house.

'There's no need to thank me. I'm doing it for Alyce. She'd never forgive me if I stopped her lessons.'

Marguerite left his office, her thoughts occupied by the fate of Biquet and the other condemned boys. Armand must have witnessed the shooting of the soldier, even if he wasn't directly involved. If he was questioned over it, who knew what else he'd be forced to reveal? No one could be expected to withhold information under torture. With Jeanne also still under arrest, their fragile network now had not one, but two deadly cracks in it. If Armand was under suspicion, then they all would be. Marguerite thought of Dorothy, so long hidden in their cellar. With this new danger, there'd be less chance of her escaping to the border. More urgently, she had to do whatever she could to save Biquet's life and the lives of his nine little friends.

Chapter 19

Marguerite took the back roads to the Villa Christelle, the Modernist waterside home that had been requisitioned by the enemy occupiers and where Etienne now lived. These days the coast was out of bounds and even if it hadn't been, the Germans had seeded landmines along the beaches and in the shallow waters, rolling out miles of barbed wire that spiralled like deadly scribbles across the sand. Blockhouses were appearing by the day, as were the concrete edifices in triangles and squares to pervert the course of any Allied tanks that might presume to land. Almost overnight, the beautiful places where people had once gathered for pleasure had been turned into fortresses, the threat of attack from both enemy and ally as imminent as the following dawn.

The villa was perched on a rocky outcrop looking out to sea like a large iced wedding cake, sheltered from behind by the shadowing hills pitted with olive trees and eucalyptus. With nothing around it but cypresses and umbrella pines, it was invisible from the road and could only be seen from a passing boat. The only approach from the land was down a steep narrow path which had been cut into the rocks countless centuries before to access the tiny natural harbour that rubbed up against the house and the freshwater spring that was said to have been used by ancient

Greek sailors to replenish their supplies. Once the house and the land wrapped itself around you, you became invisible and it was as if the world or you didn't exist.

Marguerite had no idea how Etienne had come to be granted this haven of peace and luxury, but one day it would be returned to its rightful owner. She was here to play her small part in making sure of it.

Etienne must have seen her approach, because he opened the door before she'd even reached it. In spite of everything, the nervous smile he gave her made her heart beat faster, the fine planes of his face showing softer contours in the morning light. Today, he was a world away from being a priest in his linen shirt, shorts and espadrilles, his hair brushed back from his face and still damp as if he'd just stepped out of the shower.

'Marguerite, you received my invitation.'

She wasn't there to paint his portrait and there was no time for pleasantries when the lives of so many boys hung in the balance.

'You're a friend of Otto Schmidt. Come with me. Help me to convince him to save the lives of those boys they're about to murder.'

He barely flinched at her rage, at the passion in her voice as she fought back her tears. 'Of course, but you understand the risk to yourself?'

'I don't care. You're Schmidt's confessor. Make him change his mind.'

'Give me one moment.'

He disappeared inside the villa, emerging minutes later dressed in his soutane, gripping his Bible and his rosary beads in his right hand. Once again, he was a priest, an untouchable man of God.

Together they cycled through the town, their pace relentless against the punishing heat of the day.

'Allow me to do the talking, Marguerite. He's more likely to listen to me. Try not to let him see you're upset. If he does, he'll know he's won.'

Marguerite nodded. All she could think about was Biquet's eager little face, his determination to put the world right, one good deed at a time. She hated to think what he was being forced to suffer; that he might have been separated from the other boys, that he might be frightened and alone in a dark cell.

Schmidt's office was in an anonymous apartment block situated on the edge of the town where the gently rising roads gave way to rough scrubland and the hills beyond. Set back from the coast, it lacked the panache of other areas and had a reputation for suburban anonymity. No one passing would have guessed the horrors that went on behind the solid brick façade. A cold shudder ran through her when she thought of the executions that had been ordered within its walls in the name of barbarity.

Etienne climbed off his bicycle and took her hand. 'Are you alright?'

She nodded, the careful folding of his fingers around hers creating a temporary balm. At this moment, she had no choice but to trust him.

Once inside, the junior soldier on the desk waved Etienne through as if he'd been expected, and she wondered how many times he'd visited, and what the nature of his calls had been. Was it to plead for mercy for the condemned or to absolve these murderers of their sins?

Taking the lift up to the ninth floor, they quickly found themselves in Schmidt's office. Schmidt's corpulent body rose from behind his desk as he welcomed Etienne like an old friend, his eyes betraying a moment of recognition when he realised Marguerite was there. He took a cigar from the silver box on his desk and lit it with great ceremony, buying himself time to think.

'Father, what can I do for you?' His eyes flicked once more to Marguerite's face and for the second time, he failed to acknowledge her.

Etienne waved away the offer of a cigar as Schmidt pointed to the box; an after-thought that had come too late. 'Forgive us for disturbing you, Otto. I come on a mission of mercy.'

'Then let me get you a drink.'

They took their seats on opposite sides of the desk without ceremony, the ease of their movements suggesting to Marguerite that it was what they always did. She hadn't expected such friend-liness, such familiarity on Etienne's part, and it came as a shock. All the while, she remained standing with her back to the door, deliberately unacknowledged by Schmidt as he retrieved a bottle of brandy and two glasses from the top drawer of his desk and poured himself and Etienne a generous slug.

While Schmidt was distracted, she observed the contents of his office. It was more like a gentlemen's club than a place of work, with most of the space taken up by three generous leather chairs gathered around a low table cluttered with ash trays and dirty glasses.

Somewhere in this room were the documents she needed to incriminate Schmidt and his associates for their war crimes. There was only one filing cabinet, which appeared too insubstantial to hold anything of worth, and yet the papers had to be there some-where. They were too important for him not to keep them close.

She recognised a tapestry on the wall, looted from a museum in Nice. Next to it was a painting of a reclining woman by Matisse, which must have come from the artist's home in nearby Vence. It was a thought too uncomfortable to consider given the frailty of the ageing artist. Her stomach tightened at the injustice of so much theft.

Gritting her teeth, she glanced to the right and there it was, sitting in the corner on a mahogany table whose finely turned legs were barely substantial enough to take the weight of it: a safe. The documents had to be inside. It was the only reliable place.

'Madame, won't you join us for a drink?'

Etienne's encouraging words brought Marguerite back to the moment and she realised Schmidt's eyes were on her, contem-plating her. She set her jaw, hoping he couldn't read her thoughts.

'No thank you. It's a little early in the day for me.'

Etienne leaned back in his chair, relaxed in Schmidt's company, and murmured quietly under his breath between sips of brandy so she couldn't catch his words. Whatever it was he said, it amused Schmidt, who cast a quick glance up at her and chuckled. The joke was on her, she was sure of it. She could cope with the sting of Schmidt's ridicule; it was Etienne's betrayal that hurt the most.

This cosy chat told her everything she needed to know. The two of them were as thick as thieves. Seeing them together, she realised Violet had been right; Etienne would be the best route to getting to the papers in the safe, but could she trust him? Whose side was he really on?

Schmidt swallowed the last of his drink and looked up at her, his eyes narrowed through the fog of his cigar smoke. 'The Father tells me you've come to plead for those boys' lives.'

Marguerite cleared her throat. 'They're only children. They weren't responsible for that soldier's death.'

She fought her instinct to beg for Jeanne's life along with the boys. Nicole had already been warned that any more pleading would lead to her immediate death and she couldn't risk it.

Schmidt's eyes slid to Etienne, clearly relishing the game. 'What do you think, Father? Should I save the boys or not?'

'Justice can only be served by holding the true killer to account.'

Schmidt refilled Etienne's glass and signalled for him to drink. 'An eye for an eye. Isn't that what they say?'

'You have three sons of your own, Otto. Imagine if one of them were condemned to death for a crime he didn't commit. Imagine what it would do to your wife.'

Schmidt laughed. 'No boy of mine would ever find himself on the losing side.'

Marguerite bit her tongue. He was already on the losing side and he knew it. This was why he was inflicting so much brutality on the town.

Etienne knocked back his drink and stood up to leave. 'You're a busy man. I won't keep you any longer. All I ask is that you reconsider the reprisals against those boys.'

Schmidt remained where he was, staring at the lit end of his cigar. 'Whatever happens, you'll look after my soul, won't you, Father?' He threw a look at Marguerite, as if to say, *See, I've won. I'm untouchable.*

Etienne seemed to flinch under Schmidt's question. Whatever answer he gave, it would condemn him one way or another. 'Only God can do that, Otto. We are all in His hands.'

Riled by Etienne's answer, Schmidt sat up straighter in his chair and pointed to the door. 'Leave us alone, Madame. I need to talk privately with my confessor.'

Marguerite sat on a hard wooden chair in the corridor for the next fifteen minutes, while Schmidt and Etienne continued their discussion alone. The walls in the solid building were too thick for her to hear what was said and so she sat rock still, not looking up, hoping that Etienne could work some miracle that would get the boys released and sent back to their mothers. She had to trust that he could do this, that he wasn't instead offering to save Schmidt's rotten soul.

Finally she heard the heavy tread of Schmidt's footfall as he threw the door open, his arm around Etienne's shoulder and laughing as he showed him out.

'For a Frenchman, you're not all bad, Father. I'll see you in church.'

Etienne clutched his Bible to his chest and gave a respectful nod as he said goodbye. It was only after Schmidt had closed the door that he realised Marguerite was still waiting for him. His expression clouded over when he realised she'd witnessed their exchange.

He looked straight ahead, avoiding her stare. 'Let's go, quickly.'

She waited until they were outside the building and unlocking their bicycles before she dared to speak. 'What happened? Did he agree to spare the boys?'

'Come back to the villa. We can talk there.'

126

She kept her distance all the way, observing him as he negotiated the back roads and the alleyways through the town, like a thief not wanting to be seen, avoiding the market and the shops where people would be queuing for food, where he'd be forced to face their accusing stares.

How could he have shared a drink with a mass murderer? How could he have laughed and joked with someone who had so much blood on his hands when the lives of those boys were at stake? It wasn't a game, so why was he treating it as if it was?

She followed him in silence up the grand sweep of steps into the villa. Even the rhythm of the sea, crashing against the rocks failed to soothe her. By entering this place, yet another crime was being committed. Neither of them had the right to be there when it belonged to someone else.

'Please come in. Make yourself at home.'

At home, he said, about a house that wasn't his.

'What did Schmidt say? Did he agree to release the boys?'

Etienne bowed his head, a man defeated or subservient to his master, she couldn't tell which. 'I wasn't able to convince him, not today. I'm sorry.'

Was that it? Was all hope lost? Not while they were still alive. 'What do we do now?'

She reminded him about Biquet, the sweet little boy he'd met at her studio. How could he rest, knowing his life and those of his little friends were in the balance?

'Biquet is your young assistant. I remember him. He was so proud to be helping you.' He offered a weak smile. 'I won't give up. I will keep trying. You have my word.'

She looked around, taking in the grandeur of the villa and wondered how he came to be living here. How could she trust him to keep his word when he'd made himself so beholden to the enemy he now sought to influence?

He put down his rosary and his Bible and unbuttoned his soutane, beginning his transformation from priest to man.

'Will you have something to eat?' Once again, his face was full of kindness.

'I can't stay. I need to tell the mothers of the condemned boys that today we failed to save them.'

He touched her arm as she turned to leave. 'Don't give up on me, Marguerite. While there's a chance they can be saved, I'll keep trying.'

She left him with his pledge, promising to return tomorrow. In spite of everything, he still wanted his portrait painted and she was still compelled to do it.

How could she not have faith in him when he spoke with such sincerity? And yet he was still the man she'd witnessed share a drink and a joke with the enemy while Biquet's life and the lives of the other nine boys hung in the balance. Only by painting him would she be able to interrogate his soul and discover the true nature of the man lurking beneath his soutane. She couldn't trust her heart when it came to understanding him and her mind was too confused. It would be her art that would finally tell her whether she could risk revealing her mission to him.

British Intelligence couldn't wait forever for the information. The Allied advance would be happening any time now. She had to decide whether she could trust Etienne to help her gain access to the files incriminating Schmidt for his war crimes, which she now suspected were hidden in his office safe. But by confessing her mission to him, would she be gaining an ally, or putting herself in the hands of the enemy?

Chapter 20

The sun was still on the rise, its brittle light scattering in splinters across the sea when Marguerite returned to the villa the next morning. There was no sign of Etienne as she pushed her bicycle down the narrow rocky path and the place was silent, but for the splashing of the waves, licking and pawing the rocks where they broke onto the land. This close to the water, the air was full of sea. She ran her tongue over her lips, tasting the salt and the tang of the brine and considered Gerald Mayhew's villa, wondering what he'd think if he knew his patch of paradise had been claimed by the occupying enemy and passed into the hands of a duplicitous priest.

Until that moment, she hadn't considered how a new occupier might choose to live in a house that didn't belong to them – whether they'd continue the lifestyle of the owner who'd been driven out, sleeping between their sheets and eating off their plates, or whether they'd make it over to their own taste, because in their minds, it belonged to them now and they were here to stay.

'Marguerite.'

Suddenly he was there, standing on the threshold of the villa and beckoning her inside as if he had a right to do so. She beat back the flutter of excitement that ignited somewhere inside her, steeling herself against the pull of his physical presence as she went to him, every nerve in her body telling her it was the man, not the priest who kissed her cheek and murmured how very pleased he was to see her.

Whatever changes Etienne had made inside the villa, there wasn't a mark on the white marble floors or the white plastered walls, their elegant monotony broken only by the odd tasteful watercolour study of wild lavender and yellow crown daisies, which struck her as a dull choice for someone who claimed to have a passion for modern art.

There wasn't so much as a finger smear on the panoramic windows that welcomed in the sky and the sea, relentlessly crashing against the rocks. From what she'd heard about Gerald Mayhew's wild living, it was probably in better condition than he'd left it. She took in the white leather sofas, soft as butter, the low coffee tables and pendant lights in accents of chrome and black. Faced with such elegance, she felt shabby and out of place, diminished by the environment that was meant to impress her.

'You're in time for breakfast. Would you like a cup of coffee?' Etienne lingered in the doorway watching her expression and waiting for her answer.

'Coffee?'

She gave a non-committal shake of the head, her conscience not allowing her to say yes. Accepting things that were unavailable in normal life was a betrayal of those who suffered alongside her.

He seemed hurt by her response, but attempted to cover it by inviting her to sit down before he disappeared into the kitchen, returning minutes later with coffee and two tiny cakes, things she hadn't seen or tasted since before the war. Despite her coolness, he couldn't have missed the sound of her stomach growling. She swallowed hard, her mouth watering at the smell of the cinnamon and the sugar.

Disregarding her reticence, he poured the coffee and passed her the plate of cakes, placing it on her lap as she sat on the edge of the sofa.

She looked at them as if they were evidence that a terrible crime had been committed. 'Were these gifts from your anonymous benefactor?'

'I found the coffee at the back of one of the kitchen cupboards when I first arrived and decided to keep it for a special occasion. I can only trust it's still fresh. The cakes were left on the collection plate at the end of Mass. There were twelve altogether. The rest have already been distributed. I kept these for you.'

Here, in this beautiful villa, fighting the seductive pull of the cakes, she could have been in another world, living a different life. The lump in her throat made it almost impossible to swallow as she took her first sip of coffee, closing her eyes at the unaccustomed comfort and the bitterness of it until she thought the tears would come.

When she finally gave in to it, the cake gave willingly under the soft pressure of her tongue, coating the inside of her mouth with forgotten flavours, sugar and butter and the warmth of the cinnamon, but it was sticky and cloying and she was so unused to rich food, the unlooked-for indulgence became more of a trial than a pleasure.

It was too much. She ran to the bathroom, doubled over with stomach cramps, her body rejecting everything she'd been fed with such force it was as if a fever had broken out. She leaned over the basin, shaking and damp with sweat. If she hadn't known better, she'd have suspected Etienne of poisoning her.

She washed her face and rinsed her mouth, hardly able to look at herself in the mirror. The contrast of the beautiful surroundings made it even more painful to see how rapidly she'd aged in the past few years, the shadow of her sick grandmother, whose image had horrified her as a child, was now present in every corner and crevice of her face. She'd been looking inward for so long, she'd lost the ability to see her true self. Now, challenged with the reality of the person she'd become, she was heartbroken.

'Are you alright?'

Etienne was standing outside the bathroom door, his voice full of concern.

'I'm fine.'

She couldn't say anything else without prompting his pity and she was humiliated enough without suffering that too.

She smoothed down her dress and stepped out of the bathroom, trying to summon an untroubled expression. 'We should make a start on your portrait. Where would you like to sit for it?'

Her eyelashes were still wet with tears. He looked away from her face, offering her privacy in her suffering. 'I shouldn't have made the coffee. I've been saving it for so long, but I wanted to share it with you. It was supposed to be a treat. It's the only physical pleasure I can offer you.'

His honesty was the last thing she expected, but there it was, threatening to tip her over into tears again.

'I could draw you on the terrace with the rocks and the sea as a backdrop. Or if the breeze is too much, we could sit inside and I'll capture the landscape through the window.'

'How much time can you give me?'

'As much as we need to get the portrait right. I don't want to disappoint your mother.' For all the compromises she was forced to make, Marguerite still approached each new piece of work with integrity.

'Then let's take our time in choosing the right surroundings.'

He led her around the villa, showing her every room in turn, asking her to decide where she'd most like to paint, which spot had the best light, the walls in each one revealing more uninspired watercolours of the local flora.

He led her through to a small study, the steep hill behind it sheltering it from the heat of the direct sun. The wall opposite the desk was lined with shelves of English novels that must have belonged to Gerald Mayhew, the Oscar he'd won for Best Actor in a Supporting Role before the war taking centre stage in a glass case between Austen and Dickens. He'd been forced to leave in a hurry, taking only what he could carry, which was why he must have left it behind.

'Let me show you my only treasure.'

He pulled back a black velvet curtain that covered one wall. Hidden beneath it was a painting by Josef Motz, an artist whose work had been classified as degenerate and banned by the Third Reich. The last she'd heard, Motz had been arrested at his home in Paris and imprisoned. That was over two years ago. Nobody knew if he was still alive.

She considered the painting closely, examining the brush strokes, picking up the rhythm that had dictated the artist's movements as he'd placed them on the canvas, the realisation running through her like a hot wire. This wasn't a print as she'd first assumed, but an original, and of the calibre you'd expect to see in the world's leading art galleries.

It was an exquisite creation, much smaller than his more famous work, but unmistakably by him. She recognised his bird print of a signature and knew his style too well to question whether it could have been by anyone else. Given the times they were living in, it was reasonable to assume the artwork had been taken from a private collection or from any number of galleries in German-occupied territories. If Etienne was prepared to live in a requisitioned villa, then it followed that he'd also hang confiscated artwork on its walls.

'I don't have to tell you this is a Modernist masterpiece. It was a gift from my father, just before he died. I keep it behind this curtain to protect it from the sunlight.'

She wanted to believe the story of how he came to possess it, but wasn't sure she could. 'It's remarkable.'

'I renounced everything else I owned when I took my vows to become a priest, but this, I couldn't part with. My father treasured it before passing it on to me. Whenever I doubt the existence of God, all I have to do is look at it, and there He is, displayed in every brushstroke.'

'You have doubts about being a priest?'

'I'm a man. I have weaknesses. The fact that I couldn't bring myself to part with this painting only goes to prove it.'

'Why would you choose to deny yourself so many pleasures? Isn't life hard enough as it is?'

'Faith is impossible to understand; you just have to accept it. That's the essence of it. Strength comes from giving yourself up to it.'

He turned to her, the mood suddenly broken. 'You trained in London, not Paris.'

The unexpected statement made her nervous. 'Who told you?'

'Nobody. I can see the influence of the English tradition in your work.'

'We're all influenced by those we admire.'

'But it shouldn't be at the cost of denying your own voice. You have enormous talent and a beautiful heart. These things make for great art if you'll only allow them to flourish. Whatever it is you're hiding, you should let it go.'

'It's not always easy to face who we really are. Not all of us have the strength for it.'

'You're an original talent, Marguerite. Don't bury it beneath the burden of the past.'

But she could never escape her past. The fact that Lance had tracked her down after so many years only went to prove it.

The morning turned into afternoon and evening and still they talked. When the colour returned to her cheeks, he made her a salad, using freshly picked basil leaves and tomatoes which he'd grown in pots behind the villa, fine enough and light enough for her stomach not to reject it. He prepared the food as they talked, her heart cracking open at the care he took over it, cutting the bread into thin slices, so it wouldn't be too much for her to digest.

As the hours passed, he tempted her with a little but often, encouraging her to pick over the food at will, a mouthful here, a small bite there, until by dusk, she was feeling more comfortable in her skin, the chill of the evening breeze not troubling her as they sat side by side on the terrace looking out to sea, the waves crashing on the rocks close by as if they were putting on a show just for the two of them.

She chose her moment carefully before raising the subject of the condemned boys, huddling close to his body as he sheltered her from the worst of the breeze.

'Can you try again to intervene on their behalf?'

'Schmidt came to give me his confession last night. I pleaded with him again, but I'm not sure it made any difference. The German high command is losing control. The only way they can get it back is through fear.'

'But you're their confessor. They listen to you. Surely you can change their mind.'

He leaned forward, placing his head in his hands, and suddenly she felt the rush of the breeze he'd been shielding her from.

'I did everything I could. I even offered them my life in exchange for theirs, but they know my death wouldn't carry the same resonance as that of the young boys.'

The words could have been an empty gesture, but she recognised the truth in them, that he'd been prepared to die to save Biquet and the other boys.

'How can these men be so cruel?'

'They're determined to uphold their rule of law. If they back down, people will see it as a weakness.'

'If they shoot them, people will see it as something much worse.'

He put his arms around her and held her as she cried because it was the only answer he had; the warmth of his body and the soothing pressure of his lips on her forehead the only things that stopped her feeling it was the end of the world.

Already the day was spent and they hadn't even begun to

think about the portrait. She looked up, where the mist was gathering over the distant hills, cloaking them in the mystery of evening. It was a long cycle ride home and she had to be back before the curfew.

Wiping away her tears, she climbed to her feet. 'We've done no work today, and now I must leave. I'm sorry. I've wasted your time.'

It was a moment before his replied, his voice batted here and there by the sea breeze and the beating of the waves against the rocks.

'Time spent with you is never wasted. Come back another day and we'll try again with the portrait.'

She tried not to look forward to it, tried not to count the hours and the days until she could return. She couldn't allow herself to be seduced by this man, even as he resisted seducing her. This wasn't real life. She was cultivating him to help her with her mission; that was all. She had no right to long to be in a villa owned by a stranger, and no right to want to be with Etienne. He could no more belong to her than the villa itself or the waves that threw themselves relentlessly against the rocks, threatening to overwhelm her before pulling themselves away again. And as he walked her to the gate and pressed his lips against her cheek to say goodbye, allowing them to remain there longer than he should, it felt as if it was the end of the world and at the same time, it felt as if it was just the beginning.

Chapter 21

Marguerite pushed her bicycle up the steep path that led up from the villa onto the road and began cycling at full speed. The light was already fading and she was in a hurry to get home. Despite the dusk, she soon noticed a group of boys in the distance, loitering as if they were waiting for something to happen. The youngest, who was no more than twelve, trailed behind them as if he were reluctant to be a part of whatever was about to unfold.

She knew their faces. Most of them she knew by name. Simone had taught all of them at one time or another. Some were almost old enough to begin their resistance against the enemy, rootless in the hinterland between adolescence and adulthood. She nodded to them as she approached, fighting to keep the handlebars of her bicycle steady on the uneven surface of the dusty road, conscious that each set of eyes was narrowed on her against the fading light, tracking her movements as she grew closer, until the tallest called out.

'Nazi whore.'

Marguerite increased her speed, gripping the handlebars more tightly as they spread across the road to block her way, each one of them now shouting a chorus of abuse in imitation of what they'd heard the grown-ups do; using words they were too young to fully understand the meaning of, but still, the sharpness of their tongues ran like blades across her skin.

'Out of my way please, boys. I'm in a hurry. It's not long until curfew. You should get yourselves home. You don't want to get into trouble.'

She tried to keep the fear out of her voice. They were only boys. What harm could they do? But they were more than just boys; they were young men, hardened by their experience of growing up in wartime, their reasoning distorted by constant hunger and want.

Without warning, she felt a tug on her shoulder and the sensation of falling backwards. Someone had dragged her off her bicycle and the sharp surface of the ground was coming up to meet her. She put out a hand to save herself, hearing the scuffling of feet in the dust close by as the boys continued to throw curses and insults, the echo of their laughter rattling back and forth above her head until suddenly a foot, housed in a battered shoe, flew towards her, glancing across the side of her head as it made contact with the front wheel of her bicycle.

Before she could scramble to her feet, she heard a motorcycle approaching, the crunch of its tyres sharp on the rough ground as it came to a halt beside her. She looked up, just in time to see the boys dispersing, their heels kicking up the dust as they ran, laughing all the way, the cruel words they'd used as weapons against her still ringing in her ears.

'Well, my old duck; fancy seeing you here.'

It wasn't a German soldier as she'd expected, but Lance.

He held out his hand to help her up. 'I won't ask what you did to upset those poor innocent boys.'

She used the excuse of brushing the dirt from her dress for not accepting his help in getting to her feet. 'They're full of high spirits, that's all.'

'They should show more respect to a woman.'

'They're starving and they're scared. They're only one step away from savagery and who can blame them.'

'Don't they know what a great artist you are?' There was a sneer in his voice as he said it.

'I'm nobody, Lance. They see me only as a woman who sells her work to the occupying enemy. They have a right to be angry with me.'

'Then I arrived just in time to save you.'

She clambered back onto her bicycle, ignoring the sting of her grazed palms, the tiny cuts where the gravel had dug in. 'What are you doing here?'

'I could ask you the same question, Duckie.'

She wasn't fooled by his insouciance. Everything Lance did had a purpose to it. It was too much of a coincidence that he'd come across her on this deserted stretch of road, that he'd rescued her just in time.

'Do you know those boys?'

'You seem to forget, I'm a stranger in town.' He looked her up and down and grinned. 'It's not safe for you to be out on your own. Let me escort you.'

'It's not long until curfew. You need to get yourself home.'

He grabbed the handlebars of her bicycle, pushing against them as she tried to set off.

'When are you coming back to me? I've been waiting for you.'

'I'm not coming back to you, Lance. I have a new life now.'

'You're still my wife, Duckie, and you're still a beautiful woman. To a man who spent the last ten years in prison, you're more beautiful than ever. If nothing else, these are dangerous times. You need the protection of a man. Surely this little incident with the boys has proven that to you. Imagine what might have happened if I hadn't intervened.'

She refused to be a victim of his threat. 'Go home, Lance. You're an enemy alien. Whatever you might think, it's not safe for me to be seen with you.'

He threw back his head and laughed. 'That's a good one, Duckie. Very funny indeed.'

Tired of listening to him, she yanked the bicycle from his grip and set off at full speed so he was forced to step out of her path. She refused to succumb to his coercion, and she wouldn't be drawn into his games.

Chapter 22

Marguerite was up before the light, determined to cycle into town to join the queue for food. With supplies being so scarce, people had begun queuing earlier each day, and the lines outside the shops now formed long before dawn. Many of the local mothers had taken to sending their sons to queue overnight to get the first pick of anything that was available, and yet it still proved a fool's errand with many of the shopkeepers keeping the best for themselves or putting it aside for their favourite customers. It was no wonder that even the most law-abiding citizens had been driven to use the black market.

The town was already busy by the time Marguerite locked her bicycle against a lamp post in the main square. She risked a quick glance at the mayor's office. Yves Musel was looking out of the window, his face grey and ghostly in the early morning shadows. He'd lost weight during the Occupation, just as everyone had, although he still appeared prosperous and healthier than most. Marguerite put this down to the fact that he had a well-paid position, but it was hard not to suspect he accepted favours from the German officers he entertained at his house. Most people trusted that this was all part of his job as mayor and thought no worse of him for it. Some actually pitied him for having to associate with them, grateful that he was working in the interests of the town, but Marguerite wasn't so sure. The way he'd taken over the role of mayor so soon after Monsieur Jupin's sudden death had left her suspicious.

It had been weeks since Musel had first summoned her to his office and she had no idea how his investigation was going into the mystery of her false identity papers, but he'd made it clear that if her duplicity was discovered by the Third Reich, he wouldn't stand by her. Now she wondered if he'd discovered anything at all about her, and if he had, whether he'd act on it to gain favour with the occupying enemy. He'd been his old jovial self at her exhibition. She couldn't decide if his ability to separate his work from his private life showed a man in complete control of his situation or one full of duplicity.

She nodded in his direction, but with his face set back in the shadows, she couldn't tell if he responded or not.

On the way to the bakery, she stopped to say hello to Madame Allard. The old lady had been a great friend of Simone's grandmother and always liked to pass the time of day, but this morning she seemed distracted as she clung to her shopping bag and turned her steel-grey head away, pretending she hadn't seen her. Everyone was more suspicious than ever while the fates of the ten young boys hung in the balance and Marguerite didn't take Madame Allard's snub personally until she heard someone shout behind her back.

It was only then she noticed that other people were gathering in groups and talking, comparing what they'd managed to buy at the market. She was the only one they were ignoring, or not ignoring completely. *Whore.* That was the word someone used after she walked past them, just as the boys had shouted it the night before. She was mortified when she realised it was aimed at her.

Undeterred, she joined the queue at the bakery, paying no attention to the whispers of the other women, the elbow nudging and the creeping murmurs behind her back. When it was her turn to be served, Madame Damas, whose vast proportions suggested there'd been no shortage of food at her table, folded her arms across her chest and ordered her out of the shop.

Marguerite held out the money. 'One loaf, that's all I'm asking. It's for Simone, the schoolteacher, as well as for me. Surely, you won't let the woman who educates your son go without?'

The shopkeeper's eyes were fierce behind her pebble glasses. 'I won't take the money you earned selling yourself to the Nazis.'

'It was my paintings they bought, not my body. Can you honestly tell me you haven't sold bread to a German soldier?'

But it was as if she hadn't spoken. Madame Damas simply looked beyond her, summoning forward poor old Monsieur Ames, who'd recently been widowed and was reduced to queuing for his own food. Nobody resented that he still claimed the rations for his dead wife, which she'd left him in her will.

Marguerite left the shop, ignoring the hard stares of everyone around her, refusing to allow anyone to see how stung she was. Madame Damas had supplied her with bread every day for ten years, but there would be no more.

She tried the market, shouldering her way through the crowd, refusing to flinch at the relentless shoving of baskets against her back, hoping to buy barley and vegetables for soup, but once again she was refused and there was nothing else. There was no meat, and there hadn't been fish for a long time. There was no milk or eggs, and no cheese. Even if there'd been plenty of everything, she knew she'd have been denied it.

Desperate now, she was about to try Madame Damas once more, when a little boy from Simone's class came running up to her, laughing in her face and waving a leaflet.

'What is it, Jacques? Let me see it.'

Jacques dropped the leaflet at her feet and ran to his mother who was standing some way off, watching Marguerite's every move.

Marguerite picked up the leaflet, her attention immediately caught by the image in the centre. At first she thought her eyes were deceiving her, because looking back at her from the page was her own face. The photograph was a copy of the one she'd used on the posters to advertise the art exhibition, the words beneath it an audacious piece of propaganda.

> *Be like Marguerite Segal and make the soldiers of the Third Reich welcome in your town. If you're friendly to us, we'll be friendly to you.*

No wonder everyone had turned against her. The Germans were using her as an example of friendly cooperation. Not only was it untrue, but they'd done it without her knowledge.

The mud stain on the corner of the leaflet suggested it had been trodden underfoot during a recent rainstorm, which meant it must have been distributed days ago, along with hundreds of other copies. Everyone in the town would have seen it by now and taken the message to be true. She had no means to dispute it; the battle was futile against the strength of the German propaganda machine. Simone would have to do the shopping from now on, although how she'd find the time when she spent all day at school was anyone's guess.

If this was all because her paintings had been bought by German officers, then Monsieur Boucher would also be in trouble. She dashed down the side street to his gallery, but it was too late to warn him. His windows were already boarded up, the glass lying in splinters in the gutter.

She knocked on the door, begging him to open up. When he finally answered, his face was pale and drawn, the grey pallor of worry transforming him overnight into an old man.

He peered at her from behind the half-closed door. 'Did you get the note I sent?'

'What happened to your gallery? Was it looters?'

'No, Madame. Everything's untouched apart from your work. Take a look.'

He threw open the door and let her in. Even without the light from the windows she could see her canvases had been slashed, each one ripped from the walls and stamped on.

'I'm sorry. I didn't mean to bring any harm to you or your business.' Her hands trembled as she started to clear up the mess, gathering the broken frames and the shards of glass. 'I'll take this away so you can have your gallery space back. I'll see what I can do to get your windows replaced.'

'I don't want your help, Madame. I couldn't trust where it would come from.' He ushered her out of the door, throwing the remains of her paintings into the street after her. 'I won't be tainted by your association with our enemy. My business won't stand it.'

He reached into his pocket and pulled out his wallet, counting out the commission he'd been given for the watercolour of the mimosa in the blue jug and the other paintings that had been bought by the German officers.

'Take this. I don't want it. Don't come near me or my business again.'

Marguerite stood in the street, a mass of torn canvases and broken picture frames at her feet. How was she supposed to recover from this? How was she supposed to prove to the people of the town that she was only trying to help them?

It took three journeys to carry the damaged paintings back to her studio. Each one was beyond salvaging, but she couldn't leave them in the street for the rats to chew on. They were a testament to her disgrace and had tarnished Monsieur Boucher's reputation.

It was only afterwards that she found the note he'd sent, requesting her to remove her paintings from his gallery immediately, which of course, she'd already done. Simone had left it on the kitchen dresser along with a letter from Madame Martin.

Dear Marguerite,
Please take this letter as formal notification that I no longer require you to teach drawing to the children. It isn't your

artistic ability that is in question, but I worry about the
moral corruption the children might be exposed to in your
presence. I'm sure you understand that with my husband's
professional standing being what it is, we can no longer risk
associating with you.

   Yours
   Madame Martin

Marguerite cried when she read the letter. Over the years, she'd taught Madame Martin and her children to speak English as well as drawing, and she'd considered her a friend. Apart from Yves Musel, she was the last of her clients. As the wife of the local notary, her opinion was highly respected in the town. Now she'd turned her back on Marguerite, no one else would change their view and accept her again.

The tide had already turned. Not only would it make things more difficult for her financially, but it was another blow on top of a day of terrible blows. She should have handled the situation more cleverly and steeled herself against Etienne's charm. The pull of him was overwhelming, but the price of being near him was too high. Not only was she putting her own life at risk, but she was jeopardising her mission. She couldn't risk it failing when there was so much at stake, and yet, how could she accomplish it without Etienne? How could she even begin to consider what she would do without him?

Chapter 23

As soon as she returned from school, Simone crept into the cellar where Dorothy was consoling Marguerite over the day's events.

'The people who destroyed your paintings are heathens. They know nothing about art. I commission you here and now to design the dust jacket of my next novel.'

Simone interrupted when Marguerite tried to tell her what had happened. 'I already know. Everyone's saying Monsieur Boucher's gallery was attacked because of you. No one will dare to sell you any food for risk of association.'

'Can't you speak in my defence?'

'It's only because people respect Armand that I'm not being treated in the same way.'

'Are you sure it's respect they feel for him and not fear?'

'Perhaps, but if allowing him into my bed is what it takes to keep us safe, then I'll continue to do it.'

There was more to Simone's relationship with Armand than loyalty and loneliness, but this was the first time she'd alluded to it. It revealed how closely Simone's love and fear were connected, how her instinct for self-preservation masked her vulnerability.

Dorothy's finger repeatedly pressed the Y key of her typewriter as if she were tapping out her thoughts one repeated letter at a time. 'Life is such a high-wire act. One slip and we're gone. The days are passed when we could rely on a man to act as our safety net. We have to be strong for our own sakes, and unflappable.'

There was little to eat that night. Marguerite ground the last of the hazelnuts to make flour for flatbreads and dug a small swede from the vegetable patch, which they made into a soup flavoured with the wild thyme that grew in clumps at the edge of the land.

They'd just finished eating when there was a knock on the door. Marguerite froze, hardly daring to consider what else she was meant to endure that day. Her head ached and she was exhausted from hunger and from having to make so many trips to town to retrieve her damaged paintings, which she'd piled in the far corner of her studio as if they were in disgrace for perpetrating a crime rather than being the victims of it.

'It's me, Armand. Won't you let me in?'

'There's nothing to eat, if that's what you've come for.'

Armand nodded at Simone's words as he stumbled through the door. His jaw was unshaven, the red rims of his eyes indicating his tiredness as he threw himself down in the chair next to Marguerite and buried his head in his hands.

'Jeanne is dead. They notified Nicole this afternoon. She asked me to break the news. She's in no state to come and tell you herself.'

Marguerite held Simone as she cried out, her heart turning to ice at the brutality of the crime when it had all been so unnecessary. 'How did she die?'

'The Gestapo had her for questioning in that grubby backstreet hotel we all know about. She threw herself out of the window on the tenth floor before they could torture anything else out of her. She'd already lost the child.'

If they hadn't beaten the baby out of her, she'd have had a reason to live. Marguerite fled to the garden, her stomach contracting as she brought up the swede and the thyme, the small mouthful of the flatbread she'd eaten. She should have done more to protect Jeanne and her unborn child. She should never have let her act as a courier.

When Marguerite returned to the kitchen, Simone was sitting straight-backed at the table and silent, as if she were fending off the news of Jeanne's death, refusing to allow it to become real.

Flustered by her reaction, Armand handed Marguerite a new batch of identity cards that needed altering and the bottle of lactic acid she'd requested on his last visit. 'Be careful with it. It's not so easy to come by, and if the Germans find out about it, we're finished.'

She hid the bottle and the cards in the false drawer in the dresser, her hands shaking as she fiddled with the catch. She wanted to curl up and die at the news of Jeanne's death, but she couldn't give up the fight now. Jeanne's sacrifice couldn't be for nothing.

'I'll have them ready by tomorrow afternoon.'

Armand nodded, too distracted by his own grief to thank her. 'I'll act as courier myself. I can't risk anyone else.' He watched her with a wary eye as she moved around the kitchen.

'Do you have any influence with the Hun to get the ten boys released?'

If only he knew how she'd tried, what it was she was really up to. 'Of course I don't. What do you take me for?'

'Don't make me answer that.'

'How about you, Armand? You spend plenty of time in the company of the soldiers while they drink in your bar every night. Don't you have any influence?'

'Don't be ridiculous.'

'The murder took place in your establishment. You must know something. It happened under your watch.'

'I can't be held responsible for the behaviour of my customers.'

'And nor can I be held responsible for the behaviour of the officers who bought my paintings.'

Armand pulled a hipflask from his pocket and took a large swig. He was already drunk, that much was clear.

'You know everyone in the town, Armand. Can't you quash the rumours about me? We're likely to starve otherwise.'

'People have eyes. They see it for themselves.' He took another swig from his hipflask and wiped the residue from his lips with the back of his hand. 'How's Dorothy?'

'She's holding up. Why do you ask?'

'No reason.'

'You trusted me enough to bring her here in the first place, so why the sudden question?'

Sensing the growing tension, Simone snapped out of her reverie. 'Don't, Marguerite. Not while we should be thinking about Jeanne.'

'I'm only asking a simple question.'

'Not now, please. Can't you see he's under a lot of strain?'

'I can see he's under the influence of a lot of alcohol.'

Armand shifted in his chair, pushing his face nearer to Marguerite's. 'I brought Dorothy here because she's a stupid English woman. Of all the people in this town, you speak the stupid English better than anybody.'

'It's hardly a rare skill.'

'It is here. Especially these days when everybody knows the English betrayed us, running away from Dunkirk like scared rabbits and abandoning us to the enemy.' He took another swig from his hipflask as if he were drawing on it for courage. 'People have begun to ask how you speak English so well when you claim to be from Paris. They want to know why you've never married or taken a lover.'

'Who says I haven't?'

'They've begun to comment on your odd little ways. How you like to take your tea with milk.'

'There's no tea or milk these days so it hardly matters.'

'They question why your paintings look so English.'

'Because I'm more influenced by their style than by the French.'

'*The French*, you call us, as if we were other, as if we were different to you. This is why nobody trusts you, Marguerite. You're a stranger, an outsider. The way you speak, the gestures you make when you think no one is looking. All foreign. We tolerated you until you welcomed our German invaders. Now we only look after our own.'

He thrust his fist towards her, jabbing his finger in her face. 'You've been warned. Things will only get more difficult for you if you carry on the way you are.'

'That's enough, Armand.' Simone rose from her seat and opened the front door, her fingers trembling as she gripped the handle. 'Get out of my house and don't come back until you've arranged for Dorothy's safe passage to Spain.'

After he'd gone, she turned to Marguerite, grief draining what little colour she had left in her cheeks. 'You can't tell me your German-loving priest wasn't responsible for Jeanne's death. The Gestapo paid no attention to us until you befriended him. I hope he's protecting you from his friends in the Third Reich, because nobody else will.'

Chapter 24

The air was heavy with the summer heat as they walked around the garden that night. Paralysed by the shock of Jeanne's death, Simone stayed inside, leaving Marguerite to accompany Dorothy on her nightly exercise. The resilience had been knocked out of both of them and while Dorothy wandered the garden, Marguerite sat on the bench beneath the apple tree, trying to work out how she'd made such a mess of things, the warm breeze and the soughing of the trees whispering, *I told you so.*

Dorothy was too dispirited to turn any cartwheels. Instead, she wandered along the paths, pausing here and there to take in a breath and the clear night sky, her eyes scanning the shadows in the moonlight. It was too sultry to stay out for long. Marguerite was about to suggest they went inside when she heard a sharp whisper.

'Marguerite. Marguerite. Over here, quickly.'

Dorothy was crouching beside the oleander, her arms wrapped around her knees. She grabbed Marguerite's hand and pulled her to the ground as she responded to her summons.

'Stay out of sight. There's someone there.'

'Are you sure?' Marguerite mouthed the words, forcing Dorothy to think again, but her attention had already shifted, her head tilting in the direction of the sound, eyes and ears primed. Before

Marguerite could question her again, Dorothy shot to her feet. In one swift move, she pulled a knife from the waistband of her Oxford bags and sent it spinning through the night air, throwing the full force of her weight behind it.

Both women held their breath and listened as the blade found its target, burying itself in something dense. Marguerite gripped Dorothy's arm, steadying them both as they listened for the sound of a cry, the collapse of a body in the undergrowth, but there was only silence, broken here and there by the distant hooting of an owl.

Marguerite finally let go of her breath. 'What do you think it was?'

'A man. Come on, let's find him.'

Before Dorothy could take a step, Marguerite pulled her back. 'If it was a man, he might still be there. He might be dangerous.'

'He'll be helpless by now. I never miss. You can be sure I got him, if not between the eyes, then between the shoulder blades.'

Her bravado could only have been connected to another wild story from her days in the Russian circus. Marguerite couldn't allow her imagination to put them in danger. 'Let's leave whoever it is for now. I'll check in the morning. It'll be safer.'

Dorothy sighed. 'Well, alright, but if I only managed to wound him, he'll be gone by then.'

'You're sure it was a man you heard prowling?'

'Naturally.'

There was no reason to think Dorothy had imagined it, but Marguerite wasn't prepared to tackle whoever it was alone in the dark and she couldn't risk exposing Dorothy to a stranger. And if she'd stabbed one of the neighbours while he was checking his rabbit traps, she'd never be able to explain it.

As soon as the sun was up, Marguerite returned to the garden. She found Dorothy's knife stuck in the bark of an old cork oak just beyond the boundary of the garden, the tip of the blade lodged in the trunk, it's positioning a testament to Dorothy's skill as a knife-thrower.

She looked for evidence of foot scuffs in the dry soil, snapped twigs, or the discarded ash from a cigarette, but there were no clues to suggest anyone had been prowling. Yet, Dorothy was certain she'd heard someone and her instinct couldn't be ignored. With so much mistrust and uncertainty in the air, they had to be more careful than ever.

Chapter 25

There was no sign of Etienne when Marguerite arrived at the Villa Christelle and so she slipped a hairpin in the lock and opened the door, just as Dorothy had taught her, taking advantage of his absence to search for something that would betray which side he was on. She couldn't risk asking for his help in obtaining the documents that would incriminate Schmidt and his associates for war crimes until she was certain she could trust him. She wasn't only doing this for France now, or because Violet had asked her. She was doing it for Jeanne and her unborn child and for every other innocent victim of the Third Reich.

Anything suspicious was likely to be hidden in the small room he used as a study, where his beloved painting by Josef Motz hung. The desk was clear, just as she'd expect from a man of Etienne's character. She slid open the drawers one at a time, lifting papers, examining them and putting them back exactly where she'd found them, but there was nothing to connect him with the German high command, only documents relating to church business.

Spurred on by her lack of success, she searched the large cupboard behind the desk, rifling through the shelves of table linen, bed sheets and pillow cases, working from front to back, careful to leave everything just as she'd found it.

'Marguerite, is that you?'

Etienne had returned, his cheerful voice calling out to her as if they were living a different life in a different world. She closed the cupboard, just as the study door opened and he walked in.

'There you are. I didn't expect you so early.'

His hair was wet. He was wearing bathing trunks and carrying a towel. He must have been for a swim. She tried not to show how flustered she was by his sudden appearance, and if he was surprised to see her in his study, he didn't show it. Nor did he ask how she'd let herself into the villa.

'I was checking to see what angle the light came in through the window. I thought I could paint you sitting at the desk.'

'No, I'd like the painting to be less formal.'

Her eyes followed the beads of seawater as they dripped from the ends of his hair and onto his shoulders, running all the way down to his navel and beyond, down the long line of his thighs. She longed to paint him in the nude, to allow herself the indulgence of studying every angle and contour of his body, but it would hardly be a suitable portrait to give to his mother.

She cleared her throat, forcing the idea to the back of her mind. 'You'd better put some clothes on so we can make a start.'

They decided to work on the terrace. They sat face to face, just beyond touching as Marguerite began with some preliminary sketches. For the painting, he'd chosen to wear an open-necked white shirt, pale blue trousers and espadrilles. No one looking at him would guess his religious calling.

To find a way into the portrait, she needed to find a bridge to his soul, to understand all his contradictions and discover his true nature, all the things that would also tell her if she could trust him.

'Talk to me while I draw you. Tell me about your role in the Church.'

He sat up a little straighter, as if he were uncomfortable with the turn in the conversation. 'Forget all that. I want you to show me as a man, not a priest.'

A man, not a priest.

But what nature of man was it that he kept hidden behind his clerical robes? This was what she needed to know, not only for the purposes of his portrait, but for herself and for her mission. No man had ever thrown her into such confusion and he was becoming an obsession. Beyond his undeniably beautiful body and his kindness there was someone else lurking. A man prepared to welcome the enemy at the cost of alienating his parishioners. A man not afraid to rescue an old woman from the brutality of that same enemy.

Beyond his calm exterior she sensed a complex nature and a passion he was fighting to keep hidden. If only she could understand why. If only she wasn't so attracted to him, she'd be able to see him more clearly. Art was about the representation of truth, but Etienne was so full of mystery and contradiction it was impossible to find her way through to the man he really was.

There was a look in his eyes that she struggled to capture, but she knew it would be the key to the picture. Uncertainty surely had a place in a wartime portrait. She corrected the lines she'd originally drawn around his eyes, switching her attention constantly between the paper and his face, silently willing him to keep turning over whatever thoughts were troubling him.

After an hour he began to get restless. 'Can I see what you've done?'

It wasn't usual for her to show her work as such an early stage, but she didn't refuse him. He looked over her shoulder while he considered it, the caress of his breath on the back of her neck causing her to shiver.

'It's going to be magnificent, I can see it already. But please, remove the distant look from my eyes. I want you to portray me as I am when I look at you. I want the painting to remind me forever of the time we've spent together, of the way you make me feel.'

'And how is that, Etienne? How do I make you feel?'

'Alive.'

She forced herself to look away from his steady gaze. Simone was right; she couldn't allow herself to be seduced by his charm. She needed to keep a cooler head when she was in his company. She turned over the page in her sketchbook. It was easier, quicker to begin again than to try to erase past impressions.

By dusk, she'd created half a dozen sketches. She spread them out on the table for him, conscious of having to get home before the curfew. 'I'll leave these with you to consider. When you've decided which one you prefer, I'll use it as the foundation for the painting. Let me know when you've made up your mind.'

He looked surprised at the suggestion of her leaving. 'You're going so soon? Stay and eat first.'

'I can't miss the curfew. If I'm caught, I'll be arrested.'

'Stay a little longer. I'll see you home. No one will question you while you're with me.'

So this was one of the reasons he'd befriended the Germans, to enable more freedom for himself. But what was he prepared to do with that freedom?

The sun had gone down and suddenly she felt cold. 'I have to go. Simone will worry if I'm not back by curfew.'

'Then I'll escort you. I have a little food for you to distribute, but I wouldn't want you to be caught carrying it.'

She was tempted to refuse the food until she remembered Dorothy starving in the cellar, forced to live off a share of their meagre rations. If she became ill, their situation would be even more desperate.

They rode their bicycles through the winding streets of the town, keeping quiet, so as not to draw attention to themselves, with Etienne once more the upstanding priest in his black soutane, which he trusted to make him untouchable.

Along the way, they avoided the Grand Hotel with its elegant Baroque façade where many of the German officers were living. Further inland, they made a detour to avoid the rundown back-street establishment used by the Gestapo to interrogate prisoners and where Jeanne had jumped to her death. No one of any sense went down that street anymore. The screams that rang out day and night were too awful to stand.

When Marguerite suggested they cut across the main square, Etienne insisted they take an alternative road, but the route would take them past Armand's bar and Marguerite didn't want to risk Armand seeing her with Etienne.

'The square will be quiet at this time of night and it's quicker.'

But Etienne was already pushing on. 'There's hardly any difference. Let's go this way.'

Etienne's choice of road turned out to be a good one. For once, the Bar Blanc was quiet and there was no sign of Armand.

They continued in silence until they reached the bottom of the lane where Marguerite stopped to say goodbye. She didn't want to risk Etienne coming up to the house in case Dorothy was in the garden taking her nightly exercise.

Before they parted, he handed her the package of food he'd promised. It was time to take a chance. She couldn't delay any longer. She needed access to the documents in Schmidt's safe before the Allied invasion. She couldn't risk Schmidt destroying the evidence against him before he retreated. She still didn't know if she could trust Etienne, but it was war and people were dying and someone had to be held to account for it. Putting her faith in him was a small risk to take given the sacrifices others had made.

'Is this food a gift from one of your friends in the German high command?'

'It was an anonymous donation.'

'But you do have such friends?'

His eyes remained expressionless as they searched her face in the moonlight. If that was his answer, it wasn't clear enough. She tried again. This time she lowered her voice and stepped closer so their bodies were touching.

'Would they be willing to share other things with you as well as food?'

'As I've already said, everything that passes into my hands is an anonymous donation.'

'They don't give away information when they come to you for confession?'

'What they tell me is in the strictest confidence. To reveal anything would be a betrayal of my vows as a priest.'

'Keeping their secrets is a betrayal of your country.'

When he didn't respond, she pushed a little harder. 'Would it make a difference if I told you I was working under orders from Mr Churchill?'

He stepped back from her, resisting the power of her physical presence. 'Whatever it is you want from me, Marguerite, I can't give it to you. I'm a priest. That's all I am and it's all I'll ever be.'

They lingered in silence, two uncertain figures in the dark, too frightened to reach out to one another, but not ready to say goodbye. It wasn't only Marguerite's heart that was at stake, but justice and humanity. She'd broken her cover, but it was the only way she could test his loyalty. If he wasn't prepared to help her, then she had to trust he wouldn't betray her.

She held herself apart from him, silently willing him to reveal his heart, but after an unbearable moment of tension, he climbed on his bicycle and rode away, as if the unspoken passion that bound them didn't exist.

Chapter 26

Marguerite continued up the lane, closing the gate silently behind her and tip-toeing along the gravel, so as not to disturb Simone as she approached the sleeping house and let herself in. She was in no mood to explain why she was so late.

'There you are.'

It was the second time someone had said those words to her that day. This time it was Simone, sitting at the kitchen table in the faded light, huddled in a blanket and looking stiff-limbed as if she'd been waiting for her to come home for hours.

Marguerite placed the parcel of food on the table. 'There's bread and cheese if you want it. Fruit, milk and eggs.'

'Have you been inside your studio since you got back?'

'No, why?'

'Take a look.'

Marguerite shot out of the house, stumbling along the path that led to her studio in the dark. The door was wide open and hanging at an uncertain angle where it had been forced off its hinges. Her heart stepped up its beat as she thought of the work stacked against the walls, the half-finished studies on the easels she'd left to dry, the precious materials, the brushes and oil paints, the watercolours and the rolls of canvas Etienne had given her that it had been wrong to accept, but she'd done so anyway because she'd been desperate to carry on with the work that was her only respite from a terrifying world.

Inside, everything had been turned on its head, her precious artworks thrown against the walls. Paint had been tipped, the colours bleeding across the floor and up the walls where the pots had been slung. Everything was spoiled. Everything that made her life worthwhile was ruined. She cried out, not for the loss of the work, but for the love that had gone into each brushstroke, each one a tiny prayer of hope for better times to come.

Simone stood in the doorway, watching her reaction. 'Their faces were covered. I only caught a glimpse of them. I couldn't even tell if they were men or women.'

'It doesn't matter. There are probably many more who'd like to have done this, but they lack the courage.'

'They had knives. It would have been too dangerous to try to stop them. I'm such a coward that I couldn't even fight for you. I hid in the cellar with Dorothy until they'd gone.'

Nazi whore had been scrawled across one wall. Marguerite felt the shame of it, even though it wasn't true.

'Why would anyone do this?'

'Biquet is dead. They shot him at dawn along with the other nine boys who were arrested in retaliation for the murder of that German soldier in Armand's bar. Their bodies are hanging in the main square for everyone to see. You were asked to use your influence to get them released and you did nothing.'

'Etienne tried to save them. He did his best.'

'*Etienne* now, is it? No longer *the priest*.'

Marguerite closed her eyes and there was Biquet, hanging by his delicate neck, his eager face dropped to one side, his little body dangling in mid-air. She would never close her eyes again and not see him.

Now she understood why Etienne had insisted on taking a different route. He must have known the boys were hanging in the main square. It also explained why there were no German soldiers drinking in Armand's bar. They'd have been told to stay off the streets to avoid reprisals.

There wasn't only Biquet and the other nine boys who'd been executed alongside him to mourn, but also their mothers' hearts which would have died with them. And the boys who'd stopped her in the road and abused her, friends and brothers of the ones who'd been murdered, now forced to live with the guilt of their own survival. She understood their anger and their sense of powerlessness. The heart of the community was raw and bleeding, the lifeblood seeping out of it. No wonder people had lost their humanity.

'What am I supposed to do about this?'

Marguerite put the question to the empty space. Simone had already gone back to the house and was on her way to bed in search of sleep that would never come. She wasn't aware that Dorothy had crept into the studio until she felt a steadying hand on her shoulder and heard the answer to her question.

'The mess won't clear itself up, so we'd better get stuck in.'

Dorothy stayed up all night, scrubbing away the vile words that had been scrawled across the wall of the studio and removing the precious wasted paint that had been spilled on the floor while Marguerite salvaged what she could of her art materials from the damage, straightening the edges of the torn paper and fashioning it into smaller sheets, trimming the canvas where treacherous knives had slashed it and whittling broken pencils to new points. Together they cleaned and tidied until their nails splintered and their fingers bled, but no amount of sweat and tears could remove Marguerite's despair at having failed to save Biquet and the other boys.

It was first light and Dorothy had just slipped back to the cellar when Marguerite heard a quiet knock on the door. She looked up at the window and saw the stricken face of Biquet's mother staring back at her. She wiped her hands across her apron and rushed outside to embrace her.

Madame Vuillard shied away, as if any physical contact might shatter her into a thousand shards. It was as if she was in a trance, part of her consciousness having shifted to another world where it was untouchable because any more pain would have been beyond endurance.

Marguerite's own sorrow was inconsequential to the point of shame next to her suffering. 'Please come in. Would you like a glass of milk or some fruit?' She cursed silently for having so little to offer.

Madame Vuillard's fingers clawed at her chest as if she were trying to scratch through layers of flesh and bone to dig out the pain. 'I just wanted to return this.'

The bicycle Marguerite had given Biquet was propped up against her studio wall. Marguerite recalled the delight on his face the day she'd surprised him with it, as if every birthday had come at once.

'It was a gift. You're welcome to keep it.'

Madame Vuillard turned to leave, her hand waving dismissively in the air. 'Take it. My heart can't stand to look at it.'

Chapter 27

It took a whole day of searching beyond the town and through the rough scrubland of the hills before Marguerite found the shepherd's hut where her local contact had set up camp. Like many other maquisards, he lived a hand-to-mouth existence, surviving off the land and on contributions from the local farmers who wanted to help the cause.

The more conventional resistance fighters lived in the towns, hiding behind respectable jobs, whereas men like this resorted to an undercover life, committing acts of sabotage against the enemy aided by British Intelligence. Many of them were Communists, dedicated to fighting not only their Fascist invaders, but also their own puppet government and any other institution of the Church and the State that stood in their way. Despite their conflicting political allegiances, the fight against Hitler had united disparate groups from the political right, the centre and the left against a common enemy. Once that enemy was abolished they'd fight over what was left among themselves.

Marguerite paused in the shade of a pine tree to catch her breath, keeping the shepherd's hut in her peripheral vision. It was a process of elimination that had brought her to this desolate place. The trodden down scrub around the entrance betrayed signs of its recent occupation. Her contact had to be hiding out here. Shepherds hadn't grazed sheep in this area for decades.

She knew she'd come to the right place because she could feel his eyes watching her, even though she couldn't see him. Fear had caused her to develop a sixth sense, born out of her desperation to survive. Life had never before felt this perilous. She'd never clung on to it as desperately as she did now she was faced with the prospect of losing it.

She stepped out into the glare of the afternoon sun and threw her satchel onto the bare patch of ground at her feet.

'I've brought food. From the priest.'

Slowly he emerged from behind the rock where he'd been crouching, his gun poised and ready to shoot. Anyone was capable of laying a trap these days. Marguerite understood this and didn't hold his suspicion against him.

He was wearing the same filthy clothes as when he'd approached her in the town square and she didn't imagine they'd been off his back since. His greasy hair was pulled back from his unshaven face with the same broken shoelace. She tried not to recoil at the unwashed smell of him as he drew closer.

All the while she kept one eye on him, the other primed to pick up any movements that would give away that he wasn't alone. Some maquisards lived in groups while others preferred to live like lone wolves, only connecting with others as their activities demanded. Anonymity was the key to survival when questioning under torture could break even the strongest warriors and cause them to betray their contacts.

He knelt before the bag and pulled out the bread and cheese which she'd wrapped in an old piece of linen. It wasn't much, but it was the lion's share of what Etienne had asked her to distribute. She was relieved to discover he wasn't above accepting food that had come from a German source. Unlike Simone and many others, the maquisards were happy to take from the mouths of their enemy and grow strong on it.

She watched him tear into the bread. 'I don't have a name for you.'

'You can call me Pascal.' He looked at her, his eyes still hungry. 'Do you have anything else?'

'That's all the food for now. I'll try and get more.'

'That wasn't what I meant.'

'Do you know who vandalised my studio?'

'It could have been anybody. You haven't exactly made yourself popular in the town.'

'The priest is proving difficult to break. What else can I do?'

She thought of Jeanne jumping to her death to prevent her betraying the network under torture, of Biquet and his nine innocent friends hanging in the town square. The thought of what the enemy were capable of terrified her. It couldn't go on.

'Try harder, Marguerite. Take a risk. The fight is bigger than your fear. Don't come back until you have something to give me and I don't just mean food.'

'Could you make it known in the town that I'm not collaborating with the Germans?'

Pascal chewed the bread, his eyes considering her as he slugged from his hipflask to wash it down.

'I can't tell anyone anything about you. As far as I'm concerned, you don't exist.'

Of course Pascal wouldn't stand up for her against the people of the town. It had been naive of her to ask. The mistakes she'd made had been of her own doing. She couldn't expect anyone to save her. It was the rule, not knowing any of the other links in the chain. It was for everyone's safety. And if anyone asked, there was no chain. If she was to be any use to the cause she had to survive on her wits. No one was coming to her rescue.

Marguerite had almost reached the outskirts of town when she saw Jeanne's mother trailing along the edge of the deserted road, her eyes roaming from left to right as she scanned the scrubland.

Marguerite dismounted from her bicycle and fell into step alongside her. 'Nicole, are you alright?'

Nicole kept her eyes trained on the distance, as if she were searching for something in the vast expanse of pine trees and rough grass that surrounded them on both sides.

After she failed to answer, Marguerite tried again. 'Nicole, it's me, Marguerite.' She touched her gently on the arm, trying not to startle her. 'Do you need help?'

Nicole's eyes were unfocused, the lids red and swollen from crying. 'I'm looking for Jeanne.'

The skin on her face was red and blistered from too much exposure to the sun, her lips cracked and bleeding. Marguerite took her arm and guided her off the road and into the shade of the pine trees.

'Shall we rest for a while?'

She encouraged her to sit and offered her some water. Reluctant to take it at first, Nicole eventually gulped it down, the excess running from the corners of her mouth in rivulets in her desperation to quench her thirst. How long had she been searching for Jeanne and what had she hoped to find?

'Are you ready to go home? I'll walk with you.'

'I can't go home. Not until I've found Jeanne.'

But Jeanne was gone and she was never coming back. 'You've had too much sun. You need to go home and rest.'

'I can't rest until I've found Jeanne.' Her voice was raw against the rustling of the trees, the crack and splinter of the pine cones as they released their seeds in the afternoon heat.

'I'm sorry, Nicole, but Jeanne's dead. Don't you remember? She's not coming back.'

'I know she's dead. I'm not a fool. That's why I'm trying to find her.'

'I don't understand.'

The tears were running down Nicole's face. She gripped Marguerite's hand, her fingers digging in like claws as her body doubled over with grief. 'They buried her in a ditch, but they won't tell me where. I have to find her. I have to bring her home.'

The country was littered with the unmarked graves of those the Third Reich had murdered. The realisation that Jeanne had been forced to suffer the same fate cut like a knife. What words of comfort could she offer when there were none? What was she supposed to say that would make any of it less terrible? The search would never end and none of it could ever be put right. All anyone could do was make it stop.

She cradled Nicole until she was too exhausted to cry anymore, until the sun went down, taking the fire of the day with it, and in the cool of the evening, Marguerite took her by the hand and silently led her home.

Chapter 28

Take a risk, Marguerite. The fight for France is bigger than your fear. Pascal's words wrapped themselves around her heart like a coiled snake as she cycled to the Grand Hotel, where many of the high-ranking German officers lived. Jeanne and Biquet had sacrificed their lives for the cause. She owed it to them to continue the fight. If Etienne wouldn't help her find the information she needed, she'd find other ways to get it.

Every time she closed her eyes, she saw Biquet's innocent face, full of hope for the future and desperate to please. She remembered his mother's existence, reduced to a living death, and the sight of Nicole, searching the ditches for Jeanne's body. She'd failed them all, just as she'd failed Jeanne's unborn child. Now, if she could find the information that would make Schmidt and his associates pay for their crimes, there was a good reason for her to still be alive.

If the people she'd lived among for the last decade thought she was collaborating with the enemy, she'd do whatever it took to prove she wasn't. The same people had offered her a refuge when she'd needed it, allowing her to run away from her past without asking questions. It was time to repay their generosity, even if it meant putting her life at risk to do it. So what if Schmidt was watching her? He hadn't bothered her since the day he'd searched her studio. His threat was probably a bluff; a way of primping his male pride. The world was full of men who validated themselves by intimidating women. She couldn't allow herself to be scared of him.

She didn't stop to consider the recklessness of her plan when she swung into the hotel foyer as if she had every right to be there, or while she waited to speak to the receptionist who was busy placating a junior officer demanding to be moved to a room with a sea view. It was just like the real world again, with English aristocrats and wealthy American visitors insisting on the best of everything, only this time it was the German soldiers and they weren't rich, but simply demanding, as the world turned and hung on a deadly tilt.

She'd made a poster, offering pencil portraits to German officers at a bargain price. She was relying on the men remembering her from her exhibition at Monsieur Boucher's gallery, and they knew she was friendly because the leaflets they'd distributed had said so.

While she waited for permission to put up the poster, she saw Nancy, Musel's sixteen-year-old daughter, dashing down the stairs and out of the main door, her blue polka dot skirt swishing against her girlish calves as she skipped down the front steps and onto the busy street. Before Marguerite could ask her what she was doing, she was gone.

She was so distracted by thoughts of what it was Nancy might have been up to, that Marguerite failed to notice the man come up behind her until he grabbed her arm and pulled her aside.

'We have to get you out of here.' It was Etienne, his breath hot on her neck as he led her away. 'Follow me and don't look up.'

Before they'd crossed the foyer, Schmidt stepped out of the lift. 'There you are, Father. I wondered where you'd disappeared to. I should have known a woman would have something to do with it.'

Etienne pulled Marguerite closer to his body. Any thought they had of getting away unseen was now lost.

'Marguerite is here to see Madame Danielou. She's interested in having her portrait painted. I offered to make the introduction.'

Schmidt's eyes shifted from Etienne's face to Marguerite's and back again, assessing the situation like a dog with a rabbit in its sight. 'Then we'll finish our business later.'

Etienne dashed for the lift and pulled the metal doors of the cage behind them, pressing the button and sending them clattering up through the building before Schmidt could ask any more questions.

'Madame Danielou lives in a suite on the top floor. I told her about your exhibition last time I came to hear her confession. Do you have any sketches to show her?' He spoke without looking at her, as if he felt the threat of exposure even in the small confines of the lift.

'I always carry a small sketchbook in my bag. There'll be something in there.'

'She's an acquaintance of Schmidt's, so you'd better be convincing.'

It was Madame Danielou's maid who opened the door, with a curtsey and a reverence that Marguerite thought had gone out with the Victorians. At the same time, a thin voice drifted from another room.

'Is that Father Etienne? Tell him to come through.'

Etienne went on ahead, his feet silent in the airless space. 'I have a friend with me, Madame. The artist I told you about.'

'Then bring her in. Don't just stand there; you'll wear a patch on the carpet.'

Madame Danielou lay in a large bed, her head and shoulders propped up on four peach satin pillows edged with lace. She gave a slight cough as if to present herself as an invalid when Marguerite entered.

'There you are. Sit down.'

The curtains were drawn against the sunlight and the room was heady with the artificial scent of lilacs. It was a moment before Marguerite's eyes adjusted to the gloom and she was able to take in the narrow face of the woman whose thin frame appeared lost in the vast bed. She must have been approaching seventy, her white hair pinned to her head in curls and loops, the frills on her nightdress giving her the appearance of a ghost from a bygone age.

'What do you have for me today, Father?'

'Only a prayer, Madame, and the company of my friend.'

Madame Danielou held out her hand to Marguerite, her fingers ice to the touch. 'Delighted to meet you.'

Her eyes drifted back to Etienne, her face expressionless. She either had nothing to say or was unwilling to say it in front of Marguerite.

To cover the awkwardness, Marguerite pulled her sketchbook from her bag. 'Would you like to see my work? I have some small studies here of ... '

'I should like to regain a little weight before I think of having my portrait done.' Her eyes hadn't left Etienne's face. 'I don't suppose you've brought me any fruit?'

'I'm sorry, Madame. There's none to be had anywhere.'

'That's what my maid tells me; she's probably not lying then.' She glanced at Marguerite, assessing her shabby mackintosh, the worn-down heels on her shoes.

'Have you heard the news? They caught one of those peculiar artists hiding in Marseille. He was about to board a boat to America. They should have let him go. It would have saved France the cost of feeding him in prison.'

Etienne made himself more comfortable in the chair as if the subject were part of an ongoing conversation. 'Do you know his name?'

'Man ... Mun ... something.' She smoothed the bedcovers across her stomach as she struggled to recall it. 'I don't know. These foreign names all sound the same to me.'

The scent of lilacs clawed at the back of Marguerite's throat until she thought she was going to be sick. She took deep breaths but the cloying atmosphere of the room only made it worse as Madame Danielou continued.

'I don't understand why these artists flock to France. It's not as if they can afford to live here and most of them can't speak the language.'

Marguerite cleared her throat, drawing the old woman's attention from Etienne. 'Don't you think we should value such people for their work? For the way they help us to understand the world in different ways?'

'What's there to understand? Most of it is nothing but squares and dots and odd shaped faces. What can they teach me from that?'

Marguerite shot out of the chair, not caring how rude she appeared. 'Forgive me, Madame. I must go. I have another appointment.'

Etienne stood up to join her. The corners of Madame Danielou's mouth dropped when she realised he was leaving. 'You're not going as well, are you? You've only just got here. You can't treat a lonely old woman so brutally.'

'Forgive me, Madame. I promised to accompany Marguerite to her appointment.'

'She's obviously more important to you than I am and anyone can see why.' She turned her cheek towards him, demanding he kiss it, which he obediently did, glancing his lips against the fine dust of her face powder.

'Until next time, Madame.'

She sniffed, seemingly untouched by his charm. 'Heil Hitler. Bring me some fruit when you come again.'

They took the back stairs out of the hotel, avoiding the lift and the public areas. Etienne gripped Marguerite's hand and refused to let go until they'd crossed the road and turned the corner into another street.

'What were you thinking, walking into the lion's den like that?'

'I asked you to help me and you refused. What was I supposed to do?'

'And you thought this was a good idea?'

'War drives us to do desperate things.'

His eyes were wild, searching her face for answers. 'They're watching you, Marguerite. Schmidt told me himself.'

'I'm accused of being an enemy collaborator by the people in the town. They vandalised my studio to have their revenge. I have to do something to prove them wrong.'

'You shouldn't have told me who you're working for.'

In asking for his help, she'd revealed too much of herself to him. 'How did you know where to find me?'

'Schmidt received a call in his room, informing him you were in the hotel. Why do you think the receptionist delayed speaking to you for so long?'

'What were you doing in Schmidt's room? Plotting the downfall of Europe, one prayer at a time?'

'I was taking his confession.'

'For what? For the murder of Biquet and his nine friends? They were children, Etienne, denied the privilege of becoming men. Nobody deserves to be absolved of that sin.'

'I've already told you, I can't reveal anything I'm told in confession.'

'Instead, you choose to protect a mass murderer.'

'I did everything I could to save those boys. In their world, Hitler's orders come before the word of God.'

She stopped on the pavement, her throat tightening as she thought about Madame Danielou. 'How can you stand to humour that woman?'

'I'm her priest. It's my duty to serve her. I gave her husband his last rites. She hasn't left her bed since the day he died. Her children have abandoned her. She has no one else.'

'She seems fortunate in other ways.'

'She's wealthy, if that's what you mean. She owns the hotel, but it's been requisitioned by the German high command. She's terrified out of her mind.'

'She didn't show it.'

'Why would you expect her to?'

'But the comments she made about the artist captured in Marseille . . .'

'Not everyone has your understanding of the world, or your courage. You shouldn't judge her for it.'

He started to retrace his steps back to the hotel. 'I have to go.'

She ran after him. 'Etienne, wait. Don't go back to Schmidt. It's too dangerous. Don't you know the Resistance shot that other priest for collaborating with the Germans?'

'One minute you want me to pass on their secrets, the next you want me to stay away from them. You'd better decide what it is you want.'

'I want you to stay alive.'

'Goodbye, Marguerite.'

The words were thrown over his shoulder without looking back. He was going, and there was nothing she could do to stop him. She resisted the temptation to call his name. People were beginning to turn and stare. She'd already made a fool of herself and couldn't risk drawing any more unwanted attention. She could only watch him leave and wonder what he was playing at as he made his way back to the enemy.

Chapter 29

Despite the rising summer heat, a cold chill of fear wrapped itself around Marguerite's heart and settled there. It wasn't only Marguerite who felt it, but everyone on the Cote d'Azur. Since the Allied landings in Normandy, expectation ticked in the air like an unexploded bomb. The best of the German soldiers had been sent north and the streets were now patrolled by battle-weary units from the failed Russian campaign and newly recruited schoolboys, prematurely forced to change one uniform for another. None of them wanted to be there; you could see it in their faces, but it didn't make them any less brutal in their methods.

Rapid and unexpected bursts of gunfire had become commonplace in the town. Shouting was heard on every corner and down every back alley as the German soldiers were taught how to defend the streets, the strain in their voices giving away their fear.

Anti-tank walls and ditches were being built around the small towns that spread along the coast, adding to the concrete bunkers, the trenches and the blockhouses that had already been constructed. Every patch of high ground had been honeycombed with gun emplacements. Barbed wire was appearing everywhere. The orchards and the vineyards were seeded with mines, as were the beaches, the roads and the airfields. Bombs were being planted in the sewers and in the grand hotels, ready to be detonated remotely at a minute's notice. The message to the local inhabitants and the Allies was clear; if the Germans couldn't keep the Riviera then no one else would have it either.

All the while, the Third Reich continued to tighten its grip on the people of the town, changing the curfew rules without warning. Everyone did as they were told, staying close to the buildings as they made their way to the market, skirting the sandbags piled against the hotels and keeping moving at all costs because stopping wasn't allowed and snipers were poised on every roof to deal with the slightest transgression.

The people of the town withdrew into themselves and those who had a cellar now took to hiding in it. Most were too afraid of the enemy to raise their heads, fearful of what might happen next. Others were too uncertain of their neighbours to trust anyone.

Life seemed fragile, as if they were living on the precipice of history. There was little word of what was happening beyond the town, but whatever devastation was on its way, it would ultimately be for the good, because out of the rage and the fire, peace would eventually emerge, and along with it, freedom.

Marguerite had heard nothing from Etienne since he'd rescued her from the hotel, although she suspected the food parcels discreetly placed outside her studio had something to do with him. Taking only a little for herself and Dorothy, she shared the rest with Pascal, slipping out into the hills with small packages after dark, breaking the curfew and ever mindful of the wolves who'd taken to prowling the abandoned houses, their mournful howling echoing through the night like an ill omen.

During her darkest moments, she gravitated to the cellar and the comfort of Dorothy's company. Dorothy, in her own way, had seen it all before.

'It's like act three of that famous play, by what's his name?'

Marguerite shrugged, failing to understand Dorothy's reference. 'I don't know much about the theatre.'

'Did I ever tell you about that actor friend of mine? He was a beautiful chap and as wild as they come. He was destined never to live long. It was his passion that burned him out, and my God he went out with a bang. It doesn't mean you shouldn't follow your heart, though; love and duty, given the right circumstances are one and the same. You don't have to choose between them.'

'Is this another one of your lessons, Dorothy?'

'It is, my love. Find a reason to go to him. Make it work.'

Marguerite was still honour bound to paint Etienne's portrait. It was the only excuse she had to go and see him. She didn't expect him to understand why she'd behaved so recklessly, visiting the hotel, but she could acknowledge the debt she owed him for saving her from another incident with Schmidt.

She left the house as soon as it was light, a canvas on its stretcher slung over her back, her pencils, brushes and oil paints in the basket on the front of the bicycle. He must have still been asleep when she arrived because when she knocked on the door there was no answer. Reluctant to disturb him, she sat on the steps of the terrace overlooking the sea, waiting for him to wake up and notice her. She'd wait forever if she had to, even if he chose to ignore her.

When he finally appeared, he came from an unexpected place, climbing across the rocks as he emerged from the sea where he'd been taking his early morning swim. He hesitated when he spotted her, briefly losing his balance as his foot slipped on a patch of seaweed, putting out his arms to steady himself before he continued towards the terrace where she waited. All the while he kept his head down, as if the slip had been a warning to proceed with caution.

She stood up to greet him, her arms hanging at her sides like a ragdoll, uncertain of a welcome. She'd put on the best of her shabby dresses and washed her hair, pinning it up overnight so it fell in soft curls around her face. She'd found a nub of lipstick and a little face powder in her dressing-table drawer and tried to make the best of herself, hoping to send a message that she was bothered about how he saw her.

He nodded, solemnly acknowledging her presence as he approached. It was time to prove how brave she was.

'Now you've had time to consider the sketches, I thought you might be ready for me to begin work on your portrait.'

He picked up his towel, which he'd left on a nearby chair and began rubbing his hair with it. 'You think I still want you to paint me?'

His body was lean and well toned from so much swimming. Her heart beat faster when she remembered how he'd kissed her in the park, how it had felt to have his arms around her. Despite the danger they'd been in, she'd never felt so safe.

She sank down onto the steps. 'I can't think why else you rescued me from Schmidt.'

'Can you really think of no other reason?'

'None that I deserve. My art is the only thing I have to offer you.'

He sighed and threw himself down beside her, closer than he should have done; his skin, still wet from the sea, dampening her dress, his hair thick with salt.

'Thank you for the food you've been leaving at my studio. It's helped more people than you can know.'

'Tell me. That day in the hotel – were you looking for a German officer to be your lover?'

His discovery of her in the hotel must have been lying more heavily on his heart than she'd realised.

'Do you think I'm the kind of woman who would take an enemy as a lover?'

He turned to look at her, his eyes full of betrayal. 'Why were you searching the villa that day while I was taking a swim? What were you looking for?'

At the time, he'd hidden his reaction so well, she hadn't

realised he'd seen her searching. 'I needed to know whose side you were on.'

'Do you think I'm the kind of man who would side with the enemy?'

'I don't know. That's what I was trying to find out.'

'And did you find the answer you were looking for?'

'No.'

He blinked and looked away. 'Then I don't expect you ever will, just as I'll never know who you are. Whenever I ask about your past, you change the subject.'

'Look at my art, Etienne. That's who I am. You might think I can trick your heart, but there's no deceiving your eye.'

'You wouldn't be the first woman to betray a man.'

The comment hit closer to home than he could ever know. She tried to read his expression, so full of confusion and despair and wondered if he was ever going to kiss her again, whether she was brave enough to risk everything by kissing him first.

He must have guessed what she was about to do because he pulled away and raised his eyes to the sky as if to remind himself there was a heaven up there, that his God was watching, and instantly the spell was broken, the moment passed.

He moved away and put on his towelling robe, tying the belt decisively with a double knot. 'I'd better go and put on some clothes.'

When he returned to the terrace, it was as if their earlier conversation hadn't occurred. Marguerite set out the art materials she'd brought with her and asked which preliminary sketch he preferred from the ones she'd left with him the time before, or whether they should begin again.

It seemed an impossible task, trying to focus on the middle of something when it felt like it should be the start of something else. She looked at him as he gazed out to sea, wishing she could read what was going on in his mind, his heart. Despite the protestations of his faith, she could see he was conflicted.

It was a moment before he replied, drawing his attention reluctantly from the horizon, and she realised he must have been praying.

'Could we just sit here for a while instead?'

She put aside her sketchbook and sat beside him, her fingertips barely touching his as they watched the sea relentlessly throwing itself against the rocks, both of them understanding its need for recklessness. After a while, she tried again to discuss the sketches, but he showed little interest in them.

'You've told me nothing about your early life, Marguerite. Have you always lived here?'

'Not always. I used to live in Paris.'

'But you studied art in London.'

'Yes. I admired many of the artists who'd trained at the Slade. I wanted to learn what they'd been taught.'

She felt herself growing warm under his scrutiny. Why did he need to know these things? Couldn't he just accept her in the here and now as the person she'd reinvented herself to be?

'That night, Etienne, when you accompanied me home and insisted on a detour . . . you knew the bodies of the boys were hanging in the square.'

'It would have done you no good to see them.'

'What else do you know? How much does Schmidt confide in you?'

'Don't keep testing my vows. I beg you. It'll only destroy us both. Can't we just sit here and enjoy the moment?'

There were things he was hiding; she was certain of it, but he wasn't about to reveal them, not like this. 'If you don't want to work on your portrait, then there's nothing for me to do here today.'

He reached out and took her hand. 'Must you go?'

But the gesture was too little, too late. She gathered up her sketchbook and her pencils, preparing to leave, her soul bruised with longing for this impossible man. She'd get through to his heart if it was the last thing she did. Etienne would reveal the truth of himself to her, even as he refused to help her with her mission. His god wouldn't keep them apart; He wouldn't win this battle, just as surely as Germany wouldn't win the war.

Chapter 30

Marguerite waited until Etienne was celebrating Mass at his church before she returned to the Villa Christelle. If anyone asked, she was there to work on the background of the painting. Her subject was a busy man. He couldn't be expected to be there the whole time she was working on the picture.

Once again, she used a hairpin to negotiate the lock on the door and let herself in. It felt wrong to be there without Etienne, a place that didn't even belong to him, but to Gerald Mayhew, yet the fact that it had been requisitioned by the enemy gave her the courage to push away the thought that she was intruding as she set about her task.

Knowing Etienne could return at any time, she hurried through to his study, continuing her search where she'd previously left off, exploring the boxes on the lower shelves of the cupboard, hoping to find something to explain why he'd cultivated his relationship with Schmidt.

Still she found nothing but documents relating to church business, notes from parishioners warning him off allowing the Germans into his church, others begging him to denounce people for stockpiling a harvest of cabbages, for keeping the white heads of the cauliflowers which were meant for German consumption only, letters she couldn't imagine Etienne ever acting on.

Having exhausted the study, she moved to the bedroom and began rifling through his drawers, her failure to discover anything justifying her continued search. What secrets did he have? What was he hiding?

Her questions were answered when her fingers bumped against the hard edge of a picture frame in his bedside drawer, tucked between the folds of his pyjamas. As she looked at the image a familiar face smiled back at her: Catherine, the girl she'd seen in Etienne's church. The photograph must have been taken some years earlier because she looked much younger. And she wasn't alone in the picture. She was sitting on Etienne's knee. A woman with long hair was standing behind them, her hand resting on Etienne's shoulder, her face so similar to Catherine's that she had to be her mother. Here he was, the man, not the priest, just as he'd wanted her to portray him in the portrait; and here in this picture of a close family, he was happier than she'd ever seen him.

Her hand shook at the realisation of the connection. Simone was right. The girl must be his daughter, the woman with him his lover. Where was this woman now? And had he loved her the way he resisted loving Marguerite?

She'd lost track of time while she'd been searching the villa. Suddenly conscious that she'd been there too long, she put the photograph back where she'd found it and checked that nothing appeared to have been disturbed before she left, pulling the door to the terrace closed behind her and hoping that when Etienne returned, he'd be surprised to discover he'd left it unlocked but think no more of it.

Her mind was still reeling from what she'd found as she wheeled her bicycle up the steep path to the main road. If the girl in the photograph was his niece, why did he keep her picture hidden in such a private place? And why had he been so evasive when she asked about his family on the day he showed her the frescoes?

'You look like you've got the world on your shoulders, my old duck.'

Marguerite jumped at the sound of Lance's voice. She looked up and saw him standing in the shade of an umbrella pine as she turned onto the road, his eyes hidden by the wide brim of his Panama hat. His years in prison seemed to have left him with the gift of stealth.

'What are you doing here?'

'I could ask you the same question.'

She pointed to her sketchbook and the box of pencils in the basket on the front of her bicycle. 'I've been visiting a client.'

'I'm doing the exact same thing. A little bird told me that the art dealer Etienne Valade lives around here. Perhaps you can point me in his direction.'

'He's not an art dealer. He's a priest.'

He pushed his hat onto the back of his head to get a better view of her. 'I can see you're disappointed, my old duck, but you never know; old habits die hard. He might still be able to sell a few of your paintings if you press him firmly enough.'

'I've just come from his villa. He's not there. What do you want him for?'

'Same as you, Duckie. A bit of buying and selling.'

She didn't want to talk to Lance any longer. Just the sound of his voice brought back the sensations of her old life and she refused to be that person again. She'd spent years shaking her off, and she wasn't prepared to pick her up again now. She pushed her bicycle past him and carried on along the road.

'You're wasting your time. You'll get nothing out of him.'

It was the second time he'd caught her leaving the villa. It couldn't be a coincidence. If Lance was watching her, then he'd become cleverer at it than he used to be.

Determined as always to have the last word, he followed her. 'You want to be careful, Duckie, wandering around on your own. You can't trust anyone these days. Two enemy aliens were arrested yesterday, denounced by someone who discovered them hiding in a barn. It seems he overheard them jabbering in English.'

'Why are you telling me this? You know I'm French.'

'Who'd have thought there'd be so many English still living in these parts? If they're found, they're given a slap on the wrist and put in prison. The punishment is much worse for those guilty of hiding them. They're made to face a firing squad, no questions asked.'

Had Lance been the intruder Dorothy had heard in the garden that night or was he bluffing?

'Don't waste your stories on me, Lance. I don't want to hear them.'

'I'm just saying, Duckie, you'd be far safer living with me rather than in that isolated old farmhouse with Simone. There's no saying what might be going on there under the cover of darkness.'

'You're the one who needs to be careful, Lance. You might claim to have perfected your French in Geneva, but that accent of yours is pure South London. If anyone is at risk of being denounced, it's you.'

He laughed, but it was a hollow sound, full of bravado. 'That's what I've always loved about you, Duckie; your sparkling wit and your ability to cut a man down to size. I'd ask you to marry me, if we weren't already married.' He tilted his hat lower over his face, hiding his expression. 'I'm reminding you of this, because you seem to have forgotten you're still my wife.'

He was becoming too familiar. She couldn't let him get close to her again. She couldn't trust him and he certainly couldn't trust her. She climbed onto her bicycle and began pedalling down the road, gathering speed as she went.

'Goodbye, Lance. Go back to Switzerland where it's safe. I don't want to see you again.'

'I'm your husband, Duckie. You won't get away from me that easily.'

He was probably bluffing, but if he did know about Dorothy, then he was a bigger threat than she'd imagined. He was reckless and full of spite and wasn't beyond using anything against her. She couldn't give him any reason to force her back into their old life together, and just like so many people she met these days, she couldn't be sure whose side he was on.

Chapter 31

Marguerite and Simone were in the cellar with Dorothy, poring over their bowls of barley soup and black bread. Always hungry for a good story, Dorothy was still mulling over the mystery of whether Etienne was Catherine's father or her uncle.

As far as Marguerite was concerned, it was a test of his character. A priest with a child was a priest prepared to lead a double life in the face of God. And if he'd lied to her about Catherine, what else had he lied about?

'If you want to get to the bottom of the matter, you'll have to dig deeper. You need to put yourself in the way of her. Find out who she really is.'

Simone ran her bread around the bottom of her bowl, wiping up the last of the soup. Since hearing of Jeanne's death, she'd withdrawn into herself and barely left her room. This was the first time she'd joined them for a meal or attempted any kind of conversation.

'She's the priest's daughter. I'd wager next week's food ration on it.'

Dorothy bit into the last crust. 'I wouldn't be so hasty. It doesn't fit the romantic picture I have of him in my mind.'

'He's a red-blooded male.' Simone gave Marguerite a warning stare as she said it. 'Remember that kiss in the park.'

Marguerite couldn't forget it; that was the problem. Just thinking about it made her breathless.

'You need to take direct action.' Dorothy delved into her carpet bag and pulled out a pink satin ribbon, dangling it between her thumb and forefinger. 'Take this to Catherine. No young girl can refuse you her friendship after you've offered her a frippery.'

And so this was how the next morning, Marguerite found herself standing at the door of the presbytery, waiting for someone to answer her knock. If Etienne appeared then she'd just have to brazen it out. There was no reason why she wouldn't want to bring a present for his niece when times were so difficult and small treats impossible to come by.

There must have been three bolts on the door. Marguerite heard whoever was on the inside curse over each one in turn before it was finally opened and she found herself face to face with Madame Mercier.

She took one look at Marguerite and folded her arms across her chest. 'If you're looking for the Father, he's not here.' It was an automatic response and she must have said it a hundred times.

'I'm Marguerite Segal. I'm a friend of Father Etienne. I've come to see Catherine. I have a gift for her.'

Madame Mercier's long hair was pulled tightly away from her face, as if she hadn't had the time or the patience to pin it up. 'Who is it you're asking for?'

'Catherine. The young girl I saw in the church.'

'There's no young girl here. This is the presbytery. Priests don't have children.'

So Etienne hadn't lied after all. 'She's Thierry's daughter. He told me about her.'

'You've been imagining things. A lot of women do that where the Father's concerned. He's too charming for his calling. You wouldn't be here if he was fat and seventy.'

Madame Mercier had a point, but she wasn't going to give up now. 'Has she gone back to Paris?'

'I don't know what you're talking about. Someone's been feeding you nonsense. Thierry doesn't have a daughter. He doesn't have any children. Now you must excuse me. The monsignor is coming this afternoon and he'll be checking the corners for dust.'

Before Marguerite could ask anything else, Madame Mercier had closed the door and begun turning the key in the first of the three locks. She should have realised there was no easy path to certainty where Etienne was concerned and it was going to take more than a pink ribbon to determine whether Marguerite could trust him.

Chapter 32

Marguerite and Simone were in the studio changing the names on the latest batch of identity cards when they heard a car pull up in the lane outside the house. Marguerite put down her pen and checked the window, her stomach turning over at the violence the soldiers put into slamming the doors of the black Citroën.

Simone grabbed the identity cards and shoved them in her pocket, screwing the lid on the bottle of blue Waterman ink with trembling fingers before slipping wordlessly out of the back of the studio.

Four men were already at the farmhouse door, the tallest hammering it with the butt of his rifle and shouting for it to be opened.

Marguerite stepped outside, shielding her eyes from the glare of the morning sun, determined they wouldn't see her fear.

'Can I help you with something?'

'We've come to search the house. Open up.'

It was Schmidt who spoke, his face sneering beneath the shade of his officer's cap. He kicked the door, the contact of his boot sending a thud like the sound of a base drum resonating around the formerly quiet morning.

'If you tell me what you're looking for, perhaps I can help. You might have come to the wrong place.'

'Don't try to be clever with me.'

Simone, who had entered the house via the garden, opened the door, begging them not to kick it down. Schmidt pushed her to the floor and the soldiers charged inside, a storm of boots and fists; their pistols blasted indiscriminately as Schmidt's rough voice shouted instructions to search every room.

Marguerite rushed to Simone's side and helped her to her feet. 'Are you alright?'

Simone nodded. 'Don't let go of my hand.'

They ran to the studio, where Marguerite armed herself with a knife, tucking it into the back of her skirt. If Schmidt touched them, she'd drive it through the centre of his withered heart.

Simone clung to her, flinching at every bang and smash inside the house as the soldiers turned it upside down. If they discovered the cellar, it would be the end of everything.

Marguerite squeezed her hand. 'If they find Dorothy, at least one of them will die for it, I promise.'

Desperate to know what was happening, they crept outside where the youngest soldier was searching the garden. They watched as he peered at the beds of root vegetables and salad, and at the fig tree that had failed to bear fruit for the last five years, avoiding the beehives where the swarm Marguerite had tempted had refused to settle.

He was approaching the shed when the other soldiers emerged from the house, their heavy boots throwing the gravel in all directions as they marched down the path towards the gate.

Marguerite let go of her breath. They'd got away with it.

'Search the women.'

With these three words, the world shifted to another level of terror. She'd been a fool to think it would be that easy.

The tallest of the soldiers grabbed Simone. Marguerite watched her hold herself rigid against his hands as he pressed every contour of her body, his fingers riddling beneath the edges of her underwear, forcing himself into intimate places where he should never have been. If he discovered the identity cards and the bottle of ink, they were as good as dead.

But in spite of his brutality, he found nothing and Simone remained unflinching when he finally shoved her away, disgusted by his failure.

Marguerite was next. She braced herself, feeling the sharp press of the knife tucked in the waistband of her skirt. It would only take the soldier's groping hands a second to find it.

Simone must have guessed her thoughts and before he could lay a finger on her, she began waving her arms and shouting.

'Can't you leave us alone, now? Haven't you done enough? Who's going to clean up the mess you've made in my grandmother's house? Who's going to pay for the damage?'

Her ranting went on and on, drawing the attention of the soldiers just long enough for Marguerite to dislodge the knife from her waistband and let it drop to the ground, the sound of it landing on the gravel covered by Simone's continued shouting.

Using the same distraction, Marguerite was able to push enough loose stones over it with her foot to stop the sunlight catching the blade before casually stepping away from it. Seeing she'd dropped the knife, Simone fell silent allowing the attention to return to Marguerite.

She prepared herself for the intrusion of the soldier's hands as he grabbed her, hoping he wouldn't pay too much attention to the silver filigree locket containing the camera that she wore around her neck. His breath on her face insulted her with the waft of garlic as he began his search. While the rest of them were starving, the enemy were eating cured meats and spiced sausages for every meal.

The boy they'd sent to search the garden finally re-joined them, his cheeks flushed with shame. Now he'd returned, the waiting soldiers started to make their way back to the car, as eager to leave as the women were to see them go. The soldier searching Marguerite finally pushed her aside. For all his violence, he'd found nothing.

The car doors slammed and Marguerite allowed herself to think it was over until she realised she'd lost sight of Schmidt. She ran to her studio and there he was, his vast form perched on the high stool at her work bench as he flicked through the pages of her sketchbook, the precious bottle of lactic acid she'd been using to bleach the original names from the identity cards within easy reach of his hand.

He watched her as she entered, a smile smeared across his face. 'There you are.'

He must have searched the studio while she was in the garden. She went cold at the thought of him rifling through her artwork and anything else she'd forgotten that he might find.

Without warning, he brought his fist down on a couple of clay figures she'd modelled, neither of which had been glazed or fired. She'd made them out of desperation when clay was the only material she could get her hands on. They weren't particularly good, but still the wanton destruction of them stung her.

'Would you like me to paint your portrait? Is that why you're here?'

'Still touting for business, I see. You shouldn't try so hard. It makes you look cheap.' His eyes ranged across the studio, his fingers restlessly drumming on her sketchbook until he spotted the bottle of lactic acid.

Marguerite watched him pick it up and turn it over in his hands. The small brown bottle didn't have a label and it was impossible to tell its contents. He pulled out the cork and sniffed, his nose wrinkling at the sour smell. Endless seconds passed until he replaced the stopper.

'What's this?'

Marguerite's mind raced to find an answer that wouldn't raise further questions. 'It's something I mix with the paint to create a better effect.'

It was the wrong thing to have said. She realised it as soon as she'd said it. He dangled the bottle between his thumb and forefinger before suddenly throwing it at her.

'Show me how you use it.'

She grabbed it from the air, recovering it as it almost slipped from her fingers. It was too precious to lose and probably irreplaceable given the increase in German scrutiny.

She didn't know how the lactic acid would react with paint, but as it removed ink, it was likely to bleach out the colour. She reached for a pile of watercolours and started sifting through them. 'There's a picture I did earlier. You'll see how I . . . '

He grabbed the watercolours and flung them to the floor. 'I said, show me. I want to see how you work with it.'

She selected a sheet of paper and washed a small area with water before taking up her watercolours and a brush.

'You only need the tiniest amount. That's why it comes in a small bottle.'

She held her breath to steady herself and removed the stopper, dipping the fine brush into the neck of the bottle, taking as little of the liquid as possible before replacing the cork.

Schmidt leaned over her, his rancid breath foul on her face. 'What's it called this miracle liquid?'

'It's called . . . It's just . . . blender.'

She stroked the bristles of the brush against a block of blue watercolour, and wrote *Otto*, in fine letters, forcing her wrist into the paper to stop her hand shaking.

His lip curled as he considered the work. 'So what's so special about that?'

Her mind scrambled for an answer. 'It makes it easier to apply the colour. It's not something that someone looking at a painting would really notice.'

He blinked at it, underwhelmed by what she was showing him. 'I don't see the point of it.'

Already the colour was fading where the bleaching agent in the lactic acid was beginning to have an effect. She removed the paper from in front of him and folded it before he noticed his name disappearing before his eyes.

'I used a very small amount, just to show you.'

Unimpressed, he snatched the bottle and tossed it from hand to hand. 'Anyone would think it was precious the way you watch me handle it.'

'Things are hard to replace these days.'

'Useless things like this, yes.'

'I find it helps my painting.'

'Someone's been fooling you, Marguerite. There's nothing to this at all.' He dangled the bottle, indicating he was about to drop it on the floor. 'Should I smash it? Perhaps I'd be doing you a favour.'

'I'd rather you didn't.'

He grinned. 'Then ask me not to.'

'Please don't smash the bottle.'

He held the bottle at arm's length. 'I didn't hear you.'

'Please don't smash the bottle.'

He leaned towards her again, stroking her face with his free hand, his touch like sandpaper against her cheek.

'Alright, as you asked so nicely.' He placed the bottle on the work bench, forcing a heavy kiss on her lips as he did so.

'Now what do you say?'

'Thank you.'

The words almost choked her as she forced them out, her lips soiled with his saliva.

He stood up, repositioning his trousers around his vast girth. 'See how nice you can be when you want to?'

Already he was lumbering his way out of her studio. Marguerite stayed where she was, rigid with fear and revulsion, not daring to say or do anything in case he returned. She was still in the same position when Simone came in a few minutes later.

'He's gone. They've all driven away. I don't think they found anything, Are you alright?'

'I'm fine.'

They raced back to the house and began furiously emptying the cupboard under the stairs, fighting through the disused pots of paint, throwing aside the gardening tools and the chairs, until the floor was clear and they could reach the hatch to the cellar.

'Dorothy?'

'I'm alright. Still in one piece. Bit of a close shave, though.'

Marguerite climbed down and gave her a hug. Simone followed, her voice thick with fear. 'Thank God they didn't find the cellar.'

'It just goes to show how clever you've been in keeping me hidden.' Dorothy fanned her face, trying to take the heat out of it. 'I'm not exaggerating when I say I owe my life to the two of you.'

Once they'd straightened the house, Marguerite and Simone faced each other across the kitchen table as they took stock of what had happened. Simone stared at her hands, picking nervously at the rough skin around the edge of her thumbnail until it bled.

'Dorothy believes we've kept her safe, but I can't help feeling our resistance activities have put her in danger. Think of the people we've already lost. It's a high price to pay for freedom.'

Marguerite grabbed Simone's hand to stop her doing any more harm to herself. 'It won't be long until the liberation. We just have to hold our nerve and look out for one another as best as we can.'

She didn't mention that Dorothy might have been spotted by Lance when she was in the garden, that he'd dropped hints that he wasn't above betraying her. Simone already had enough to worry about without this added complication.

'Armand's been trying to find her a new place, but nobody will take her. The situation in the town is much worse since Biquet and the other boys were executed.'

The Third Reich knew they were losing the war and were determined to make everyone suffer for it. Vienna had been heavily bombed by the Allies along with many German cities and other strategic sites. It might have been the beginning of the end, but no one knew how long the fighting would last or what atrocities were still to come.

'Thank God I managed to hide the identity cards and the ink alongside your pistol in one of the beehives. That dopey child they put in a uniform was probably too scared of bees to go near them when he searched the garden.'

Marguerite was grateful for Simone's quick thinking. She just wished she'd had the presence of mind to hide the lactic acid too. If Schmidt had worked out what it was used for, it would have been the end of all of them.

Chapter 33

The note from Etienne inviting her to the Villa Christelle was delivered after the curfew. He must have written it during the loneliest hours of the evening, when there was only a long night of emptiness ahead and no promise of respite with the coming of the new day. There were no clues as to who'd delivered it when she found it on the doorstep the following morning, weighted down with a stone to stop it blowing away.

He wanted to continue the work on the portrait. For all the fits and starts and the complications, neither of them could leave it alone. It was the only thing they had that the world couldn't intrude upon. How easy it was for them, sitting in the beautiful villa with the sun shining and the waves crashing against the rocks, to imagine there was no war; that life was still going on as it always had.

But for Marguerite, the pretence couldn't last, not with German planes flying back and forth across the sea, and the random gunshots in the hills that made her mourn for whoever had just lost their life. Nor could she stop worrying about the victims thrown into the backs of the vans that rattled along the coastal road, wondering which building they were being carried off to for questioning, knowing that whichever one it was, they wouldn't get out alive. While she was with Etienne, she could pretend none of these things were happening, but the pretence only lasted for a heartbeat, because beyond that brief moment, the horror of it remained with her constantly.

She set off for the villa almost immediately, full of hope and trepidation, wondering if it was the priest or the man who'd be waiting for her – the befriender of Nazis or the art lover. How would he ever reconcile these conflicting parts of his character, and if he did, would Marguerite ever be able to forgive him for it?

It was the man, not the priest who greeted her, fresh from his morning swim, the saltwater glistening on his skin in the sunlight. As he took her hand, no man had ever seemed more alive to her, so vital.

'I have something to show you. Come inside.'

There was no hint that he was pleased to see her and she wouldn't humiliate herself by demanding more attention than he was prepared to offer freely.

He avoided looking at her as he spoke. 'Schmidt paid me a visit last night.'

'He behaves like he's your best friend.'

She failed to keep the edge out of her voice. If Etienne noticed it, he chose not to respond.

'He's very fond of a good French brandy. He brought me a bottle as a gift. I insisted on sharing it with him, just as any friend would. For a man of his build, he doesn't hold his liquor very well. He passed out before we'd even drunk three-quarters of the bottle.'

'How much of it did you drink, Etienne?'

He gestured with his finger and thumb, indicating a small measure.

'Schmidt had come straight off duty and had his briefcase with him. While he slept off the brandy, I took the opportunity to see what papers were inside.'

By now they'd reached the study. Etienne unlocked the desk drawer and removed a roll of film which he handed to her.

'The briefcase contained documents detailing the forthcoming movements of German troops across the whole of the Cote d'Azur, so I photographed them.' His eyes flicked away from her face. 'I take it this is the sort of information you were hoping I could supply you with.'

She thought her heart would burst. The urge to throw her arms around him and kiss him was almost too much. She slipped the roll of film into her bag, securing it in a zipped pocket, overwhelmed that he'd taken such a risk, that he'd done it because she'd wanted him to.

'One day, Etienne, the world will thank you for what you've done.'

'Perhaps, but I did it for a more personal reason. I want you to have faith in me.' He looked away, reluctant to meet her eye. 'I have a confession to make. I can't stand for there to be a lie between us.'

He pulled aside the black velvet curtain, revealing the painting by Josef Motz. 'I once told you this painting was a gift from my father before he died, but it was untrue. Our gallery specialised in Modernist works such as this one. My brother Thierry and I shut down the business as soon as the Germans marched into Paris. Knowing they viewed such art as degenerate, we were sure they'd have confiscated everything in the gallery and either sold it abroad for their own profit or destroyed it. During those frenzied few days, as the Germans gained a stranglehold on the city, we managed to return most of the work to the artists we represented.

'Before the war, I was honoured to call Josef Motz my friend. He was arrested shortly after the fall of Paris. I haven't been able to use my influence to get him released from prison, but the night he was captured, Thierry and I helped his wife and daughters flee France. This was the only painting of Josef's they had. Josef's wife didn't want to risk being caught with it in her possession as she fled the country and so she asked me to look after it.

'I'm pleased to say the family are now living safely in England, thanks to the kindness of a mutual friend who opened their home to them.'

She wanted to believe him, just as she'd wanted to believe the painting had been a gift from his father. 'It explains why it's so different to all the other pictures in the villa.'

'They're not my choice. They were bought by Laura, Gerald Mayhew's wife. She has very different taste to him. They argue over it all the time.'

'You know the people who own this villa?'

He seemed bewildered by the accusing tone of her question. 'We became friends when I lived in Paris. He bought paintings from the gallery for his London house. He asked me to move into the villa when he was forced to flee France, trusting me to take care of it until after the war. While I'm living here, it's less likely to fall into enemy hands. The Germans wouldn't want to be seen to be turning out a priest.'

The villa hadn't been passed to him by the enemy. He was protecting it from them for a friend. She wanted to believe him, just as she wanted to believe how he came to have the Motz painting. Still, she couldn't forget the photograph of him with Catherine and the woman Marguerite assumed to be his lover, which she'd found hidden in his bedside drawer. Nor could she forget how friendly he was with Schmidt, how he'd laughed as he'd sat at his desk and drank his brandy while the boys' lives were hanging by a thread. And yet, perhaps his relationship with Schmidt was all part of his game. Her head told her one thing, but her heart told her another. Which one should she trust?

'You and your brother must have taken great risks to help the Motz family escape.'

'It was mainly Thierry's doing. As soon as war broke out, he sent his wife and children to live in safety in Spain while he stayed behind to work for an underground resistance network in Paris.'

'Catherine, the girl I saw at the church. She isn't Thierry's daughter then?'

He'd blundered; she could see it in his face as he fought to recover.

'Catherine? Yes, of course. I'd forgotten you'd seen her. She's his eldest daughter. She insisted on staying in France when her mother and her younger sisters left.'

He was lying, just as Madame Mercier had been lying. But perhaps Madame Mercier had been lying a little less than Etienne. She stored away her suspicions to consider later.

'I promised Josef that if anything happened to him, I'd do everything I could to look after his family. I want to continue to honour that promise. I intend to keep this work safe until the day it can be sold through a reputable gallery in an unoccupied country. The money from the sale will help to secure a decent future for Josef's wife and their children, should Josef not return.'

She framed the next question carefully, preparing to tread on sensitive ground. 'Where is Thierry now? Is he safe?'

'He's missing. Shot, for all I know. I might never know his fate.'

'I'm so sorry, Etienne.'

She put her arms around him and held him tight. It was all she could offer to soften the pain even if it only lasted a moment.

'I have God to thank for giving me the strength to continue the fight against Fascism.'

'How can you believe in a god that allows such suffering in the world?'

'My faith is tested every day. Learning to overcome doubt is what strengthens it. That's the purpose of temptation.'

'It's love that gives us strength, Etienne, not doubt.'

There was no disputing her argument when they were both living proof of it. He pulled her closer and suddenly it was as if they were back in the park, two strangers clinging to each other for safety in the dark. Only now they weren't strangers.

At that moment, nothing else mattered but the sound of his heart beating against her chest. She didn't need his words of love because she could feel them in every pulse of his body. And the kiss when it finally came was laden with so much more intent as his fingers fumbled to unbutton her clothes.

Struggling to pull the stubborn dress over her head, she took a step back to untangle it, but it was a mistake. A single moment apart from her was all it took for second thoughts to creep into Etienne's mind and before she could convince him to stay, he'd fled the room, cursing his own weakness and begging her to forgive him.

He wasn't coming back. She pulled on her dress, fastening the buttons he'd struggled to negotiate, wondering how she'd ever have the dignity to face him after so much humiliation. When it came to it, he hadn't trusted her enough to love her.

He'd said his faith grew stronger the more he tested it, which meant she was nothing more than a part of his game with God, a temptation to be resisted, and instead of experiencing real love when she'd offered it, he'd retreated to his religion.

She found him on his knees on the terrace. He'd put on his soutane and was gazing out across the unruly sea, praying to his god for forgiveness and she knew she'd lost him. Despite his moment of weakness, he was never hers and he never would be. She'd captured his heart, but God would always have his soul.

He stood up; his eyes narrowed against the sun as he turned to her, his expression a combination of so many things, and she knew what she had to do.

'I've come to say goodbye.'

'You're leaving already?'

He wasn't going to stop her, however much she wished it. 'I should pass on the roll of film to my contact. The sooner it reaches the right hands, the more useful the information will be.'

'Yes, of course.'

'There's one more thing. I've been asked to photograph the documents detailing the transportation of the victims Schmidt and his associates have sent to the prison camps. I need to get to them before they destroy them, which they're bound to do before they retreat from the Allies. I believe they're in the safe in Schmidt's office. I need the combination to the lock. Can you get it for me?'

He considered her request, his face registering the danger, not only for himself, but for Marguerite too. 'Yes.'

He bowed his head when she thanked him, once more the priest, just beyond touching distance, but a world removed from her.

'What we did just then was a moment of weakness on my part. I should never have allowed it to happen. Please forgive me.'

'Don't be sorry. I couldn't bear to think you regretted it.'

'No, it's not that. It could never be that. It's just . . . ' He cleared his throat, his eyes intent on her. 'It's best if we don't continue to work on the portrait.'

'If that's want you want.'

'We can never be lovers, Marguerite, however much we both wish it.'

She looked out to sea because it was too painful to witness the sadness in his eyes. 'I have to remind myself that you're a priest a hundred times a day. It doesn't stop me longing for things to be different.'

He nodded, no longer looking at her, and once again they were strangers.

As she walked away, it would have been easy to pretend that what had passed between them had never happened, if it wasn't for the press of his body, which she could still feel against her skin and the echo of the words he'd whispered between kisses that she'd never forget; *I love you, I love you, I love you.*

Chapter 34

Marguerite began the journey to Pascal's camp, pushing her bicycle when the terrain became too steep and the scrubland beneath her feet too rough to ride over. She continued through the heat of the morning, focusing on the task in hand; tears scorched her cheeks as she tried not to dwell on what had been won and lost over the course of an hour. Etienne had never been hers to love and would never be hers to keep.

Pascal was still asleep when she arrived. Reluctant to disturb him, she waited in the shade of a pine tree until he finally emerged from the old shepherd's hut, unfurling like a wildcat from the cramped interior of his den, the smell of sweat and unwashed clothes wrapped around him like a fog.

She didn't ask what he'd been up to during the night that had caused him to sleep so late. These days, evidence of sabotage was everywhere, train tracks damaged to prevent the movement of German troops and supplies, roads and bridges undermined for the same reason.

He looked surprised to see her and it took him a minute to shake off the effects of his sleep. Before he could ask what she wanted, she offered him the roll of film.

'This might be useful. It contains photographs of the documents detailing the planned enemy movements over the whole of the Cote d'Azur.'

He took it from her outstretched hand and shoved it in his trouser pocket. 'Good, but it's not what you were asked for. Time is running out. You need to photograph the documents incriminating Schmidt for his war crimes before he destroys them.'

'I'm working on it.'

'Did you bring any food?'

'There's bread and cheese.'

It had been a risk carrying illicit food in daylight. If she'd been stopped and questioned, she wouldn't have been able to explain where it had come from. She couldn't have passed it off as part of her ration. It was too good and there was too much of it, and if she'd said she'd bought it on the black market she'd have been arrested.

He unwrapped the cheese and ran his knife along the hard edge of the rind before tossing it aside. 'You're turning into quite the hero or maybe you're just a pest. I haven't made up my mind yet.'

The words were more tribute than she needed and she had to look away, knowing he wouldn't respect her if he saw her tears.

As she started to wheel her bicycle down the hill he called to her. 'You know the bar on the Chemin de la Cigale?'

'I don't go to bars. They're full of German soldiers.'

'Meet me there on Friday night.'

His tone suggested it was an order rather than an invitation and Marguerite knew better than to refuse him.

Chapter 35

The rain had begun to spit, piquing the night-time air with the smell of wet pine and damp roadside dust, when Marguerite arrived at the place on the Chemin de la Cigale where Pascal had ordered her to meet him. The bar was in the back room of a small house, ill-lit and with a low ceiling and a filthy floor, where cockroaches moved like shadows and men gathered in clusters around half a dozen tables to play cards and exchange views in low murmurs.

She knew the bar by its reputation, or rather through rumour, as few people admitted to having direct experience of visiting it. It wasn't a place you entered unless you were invited. Even the German soldiers stayed away, deterred by the lack of women and imported beer. It wasn't an illegal establishment, but it was very close to the bone and it made itself unwelcoming for a reason. Only those who met there regularly to plan and to plot knew what that reason was and it hadn't taken Marguerite long to work out that Pascal was at the centre of it.

Every head in the bar turned as she entered, screwing her eyes against the light of the oil lamps after the darkness of the blacked-out streets. Pascal was sitting on a high stool at the bar. He raised his arm and made a great show of waving her over, pulling up a seat next to him and ordering her a shot of eau de vie, made in the illegal still that had been hidden in the cellar for over fifty years.

He pushed the glass, thick as a bull's eye, across the bar and looked at her as he raised his own to his lips, pouring the shot down his open throat without swallowing. Every pair of eyes in the bar was on her, waiting to see how she reacted to Pascal's challenge. The alcohol was pure enough to take down any man not used to strong spirits, but now wasn't the time to hesitate.

He pushed the glass closer to her. 'Drink it. It won't kill you, although I can't promise it won't make you blind.'

Marguerite picked up the glass and tipped her head back, swallowing the drink in one gulp before casually placing the empty glass on the bar in front of her, fighting the urge to react as the alcohol burned her throat like the devil's breath.

Quietly, the murmur of conversation began up again as the men turned their attention back to their card games. If she'd impressed them, they weren't about to show it. She nodded to the barman, ordering another couple of shots for her and Pascal. When she dug in her purse to pay, the barman shook his head.

'No charge.'

Pascal slapped her on the shoulder. 'Now you're my friend. Now they've seen you here with me, there won't be so much trouble for you.'

'Now they think I'm your lover.'

'It's better than them thinking you're a Nazi whore.'

She wanted to thank him, but knew he wouldn't appreciate communication on those terms. It wasn't how it worked.

He swallowed the second shot, wiping his lips with the back of his hand. 'A British agent has been captured by the Gestapo. A woman. They shot her at dawn.'

'What was her name?'

'Don't ask me.'

Marguerite knocked back the second drink, refusing to flinch as it travelled to her stomach, burning every part of her insides it touched. She forced herself to sit upright on the stool as the alcohol smeared her perception of the world around her, the floor tilting every time she moved her head.

She thought of Violet, so young and brittle and doing a brave job in a frightening world. It might have been her who'd been shot, or any number of other women like her. No one was safe, however careful they were, however clever.

If it was Violet who'd been captured, she might have been forced to reveal her contacts under interrogation, which meant Marguerite was in more danger than ever.

When Pascal was invited to join a game of cards, she used the opportunity to slip away, not bothering to interrupt him to say goodbye and keeping her eyes focused on a straight line to the door.

The barman raised his hand and waved as she left. Nobody else in the room seemed to notice her go, or perhaps they didn't think it worth remarking on. Even Pascal kept his head down, his eyes examining the cards he'd been dealt, splaying them in his fingers like a man intent on winning.

Too drunk to climb onto her bicycle, she pushed it all the way out of town, the rain and the pin-sharp air helping her to shake off the worst effects of the eau de vie until by the time she turned onto the lane for home, her head was clearer, her resolve to hold on to life firmer than ever.

When she approached the house, Dorothy was sitting on the doorstep smoking an improvised cigarette of parched vine leaves and dried mint, her face hidden behind the shadows of the old house.

Marguerite strained to sound sober. 'Dorothy, you shouldn't . . .'

'I know. I just wanted to see you come home safely.' She held out her hand, asking to be pulled up from the step, her eyebrows rising at the alcohol fumes on Marguerite's breath. 'I don't suppose you've got any more of that fire water.'

Marguerite shook her head, suddenly queasy, her head beginning to thump with dehydration.

'Shame. I could do with a good degreaser for my typewriter keys.'

Chapter 36

Etienne was the only person likely to know anything about the British agent who'd been shot. It was the sort of thing Schmidt would have bragged about to unsettle him, a deliberate ploy to scare them all.

He must have seen her approaching the villa, because he dashed out onto the terrace before she'd locked up her bicycle.

'Thank God you're safe. Schmidt has just left. He came to give me his confession. He told me about a British agent they discovered. They tortured her and then shot her. I thought it was you.'

'But it wasn't. I'm here, safe.'

'I asked who the agent was, but he wouldn't tell me. It was as if he was taunting me, taking pleasure in my desperation for an answer.'

She remembered her meeting with Violet, how it had taken all the young woman's determination to overcome her fear. 'Perhaps she was strong enough not to give her name.'

'What if it had been you, Marguerite? I can't stop imagining what they might have done to you.'

She took his hand, refusing to let go when he tried to pull away, until his fingers gently curled around hers and they finally found their way home.

'I don't know who you are, Marguerite, but I can't stop myself loving you, however much I try.'

She couldn't stand to see him so tormented, but he'd said he loved her. No one had said those words to her since she was a child.

'I took a vow never to love anyone but God. My life has been given over to Him for so many years without question, but when I saw you in the park that night something broke inside me. Realising you were in danger, I stepped forward to protect you and when you asked me to kiss you, it was as if a prayer had been answered. And as I kissed you, whatever had broken was suddenly mended.'

'It was quite a kiss.'

'Afterwards, I tried to put you out of my mind, but suddenly your face appeared on posters all over the town. It was as if you were summoning me, telling me you needed me.'

'I was, and I do need you.'

'I shouldn't have gone to the exhibition, but I couldn't stop myself. That night, I saw what no one else saw in your work. I saw your soul laid bare and suddenly this terrible world was full of possibility.'

They sat on the rocks, allowing the sea to splash against their feet, inviting the hypnotic rhythm of the waves to soothe them. Gradually, they began to talk, timidly at first, as strangers do, making tentative steps towards understanding. As the morning drifted into afternoon, she avoided his direct questions about her former life, turning the subject back to him every time he mentioned her past.

She couldn't tell him the truth about herself and what she was running away from. She wasn't ready to shatter his illusion of her. He'd only see the part of her she wanted to be true. There was no way of knowing what would happen next. He didn't need to know who she really was. If she were to create a fantasy for both of them out of their time together, she had to put boundaries around the truth.

The afternoon drifted into evening as they talked, or sat in silence on the terrace, the twilight drawing in by the minute until she had no choice but to leave. It was one thing to risk breaking the curfew to visit Pascal in the hills where there were few patrols, but here on the coast, she was likely to be caught and she couldn't risk being arrested.

He looked at her, his eyes wide in the fading light. 'Why don't you stay? You can use the guest room. That's if you can stand the company of those dull watercolours on the walls.'

Her heart wouldn't stand being so close to him while having to remain apart. 'I don't think it would be a good idea. Simone will worry if I'm not home before the curfew.'

'I can arrange for a note to be sent, to let her know you're safe. I want you to continue with the portrait. We can work on it tomorrow. We won't be disturbed.'

If she was worried by the thought of staying, the thought of abandoning this temporary paradise and returning to her real life was even more terrible. She wasn't used to being treated by someone as if they cared and it wasn't a seduction. Many men were capable of that kind of behaviour but this was different. She was too vulnerable to allow herself to succumb to his kindness and yet she gave into it anyway.

He fetched a blanket and put it around her shoulders while they continued to sit on the terrace. 'If we were in a different world, I'd light a hundred candles and build a fire to keep us warm, and we'd watch the flames dance in the sea breeze while we told each other our secrets.'

It was the notion of a dreamer and a romantic, but the idea only reminded her of the reality of their situation. The blackout was enforced with an iron fist. German planes would sweep over the coast as soon as it was dark, shooting at windows and dropping hand grenades on anyone showing a light. A fire, even a single candle was out of the question.

And if it wasn't the Germans, it would be the Allies, dropping bombs indiscriminately along the coast on innocent people, turning to tatters their already ravaged lives.

He whispered as if he were unwilling to be overheard. 'One day, freedoms will be restored and the world will be returned to how it should be and once more we'll be able to be who we truly are. Until then, we should hold on to moments like this and pretend it's already possible.'

They continued to sit in the twilight, looking out to sea, watching the ragged edges of the coastline turn to shadows while she remembered how once the lights would have lit the bends and dips of the land, glinting like diamonds strung against the black velvet night.

After a while he reached out and squeezed her hand. 'Today has been a good day and I want to thank you for it.'

In spite of his god, he was lonely. War had torn him from his family and the gallery he'd loved so much. With his brother lost, his life could never go back to how it was, just as it never could for so many. Tonight, somewhere across the bay, ten mothers were mourning the murder of their sons, shot in retaliation for the death of a German soldier that hadn't been their fault and the broken hearts of those grieving women would never mend. Nicole was also out there somewhere, travelling the broken road of her soul, searching for Jeanne's grave and refusing to accept it would never be found.

Suddenly cold, Marguerite got up from the chair and pulled the blanket more tightly around her shoulders. 'If we're to catch the best of the early morning light, I should go to bed.' Even in the dark, she couldn't hide the fact that she was trembling.

He led her back through the villa, showing her to the room next to his, inviting her to help herself to anything she wanted before saying goodnight.

With the bedroom curtains closed against the night, she turned on the lamp. There on the pillow, he'd placed a pair of pyjamas and on the dressing table, a sponge and a bar of soap such as she hadn't seen for years. She picked it up, running her fingers over the cool marble texture of the bar and held it to her nose, breathing in the delicate rose scent, so faded now that it must have been left behind by Gerald Mayhew, who couldn't have known how precious a commodity it was to become. It might not have been at its best, but it was real soap and just the thought of using it brought tears to her eyes.

She was unbuttoning her dress when she heard Etienne's gentle knock. She bunched the loose fabric in her hand, pressing it to her chest where her heart had begun to beat with a steady thud and opened the door.

His eyes travelled from her face, down the line of her neck. 'I'm sorry to disturb you. I thought you might like a bath. I've run the water and laid out fresh towels.'

'Thank you.'

She listened to his footsteps as he walked away, catching sight of herself in the dressing-table mirror, trying not to revel in the luxury he'd laid out for her, hoping that there might be a little shampoo in a bottle beside the bath.

An hour later, her skin tingling from the hot water, her hair fresh with the scent of Gerald Mayhew's apple shampoo, Marguerite crept out of the bathroom and tip-toed across the landing, wrapped only in a bath towel and feeling partly restored to the person she once was. She was clean, even if she wasn't beautiful, fresh, even if she was no longer young. Her toes clenched on the cool marble floor as she hesitated outside Etienne's bedroom door, listening to see if he was awake and bracing herself for what she hoped would follow, before she knocked gently. It had been so long since she'd done this and he probably wouldn't want her. He'd turn her away like the fool that she was because she'd misread his attention.

A moment passed before she heard his approaching footsteps and saw the door handle turn, and suddenly there he was, standing before her, his tall figure no more than a still shadow in the dark. When she didn't move, he lifted his hand to her face and stroked her cheek just as he'd done when he'd wiped the charcoal from her face in her studio. Then, he'd touched her without thinking, this time the movement was slow and deliberate. And when she didn't back away, he opened the door wider and invited her in. The words uttered under his breath, *may God forgive me*, were carried away on the night-time breeze.

Chapter 37

She woke to the sound of the sea crashing against the rocks, feeling the heat of the early morning sun streaming through the window and the cool embrace of the white cotton sheets before she remembered where she was.

He'd been the kindest lover she'd ever known. She'd cried in his arms, mourning the tenderness she'd been missing for so many years, clinging to him through the darkest hours as he slept and forcing herself to stay awake, not wanting to miss a moment of being with him while she waited for the lilac dawn to tip-toe across the sky and peel back the night, not knowing what the new day would bring.

Despite her attempts to stay awake, she must have fallen asleep sometime before sunrise. Now, the space in the bed beside her was empty and there was no sign of Etienne. She slipped on his robe and went to look for him, her stomach turning over at a sudden burst of familiar laughter in the living room.

The crease between Etienne's eyes deepened when he saw her. 'Marguerite, there you are. There's someone here. An Englishman. You might want to put some clothes on.'

'Hello, my old duck. Fancy seeing you here.'

Marguerite faltered, running her fingers through her sleep-mussed hair as she found herself face to face with Lance, her mind working overtime to come up with an excuse for her being there.

'Etienne has commissioned me to paint his portrait.'

'A study in rumpled bed sheets, is it?'

He leaned back on the sofa and lit a cigarette, an empty brandy glass beside him. He'd already made himself at home, just as she'd seen him do so many times before in so many different places. His self-assurance knew no bounds, even in wartime.

'Don't worry, Etienne. I won't play the jealous husband by challenging you to a fist fight. Duckie and I haven't been a proper man and wife for years. A long prison sentence will do that to a marriage.' He turned to her, the white heat of rage burning in his eyes. 'Now I understand why you've been so reluctant to return to my bed, my old duck.'

Already Etienne had moved to the other side the room, putting himself as far away from Marguerite as it was possible to get. She tried to catch his eye, but he refused to look at her.

She pulled Etienne's robe closer to her body as it threatened to fall open. 'What are you doing here, Lance?'

Lance reached for the brandy and poured himself another glass. His years in prison hadn't broken him of his habit of drinking before breakfast.

'Talking of betrayal, my old duck, I've been thinking about who it was who shopped me over my little scam all those years ago, and I've got a pretty good idea.'

Etienne stared out of the window, his eyes scanning for anyone who might be approaching the villa. 'It's not safe for you to be in enemy territory, Lance. You should leave France as soon as possible.'

'I'm just here to do a bit of business. The Boche'll respect that.'

Lance had already said too much. Marguerite couldn't risk him revealing anything else. 'I wouldn't count on it. You should take Etienne's advice and go.'

'Not until I've finished what I came here to do.'

'You didn't say why you wanted to see me.' Etienne's expression was unreadable as he faced Lance, dragging his eyes for barely a second from the window.

'I'm here to buy up any degenerate art that happens to be going cheap. There's a big market for it in Switzerland. As you ran that famous little gallery in Paris with your brother, I thought you'd be the man to see about it.'

'We closed the gallery years ago. There's nothing I can do for you.'

Marguerite jumped in. 'It's too dangerous, Lance. Degenerate art has been outlawed by the Third Reich. You don't realise the trouble you'd be getting into.'

'What happened to your sense of adventure? You never used to say no to anything.' He glanced at Etienne. 'It seems you still don't.'

Etienne was growing increasingly uncomfortable. She could tell by the way he kept watch at the window and refused to sit. The revelation that she was married had destroyed him. She knew every nerve and sinew in his body and she knew how to read him. He tried to look in control but his soul was bleeding. However he tried to hide it, she could feel it. She knew him. She was him.

Lance knocked back his drink and rose unsteadily to his feet. 'I'll talk to you about stealing my wife another time, Etienne, old chum.' He patted him on the shoulder as he staggered towards the door. 'And we'll continue our conversation about our little business venture when you've had time to think about it. I'm sure you could lay your hands on the type of paintings I'm after if you put your mind to it.' He threw a look at Marguerite. 'You owe me that much, at least.'

After Lance left, Marguerite joined Etienne at the window. Together they watched him stumble across the terrace and up the narrow rocky path, the tension growing more brittle between them with each breath. When she tried to touch him, he folded his arms across his chest, as if he were forming a barrier around his heart.

'Why didn't you tell me you're married?'

220

His manner was as cold as ice; the love and understanding they'd tentatively built between them had been demolished. There was no excuse for her duplicity and nothing she could say to make it right.

'It was years ago. The girl who married Lance Holmes isn't the woman I am now. I haven't been her for a long time.'

'I remember Lance's court case. It caused a great scandal in the art world. He was jailed for selling forged artworks. His wife was an artist. Her name was Daisy Hamilton. It was said she fled the country on the day he was arrested and hasn't been seen since.' He looked at her, as if none of it was making sense. 'Lance said you're his wife, but you're French. Daisy was English.'

He was pleading with her to tell him he was mistaken; she could see it in his eyes. But the truth was out and there was no going back on it.

'My father was English and that's where my nationality lies, but my mother was French. Half my childhood was spent in London, the other half in Paris. I'm fluent in the languages and habits of both countries and can pass myself off as a native in either one. If there's a divide in me, I don't know where it is. I can't point to where the English in me ends and the French begins and I don't want to, because it's who I am.'

Etienne was silent while he took it all in. 'When I said I didn't know who you are, I didn't realise how true it was.'

'I'm the woman you fell in love with through her art. That's where you saw my soul laid bare; that's the truth of who I am.'

'You're married, Marguerite. I broke my vows for you and all the while you were deceiving me.'

'I was nineteen years old when I met Lance and heartbroken over the death of my mother. I was living alone in London and struggling to make a living as an artist. It didn't take much for me to fall under his spell. He was a successful art dealer. I naively thought he was the route to my success. At the time, I had no idea he was selling forged artworks. I'm ashamed of my association with him, which is why I left England and changed my name. But as much as I want to, I can't change the past. I can't stand to think of the innocent people Lance swindled, the customers I helped him to cultivate, when all the while he was selling forgeries. All I can do is to try to atone for the part I unwittingly played in enabling his crimes which is why you find me here now, risking my life to obtain information from the enemy to help us win the war.'

'Now you want me to believe you're a hero.'

'I'm not a hero, but I've learned that if you hide your fear well enough, people don't know you're scared. With practice, you can even deceive yourself. I buried who I really was during the years I was with Lance, believing him when he said he could help build my reputation as an artist, just as I changed my identity to enable me to begin again when I left England. That's why I find it hard to express who I am through my work today. Only you spotted the real me beneath the façade, Etienne.'

In running away from Lance, she'd condemned herself to living with the identity of a woman who'd died in a fire in an apartment block in Paris in 1932. She'd chosen her because of the similarity in their dates of birth and the closeness of their names, but however many years she lived, she'd never come to terms with being Marguerite Segal and not Daisy Hamilton.

She'd never expected to get away with hiding forever and she'd never dared to look too far into the future, knowing that one day, Lance would be released from prison and come looking for her. She'd always hoped for a miracle that might change things, even though she knew it was impossible. For years, she'd managed the situation day by day, always hiding, always looking over her shoulder, until the war came along and made her position so much more dangerous. It was only the arrival of Violet with her request to help British Intelligence that had given her a means of restoring her self-respect. Now, just as she'd found a path to a more certain future and the chance of happiness with Etienne, Lance had put everything in jeopardy.

She wanted to throw herself at Etienne's feet and beg, if not his forgiveness, then his understanding, but it wouldn't do any good. And if she professed her love, it would only sound like another lie.

'I'm sorry I deceived you, Etienne. I wanted you to see me as the person you could love, rather than the person I really am.'

When she came back from putting on her clothes, he was still staring out of the window, as if one look at her would be enough to destroy him. He didn't move while she gathered together her painting materials and prepared to leave, and he didn't reply when she stood in the doorway and said goodbye. She didn't ask if she should come back another day to continue the portrait, because it would have been impossible to carry on, knowing the happiness they'd come so close to achieving had been destroyed.

Chapter 38

Marguerite's response to Etienne's rejection was to start painting in a different way. She put aside her experiments with botanical subjects and reverted to larger canvases, using the materials Etienne had given her, which she'd salvaged from the vandalism to her studio. Now, the rich colours of the oil paints beckoned to her and she streaked her canvases with smoky greys and royal purples, the formless shapes throwing open the possibilities of interpretation, leaving the viewer to make of them what they would, to prise apart the meaning which was there if you knew where to look for it, if you knew how to see it. To Marguerite, it felt like she was cutting open her heart and allowing the thick arterial blood to flow and congeal on the surface of each new raw and bleeding canvas.

Simone, who understood her painting better than anyone, swore when she saw the first three canvases propped against the studio wall to dry.

'What are you playing at, Marguerite? Don't you know what people will read into these images? They'll see straight through to your heart now you've smeared it everywhere for all to see.'

'This isn't me.'

Marguerite sobbed, only realising she was crying as she began to speak. She'd cried as she'd painted them, rapidly, in a frenzy

224

of feeling over an intense couple of days. Now she was destined to cry all over again every time she looked at them.

'This is war. This is circumstance.'

'No, Marguerite; this is Lance's doing. He's the one who ruined everything for you with Etienne. How many times are you going to let him get away with destroying your life before you finally put a stop to him?'

Dorothy, who had heard the shouting from the cellar, tip-toed into the studio, as if treading quietly meant she couldn't be seen. She gaped at the blood-red canvases.

'Oh, my love, what has he done to you?'

The paint was still only touch-dry when Lance appeared, slipping in quietly as before, but for the squeak of his plimsolls on the stone floor, his laugh cracking the silence like a roll of thunder as he announced himself.

Simone had cycled into town to buy bread only a few minutes earlier, having eventually negotiated Dorothy back into the cellar. The timing of Lance's appearance seemed too much of a co-incidence and Marguerite suspected he'd been watching the house, waiting until she was alone before he visited. If this were the case, then it was almost certain he'd seen Dorothy.

He lit a cigarette and surveyed her new paintings. 'Blood and guts. You haven't lost your old vigour, my old duck.'

'Art is a journey. It changes as we do.'

She put down the paint bush she'd been cleaning and wiped her hands on a rag, the paint beneath her fingernails set like ridges of dried blood. 'You've been told not to come here. Simone will be furious if she catches you and I never want to see you again.'

'I'm on a mission of mercy, old duck. I've come to warn you of danger.'

'Don't tell me you've realised there's a war on.'

He took a long pull on his cigarette and threw back his head, releasing the smoke in rings with carefree ease.

'Funny you should mention it. That's what I want to talk to you about. Not war exactly, but Etienne Valade.'

'What about him?'

'He's in love with you, if you didn't know it. That morning at his villa, his face was ablaze with desire every time he looked at you. He tried to hide it, but the poor weak fool is a hopeless case.'

'Don't be absurd. He's a priest.'

'It didn't stop him taking you to his bed.'

'I was there to paint his portrait.'

'It's usually the sitter who's naked, not the artist. You had nothing on beneath that robe. Don't think I didn't notice.' He studied her face, taking a long drag on his cigarette. 'You always did have a knack of making men fall in love with you.'

'Not all men, Lance.'

He shrugged, absently flicking his ash into a coffee cup. Irritated, she snatched the cup away.

'Please don't do that.'

He sniggered at her annoyance, belittling her response, just as he always did. 'You used to tell me off all the time. Old habits die hard.'

'Not all of them.'

She turned from his gaze, busying herself with cleaning her paintbrushes, jabbing them repeatedly in a jar of turpentine.

'I don't believe you risked Simone's anger just to come and tell me you think Etienne Valade is in love with me. There must be something else.'

He looked around for somewhere to flick his cigarette ash, finally tipping it into the palm of his hand.

'Quite right, Duckie. I didn't only come to tell you that, although I thought it might amuse you. I've come to warn you to stay away from him.'

'Why would I do that?'

'It's too dangerous for you to associate with him.'

'You're only saying this because he refused to help you to trade in degenerate paintings. That's what's really bothering you. Or are you jealous?'

'Of course I'm jealous, but it doesn't change the fact that he's too pally with the Germans. No self-respecting Frenchman will set foot in his church. It won't do you any good to get too close to him.'

She considered what might be the real reason Lance was here, why he'd been released from prison early and why he'd suddenly appeared, seemingly out of the blue. Was he answerable to the same people in London as her? And if he was, would he reveal it? And did he know she was part of the same network?

Was he warning her to stay away from Etienne because he'd been brought in to take over her assignment? After all, the three of them were connected by art in the same way; the links could just as easily be forged one way or the other. As a man, Lance was less likely to be suspected of being an enemy collaborator than she was. It was unfair, but it was true. There was no getting away from the fact that sex came into everything and in wartime, it was just another weapon.

'You forget I've been commissioned to paint Etienne's portrait. I can't abandon it. I need the money.'

He made a great show of brushing the cigarette ash from his hand onto the floor. 'Then don't say I didn't warn you, my old duck.'

She refused to rise to the annoyance. 'You need to leave now. You know what will happen if Simone catches you here.'

'Did you hear the news? Another enemy alien has been caught. This one was hiding in the cellar of a bookshop. It seems there are a whole collection of English literary ladies at large. Who'd have thought it?'

'I told you to leave.'

'Imagine, all those dotty English women, crawling out of cellars and chatting in gardens in the dead of night and giving themselves away. They don't realise how far their high-pitched voices carry.

Imagine what a catastrophe it would be if any of them came to the attention of the wrong people.'

It must have been Lance who'd spotted them that night in the garden. She suspected he'd been watching her and this only went to prove it. For the first time, Marguerite regretted the fact that Dorothy's knife had failed to find its target.

'I told you to leave.'

'There's a way to prevent anything awful happening, my old duck. I just need a favour, for old times' sake.'

'What is it you want?'

'If the priest won't supply me with degenerate art then you must.'

'Don't be ridiculous. How do you expect me to lay my hands on such work?'

He waved his arm around her studio. 'You have paints, brushes and canvases. I'm sure you can knock out a Miro without too much trouble. Even a Chagall or a Van Gogh wouldn't be beyond your talents.'

The door to the studio banged open as Simone stormed in, her face red and sweating from cycling from town in quick time. She threw a fierce look at Lance.

'I told you not to come here again. Don't you understand, even when I say it in plain English?'

Marguerite placed a hand on her arm to calm her down. 'He's just leaving.'

'Why are you making excuses for him?'

'I'm not.'

'You know the dangers of him being here. Hasn't he done enough damage to you already?'

Marguerite turned to Lance who was casually lighting another cigarette, his eyes examining the fresh canvases drying against the wall.

'Look at the upset you've caused.'

He waved his cigarette in the air, his words aimed at Simone, even though he didn't look at her. 'I came to warn Duckie against associating with Etienne Valade.'

Simone picked up an earthenware pot from a shelf and smashed it to the floor. 'Her name is Marguerite, not Duckie. And if I catch you here again, I'll shoot you.'

Lance stared at the pieces of broken pot at his feet. 'If you're going to slurry the conversation with honesty, she's not Marguerite either, is she? I suppose the French alias was your idea.'

Tears of anger were brimming in Simone's eyes. Marguerite knew she wouldn't want him to see them. 'Get out, Lance. Don't come back again.'

He held up his hands, feigning an innocence that fooled nobody. 'Don't let me keep you from your painting. You know what you have to do.'

This time, Marguerite didn't bother to see him off down the lane. Simone was too overwrought to be left. It seemed to be more than just Lance's presence that had upset her. Once he'd gone, Marguerite closed the studio door and locked it. She pulled a clean handkerchief from her pocket and thrust it into Simone's hand.

'What's happened?'

Simone's fingers curled around the smooth linen like a drowning child grasping for a lifeline.

'Armand has been arrested.' She almost choked on the words as she forced them out. 'I'd just reached the outskirts of town when I saw Yvette, the woman who works in his bar. She was on her way to tell me the news when our paths crossed. Four of them came this morning to search Armand's rooms. That German soldier who was killed in his bar. They found his pistol wrapped in an overcoat at the bottom of Armand's wardrobe.'

'That doesn't prove Armand had anything to do with the soldier's death. You know how he likes to collect weapons for the cause.'

'Biquet and the other nine boys they rounded up didn't have anything to do with that soldier's death either, but they executed them for it anyway and hung their bodies in the town square for the seagulls to peck at.'

After the boys had been murdered, the Germans had let the matter drop. They'd had their retribution and were waiting for the resentment to boil over in the community at the injustice of it, knowing sooner or later, someone would betray the true killer.

'What prompted them to search his rooms after all this time? They must have questioned Armand about the murder when it happened and been satisfied with his answers, otherwise they'd have arrested him then.'

Simone blew her nose, chafing the soft skin above her lip with the handkerchief. 'He was denounced by Gabrielle Damas whose mother owns the bakery. According to Yvette, he'd been sleeping with her, taking her back to his rooms night after night. She must have found the pistol or perhaps he showed it to her, primping his male pride.'

It hardly surprised Marguerite that Armand had been unfaithful to Simone but it wouldn't do any good to say it. 'I'm so sorry.'

'It seems everybody knew. It had been going on for months.' Simone shrugged, as if such a gesture would shed the pain and the humiliation. 'Now he knows how it feels to be betrayed.'

'Why would she denounce him like that? Doesn't she understand the consequences?'

'Probably not. Her head is as thick as the dough her mother sets to rise each day in the bakery.'

The betrayal wasn't just a sign of Gabrielle's moral character, but also of her desperation. People were starving and they were short of money. The financial inducements the German authorities offered for information were too tempting for many to ignore. It could mean the difference between eating and not eating, the difference between being able to afford medicine for a sick child or watching them suffer and die. Gabrielle had a baby and no prospect of a husband. The father was an Italian soldier who'd been forced to flee when the Germans marched in. He'd promised to marry her and had probably meant it, but circumstances were different now. Whether he loved her or not, however much he wanted to look after Gabrielle and the child, it was impossible for them to be together.

With Armand arrested, they had to think about the danger to themselves. It felt callous to mention it to Simone at such a time, but it couldn't be avoided.

'What shall we do about Dorothy? If Armand mentions her when he's questioned, they'll come looking for her.'

It wasn't only the threat Armand now posed, but also Lance. He'd dropped enough hints for Marguerite to suspect he knew they were hiding her. She couldn't let him blackmail her into forging paintings for him, but nor could she risk Dorothy being denounced.

Simone thrust the handkerchief into her pocket, the search for a solution focusing her mind. 'I don't know who to trust. I don't know anyone who might be willing to take her to the border. Armand was always careful never to tell me the names of anyone else in the network. It might be safer to leave her where she is. She wasn't discovered last time the house was searched. If it comes to it, we'll hope for the same again.'

It seemed wrong to be doing nothing at such a time, but it was the best way. To move Dorothy was to risk exposing her, and they worried she wouldn't have the strength to stand up to an arduous journey on foot to the border and beyond. She'd been hiding for so long, her resilience had weakened, along with her physical strength. Gone were the nights when she'd turn cartwheels along the garden path. Even the progress of her new novel had slowed. The tapping of her typewriter was heard less often and the last sheets of paper Simone had scavenged from school remained blank.

Lately, Marguerite had heard her talking to herself in the cellar. Not the usual muttering you'd expect from an author plotting her novel, but something more like conversation, as if she were recounting things that had happened in her life, her sentences peppered with laughter, pauses and interjections. It seemed such a private exchange that Marguerite had shied away from mentioning it.

And so for now, they agreed to do nothing about moving Dorothy. They'd wait to see what would happen to Armand, wait to see if the soldiers would come and search the house. Marguerite would wait for Etienne to get the combination to Schmidt's safe and all the while she waited, she'd try to anticipate Lance's next move.

The uncertainty couldn't last forever. It was only a matter of time before the Germans were driven out, but if they were crushed, what would happen to Etienne? So many people in the town thought he was an enemy collaborator. Would they turn against him like they turned against the other priest, shooting him in the cool light of day?

It would only take one angry man with a gun and a misplaced desire for revenge, someone prepared to kill him in cold blood because of the church he represented without knowing where his true loyalties lay. Marguerite was desperate to see France liberated through an Allied victory, but it would be no victory if Etienne's life was one of the sacrifices that were made for it.

Chapter 39

Pascal was emerging from the shepherd's hut when Marguerite arrived. It was already midday and the sun was high in the sky, the air scented with wild rosemary and thyme, lavender and myrtle as it baked in the heat. He yawned, running his fingers through his beard. She stepped back, hoping he wouldn't notice her face turn pale at the stench of his unwashed clothes, the smell of fried onions matting his hair.

'There's something I need to ask you. Lance Holmes, the Englishman. He keeps appearing in unexpected places. Is he working for the same people as us?'

'I'll find out.' He combed his hair with his fingers and tied it back with a shoelace. 'We need you to photograph the German plans showing where the mines have been seeded along the beaches and in the coastal waters.'

'Where will I find them?'

He shrugged, as if the question wasn't his to answer. 'Ask your German-loving priest and don't forget the other documents you've been asked for. Time is running out.'

He disappeared into his shepherd's hut, his head and shoulders stooped as he bent his way back into the darkness. It was no use waiting for him to come out again. He'd told her everything she needed to know. The rest was up to her.

If the Allies were planning to come in by sea, they'd need an entry point where they stood a chance of not being blown up, which meant knowing which beaches and stretches of coastal waters had been mined and which ones were safe to navigate. The sudden call for the information suggested the liberation was imminent. Now, it was more urgent than ever that she photographed the documents in Schmidt's safe incriminating him and his associates for their war crimes before he destroyed them.

The house was quiet when Marguerite returned later that afternoon. Simone should have returned from school hours ago, but the quiet humming she expected to hear as she went about her daily tasks was noticeably absent. She checked every room in the house, calling her name, the creeping dread growing stronger each time she failed to reply. Simone wasn't there.

They always told each other where they were going and what time they'd be home so the other wouldn't worry. This had become even more critical since Armand's arrest. More than twenty-four hours had passed since he'd been taken in for questioning. It was enough time for him to betray them. No one had been to search the house yet, but that didn't mean it wouldn't happen.

Marguerite knocked on the door to the cellar. 'It's me, Marguerite. Can I come down?'

'Is everything alright?'

Dorothy must have heard the fear in her voice. They hadn't told her that Armand had been arrested. There was no point worrying her when there was nothing she could do, but she must have guessed something was wrong.

'Did Simone say anything to you about where she was going after school? I'd expect her to be back by now.'

'She didn't mention anything. Should we be concerned, do you think?'

'She probably had to stay behind and forgot to tell me, that's all.'

Marguerite cycled to the school, stopping familiar faces along the way to ask if they'd seen her, but nobody had. The building had been locked up for the day when she arrived and the place was deserted. With the stepping up of German patrols, no one spent time away from their home more than they had to. These days, the town was like one large open prison.

She carried on to the headmaster's house, hoping he could explain where she was, desperate for him to say one word that would make everything alright.

He looked surprised to see her when he opened the door. At first, she thought she'd come to the wrong house. He'd aged ten years since Marguerite had seen him the previous summer, his slight figure slowly collapsing under the weight of his burdens. When she asked about Simone he shrugged, more sorry than annoyed.

'I thought you'd come to tell me where she was.'

She hadn't turned up for school that day, which meant she'd been missing since she left home that morning. Marguerite's heart beat faster as she thought of Jeanne and Biquet and Armand and the hundreds of others who'd disappeared. This was how every tragedy began, with a silent and unexpected absence.

She rushed back to the house on the slim chance that Simone had returned home and was safe. But of course she wasn't there and the place was just as Marguerite had left it. The emptiness wrapped itself around her, fear clawing at her throat. If they'd arrested Simone, what terrible things were they doing to her? And what else would follow?

Armand must have mentioned her name when he was questioned. If he'd also mentioned they were hiding Dorothy, it would only be a matter of time before they came for her, before they came for both of them.

She knew the brutality they used on prisoners to extract information, pushing them to the point when they'd be desperate to denounce someone just to make it stop. She couldn't blame

Armand. He didn't start the war, and whatever was happening to him now, he didn't deserve it and neither did Simone. All any of them had tried to do was fight for their freedom in their own small way. Their only weapons were their resilience and their determination. Now even this was being squeezed out of them as their circumstances grew more dangerous by the day.

It was time to tell Dorothy. Her life was in Marguerite's hands and she deserved a say in what happened next.

Dorothy reacted to the news with her usual English astonishment. 'What do you mean, she's missing? She can't be. She was perfectly fine when I last saw her.'

'She didn't turn up for school today. No one's seen her since she left the house this morning.'

'Then I was probably the last person she spoke to.'

Marguerite had left the house to visit Pascal before Simone was out of bed. She hadn't even said goodbye to her.

Dorothy stroked her muskrat coat, which had grown rancid in the damp cellar. 'We shouldn't get ahead of ourselves. It doesn't necessarily mean something terrible has happened. She might just have fancied a day off. We all like to play truant from time to time.'

'Armand has been arrested. It's too much to hope that Simone's disappearance isn't connected. They'll have questioned him by now.'

Dorothy appeared to shrink before Marguerite's eyes. 'I see. Then it's my fault. I've brought such trouble to your door.'

'It's not your fault, but if Simone has been arrested, there's every chance they'll come and search the house again. We have to decide what to do. You can carry on hiding here at the risk of being discovered, or I can try to find a way of getting you to the border, but I can't go with you. I have to stay here in case Simone comes back.'

'I won't leave you alone to face whatever's coming. Not now. You've been too good to me for that. Whatever we have to face, we'll face it together.'

236

Chapter 40

It was after dark, the blackout coating the hot summer evening like an ominous threat. Even the stars seemed to shy away from the sky, as if by showing themselves, they too would be guilty of a transgression. Having left Dorothy sleeping in the cellar, Marguerite had crept into the garden and was sitting on the bench beneath the apple tree where in happier times she'd liked to sketch. Now all she could do was look up at the blank sky, watching the dark smudges of the bats as they flipped and dashed against the night like cloaked acrobats.

There'd been no Allied bombing that night and even the German planes were quiet. Usually they patrolled the sky, checking for lights on the ground, shooting at anything that offended them, as if war were nothing but a fairground game, and life as cheap and easily dispensed with as a coconut knocked off its shy. Tonight, it seemed the fun had gone out of killing, even for the enemy gunners, as if a change in the direction of the wind had brought on a different mood.

And so instead of the steady throb of engines, it was the quiet rustle of trees that distracted Marguerite's mind from Simone's plight, the gentle shift of the nimble branches as they knocked against each other, bark to bark, and the insistent rasp of the cicadas, forever invisible in the grass in spite of the song and dance they made, as if life were a circus and there was something to laugh about.

After a while, she became aware of a different noise cutting through the familiar sounds: the unmistakable approach of tyres treading over the dirt and stones that made up the surface of the lane. It was the dead of night and someone was coming. And it was the worst time of all for someone to come.

She stayed exactly where she was on the bench, her back rigid with fear, her ears primed for every sound, her eyes almost blind in the dark. And there it was, just as she'd been dreading – the sound of the gate opening, the hinges squeaking in complaint at being disturbed, just as they'd come to rely on, then the sound of boots on the gravel, the crash and give of the sharp stones serving as a second alert. How many sets of boots? She tried to count them but she was in too much of a panic to focus, her mind smeared with fear that sent her blood rushing.

Whoever it was had reached the front door. She heard the brittle clang of the bell echoing around the garden, creeping around the stone corners of the house and sneaking in through the windows. She thought of Dorothy, hidden in the cellar like a hunted animal gone to earth and knew there was nothing she could do to save her.

Everything was silent now, while whoever was there waited. And they waited with more patience than she expected. A minute passed, perhaps two. Her mind was too confused to count time. She expected the shouting to have started by now, the sounds of fists banging on the door, the echoing thud of boots kicking the old, weathered wood like last time. But there was only silence, which was worse, because with silence comes anticipation, and with anticipation comes the greatest fear.

And still the silence went on. It was a trap. They were waiting for her to give herself away, and then they'd goad her, telling her what a fool she was, that she got everything she deserved for giving herself up. There's no more admission of guilt than that. It would be written all over her face: shame, resignation, fear. Who could tell the difference between any of these things? And when you're the conquering enemy, so used to being on the winning side and knowing you were about to lose, who would care?

'Marguerite?'

One set of footsteps. One voice that was familiar and measured. Etienne.

As soon as she realised who it was, she crept through the garden, taking each step tentatively until she was sure it was him. He must have recognised the sound and rhythm of her movement before he saw her, his voice a symphony of relief.

'Thank God you're safe.'

She was in his arms before she could take another breath, the strength of him wrapping around her. His touch was too much for her to do anything other than exist. To think, to speak would be to move into uncharted territory. To remain like this forever would be everything she wanted. She needed the world to stop now, because there was nothing else.

'Schmidt told me they'd arrested Simone. I came as soon as I could to let you know.'

She'd guessed Simone's fate, but with Etienne's confirmation it was indisputable.

'What did they arrest her for? Did he tell you?'

'She's been accused of buying a piece of fish on the black market.'

'That's ridiculous. She's too principled to do such a thing. She won't even touch the food you send this way.'

He sighed, defeated by the madness of it all. 'That's all I know.'

She sank onto the bench, trying to take in the news. 'Buying fish on the black market isn't such a serious offence. They'll let her go, won't they?'

'I can't make that promise. Everything is so uncertain. I'm sorry.'

It was such a small transgression and the accusation would have been unfounded. They'd let her go, they had to. It was

239

unthinkable that they wouldn't. Marguerite wouldn't give up on her. She'd fight for her to the death.

'There's something I have to ask you.'

'I've already tried to use what little influence I have to get her released, but Schmidt wouldn't listen. He's scared of showing any weakness. They're losing the war and he knows it.'

'I know you'd help her if you could. It's not that. I need information.'

Her voice was barely a whisper as she explained her quest for maps identifying where the mines had been laid on the beaches and in the coastal waters. She didn't have to say why they were needed. It was obvious what the Allies were planning. Liberating France of its occupying enemy was the only way to free Simone and it couldn't come soon enough.

'I'll see what I can do.'

'And the combination to Schmidt's safe. I still need that too.'

'It's written in a notebook which he keeps in his desk drawer. I have to find a way of getting to it without him finding out.'

'Don't do anything to make him suspicious.'

'It's a chance I'll have to take.'

This wasn't the reassurance she needed. She was desperate for any comfort he could give her, willing him to say he'd forgiven her for not telling him she was married. More than ever, she needed to hear the kind of things lovers say when there isn't a war on, but those conversations were impossible now and the words would never fall from Etienne's lips.

'We have to say goodbye now, Marguerite.'

It wasn't safe for him to stay too long. Even in this remote place, they couldn't be sure who might be watching and listening. If Gabrielle had betrayed Armand, even though they were lovers, there was no saying what neighbours would be prepared to do for the sake of a square meal or a few extra coins in their pocket.

'But I'll see you again soon.'

She wasn't ready to let go of him. The world was too lonely and dangerous a place. Now Simone had been arrested, he was all she had to hold on to. 'We can't end things like this when we mean so much to one another. Love is as precious as life, Etienne.'

'Seeing you here has been everything, but it can't happen again. I'm a priest. What we have between us is a sin. It has to stop.'

'I should have been honest with you from the beginning. I don't expect you to trust me, but you must believe my love for you isn't a lie.'

'I don't doubt your love, Marguerite, but look around you. Look at all the suffering. God is punishing us.'

'War is making us suffer, not God. You once told me that God is reflected in art. That's where your god lies, not in judgement. No god worth putting your faith in would punish you for loving me.'

'It's tearing me apart. I made my vows to God. I dedicated my life to serving Him. I can't do it with you in my heart.'

'Then choose between us. Choose me.'

'I'm sorry, Marguerite. I've already chosen.'

This couldn't be it. It couldn't end like this. 'Give me one more night, Etienne, one more morning of waking up with you.'

One more night that would lead to another and another after that until they had forever. But even as she said it, she knew it was impossible. Their love had been a dream, but dreams are fleeting and intangible, and in the morning there's nothing left but a sense of loss for what might have been. Now that dream was gone and there'd be no more mornings.

'Let me go, Marguerite, for my sake.'

'I'm not giving up on you, Etienne. This isn't the end. You will come back to me.'

'I can't, Marguerite.'

'Then wherever you go, I'll find you.'

If this was to be his lasting memory of her, she had to make it a good one, and so she gave him a kiss to carry with him and

241

forced herself to smile through every layer of grief that weighed her down, because there'd be time enough for tears after he'd gone.

She stayed on the bench long after he'd said goodbye, listening to the sound of his bicycle disappearing down the lane, the darkness gathering around the space where he'd sat beside her, still feeling the touch of him on her skin, the way he'd patted her hand and kissed her cheek, his gestures spent of their former passion. He was no longer her lover, but a devout priest, a brother.

It was a mistake to love during a war, because to love was to lose. To give your heart, is to risk everything, even life itself. And whatever happened now, Etienne would always be a priest and Marguerite would always be the woman it was impossible for him to love.

She wouldn't cry anymore. If she gave in to her emotion, it would be the end of her and she had to stay strong for Dorothy and Simone. Everything was changing so fast and nothing was getting better. It felt as if the war would go on like this forever even as it rushed towards its shattering conclusion.

Chapter 41

It was impossible to sleep. Marguerite lay awake, listening to the night-time sounds transform themselves into the refrain of a new day; the chorus of birds brought a sad lament where once there'd been a promise of hope, and the sun, rising by degrees, failed to shed its light on the shadows in her heart.

At first, she thought she'd imagined the sound of the tyres ripping up the stones and the dirt in the lane, the heavy chug of an engine grinding to a halt at the front gate. She climbed out of bed and peered through a gap in the curtain just in time to see a German soldier jump out of a truck, his door slamming against the early morning silence.

Simone must have broken under questioning and he'd come to search the house, catching them before they were fully awake. It wasn't her fault. They'd have done such terrible things to her.

She threw a cardigan on top of her nightdress and ran downstairs. If she was quick, she might make it to the cellar. If she was lucky, he wouldn't spot the hiding place. They'd got away with it before. She had to trust that this morning their luck wouldn't run out.

By the time she'd reached the kitchen, the soldier was hammering on the door.

'Marguerite. Open the door. It's me, Hans.'

It was the young officer who'd bought the painting of the mimosa in the blue jug. Marguerite froze, her toes clenching on the cold stone flags. It had to be a trap. They'd sent him because he knew her.

'Step outside, please.'

Perhaps he'd do her the kindness of shooting her on the spot. It was the least he could do after she'd let him have the painting.

'Please hurry. I can't stay any longer.'

The truck's engine was still running. She could hear Hans' heavy boots on the gravel backing away from the house.

'Marguerite, I beg you.'

There were tears in his voice. A young man's tears.

She opened the door a fraction and there he was, his uniform pristine and his stomach full of breakfast. At the sight of her, he fell to his knees.

'They made me do it. I'm sorry.'

There was a canvas sheet on the lawn, a body wrapped inside it. Marguerite ran outside and knelt before it, unfolding the fabric from the head, too afraid to breathe, too angry to care that she was about to be shot.

Simone's beautiful face looked up at her from inside the canvas. Her unblinking eyes would never reflect her smile again or narrow against the sun.

'You have to forgive me, Marguerite, because I'll never forgive myself.'

She cared nothing for Hans' guilt, for the trauma of this man-child who'd broken their lives in two, never to be mended. It was an insult that he should consider that she could.

Tears ran down his face, staining the uniform that had made him a killer, and it was all she could do not to run at him, to grab the bluntest knife and ram it into his heart. But vengeance would be got another way and on a grander scale.

She looked him in the eye and cursed the good Catholic boy

he claimed to be. 'Your god will never forgive you for this and neither will I.'

The dust thrown up by the tyres of the retreating truck had hardly settled when Dorothy appeared, alerted by the sound of Marguerite's cries. She found her lying across Simone's body, which was still perfect, but for the life that had been taken out of it.

They held each other tight as they cradled Simone, channelling their grief through one another like a Greek chorus, releasing it in great bursts into the morning air. It didn't matter if they were seen or heard. The worst had already happened. Nothing more terrible could be done to them.

A smear of blood marked Marguerite's face when she retracted herself from Simone's body. It was a single shot to the heart that had killed her. She was thankful for that at least.

'I wanted her back so desperately, but not like this. What do I do with her now, Dorothy? I don't know what to do with her.'

Dorothy kissed Simone's face, which was as beautiful as ever. 'This can't be true. I won't let it. Something must be done about it.' She scrambled to her feet, delirious with grief as she turned this way and that. 'We'll go and sort this out right now. There must be someone we can speak to. They can't be allowed to do this.'

But it was done, and it couldn't be taken back. Marguerite grabbed Dorothy to steady her, their bodies clinging to one another, cold and rigid with shock. The war had gone on too long and now it might as well never end.

Marguerite cycled into town, not looking left or right as she negotiated her way through the narrow streets to Monsieur Rayon, the undertaker who would know what to do, because she didn't, because her head was in a spin, her heart a dropped stone. There was no point going to Etienne for comfort because he was a priest and his god didn't exist, and how could she break that news to him when they'd already destroyed each other?

Monsieur Rayon gave her his last drop of Armagnac to stop

her shaking and held her while she cried, the sympathetic twitch of his eyelids no less genuine for having seen it all before.

'This is a great tragedy, Madame. Simone was loved by everyone in the town.'

Suspended in her grief, she sat in the dim light of his mahogany panelled waiting room, staring at the dust that had gathered between the fringes of his downtrodden rug while he made sure Simone was taken away by careful hands, her death registered at the mayor's office. For something so monumental, it was a small administrative formality that marked Simone's murder, signified only by one more sheet of paper. One more name added to the list of so many others on the unjust pile.

Afterwards, Marguerite buried herself in the cellar with Dorothy, a flayed animal, incapable of licking its wounds, unable to comprehend anything through the fractured prism of her grief. How was she supposed to accept that Simone was gone? How could she continue the fight without her loyalty and her love?

Seeing her like this caused Dorothy's rage to set in. The muskrat coat was sent flying across the cellar as she raved, cursing every war-hungry man on the planet.

'If only I had a magic wand. I'd wave it across the whole world and make everything alright. I'd fill every heart with love until there was no room for hate and there'd be no more war. I'd bring back everyone we've ever loved and we'd never lose them again.'

As a wish, it was a good one, but without the magic, it would never come true and so there had to be another way.

'Chin up, my love, and best foot forward. Hiding's no way to go on when there's a war to be won. It's time to make the bastards bleed for what they've done.'

Acting on Dorothy's advice, Marguerite dragged herself out of the cellar and forced herself to work, because putting food on the table was the only way to ensure they'd survive. And it was only by surviving that she could avenge Simone's death.

She started by tending the vegetables in the garden, the exercise helping her to batten down her rage before she returned to her studio to work on another abstract study of war and illicit love, burying her grief deep in the straight lines and rolling curves of the brushstrokes, manipulating the paint to bend to her despair, knowing Simone would have scolded her for exposing herself with such brutality, acknowledging that she'd also be proud of her for being brave enough to finally reveal her true self in her art.

Despite her determination to work, every other minute something would catch her attention, a bird hopping in a nearby hedge, the stuttering engine of a plane flying overhead, and she'd rush to the gate and look down the lane, searching for a sight of Simone making her way back to her, a smile pinned on her face, one hand raised in her usual wave. But it was never Simone because it never could be, and with this knowledge each day seemed longer and darker than the one that went before it.

She worked herself to exhaustion, but still she couldn't sleep while all around her, the echoing call of the wolves and the steady circling of raptors provoked unimaginable horrors. And in the aching solitude of the early hours, Marguerite drew thanks that at least the German soldiers hadn't come to search the house. Whatever Simone had told them before she was murdered, she hadn't mentioned Dorothy or the pistol, still hidden in the leather purse in the beehive at the bottom of the garden. And by not mentioning these things, she'd kept the secret of who Marguerite really was, and in doing this, she'd kept her purpose alive.

Chapter 42

It was the third day when they ran out of food. Marguerite had no choice but to cycle into town to queue for her bread ration. Along the way, she was conscious of the looks on people's faces as they turned from her; each one unable to cope with the grief that scarred her as deeply as stab wounds, terrified that it might be catching.

Locking her bicycle in the town square she spotted Nancy standing next to the fountain, laughing with two young German officers.

She pretended to busy herself with her bicycle while she kept an eye on her, trying to work out if she was passing the time of day so as not to annoy them, or whether there was more to it. After five minutes, it was obvious that Nancy wasn't talking to them under sufferance and had no intention of giving up their company.

At sixteen, Nancy might have thought of herself as a woman, but there was so much of the child still in her that Marguerite couldn't stand by and see her fall victim to their charm. She'd have smiled and blessed their innocent flirtation if it had been a local boy, but it wasn't, and this situation wasn't only saddening, it was dangerous.

Marguerite walked over to the fountain, pretending to suddenly notice her. Nancy at least had the good grace to blush when she realised she'd been caught.

'Nancy, I'm so glad to see you. Would you give your mother a message for me?'

Nancy nodded, squirming as the two German officers sniggered. 'Of course, what is it?'

'Walk around the square with me while I explain it to you.'

Nancy frowned, but was too well brought up to refuse. She followed the summons to the far side of the square where Marguerite positioned them out of sight of the soldiers, whose eyes seemed reluctant to leave Nancy's figure even for a second.

'What is it you want me to tell my mother?'

'Nothing. I wanted to warn you about being seen with German soldiers. People in the town won't look kindly on you for it.'

Nancy cast a look over her shoulder, her eyes briefly scanning the square for a sight of the young men. 'You're in no position to warn me against such things.'

'I'm more qualified than anybody. You don't want to suffer the contempt of the town the way I've had to.'

'I'm grown up now. I can do as I like.'

'If you're grown up, you'll understand the responsibility you owe to others. Not long ago, I saw you coming out of the hotel where many of the German officers are staying. I beg you not to put yourself in danger. If nothing else, think about your father's position. As mayor, he needs the support of the people of the town. It's not easy for him, having to manage relations with the Germans on everyone's behalf.'

It was the mention of her father that seemed to enrage her, but instead of shouting or waving her arms as she did as a child, Nancy's eyes burned with cold fury.

'You don't know anything about it. Please go away and leave me alone.'

After Nancy had returned to the soldiers, Marguerite left the square to join the queue for bread. Since she'd been seen with Pascal in the bar on the Chemin de la Cigale, Madame Damas had grudgingly agreed to serve her in the bakery again.

By now, she was too late for anything other than the stale scraps of what was left, but the disappointment of it barely crossed her mind. She could only think about Nancy's reaction and how little she understood about the danger she was putting herself in.

She'd just finished queuing at the market for a few ounces of barley and polenta when a young woman approached her. Marguerite had often seen her around the town, but didn't know her name. She looked about twenty-five, but was probably younger in the way that everyone looked older these days, her steady stride giving away her sense of purpose even though she kept her head down. Her light woollen coat was a shadow of its former smartness, her cotton gloves and brightly coloured rayon scarf indicators of her struggle to maintain her pre-war style. She fell in step with Marguerite as she crossed the main square.

'Are you the woman who paints?'

Marguerite gave her a distracted nod as she fumbled in her bag for the key to unlock her bicycle. Already the woman had begun to walk away, but not before Marguerite felt the tug of cold fingers on her hand as a folded sheet of paper was pushed into her fist. She took it without acknowledgement and slipped it into her pocket, not daring to look at it until she was back in her studio with the door locked.

Dear Madame,
Please come to my apartment at midday tomorrow. I would like you to make a pencil portrait of my dog because he is very dear to me.
A friend.

The address had been included on a separate slip of paper tucked inside the folds of the first.

Not knowing what to make of it, she showed it to Dorothy, who frowned at the small writing, her eyesight no longer being what it once was.

'It's a strange way to make an approach, but then we're living in strange times.'

'Do you think I can trust her?'

Dorothy puffed out her cheeks and blinked two or three times while she thought about it. 'There's only one way to find out.'

Commissions were so rare these days that Marguerite couldn't afford to turn down the work, and so she pushed her doubts to the back of her mind and prepared herself for the new task.

Chapter 43

The woman who'd passed her the note lived in a small apartment on the outskirts of the town. There was no one in the street when Marguerite arrived, or if there was, they went to a lot of trouble not to show themselves. Suspicion was rife everywhere. The sums of money offered by the Third Reich to anyone willing to denounce their neighbours were significant enough to be irresistible to the desperate and these days people rarely risked communicating with strangers. Most no longer even trusted close friends with their opinions. People had been divided as they'd been conquered and the atmosphere was thick not only with fear, but also with loneliness and uncertainty.

She must have been looking out for Marguerite to arrive, because she opened the front door before she'd even reached it and ushered her inside with a sharp gesture.

Seeing her properly now for the first time, Marguerite was shocked at how pale the woman appeared, even by the standards of today's suffering. Her skin was stretched across the sharp bones of her face, her eyes shadowed as if she were recovering from a long illness. Marguerite followed in silence as she led her through the apartment into the bedroom.

'You were recommended to me by Father Etienne. He said you were good at taking photographs.'

'Your note said something about a portrait of a dog.'

Marguerite scanned the room, expecting to see the little creature sleeping at the bottom of the bed or sprawled on the rug beside the unlit fire.

'There's no dog.'

Of course there wasn't a dog. Nobody could feed a dog these days. She should have realised this before she came. Marguerite remained silent, fearing she'd walked into a trap.

'You're probably wondering why I asked you here.'

Marguerite nodded, committing herself to nothing.

'Father Etienne was a great help to me recently when I was ill.'

It explained the lack of colour in her face and the way she moved, as if any part of her might break at the slightest knock.

'I wasn't ill exactly, but what happened has left its ill effects.' She challenged Marguerite with a cold look. 'This is no world to bring a child into, don't you agree?'

'It's not something I could imagine doing.'

'The war has changed everything. These foreign men we're now expected to obey. They occupy our town and think everything is theirs for the taking and so they take it, even when we say no.'

She paused, as if she were gathering the courage to continue. 'It wasn't an easy choice, but when it came to it, I couldn't bring myself to have the child. I couldn't spend the rest of my life knowing every time I looked at him or her, all I would see would be the face of my enemy attacker.'

Marguerite listened without judgement, a silent confidante to the stranger who needed to talk about her trauma.

'I went to one of those backstreet places. I knew it was a risk, not only to my body but also to my life. I'm sure I don't have to tell you that it's a capital offence these days to terminate a pregnancy. The woman assured me she'd relieved hundreds of women of the same problem. My predicament wasn't a unique one, you see. It's what comes of being a woman in enemy-occupied territory.

253

'She said there'd be bleeding afterwards. I was so scared, I didn't take in most of what she said, but I'd talked to other girls about it and knew what to expect. On my way home, I began to lose a lot more blood than I should have done. I knew I was going to collapse and there was nothing I could do to prevent it. I was leaning against a wall just three streets from here, waiting for the world to come back into focus when Father Etienne found me. I would probably have died on the spot if he hadn't carried me home and called a doctor.'

She sank onto the bed, drying her eyes on a crumpled handkerchief. 'I'm sorry; you didn't come here to listen to this and it's not the reason I invited you. The point I'm trying to make, is that if we want to live in a world where we have the right to choose the fathers of our children, a world that's safe to bring those children into, then this war has to end.'

Her eyes flicked to Marguerite's bag where she'd stowed her sketchbook and pencils, expecting to begin a preliminary drawing for the portrait.

'Have you brought your camera?'

Marguerite nodded, her fingers automatically drifting to the silver filigree locket she always wore around her neck. She didn't usually work from photographs, but if that was what she wanted, she'd do her best once she knew who the subject of the portrait was to be.

The woman dragged a leather satchel from under the bed and pulled out a pile of documents.

'Photograph whatever you need. Please be quick. I'm due back at work in twenty minutes and I have to return those papers to Gestapo headquarters before anyone notices they're missing. I'm only a secretary. I'm not supposed to remove anything from the building. I'm going to wash my face. You know the way out. We won't see each other again.'

Marguerite nodded, meeting the woman's eyes, grateful for the risk she'd taken. Her thanks would have been inadequate and it would have been wrong to forge any kind of connection between them given the circumstances.

Once the woman was gone, Marguerite set about photographing the documents. Among the memos and lists of orders were the plans showing where the mines had been seeded on the beaches and in the coastal waters.

She worked quickly, holding her breath to steady her hands as she photographed the maps, careful to catch each section so not a single landmark or reference was missed. Once she'd captured everything, she returned the papers to the satchel, checking each corner and pocket, hoping to find the combination for Schmidt's safe, but it was too much to expect to find that too. Conscious that she'd already taken too long, she left the apartment, the camera concealed in the silver filigree locket around her neck.

Once outside, she climbed onto her bicycle and pedalled at full speed. She didn't glance over her shoulder because it wouldn't do to look back. If she was to avenge Simone's death, she had to keep moving forward, because this was how they would win the war. Etienne had been as good as his word in getting her access to the maps showing the mines in the coastal waters. Now all she could do was hope he could get the combination for Schmidt's safe. The Allied invasion was getting closer and there wasn't much time left.

Chapter 44

To minimise the risk of being caught, Marguerite waited until nightfall to take the photographic film to Pascal. Having done the trip so often, she'd worked out an efficient route that avoided the main roads, and had become adept at negotiating the rough tracks and sharp inclines in the dark. Dressed in black, she was just another shifting shadow among the trees, undetectable but for the inevitable snap of twigs beneath her feet and the crunch of last year's fallen pine needles.

Pascal wasn't at the camp when she arrived. It was important to pass on the film in person. Knowing she might be in for a long wait, she walked another circuit of the hill, checking for signs of anyone who might be approaching. These days, she found it impossible to shake off the feeling that she was being watched.

She was on her second lap when she heard a voice calling from behind.

'No need to ask what brings you here, Duckie.'

She turned around, narrowing her eyes against the dark, focusing on Lance's familiar figure as he came towards her, the pinhead light of his cigarette a red glow in the black night.

'Put that cigarette out. You'll have the German gunners down on us.'

He dropped the cigarette to the ground, not bothering to extinguish it. 'You never were one for taking chances.'

'What are you doing here?'

She tried to keep the worry out of her voice. No one knew she was coming here, so he must have followed her unless he had a pre-arranged meeting with Pascal.

'I'm here to take whatever it is you've brought with you. It's my job now to pass things on to the folks in London. Your work has made a great impression on them. I wouldn't be surprised if you weren't awarded a medal at the end of it all.'

Whatever it was he'd come here to do, she hadn't been told about it. 'How did you know where to find me?'

'Don't be so suspicious. I'm still your husband. What do I have to do to make you trust me?'

'I know you too well to trust you.'

'There's a war on. You can't expect to know everything. It's not how these things work.'

This much was true. The rule was that you never had more than one contact, one link in the chain. It was the only way to protect everyone.

'Have you done those paintings for me yet? I'm rather in the mood for hanging a Van Gogh on my bedroom wall.'

'I won't forge any paintings for you, Lance. I wouldn't do it for you in the past and I won't do it for you now.'

'We'll discuss it later.' He held out his hand, a child begging for sweets. 'What have you got for me?'

Marguerite hesitated; the silence was finally broken by the steady tread of boots, the regular rhythm suggesting it was someone who knew the ground intimately.

Lance was still holding out his hand. 'Whatever it is, give it to me, quickly.'

It was Pascal approaching, his voice sharp in the night as he called out, his pistol pointing at Lance. 'London has no knowledge of Lance Holmes being here, Marguerite. He doesn't work for them.'

Lance let out a bark, seemingly untroubled by the fact that there was a gun pointing at him. 'You're not going to take the word of a Frenchman over mine, are you, Duckie?'

'I'd trust him with my life.'

'Which life is that, Duckie? Your old life or your new life?'

His comments were enough to enrage her. 'Who supplied you with the papers that enable you to roam so freely here, Lance, if it wasn't the British? Who supplies your cigarettes and the petrol for your motorcycle?'

'I told you before, my old duck. I have friends in high places.'

'You mean you're working for the Germans.'

He cast a wary glance at Pascal, who was as still as a monument, his pistol trained on Lance's temple.

'If the Frenchman lowers his gun, I'll explain how you came to be involved in all this in the first place.'

Violet had approached Marguerite out of the blue. She'd been living covertly for so many years. Even now, she had no idea how British Intelligence had found her. Whatever Lance told her, she'd assume it to be a lie or a half truth, but she wanted to hear it anyway. She buried her hands in her coat pockets and nodded to Pascal to lower his pistol.

'Go on, Lance. But remember; whatever you say, it'll only take a second for Pascal to raise his gun to your head and fire it.'

Lance laughed; even now he was full of bravado, full of absolute confidence that he could talk his way out of any situation.

'It was the summer of 1939, just before the war broke out. Nobody believed it would actually happen, not in France or Britain, and anyone who was anyone was spending the summer on the Riviera. Cannes was planning its first film festival and everyone was desperate to rub shoulders with the American film stars.

'You remember Diana? She was one of the London crowd I used to gad about with. Lovely girl. Rich as they come, but nobody held it against her. Her uncle had rented a villa in Nice and she'd offered to act as his hostess for the summer. Funny set-up, if you ask me, but there you go. Anyway, it was Diana who spotted you. You were sitting on the rocks overlooking a deserted beach on the outskirts of Cannes.'

Lance was always full of stories and this one seemed a little too neat. 'How do you know all this?'

'As soon as she got back to London she came to see me in Wormwood Scrubs. Obviously, I couldn't deny or confirm whether it was you she'd seen because I'd heard nothing from you since the day I was arrested. But I knew Simone had a house down here and you two were always as thick as thieves, so it didn't seem completely impossible that you were hiding here.

'Diana didn't bring it up again and I thought she'd forgotten about it. Nowadays, her father's something big in Churchill's government, so I can only assume she mentioned you to him. They'd have been desperate to find the right kind of agents to operate in this part of France and you'd have been the perfect candidate.'

He wiped the sweat off his brow, as if he'd been talking for his life. 'So there you are, my old duck. It was pure chance you were spotted.' He reached out his hand, encouraging her to step forward. 'Anyway, I've enjoyed our little chat, but I really must be moving on, so if you give me whatever it is you have, I'll make sure Diana's old dad gets it. Churchill will thank you himself one day. As I said, there's sure to be a medal in it for you. You can't ask for more than that, can you?'

Lance was never a man to be crossed and prison seemed to have made him more ruthless than ever. She dreaded asking the next question, but she had to know.

'Did you have anything to do with Simone's arrest and execution?'

'She had no right to order me out of your studio like that. You're still my wife, for God's sake.'

'She was the only friend I had in the world.'

'She was the one who betrayed my little forgery scam to the police all those years ago, Duckie. I was doing very nicely until then. Ten years of my life that cost me. Not to mention a considerable fortune. You didn't think I'd let her get away with it, did you?'

That he'd acted with such inhumanity against Simone, all because of a long-held grudge, appalled her. But this was the man he truly was.

'What did you say to have her arrested?'

'I was just an innocent bystander who happened to see her haggling over the price of a piece of fish in the street. She disposed of the evidence down the nearest drain when she realised I'd seen her, of course.'

'You mean there was no evidence.'

He shrugged off her comment.

'They wouldn't have shot her just for that. What else did you tell them about her?'

'Stop wasting time, Marguerite. Just give me whatever it is you have and I'll be on my way.'

He sidestepped Pascal and grabbed her wrist, forcing her bag from her shoulder, but Marguerite was quicker off the mark. She should have put a stop to him a long time ago. If she'd listened to Simone's advice, she'd still be alive.

Before Pascal could take a fresh aim, Marguerite pulled her pistol from her pocket and shot him through the heart.

'It wasn't Simone who betrayed you all those years ago, Lance, it was me.'

For a second, it was as if the bullet hadn't touched him. He stared at her, his face as vital as it had always been, but for the look of shock that replaced his usual attitude of complacency. But it didn't last. He didn't even have time to reach for his chest to stem the blood before he stumbled, first forward and then back, his knees collapsing under him, bringing him down like Jack too long out of his box.

Marguerite stared at him on the ground, not quite dead and cursing. 'I'm sorry, Lance, but it was the only way to stop you.'

She braced herself to take a second shot, putting a bullet neatly through his brain. 'That one was for Simone.'

Pascal turned his head from side to side in disbelief. 'Was he really your husband?'

Marguerite nodded, unable to summon any words.

'You have terrible taste in men.'

She stood over Lance, watching a dark red patch spread across his chest, the blood from the head wound creating a halo around him in the dirt, making him appear like no angel anyone had ever seen. But he was still now and silent, and would inflict no fresh acts of harm. He couldn't blackmail her into forging artworks and he wouldn't expose Dorothy. After years of hiding, she was finally free of him.

Pascal disappeared into the shepherd's hut, reappearing a moment later with two spades. He thrust one at Marguerite.

'We have to bury him, but not here.'

They dragged Lance's body to the other side of the hill where the woodland was dense and untravelled, the ground uneven enough for no one to notice a fresh grave even if they stumbled over it. As Pascal set about finding the right spot, pacing out the area they needed to dig, she guessed it wasn't the first body he'd buried there.

He looked up at her after he'd made the first strike in the soil. 'Are you alright?'

She nodded. 'Yes, just a bit cold.'

'It's the shock. It always gets you like that the first time. Start digging. It won't help, but the work will take your mind off it.'

They dug the makeshift grave and rolled his body into it. She was too tired even to bid Lance farewell. She just wanted the job finished. She threw the soil over his head, watching his face disappear with every spade she tipped and felt only relief at seeing him gone.

He'd never loved her. That much she now understood, having experienced with Etienne what love truly meant. As a young woman she'd been flattered by his attention, by his determination to put her at the centre of his life. It hadn't taken her long to realise that it wasn't her he'd wanted, but her talent as an artist.

261

They'd only been married a few months when he asked her to start copying the work of established painters for him to pass off as originals. When she refused, he insisted he'd meant it as a joke, that he'd been testing her integrity and she'd wanted to believe him. It was only later, after he'd proven to have a remarkable ability to track down previously unknown works by Turner and Constable, which he sold for extravagant sums, that she became suspicious.

One day she found a receipt for artist materials in his jacket pocket. The receipt gave the address of the studio where the order was to be delivered. When Marguerite tracked it down, it led her to Hector Travis, a notorious art forger whom the police had been trying to capture for decades.

Even after all these years, having mulled it over in his prison cell, Lance hadn't worked out that she'd been the one to send the anonymous note alerting the police to the forgeries and to the whereabouts of Hector Travis.

She'd left the country as soon as they were both arrested, not wanting to face the wrath of any associates they might have, changing her name in the hope that Lance wouldn't find her when he came looking for her, as she knew one day he inevitably would.

By the time they'd finished burying him, Marguerite was too exhausted to think of anything, even the fact that Lance was dead and that she'd been the one to kill him. Her hands stung, the blisters on her palms raw and bleeding where the handle of the spade had dug in every time she'd thrust it into the soil. But he was gone and he would never come back, and now she had to learn to live with the knowledge of it.

Pascal offered her a slug of brandy from his hipflask. She knocked it back, feeling the alcohol scorch the back of her throat, her eyes stinging as it brought water to her eyes. It hadn't crossed her mind that she should cry for Lance and these were the only tears she'd shed for him.

Day had already begun to break as they sat on the rotting remains of a fallen tree near Lance's grave, the first rays of the sun making perfect circles at their feet as they poked through the canopy of leaves above them, a gentle breeze offering a hushed applause at their night's work. She wondered if she should memorise the exact location of Lance's last resting place, whether in years to come, she'd feel inclined to come back. There was nobody else who'd want to mark his passing. His shining star had begun its descent the day he first commissioned Hector Travis to forge a painting. Now, he'd been nothing but a seedy ex-convict, hustling for every penny he could lay his hands on.

It was turning into a beautiful morning, the sun growing brighter and bolder as the earth turned, reminding her that life was moving on and that to remain still would be too dangerous.

Pascal lit one of Lance's cigarettes which he'd had the foresight to remove from his pocket before rolling him into his grave. He took a satisfied drag, reeling at the power of the tobacco he was no longer used to.

'Why would your English husband be on the side of the enemy?'

'Lance was only ever on his own side.'

He took another drag on the cigarette, savouring it for a while before he spoke. 'If Lance was an enemy agent, the Germans won't like it when they realise he's missing. Even if they can't prove he's dead, they'll assume he is and act accordingly.' He flicked the ash onto the ground, smearing it with the toe of his boot. 'Does anyone know about your connection to him?'

'Only Father Etienne Valade.'

'Then you'd better hope you can trust him.'

The cigarette burned to a stub. Pascal took a final draw before extinguishing it between his finger and this thumb and stowing it in his pocket. 'You should stay away from here for a while. You told me Schmidt is watching you. Don't do anything to arouse any more of his suspicion.'

She handed him the film from the camera and nodded, knowing he was right, but without Pascal, she was even more alone. Suddenly things were more dangerous. Now was the time for the true reckoning. All she could do was hold tight to the love she felt for Etienne, in spite of his rejection of her, and hope he'd remain loyal. As a lover, she'd broken his faith, but she had to trust he'd remain steadfast and find a way to get her the combination to Schmidt's safe.

Chapter 45

It wasn't until Marguerite got home that she realised she was covered in blood. It must have splattered from Lance's heart as she shot him at point blank range. She'd been too preoccupied to notice at the time and had cycled back with the tell-tale signs of murder all down her front.

She unbuttoned the dress and stepped out of it, throwing it into the kitchen sink and steeping it in cold water. However much she scrubbed, there'd always be a clutch of brown stains to remind her of what had happened. And the memories, the sensations of it would stay with her forever. She watched, trembling in her camisole and knickers as the water slowly turned to rust and the blood began to lift, sickened by her ability to kill.

Dorothy must have heard her come back, because a few minutes later, Marguerite heard the coded knock on the floor that was a sign she wanted to talk. She ran upstairs and threw on a clean dress before slipping into the cupboard under the stairs and joining her in the cellar.

Dorothy was horrified when she saw the state of Marguerite's hands. 'I won't ask what you've been up to.'

'I've been digging over the soil in the garden ready for the late summer planting.'

'Of course you have. It's the sort of thing everyone does in the dead of night.'

There was no point telling Dorothy who'd denounced Simone, or how she'd made him pay for it. It would be too much for her to dwell on during the lonely hours she spent in the cellar and in any case, Marguerite wasn't in the mood to talk about it.

The shock that she was capable of murdering a man in cold blood took a while to sink in. She lowered her eyes every time she passed the mirror in the hallway, unwilling to acknowledge the face of the killer that would stare back at her. It wasn't what she'd done that appalled her, but her lack of repentance. After all, she'd been driven to it out of desperation, out of a need to avenge Simone's murder and to protect Dorothy, as well as for herself and for France.

It was the following day when Marguerite found a note pushed under the door.

Dear Madame,
Please come to the presbytery as soon as you can. It is urgent.

There was no signature and she didn't recognise the handwriting. She set off straight away, cycling through the town at double speed, arriving at the presbytery forty-five minutes later, taking the time to catch her breath while Madame Mercier went through the ritual of negotiating the three locks. This time, the housekeeper didn't leave her standing on the doorstep, but invited her inside.

'Thank God you've come. Father Etienne asked me to contact you if anything happened to him. He said I could trust you.'

'Where is he?'

'He's gone.'

Hearing these words, Marguerite's world collapsed a little further. Now there was nothing but ruins. 'What happened?'

'Schmidt returned to his office while Etienne was there. Etienne admitted to helping himself to his brandy, but thinks Schmidt might have guessed he was searching his desk.'

'Have they arrested him?'

'I don't know. They followed him here after he left Schmidt's office. He fled as soon as he realised they were at the door. As he ran, he asked me to let you know he has the code.'

It had to be the combination to Schmidt's safe. He'd done as she'd asked and was now facing the ultimate price for it. 'Was he able to pass it on to you?'

'There was no time. The Gestapo were beating at the door, demanding I open it before they broke it down. He had to run for his life.'

She had to find him; she had to make sure he was safe and get the combination from him. 'Do you know where he might be?'

'If he got away, he could be anywhere. The Gestapo have been suspicious of him for a long time and were waiting for an excuse to arrest him. They didn't understand why he was living in a villa on the coast rather than here at the presbytery. They wouldn't believe he was simply looking after it for a friend. It wouldn't have taken much for them to guess why the access it gave him to the sea might be useful. I told him not to take so many risks, but he wouldn't listen.'

Marguerite thought of all the things Etienne had done to help her: the documents he'd photographed from Schmidt's briefcase, the access to information he'd enabled from the young woman who worked as a secretary for the Gestapo, the food he'd redirected to those most in need of it. If he'd been arrested, he could be shot for any one of those things.

Madame Mercier wrung her hands. 'I have to find somewhere to hide Catherine in case the Gestapo come back. Even if they don't, another priest will be sent to replace Father Etienne. I can't risk her being discovered. Not every priest is an anti-Fascist.'

'Catherine? The young girl I saw in the church?'

'Father Etienne said if anything happened to him, I was to ask

267

you to make up her documents. Now she's sixteen she needs an identity card and a ration book. I can't apply for them through the authorities because I have to keep her Jewish identity hidden. I've bleached her hair, so she passes as French if she happens to be seen, but it's not enough to keep her safe.'

'She's not Etienne's daughter?'

'Her parents were Etienne's dearest friends. When Paris fell and the round-ups began, he helped them to settle in Nice. That was before the Germans took over the Occupation from the Italians, when it was still safe for them to live there. Catherine has always had a special place in his heart. You must forgive me for denying her existence when you were kind enough to bring her a pink ribbon but nobody could know she was hiding here. It was the only way to protect her.'

So the woman in the photograph was Catherine's mother, and Etienne's dearest friend. Not his lover as Marguerite had assumed. He must have been hiding the photograph because Catherine and her mother are Jewish and in hiding themselves.

Etienne had told Madame Mercier to trust her, so there was no reason for her to lie. 'I'll take Catherine. She'll be safer with me than here at the presbytery.'

'Bless you.' She took Marguerite's hand and kissed it. 'Etienne planned to get her out much sooner, but with the Germans increasing their patrols of the coastal waters it was too much of a risk to keep running the feluccas to Gibraltar.'

'Feluccas?'

'It was how he saved the children. He helped dozens to escape, perhaps fifty or a hundred before it became too dangerous.'

All this time he'd been hiding in plain sight, befriending Schmidt so he wouldn't guess what he was up to. No wonder he'd been reluctant to help her find information when she first asked him. If he'd been discovered, it would have jeopardised his own covert work.

'How did he know to tell you to come to me for forged papers?'

'That night he rescued you in the park from the German patrol. He was there to collect the papers from you. I was too sick to go and so he stepped in.'

Suddenly it was all beginning to make sense. 'You were my regular contact, the one I passed so many identity cards on to?'

'I was always careful not to show you my face. My only worry was that you might recognise my figure when you saw me in the church with Catherine the day you came to look at the frescoes.'

It had never crossed Marguerite's mind that Etienne's stern housekeeper could have been part of the resistance network.

'That night in the park. Why didn't he ask me for the papers after the soldiers had gone?'

'You were too known to each other by then. He didn't want to compromise you by being able to identify him if you were ever questioned. He didn't guess you were the forger and not just the courier until he saw your work at the exhibition.'

Etienne had been protecting her from the first moment they'd met, even though she hadn't realised it. Wherever he was, she had to find him and get the combination to Schmidt's safe from him. They'd gone too far to fail now.

'I'll come back for Catherine as soon as I've made her an identity card. We can't risk her being stopped and searched without one.'

'There's something you should know about her first. Catherine's parents went into hiding as soon as the Germans marched into Nice, but someone must have denounced them and they were taken during that terrible night last September when so many were rounded up.

'Catherine hid in a cupboard in their apartment and wasn't discovered, but she witnessed her parents being dragged away at gunpoint. Etienne found her when he visited three days later. She was still hiding in the cupboard, too terrified to come out, delirious with dehydration and starving.

'Etienne brought her here to keep her safe, but the poor child hasn't said a word since. It's as if the shock and the grief have taken away her ability to speak, or she's chosen to close herself off from a world which she considers too brutal to engage with.'

How had the world come to this, where the people who should be cherished were treated with brutality? 'I'll do everything I can for her. You're not alone anymore, Madame. I'm here to help.'

Chapter 46

It was almost dusk by the time Marguerite returned to the presbytery to collect Catherine. She'd worked so quickly, the ink was only just dry on the identity card when she slipped it into an envelope and taped it to the small of her back, where she hoped it would be missed if she was stopped and searched.

When Marguerite arrived, Catherine was sitting on the edge of the bed ready to leave. She was dressed quietly in low-heeled shoes and a mackintosh, so as not to draw attention to herself and would be travelling only in the clothes she stood up in to avoid any suspicion that she was on the move.

'This is Marguerite, the woman I told you about.' Madame Mercier gripped Catherine's hand, reluctant to let her go. 'She'll be looking after you until things are safer.'

Catherine's curls were brittle on the ends from so much bleaching, her eyes blank with what could only have been fear or resignation to whatever fate she was expecting.

Once Marguerite had added Catherine's fingerprint to the identity card and given it time to dry, the young girl climbed on the back of Marguerite's bicycle, and they set off, wheeling through the back streets of the town where they were less likely to be stopped by a German patrol. The Allied bombers had visited early that evening and the streets were quiet, most people having fled to their cellars or to the bomb shelters as soon as the enemy planes had begun rumbling overhead.

There were no longer any air-raid warnings. Now the Allies had stepped up their attacks, the Germans preferred to abandon the civilians to their fate, which left Marguerite and Catherine unprepared, when for the second time that evening, the sky became shadowed with the burden of another wave of Lancaster bombers, the guttural sound of their engines, and the whisper and pound of the bombs dropping in the distance making the journey more terrifying than it already was.

Marguerite kept her head down and pedalled for dear life as she turned onto the final stretch of road where she'd encountered Violet, who might have been shot for all she knew. The nature of her undercover work meant Marguerite would never know her real name and she could never properly mourn her for the person she truly was.

The sound of a motorcycle approaching in the distance wrenched Marguerite from her thoughts. This time it wouldn't be Lance, which meant only one thing. She whispered over her shoulder to Catherine, urging her to stay calm as the German soldier circled them on his motorcycle before ordering them to pull over.

Marguerite's heart beat with a steady thud as he climbed from his motorcycle and approached them. He looked as if he should still be at school, his ill-fitting uniform hanging off his shoulders proving he still had to grow into it. He was the worst kind of recent recruit, his youth and inexperience putting him out of his depth and making him reckless and volatile.

'Papers.'

He barked the instruction in a barely broken voice, the adolescent pimples on his cheeks firing red and angry. Marguerite set her face to mask her fear and held out her identity card, encouraging Catherine to do the same, praying that the fading light would disguise any hints that her forger's hand had been at work.

He stared at the papers, straining to find fault. The ink on Catherine's identity card would be dry by now, but would it still smell fresh? Could any smears that might have resulted from her hurried work be put down to the hands of a clumsy official?

Marguerite watched as he pushed his nose further into Catherine's card. If the ink still had a scent, he'd surely notice it.

'When was this card issued?' He looked up, his eyes burning into Catherine's face.

Marguerite jumped in. 'Four weeks ago, on her sixteenth birthday. It says so on the card.'

There was nothing he could challenge. The photograph was a recent one, and the fingerprint hadn't smudged. Her physical description was correct. What else could he find to pick on?

'Why are you out at this time of night?'

Once again, he fired the question at Catherine who stared at him, her jaw slack with her attempts to answer until Marguerite came to her rescue.

'We haven't broken the curfew.'

He must have sensed something wasn't right, because his eyes remained on Catherine, probing every dip and contour of her young body beneath her mackintosh.

'Didn't you hear the English bombers flying over? Don't you know they're trying to kill you?' His hand drifted to the pistol in his belt. 'Do you want to die?'

Marguerite gripped the handlebars of the bicycle, her right foot poised on the pedal, ready to push off.

'We had no warning of them. We're just on our way home now.'

He leaned in closer to Catherine's face, revelling in her fear, his fingers stroking his pistol. 'Why doesn't she answer? Doesn't she understand what I'm saying?'

Catherine's breath was coming quicker. She was beginning to panic, her fingers digging deeper into Marguerite's waist as she held on for dear life. Marguerite had to think quickly.

'No. She's deaf.'

The soldier stepped back as if he'd been told she had a contagious disease, his desire for her falling from his eyes quicker than a stone dropped into the abyss.

'Then what are you doing here? Go home now.'

Marguerite didn't need telling twice. She pushed down hard on the bicycle pedal and they were off, Marguerite negotiating Catherine's extra weight as best she could, pushing her speed until she turned onto the lane that led to the house, breathless and exhausted, but almost home. All the while, she tried to stay calm, despite the constant rumble of the planes overhead, not wanting the young girl to sense her fear. If Catherine was going to trust her, she had to believe Marguerite was capable of protecting her.

Once inside, Marguerite locked the door behind them and led Catherine down to the cellar. It wasn't safe above ground while the Allied bombers were so close and while someone might see her.

Dorothy stood up to greet her as soon as she entered. 'Welcome, my dear. I'm delighted to have you. Do you know how to play gin rummy? Never mind. I'll teach you.'

While Marguerite made up her bed, Dorothy explained the rules of the card game, not the slightest put off by Catherine's failure to respond.

'I can see we're going to be great friends. I love nothing more than to talk, and you appear to be a great listener.'

As the bombs rained overhead, Marguerite sheltered in the cellar with Dorothy and Catherine. Here in this sanctuary, she could stay captured in the moment and pretend time wasn't moving on. As soon as the raid was over, she would have to venture into a world where Etienne's disappearance would become a reality and where his fate would eventually be decided – where she might have to face the prospect of a life without him.

Catherine was safe for now, but where was Etienne? And how was Armand standing up to interrogation since being arrested? Had he denounced Etienne to make the torture stop? And if he had, who would he be prepared to denounce next?

While there were no answers to these questions, none of them were safe. Every second that passed only seemed to increase the danger they were in. At any minute, Armand could be forced to reveal Dorothy's hiding place in the cellar and Marguerite's activity as a forger. Liberation was coming, but she couldn't rely on the Allies rescuing them in time to save Etienne. While there was a chance he was still alive, she had to find him and hope he was able to give her the combination to Schmidt's safe before the papers inside it were destroyed.

Chapter 47

The Allied invasion began in the sultry heat of the night, the screech and rush of the missiles coming in great strings overhead like beads on a rosary and creating an early dawn of flames. Bombs were not only dropping from above, but missiles were coming in from the sea as the Allied warships in the coastal waters shelled the gun emplacements and the blockhouses along the beaches with abandon, the vapour and dust blinding everyone to the destruction.

But it wasn't only the Allies who were to blame for the mess. The enemy refused to give in, as hour after hour, Messerschmitts dive-bombed the ships at anchor and Junkers 88s bombed the beaches, tracer bullets streaking through the sky in response.

From her bedroom window, Marguerite watched the fires raging in the hills where the Allies had overshot their targets. She could see the olive groves and the vineyards burning; hear the crackle and the spit of dried scrubland as the flames spread, the air stinging with the bitter smell of scorched pine and eucalyptus, lavender and thyme, of paradise laid to ruin.

Hours later, still unable to sleep, she sat at the kitchen table waiting for it all to stop. With only the surrounding fires for light, she'd left the window shutters partly open, the angles creating tilting shadows across the floor, the smell of the burning hills acrid at the back of her throat. The air was still and sultry, the rasping chorus of cicadas inaudible beneath the rumble of war.

Closer to home, nothing stirred; not even a leaf on the tallest tree dared to blow for fear of drawing attention to itself. And so the squeal of the front gate was even more alarming when it came, the crunch of the gravel giving away otherwise silent feet.

Marguerite held her breath, her heart banging in her chest. Only those sanctioned to do harm were allowed to move about at this time of night and only the most reckless would venture out during a battle. If only she hadn't left the shutters open, she could have made the house appear uninhabited, as many were in this isolated place.

What kind of invader was approaching: enemy or ally? Whichever one it was, it was too late to hide.

She stayed exactly where she was, her fingers curled around the pistol stowed in the pocket of her dress, the cold steel of its barrel pressed against her thigh. Like the poor hunted rabbits in the hedgerows, she hoped that if she didn't move, they wouldn't spot her. She blinked slowly, willing them to go away, counting down from ten for no reason other than to give her mind something to focus on while she waited.

Whoever was out there must have reached the house by now, but still they hadn't made themselves known. She'd expected a knock on the door, a fist shrouded in a leather glove; rifle butts hammering like before, heavy boots kicking against the wood. She expected the shouting of orders, the snatch of a pistol being pulled from its holster, revenge for killing Lance, but there was nothing, only the steady thud of her heart and the distant roar of the burning hills.

Eventually, a voice made itself known, the words flinty against the edges of the darkness, a fingernail tapping on the kitchen window.

'Marguerite. Are you there? It's me, Pascal.'

A wave of relief passed through her. 'Thank God.' She opened the door and let him in, relieved to see a familiar face. 'What's happening? Have the Germans been driven out?'

'A few have fled north, but most are digging in; some have buried themselves in the foxholes and the trenches in the town and in the surrounding villages. The local resistance fighters are retaliating with snipers and ambushes.'

He emptied the large canvas bag he'd been carrying, placing packages of cheese and meat, fruit and vegetables on the kitchen table, bottles of wine, eggs and chocolate.

'I stole some of the German supplies on my way here. Help yourself.' He pushed a loaf into Marguerite's hands.

Marguerite tore off a corner of the bread and slid it into her mouth before handing the rest of it to Pascal, who ripped it apart with his grubby hands.

'Will the fighting go on much longer?'

'Word has it that the French soldiers who landed in Saint-Tropez alongside the Americans have torn down the swastikas from the public buildings and replaced them with the *tricolore*. There are barrage balloons in the harbour and on some of the beaches, sending the message to the Luftwaffe that the land has been reclaimed by the Allied warships. The American soldiers are kissing every Frenchwoman they can get their hands on and marauding as if they own the place. But the street fighting continues along the coast and in the villages inland. Each patch of land is being hard won with hand-to-hand combat. It could go on for weeks.'

And so the heavy stamp of one nation's army boots was steadily being replaced by another. The towns that were slowly being liberated were still occupied, with control shifting from the Germans to the Americans. If Etienne was still alive, would the situation be better or worse for him? Was it safer for him to be captured by the enemy or condemned as a collaborator by his own side, which was surely what would happen once the French were back in charge? The label of German-loving priest wouldn't be an easy one to shake off and it was only a matter of time until the reprisals began.

'Will the Gestapo release the people they arrested?'

'Rumour has it they've shot the prisoners they suspected of betraying them, even their own officers. There was one in particular, a great sweating pig of a man called Leo Klarsfeld who negotiated a deal with the local Resistance. The grand hotels had been planted with bombs with remote detonators. They were all to be blown up at the same moment, just as the Allies landed on the beaches. Klarsfeld agreed not to detonate them if his soldiers were given safe passage to leave the area.'

'What happened?'

'The hotels and the soldiers were saved. Klarsfeld was shot by one of his superiors for disobeying orders.'

Pascal took another mouthful of bread, hardly taking the time to chew it before he forced it down. 'Klarsfeld was the one who gave the order for the execution of those ten boys in retaliation for the German soldier who was shot in a local bar, so don't feel sorry that he was made to suffer for the consequences of his one selfless act.'

Finally, some form of justice had been served for the murder of Biquet and nine little friends. It wouldn't give them their lives back, but at least it was something.

He swallowed a hard lump of crust. 'Armand has been executed. They shot him yesterday morning at dawn.'

The news wasn't unexpected, but still it came as a blow. What had he told his captors under torture, and had it put everyone in more danger? She should have been sorry for him, but she was more concerned for the safety of those still living. Armand had always been reckless. He'd never made a secret of the fact that he and Simone were lovers and yet it hadn't stopped him betraying her with another woman. In spite of Marguerite's disapproval, she knew death was too high a price to pay for his infidelity.

'Did they have any proof he'd killed that German soldier in his bar?'

'They didn't need proof. What do you take them for?'

'Where have they buried him?'

Pascal shrugged as if it hardly mattered. 'Probably in a ditch where no one will find him.'

She hoped he'd been laid beside Jeanne, so they wouldn't be alone as well as lost. She thought of Lance, buried in a shallow grave in the hills. At least if it came to it, she knew where he was. The spot was marked, even if only on her own heart.

She helped herself to more bread while he poured them each a slug of brandy from his hipflask, his mood darkening as he concentrated on his task. He cleared his throat, paving the way for yet more bad news.

'Yves Musel has also been killed. Three German soldiers stormed into his office and shot him in cold blood two days ago. They didn't even give him a chance to answer for himself.'

Marguerite gulped the brandy to stave off the shock. 'They shot the mayor? But he'd built such good relations with them.'

'He worked for the same people as you. Who do you think covered up the evidence of your false identity? How do you think you were recruited to the cause in the first place?'

So Lance had lied to her. She hadn't been recruited after being spotted by his friend Diana before the war. It was all down to Yves Musel.

She thought back to that day when he'd called her into his office to question her about her papers. It had felt like an interrogation. He must have been testing her, seeing how she reacted under pressure. Ever since, she'd seen him as a threat. She hadn't had the slightest suspicion he'd been covering up her false identity, helping her to survive by paying well above the usual rate for the drawing lessons she gave to Alyce.

'Poor Celeste. Poor Alyce and Nancy. How will they survive?'

'They'll be taken care of. Nancy intends to continue as part of the network.'

'Are you saying that Nancy . . . ?'

'She was her father's eyes and ears. No one suspected her of being anything but a silly love-struck girl, flirting with the German officers for attention. It wasn't chocolate and sauerkraut she was after, but information.'

Marguerite remembered the conversation she'd had with Nancy in the town square, warning her off mixing with the soldiers. Even she'd been taken in by her.

'Poor Musel. What a brave man he was.'

Pascal poured them each another brandy. 'He could have hidden in the shadows like many of us, but he chose to keep a public face. He thought if he was seen to cultivate the German officers as friends, they wouldn't guess whose side he was on.'

'Who betrayed him?'

Pascal shrugged. 'He might have betrayed himself without realising it.'

By befriending the Germans, Musel's game had been similar to Etienne's and there was no saying he hadn't suffered the same fate.

'Is there any word of Father Etienne Valade? They were after him. Do you know if they've shot him?'

Pascal must have heard the desperation in Marguerite's voice. 'Forget about him. You should leave this house and not come back. It's not safe for you to stay here. Go to another town. They could come searching for you at any time.'

'I've evaded the Gestapo so far. I can wait it out a bit longer.'

'It's not only the Germans you need to worry about, but those closer to home. Your actions haven't exactly made you popular with the people in the town.'

'But when the Resistance know what I've done, surely . . . '

'They won't invite you to prove your allegiance to the cause, Marguerite. They'll simply shoot you. You'll be safer anywhere other than here.'

'I can't leave. Not until I've found Etienne. He risked his life to get the code to Schmidt's safe so I can access the papers that will incriminate him for his war crimes. I still need that code. I can't give up the search now.'

'Your loyalty puts you in danger. You should think of yourself.'

'I still have a duty to France. And I'm nothing without the man I love.'

Without warning, he reached across the table and kissed her with a passion she'd hardly have expected from him. 'Forget the priest. If I survive the war, I'll marry you myself.'

It might just have been the gesture she needed. Flustered and appalled by his actions, it was the first time in months that Marguerite had laughed.

He looked up at her, his eyes bright in the dim light. 'I don't know why you think that's so funny.'

'I'm flattered by your offer, but if I'm to complete my mission, I have to find Father Etienne Valade.'

'Are you sure he's still alive?'

There was something about the way he phrased the question that stopped Marguerite's heart. 'Do you know something?'

'There are rumours of a priest being shot. I don't know any more than that.'

It didn't mean it was Etienne. There was more than one priest in the town. He couldn't be the only one in the Catholic Church prepared to stand up for the fight. And even if it was him, just because he was shot, it didn't mean he was dead. If he was still alive, she'd track him down. She'd scour the town and not give up until she'd found him.

Chapter 48

The killings of Armand and Yves Musel following so rapidly on one another's heels showed how quickly things could change. Musel had been the biggest shock. How could Marguerite have misjudged him when the evidence of his allegiance was there all along? How could she have taken him for granted and what could she have done to save him? Good men, righteous men were dying every day and there was no end to it.

If Etienne was in prison, would he be released now the Allied invasion was underway? Would he get the code to her, or would the Resistance kill him first?

Before going in search of him, Marguerite slipped down to the cellar, taking the food that Pascal had brought.

Dorothy was sitting up in bed, her hollowed-out eyes betraying her lack of sleep. She put her finger to her lips as Marguerite entered, drawing her attention to Catherine who was curled up in the bed they'd made up for her, sleeping the sleep of the innocent.

'It's begun,' Marguerite whispered, trying to keep the fear out of her voice. 'It's the beginning of the end. You'll soon be free to return to Edith.'

Dorothy was quiet, her upright body sagging when Marguerite

mentioned Edith's name. 'There's no looking back for me. Once this is over, I'll return to England.'

'After everything that's happened, surely it's worth trying to win her back?'

'Some of us are destined to carry the loss of a lover with us always. Not many people would understand how I feel, but you do, Marguerite. The despair hangs over our hearts like a shadow that darkens everything we do, dampening every joy, every thought and action. The grief we endure cuts very deep and it never goes away, however much time passes.'

'I'm sorry, Dorothy.'

'Today would have been our anniversary. If she hadn't left me, Edith and I would have been together for twenty-five years. It's a long time to share your life with someone, although the time flew by. Missing her isn't an easy thing to shake off. There are moments when I long for her so much I lose all sense and reason. The need to be with her is very great.'

'Then why not give yourself another chance of being reunited with her?'

'I've thought about Edith so much lately and come to realise that although she's gone, she hasn't really left me. And there's no point going to where she is, because she isn't there.'

The words were making no sense. 'Has she gone back to England?'

'No, my love.' Dorothy formed a fist and placed it against her heart. 'She's in here.'

'You've accepted that she chose to leave you?'

'She never meant to leave me. Edith died in the summer of 1938. It was her heart, you see. Her beautiful great big heart finally gave out. I sprinkled her ashes on the hillside where we'd lived happily in our little villa for so many years. Knowing she'd always be there was the reason I chose to stay when the British were told to leave at the outbreak of the war. I couldn't find it in my heart to abandon her.'

'I had no idea.'

'Of course you didn't. You have your own sad story. You don't need to know mine as well.' She sighed, casting her eyes around the cellar. 'Sitting here for so many days and weeks, I've come to realise I'm not alone. Edith hasn't been left to forever roam that hillside where I scattered her ashes, because she's here with me and she always will be.'

'She's the person I've heard you talking to before Catherine arrived?'

'You might think I'm a sentimental fool, but talking to her, laughing over our old jokes has brought me no end of comfort.'

'You're not a fool. You're the wisest woman I know.'

'I wouldn't go as far as to say that, but I know that when I eventually leave, I won't be leaving Edith behind. I'll be taking her with me.'

She took Marguerite's hand and gave it a squeeze. 'Wherever Etienne is and whatever he is, you must find him and you must fight for him. Don't give up. Love is a rare and precious thing and you must hold on to it and never let it go.'

Chapter 49

Daybreak when it finally came hardly seemed real, obscured as it was by the black smoke; the earth, thrown up to the sky by the shelling, added to the murk and the disorientation of the new morning. It was impossible to know who was coming and who was going, who the destroyers were and who had been destroyed.

In the distance and through the haze, men dropped from the sky, the white mushrooming arcs of their parachutes swaying in the wind. At another time and in another direction, there appeared strips of silver foil, flashing and blinding as they hit the odd glint of sun sneaking through the smoke in unexpected fits and bursts to confuse the enemy radar. It was all happening at once and then not at all. One moment there was something and then there was nothing. It was happening to the north or perhaps it was nearer to Genoa. It was impossible to tell and it was too disorientating to analyse.

Marguerite cycled through the town while the rest of the population slept off the bombing raids, conscious that there was no timetable to the street fighting which could erupt at any moment. Even at this quiet time, there was a bubble of expectation in the air; a sense of fear and jubilation mixed with the smell of cordite and burning buildings.

Even before their arrival, the Allies had put their dirty boot stamp on the paradise that once was. Marguerite took it all in: the holes blown in the sea wall that created another disaster waiting to happen, the scrawls of barbed wire scuttling across the sand like deadly insects, torn limb from limb, the once elegant palm trees ripped apart by gunfire, jagged and weeping at the edges.

The block houses which had been built as a line of defence by the Germans had already been demolished by the carpet bombing. Treated to the same punishment, the gun emplacements were derelict and the anti-tank walls were crumbling into the sand.

Despite the perfection of the sunshine and the blue sky, the atmosphere was heavy with the pinch of desolation, with the stench of regret and humiliation that would continue to cast a long shadow over what was once a playground for the rich. How would they ever move on from this? How could they ever become a community again when the need for revenge was still so ripe?

There was an eerie silence as she approached the town, taking the narrow streets for cover and cycling close to the buildings, every breath containing the seep of methane from the erupting sewers. Everywhere she looked there were dilapidated buildings and bombed streets, the art deco villas perched on the hillsides, chipped and cracked like broken teeth.

The sky was free of birds and even the rush of waves had dropped to a whisper as if the Mediterranean were holding its breath, waiting to see what would happen next. Whole streets were unrecognisable thanks to the Allied bombing. Monsieur Boucher's art gallery was a ruin, as was Simone's school; the mayor's office and the once fashionable hotels were sandbagged up to the hilt. This wasn't home anymore, this was a battlefield.

People were sheltering in the bombed-out remains of their homes because there was nowhere else to go, their expressions betraying relief and trauma, disbelief and the worry of what might come next. Every street revealed the prone figure of a woman, stick thin and hunched over a broom, sweeping up the rubble and the dead rats, battling to brush into a corner the memory of the horrors that would haunt her forever.

Old habits hadn't left them. Everyone still looked over their shoulder. Fear was the one emotion they all had in common, the warm breeze carrying the ashes of what was lost and the memory of what could never be taken back.

Marguerite kept going, her eyes scanning left and right for signs of sudden movement. Maquisards were hiding in the shadows and around corners; she could sense them, even if she couldn't see them. The eyes of the snipers were on her, their bodies silent as they perched on the roofs and the parapets, as still as hawks stalking prey. She didn't have to look up to know they were there and she could only hope they wouldn't shoot.

Any one of them could have been Pascal who had disappeared last night as swiftly as he'd arrived. If it hadn't been for the food and the heavy weight of the bad news he'd delivered, she'd have wondered if he'd been there at all. She could only trust he knew how to keep himself safe, trust in a world where to trust was to risk everything.

Now, finding Etienne was all that mattered. Searching the desolated town, she spotted him a hundred times, standing on the rocks above a broad sweep of beach or at the water's edge, looking out to sea, the waves encroaching on his boots as if the mermaids were tempting him in. But it was never him. The men were never tall enough or they were too old or too young. They never held themselves in quite the same way as Etienne; their faces could never match his expression.

She heard his voice carried on the wind, but every time she turned to look, her eyes narrowing against the brightness of the perfect sky, he wasn't there. The sound had been nothing but the catch of a wave on a jagged rock, the echoing cry of a gull as it passed overhead, or the fronds of a surviving palm, whipping each other in the relentless breeze.

Each time her senses deceived her, the despair peeled away another strip of her thinning soul. If Etienne wasn't here, then where was he? And if he was here, how long could he be expected to survive with landmines primed on the beaches and in the streets, with the Resistance determined to kill him and the enemy out to capture him? There was no satisfaction to be had in not seeing him, no comfort to be drawn from the possibility that if he wasn't here then he must be somewhere else just as dangerous.

The sun was already turning up its heat by the time she reached the hotel where the Gestapo interrogated their prisoners. If Etienne had been arrested, there was a chance he might be there. She glanced up at the high floors, allowing herself a moment to remember Jeanne, who'd shown such courage in throwing herself from a tenth-floor window to avoid betraying anyone under torture. Or perhaps it was grief that had compelled her to do it. Who could blame her after the murder of her unborn child?

A young German guard, a man taller than any she'd ever seen, dropped his hand to his pistol as she pulled up her bicycle in front of the main door, a door that until the Occupation had led into the Baroque-styled foyer of one of the grand hotels. Now instead of roses and amber, the building had nothing but the smell of death about it.

'I'm looking for a priest. His name is Father Etienne Valade. Is he here?'

The soldier looked bewildered as he stared at her; the unaccustomed summer heat slowing his reactions.

'It's important that I find him quickly.'

He unlocked his eyes from her face and looked her up and down. 'You shouldn't be out on the streets. It's not safe. The Americans are on their way and they're determined to kill everyone, especially the women.'

'Could you find out about the priest? You must have a list of prisoners. Shall I write down his name so you don't forget it?'

He folded his arms across his chest and spread his legs, his broad form occupying more space than she thought possible.

'If you want company we could go upstairs.'

There was a double meaning to his suggestion. To a man like this, sex and death were inseparable, interchangeable. She fought to keep her voice steady. 'I need to find the priest. It's very important.'

His eyes slid down her body once more. 'If you need to make a confession, you can tell me.'

'How can I find out if he was arrested? I don't have much time. I've heard you keep accurate records of all your prisoners.'

'What's your name?'

'My name is Marguerite. The man I'm looking for is Father Etienne Valade. Have you heard of him?'

'How is it that you French women have such pretty names? Is it to help you seduce every man you meet?'

She fantasised about charging at him, knocking him off his feet, beating his chest with her fists until he couldn't breathe, but he was the size of a beast and would easily overpower her, and any direct action would only get her arrested; she'd never find Etienne if they locked her up. It was best to save her rage for someone who really deserved it.

'I need to find the priest. Can you help me?'

'I'm only a guard. I'm here to guard until the Americans come and then I will fight. We will kill every one of them. They will not take this land from us.'

He'd been brainwashed or drugged. It was the only explanation for the inhuman look on his face. This was how Hitler kept his rank-and-file soldiers obedient. 'Is there anyone else here who can help me?'

'There are only guards here. We can't let anyone in or out.'

It was hard not to scream with frustration. 'Thank you.'

She straightened her bicycle and pedalled away, ignoring the soldier who kept on firing questions at her retreating figure, wanting to know where she lived and when she was free. But Marguerite would never be free, not until the enemy had been driven out, and Etienne was safely back with her.

Chapter 50

Time was ticking by. If she couldn't determine whether Etienne was being held prisoner then she had to keep looking elsewhere. She headed to the Villa Christelle, wishing she'd gone there first instead of wasting time with the German guard. The morning was passing and the streets were getting busier as the market stalls and the shops did their best to keep people fed with whatever they had. The sun was already high in the sky, its heat burning the back of her neck as she crouched over the handlebars of her bicycle, pushing on ever faster.

Determined to stay out of sight, she slipped off the main road and made her way along a narrow dirt track, continuing through the brittle scrubland of myrtle and broom, the lizards scurrying in fits and starts as her wheels threw up the dust.

The Villa Christelle appeared deserted as she approached, leading her bicycle down the steep path that led to the terrace. Even though it belonged to Gerald Mayhew, she would always associate the villa with Etienne. He'd looked after it with such care, keeping it safe until its true owner could return. No one would ever have guessed he'd been using it as an escape route for so many vulnerable children.

'Etienne?'

Her voice echoed as she called his name, the sound drowning in the waves as it was swept out to sea. On every other occasion, her stomach had fluttered as she'd made her way there. Just the thought of seeing Etienne had made her heart fly and the time they'd spent together had been the happiest of her life. Now, as she stood on the terrace taking it all in, she felt an overwhelming sense that something had been lost that could never be regained.

Every window was broken, the smooth white walls cracked and splintered where the Allied warships had fired indiscriminately along the coastline, targeting any building that stood out against the rocks.

She thought of Gerald Mayhew, who was probably entertaining the troops somewhere abroad, doing his bit for the war effort. One day he'd come back and be made to face the heartbreak of the destruction.

Inside, the marble floors were pockmarked with bullet holes, the walls and the doors looking as if they'd been used for target practice. This wasn't damage caused by guns at sea. The place had been ransacked, probably by the German soldiers who knew their days in this stolen paradise were numbered. The white leather sofas were soiled with muddy boot prints, red wine streaked across the cushions as if a whole bottle had been slung with determination. There were cigarette burns in the leather and on the rugs. The floral watercolours on the walls had been shot, the glass from the frames lying in splinters on the floor. The beds had been stripped, the sheets and pillows left in piles and stinking of urine, the curtains shredded as if someone had taken a knife to them.

'Etienne, are you here?'

Marguerite walked from room to room, searching against hope for her lover, sickened by the devastation, hearing the jeers in the back of her mind, imagining the drinking songs that would have been sung as the soldiers did this. She felt the lingering smoke of German cigarettes catch at the back of her throat, the familiar smell stinging her nostrils. It was all so much worse because the destruction had been deliberate, as if they'd sensed the illicit love that had grown within the walls and been determined to desecrate it. It wasn't a love that should have been allowed, and so they'd chased Etienne away and destroyed the place that held her memories of him. And now he'd gone, every other feeling had gone too.

She crept through to the study, remembering the day Etienne had given her the film containing the images of the documents in Schmidt's briefcase showing the troop movements across the region, and how in handing them over, he'd fought his passion for her.

Now, the smooth polished surface of the desk was scratched where someone had taken a knife to it, the leather chair where he'd sat for so many hours attending to church business, slashed. She cried as she stared at the empty space on the wall where his precious painting by Josef Motz had once hung, wondering whether the soldier who'd looted it had understood its true meaning.

The books on the shelves had been tumbled to the floor and beneath the dusty, uneven piles lay the case containing Gerald Mayhew's Oscar, the glass smashed, the gold statue discarded as if it were a piece of bric-a-brac, a misjudgement that might just have saved it.

She picked it up from the rubble and brushed the dust from it. The gold surface was grubby from being manhandled and badly scratched, but it was still in one piece. Whoever had picked it up hadn't paid enough attention to it to realise it was the real thing.

However much she searched, she couldn't find any clues to where Etienne might be. Perhaps he'd guessed that one day he'd be arrested and cleared everything out. She imagined him going from room to room, removing every trace of the life they'd shared, the rumpled sheets that smelled of their lovemaking, and the tray laid for a late breakfast, the preliminary sketches she'd done for his portrait that never became more than a concept, because they couldn't be alone for any length of time without touching. Or perhaps Madame Mercier, loyal and loving as any mother, had visited when no one was looking and removed all traces of him.

But for her memories, it was as if Etienne had never been there. As if the love they'd shared had never existed. Without his presence, there was no point in staying. The place was empty and she didn't belong there. She never had. She was just as much an intruder as the soldiers who'd left their muddy footprints behind, as unwelcome to Gerald Mayhew as the men who'd slashed the furniture and spilled the wine.

There was nothing here for her now beyond sentimentality. She allowed herself one more minute to stand on the terrace and look out to sea, to walk the rooms once more and say goodbye, to thank the place for taking such good care of them, for being somewhere they hadn't had to hide their love.

Finally, she walked away, resisting the urge to look back. In spite of everything, the villa had survived and there'd be a future for it. A little love and care was all it needed. One day, she might be ready to share the love story that was attached to the place, but not yet, because first she had to know how it ended and to do that, she had to find Etienne.

Chapter 51

Perspiration ran down Marguerite's face as she cycled back into the town. This time she took the main road, swerving the bomb craters and the fallen trees, unflinching in the heat as the sun burned her head and the back of her neck. There was no shade to be had anywhere. Much of the scrubland had been reduced to scorched earth where the fires started by the naval guns had burned themselves out, leaving nothing but ashes. Paradise had fallen and been laid to ruin, not only by the enemy, but also by the Allies. Tonight there would be more explosives, more fires. How much more had to be destroyed before nature was allowed to heal? How much more damage would they have to suffer in the name of rescue?

It was the burst of a single gunshot that brought her back to the present danger as she entered the town, turning onto the grand boulevard lined with elegant cafés and grand hotels. She looked left and right. The street was empty and silent now, but for the echo of the gunshot still ringing in her ears. She steadied her breath and listened to the particular form of silence: hollow and full of trepidation. The street was deserted for a reason. Whatever was going to happen next was out of her control. She pushed down hard on her pedals and cycled onwards, determined to get out of the centre of danger as quickly as possible, until the shock of another gunshot cracked the silence wide open, the bullet just missing her shoulder and almost sending her flying from the saddle.

The human hunt was on and she was the moving target. She steered towards the edge of the pavement, pushing herself up against the sandbagged buildings and kept going, head down, her shoulders hunched for no reason other than that was where the fear was lodged – tightly held between head and heart.

Never had any street been so long, so treacherous, but still she kept pedalling, her heart flinching at the sound of a German voice cursing from somewhere behind a shuttered window as a hand grenade flew over her head. It made no sense to keep riding in the direction of where it was about to land, but fear had conditioned her legs to keep going, no matter what, even if they carried her into danger.

But the grenade was only a prelude to greater things, as its blast detonated the explosives planted under a manhole cover by the German army in preparation for their retreat. Suddenly she was drowning in black smoke, the sky full of rubble and shattered pipe, sewage and water. Dead rats were flying into the air and raining down, their dense bodies hitting the ground until it wasn't only rubble and dust landing at her feet, but blood and fur, teeth and claws. With the floodgates open, hundreds of surviving rats poured out of the holes in the sewers, scurrying in all directions, their panicked screeching scraping the insides of her ears.

Everything depended on getting out of the street, away from the vermin before they ate her alive, away from the German soldiers before they shot her to pieces. There could have been one or a hundred men, watching and waiting with guns and hand grenades, fingers poised over detonators. She leaned into the bicycle and pedalled for her life. On and on she went until without warning her wheels stopped turning, as if someone had pulled on the brakes.

Her body lunged over the handlebars at the force of the sudden stop and she began falling headlong into the road until a strong pair of arms grabbed her around the waist and wrenched her from the saddle, dragging her from the bicycle and across the street. She kicked and screamed, jabbing her elbows into the thin flesh of whoever had overpowered her, but their grip tightened with every step as they lugged her into one of the hotels and dropped her onto a sofa in the foyer. Desperate to escape, she scrambled to her feet, but he'd already locked the door behind them.

'You have to stay off the streets. Don't you know there's a siege?'

It was a maquisard, his face smeared with years of dirt from living in the hills, his eyes wild with the instinct to fight.

'I'm looking for Father Etienne Valade. I was on my way to his church until you abducted me.'

'You have to wait. The Americans are on their way. We're trying to clear the streets for them.'

He was dressed in combat trousers and carried a British gun; his determination to win came off him in waves. This was the moment he'd been trained for, the moment he'd been anticipating for years.

'I need to find the priest. Please unlock the door so I can collect my bicycle before someone steals it and then I can be on my way.'

'If you leave, the Germans will shoot you. I risked my life to save you. I can't let you out.'

She was shaken to the core, but she wouldn't let him see it. The rats dropping on her head, jumping onto the wheels of her bicycle and running up her legs, had been worse than any explosion, worse than the threat of any sniper.

'I'm grateful to you for saving me, but I must go now. My bicycle . . .'

'No.'

'You don't understand. I'm an agent working for British Intelligence. I have a job to do. I order you to let me go. I need to get the code for a safe. There are documents I need to procure.'

'Show me your badge.'

'I'm undercover. I don't have a badge. It would give the game away.'

'Then why should I believe you?'

Marguerite scanned the hotel foyer. There had to be a way to escape, but the building had been built during the Belle Époque and was like a fortress.

He must have guessed her intention because he took her arm and led her into the lounge, the firmness of his grip giving her no choice in the matter. 'Wait here. You'll thank me when all this is over. You'll probably even want to kiss me.'

This was unlikely, when all she wanted to do was punch him, but there was no point saying it as he'd probably have taken it as encouragement.

In the lounge, the plush velvet sofas, Abusson rugs and silk drapes were a reminder of the glamorous world that had been so rudely interrupted, the film of dust on the chandeliers and the piano indicating its fall from grace. Despite the display of stoic grandeur, the room was unoccupied, but for one tiny figure sitting in a leather wing-backed chair in the corner facing away from the window. Marguerite recognised her as Madame Danielou, the owner of the hotel commandeered by the German high command. Her face cracked into a faint smile when she saw Marguerite.

'There you are, my dear. I don't suppose you've brought me any fruit?'

'I'm afraid not. Have you seen Father Etienne recently?'

Madame Danielou leaned back in the chair, her legs swinging because they were too short to reach the floor. 'Not since I moved to this hotel. Mine was bombed, you know?'

'I'm so sorry.'

'Don't be. Thirty German officers were killed. Lucky for me, the bomb landed while I was attending Mass. It was the first time I'd left my bed in years. It must have been God's will that I was saved.'

'Who said Mass? Was it Father Etienne?'

'I didn't go to Father Etienne's church. It's full of Germans, you know.'

'When did you last see him?'

The old lady's eyes drifted to a console table where a redundant cake stand had been granted a second life as an ornament. 'What I wouldn't give for a piece of fruit.'

Marguerite sympathised, her eyes scanning the room, looking for a way out. She couldn't waste any more time.

'Do you know how I can get out?'

'The streets aren't safe. You're better off waiting for the Americans to come.'

'I know, but I really have to go.'

Madame Danielou's tiny fingers drummed the arm of the chair. 'The kitchen is in the basement, through there and down the back stairs.' She nodded to a side door, hidden behind a decorative screen of green watered silk. 'There's an exit next to the cold store. Give it a hard shove. It's never locked. The people who work in the kitchen use it to slip outside for a cigarette from time to time.'

'Are you sure?'

'Of course I'm sure. Marcel, one of the porters, showed it to me the other day when I went in search of grapes.'

'Thank you.'

Marguerite planted a kiss on the old lady's powdered cheek before creeping out of the side door and down the back stairs to the basement. Following the directions, she was through the kitchen and had slipped out the exit within minutes. Despite a number of wrong turns, none of the kitchen staff stopped her to ask what she was doing. In a world driven by fear, people had learned to look the other way from anything out of the ordinary and for once, Marguerite was grateful for the freedom the trepidation of others granted.

The street outside the hotel was quiet now and still, the escaping rats having retreated to the shadows, but for the hungry few who remained to feast on their dead companions. For every dead rat there seemed to be three live ones devouring it. Beneath the shifting carpet of vermin, the debris from the explosion covered the street, not only rubble and earth, but raw sewage, the stench of the seeping gasses even more appalling than the sight of it, the meat flies creating a deafening hum as they hovered in great clouds above the ground.

Marguerite's bicycle lay on its side beyond the kerb, the right pedal pointing into the air as if to flag her down. She pressed her body against the hotel wall, out of sight of the maquisards who were watching the street from the roof. To retrieve the bicycle, she'd have to tread through the feasting rats and the sewage. She'd have to risk a German sniper spotting her, risk being manhandled to safety by a freedom fighter intent on saving her.

She scoured the ground nearby until she spotted a sheet of corrugated metal which must have blown off the roof of a small outbuilding in the blast and shrugged it across her shoulders, using it to shield her as she dashed into the road, taking great strides to avoid the rats, her mouth closed to stop her swallowing the flies batting her face. All the while, she kept her eyes fixed on the bicycle and bit down hard on her resolve.

It was only a few steps to the bicycle; five, and then four, and then three. Then it was only a matter of a quick bend of the knees to grab the handlebars, without looking down at the sets of gleaming rodent eyes peering up at her. She moved swiftly, not giving the rats time to bite, driving them back with the flick of a foot, holding her breath so as not to taste the stench, and throwing off the metal shield as she clambered onto the bicycle and pedalled for her life.

If the maquisards saw her from the hotel then they must have decided she wasn't worth risking their lives for a second time and any Germans must have already fled. She didn't look up to find out or down at the ground as the bicycle wheels bumped over the bodies of the rats, her eyes steady on the path in front of her as she swerved to avoid the rubble. It was twenty seconds or perhaps thirty until she turned off the road into the nearest alley and away from the worst of the devastation, the rats and the meat flies thinning out with each wheel turn, the stench fading with every patch of fresh ground she covered, with each breath of air that filled her lungs.

Even when she was clear of the worst of it, she kept going, not allowing herself to dwell on the horror or on how close she'd come to death, conscious that eyes might still be watching, gun sights trained on her retreating figure, waiting for a fleeting hesitation.

Calmer now, she wound her way through the narrow passages that ran behind the hotels and apartment blocks, slipping around the perimeters of gardens and children's playgrounds as she continued through the town to Etienne's church. Still there wasn't a soul to be seen beyond the makeshift camps of those bombed out of their homes, the small family groups huddled in shadows, retreating from the world with an expectation of worse to come. It was slow progress but the safest route, assuming most attention was on the wide boulevards and grand buildings. Victory was so close now she could almost taste it. And nothing was going to get in her way of her finding Etienne and the code he'd risked his life to obtain for her.

Chapter 52

It was almost afternoon by the time Marguerite reached the presbytery. She'd been on the move since before daybreak. Her stomach rolled with hunger, her hands shook and her head ached with dehydration, but there was no time to stop.

Whoever came to the door after she'd knocked went through the endless ritual of undoing the three locks, testing Marguerite's patience to breaking point.

'Madame Mercier, is that you? It's me, Marguerite.' She needed to know if she'd heard from Etienne since they'd last spoken, if he'd left any clues as to where she could find him.

The door finally opened. 'Can I help you?'

The priest who stood in front her was a stranger. He was younger than Etienne and shorter, his expression one of forced kindness as he tried to hide his irritation at having been disturbed, of being made to face the street when there was danger out there.

'I'm looking for Father Etienne Valade. Is he here?'

The false expression fell from his face at the mention of Etienne. 'There's no one here of that name.'

If he wasn't here, she didn't know where else to look. She had to find him before the Germans began their retreat, before Schmidt destroyed the incriminating papers in his safe. Already, she could hear the distant rumble of the American tanks as they approached the town; the groan of their planes scouting overhead.

'Do you know where he is? I have to find him.'

His eyes scanned the street, his weight pushed back on his heels as he leaned into the shadows of the presbytery. This wasn't a man who was prepared to put himself in danger.

'He's not welcome here. I have to rebuild this congregation from nothing, thanks to him.'

He started to close the door. Marguerite wedged her foot against it. 'Can I speak to Madame Mercier?'

'She's gone back to her family in Lyon. Don't ask me where. She left before I arrived.'

He pressed the door against her foot with increasing force until she removed it. 'Would the Monsignor know where he is? How do I contact him?'

Already he'd closed the door on her, his muffled voice travelling down the hallway, apologising to someone inside for the disturbance before he moved out of her hearing. As a priest there was no war for him to fight. Whether the battle for freedom was lost or won, it would make no difference to him.

What now? Where else could she try? She'd been everywhere she could think of and there was no sign of Etienne and no evidence to suggest he'd been to any of the places she'd expect him to be if he was still alive. It was as if he didn't want to be found, or else he no longer existed. Exhausted, she stumbled into the church, craving the cool embrace of the ancient walls. If anywhere could help her to think more clearly then it would be here, where every stone held the memory of Etienne's presence.

The place was deserted. She sat on one of the pews at the back, just as she had on her previous visit and breathed in the silence, the reek of dust and incense. Nothing had changed and yet everything was different without Etienne. The love had gone from the place, just as it has slipped from her life and all that was left was emptiness.

Where else? Where else should she look for him other than in her heart? He had to be somewhere she hadn't thought of. He still had to be alive because the alternative was unthinkable.

There was no point in lingering when there was still time to search for him. As she stood up to leave, she remembered the frescoes in the crypt, how safe she'd felt in the deep vault of the church with Etienne where no one could touch them.

It was the perfect hiding place. How had it taken her so long to realise it? Where else would he wait for her to hand over the code but in his own church, secure in a place that few other people knew about?

Her legs shook as she made her way through the secret passages and down the stone steps, made uneven by centuries of wear. The door to the entrance was open. Whoever had last brought him food must have forgotten to lock it. In spite of the slip, he'd still be safe here. The place was like a labyrinth. Anyone searching the church was unlikely to make it this far.

She pushed open the heavy wooden door and descended yet another set of ancient steps, her eyes slowly growing accustomed to the dark. The air, left so long undisturbed, had settled against the stone walls and was cold to the touch as it came up to meet her.

'Etienne?' Her voice sounded flat among the ancient stones. 'It's me, Marguerite. Are you here?'

And there it was, the sound of a boot shifting across a stone flag. The breath caught in Marguerite's throat. 'Etienne. It's alright. You can come out.'

More footsteps followed as a tall figure appeared from the deepest shadows, the face indistinct in the darkness.

'Etienne, is that you?'

He was reticent at first, and then bolder as he raised his arm and pointed a gun at her. Not Etienne, but a German soldier.

Marguerite's heart plummeted as she raised her hands. 'I won't harm you. You can put the gun down.'

But her words had no effect. He waved the gun, ordering her

to sit on the floor while he relit the candle that he must have blown out when he heard her approach. She considered his face as the light filled the small corner of the crypt. He must have been about thirty, his sallow skin and the dark rings around his eyes indicating months of sleep deprivation and hunger. His unshaven jaw suggested he'd been hiding for at least three days. His uniform was stained and shabby as if he'd crawled on his knees to get there.

'Do you have any food?' His voice was hoarse and rough around the edges, making it impossible to judge his mood.

'No, but I can go out and get you some.'

She climbed to her feet, seeing it as an excuse to get away, but already the gun was pointing at her face.

'Sit down.'

'If you're hungry, I could ask the priest for food.'

'No. You stay here with me.' He grabbed her bag from her shoulder and rifled through it. 'You must have something to eat.'

He was still for a moment, his fingers rubbing against something in the bag. His eyes narrowed on her as he pulled out her gun which she'd buried in the zipped pocket.

'Why do you have a gun?'

'Because there's a war on.' As he shoved it in his belt, Marguerite realised her last defence was gone.

He slid down the walls opposite where she sat, collapsing in a heap, still within touching distance, his knees tucked under his chin. The minutes ticked away while he stared at her, the uncertainty in his eyes making him unpredictable.

'What's your name?'

'Marguerite.'

If she could make him realise she had nothing against him, perhaps he'd let her go.

'What's happening out there? Have the Allies gained control of the streets?'

'They'll be here any minute.'

'And the German soldiers? What's happened to them?'

'Some of them have gone north.'

'And the others?'

What did he want her to tell him? What did she need to say to get herself released? She wasn't interested in seeing him captured. She just needed him to let her go.

'If you give yourself up, the Allies will treat you well. They'll feed you. You won't be harmed.'

'Only cowards give themselves up.'

'And a wise man knows when he's beaten.'

She saw it coming, but had no way of dodging the blow as the barrel of his gun landed with force against her cheekbone. She swallowed the blood gathering at the back of her nose.

'Did the army train you to hit a woman?'

He visibly shrank at her comment, covering his face with his hands. 'My mother would be ashamed of me for what I just did.'

'Then let me go. It would make her more proud of you than holding me captive.'

He crawled back into the corner like a beaten animal, his gun pointing at her. She was tempted to run, but didn't trust him not to shoot. She stole a look at her watch, her cheek throbbing as she moved her head, the skin tender where the bruise was beginning to spread.

Ten minutes passed and then twenty. Already the candle had burned down to a nub. He lit another from its dying flame.

'Why did you come down here? What were you looking for?' His eyes were trained on her, the barrel of his gun still pointed at her forehead.

'I was looking for Father Etienne Valade. This is his church. He brought me down here once to show me the frescoes on the walls.'

'Why did you think he was here?'

'I've tried everywhere else.'

'Why do you want to find him?'

'Because I love him.'

'You said he was a priest.'

'He's also a man.'

He turned his eyes from her and stared at the floor. 'My wife was killed when the Allies dropped their bombs on Hamburg. Also, my two little boys.'

'I'm sorry. This war isn't your fault. You didn't deserve to lose the people you love. None of us do.'

A sob escaped from deep inside his chest and she realised he was crying. This battle-weary warrior was as broken as everyone else.

'You didn't tell me your name.'

'Ulrich.'

She reached out and placed a hand on his leg to soothe him, but he shook her off, his bravado suddenly restored by her touch.

'Don't talk any more. If you say another word, I'll shoot you.'

There was no plan; that much was clear. He had no idea what to do with her, how to save the situation with grace. All she could do was watch for a change in his mood and wait, hoping for an opportunity to escape.

Time ticked on and still they remained in silence. The second candle burned itself out and he lit a third. Every minute she remained trapped was a minute not spent searching for Etienne, another minute in which she'd failed to get hold of the code. She had to win Ulrich round if he was to let her go. She had to keep him talking.

'How long have you been down here?'

He shrugged. 'Days.'

'Without food or water?'

'It was worse at the Russian front. Then we had to suffer the cold too.'

'Where's the rest of your unit?'

'Gone. They left without me.'

'It's not too late to follow them. The streets are quiet. If you're quick, no one will see you. Would you like me to go outside and have a look? I can get food while I'm there. You'll need your strength if you want to catch up with your unit.'

Her hope of release was beginning to build. She was getting through to him. Already his body was growing tense, ready for action. Slowly she stood up, risking a move towards the door. 'I won't be long, Ulrich. I'll be back soon. I promise.'

'Don't use my name. I didn't say you could call me by my name.' Suddenly the crypt was filled with the sound of his voice. 'You go nowhere until I say.'

She wanted to cry with frustration, to stamp her feet and scream at the injustice of being held captive. The afternoon was long gone, the evening almost spent.

'Stay here if you want to, but you have to let me go.'

'No.'

'People will come looking for me when they realise I'm missing. I have friends patrolling the streets, guerrilla fighters. They've been armed by the British. They won't forgive you for holding me captive.'

'You're lying.'

'Do you want to die a coward in the eyes of your enemy?'

He raised his gun to her head. 'Do you?'

Marguerite sank to the floor. The situation was growing more urgent by the minute 'We can't stay here forever. If we both walk out now, we can walk out alive.'

'Not now. Tomorrow. At daybreak.'

'What's the difference? Why not now? Why wait?'

Daybreak would be too late. The Americans would have arrived by then and Schmidt was likely to have fled, having destroyed the documents incriminating him and his associates for war crimes.

'The lazy Allies will still be asleep at daybreak. I have a better chance of escaping them.'

She buried her head in her hands in despair and sobbed. She had to get the code before it was too late. 'Do you want my body? Is that what it will take for you to release me?'

She held back her disgust as she said the words, but if she could get him into a vulnerable position, she might be able to disarm him.

'If I wanted you, I would have taken you already.'

Another hour passed, another candle burned down. Marguerite remained still, silent, willing him to fall asleep. Then she could slip quietly away without him noticing, but hunger had made him wild, and instead of resting, he paced the confines of the crypt, spinning his gun in his fingers, all the while keeping one eye on her. He'd gone mad, she was sure of it, and this made him volatile. One wrong move and she'd be dead, shot at point blank range, just as she'd killed Lance.

A quick glance at her watch told her it was 9pm.

'Why do you keep looking at your watch?'

'To see what time it is.'

He lunged forward and ripped the watch from her wrist before throwing it to the floor and stamping on it. 'No more.'

Once again, he began pacing up and down. She watched helplessly as another candle burned itself out and then another, the soldier's gun still pointing at her. She was weak with hunger and thirst, her determination to escape almost spent, but she couldn't give up.

'It's getting airless down here. We need some fresh air.'

'No.'

If only he hadn't taken her gun, she'd have risked shooting him by now. She thought of ways to overpower him, but despite his hunger and fatigue, he was much bigger than her; the force of his body alone would be enough to defeat her. And he still had his gun poised. She closed her eyes, feigning sleep, hoping to catch him unprepared and all the while trying to work out how to outwit him and get away.

Eventually, the pacing stopped. She could sense him creeping closer, the smell of him growing steadily stronger the nearer he came. She opened her eyes. There he was, crouching in front of her, his face almost pressed up against hers, his sour breath making her retch.

'Wake up. We go now.'

How many candles had burned down? The darkness, hunger and exhaustion had caused her to lose all sense of time. Her watch, the last gift from her mother before she died, lay in pieces on the floor, a victim of his vengeance and his great army boot.

He grabbed her and pulled her to her feet, his fingers digging into the fleshless bone at the top of her arm as he dragged her out of the crypt and through the church, the two of them blinking in the light of a bright new day, the barrel of his gun cold against her temple.

Whatever he did now, release her or kill her, she was too late. The Allies were probably already here, reclaiming the streets. Schmidt might already have fled, having destroyed the documents that would incriminate him for his war crimes.

Together they crept out into the silent morning, defeated invader and captive. Ulrich's eyes darted here and there as they crossed the square where Etienne had saved the old lady from the taunting of the German soldiers. Where was he now when she needed him? Where was Ulrich's dignity as he hid behind her to save his own skin?

'Drop the gun and let the woman go or I'll shoot.'

The voice of an American soldier came from somewhere behind a cluster of lime trees in the corner of the square, shattering the brittle morning peace. Ulrich's grip tightened on Marguerite's arm.

Marguerite scanned the empty square but her rescuer remained out of sight. She watched Ulrich from the corner of one eye, not daring to move her head. 'You should do as he says.'

A sweat had broken out on Ulrich's face. Even in the open air, he smelled of filth and blood, like the rats that had been blown from the sewers.

'Let me go, Ulrich.'

His grip grew tighter as she hissed at him, the barrel of his gun pushing harder against her temple.

'Put your gun down or I shoot the woman.'

Marguerite's heart clenched. 'Don't be a fool, Ulrich. If you shoot me, you'll be dead before I hit the ground.'

The American soldier stepped forward from behind a lime tree. 'You have until the count of three to let her go and then I'll shoot.'

'One.'

Marguerite took a deep breath. If he missed the German soldier, the bullet was likely to hit her. 'Let me go, Ulrich. For my sake if not for yours.'

Ulrich sobbed, the tears coming down his nose in streams, his grip tightening on Marguerite with each breath.

'Two.'

There was a loud crack. The grip on Marguerite's arm released and Ulrich hit the floor, the blood from the fatal bullet wound pouring from his skull.

'What the hell happened?' The American soldier raised his hands. He hadn't even taken aim.

Marguerite looked around for her saviour, spotting Dorothy's familiar form as she stepped out from the shadows, her gun poised and ready to shoot again.

'We don't play fair with the Germans. They've never played fair with us.'

She ran her fingers through her grey curls, which had grown unruly for want of a haircut and frowned at Marguerite. 'Why didn't you kill him?'

'He took my gun.'

Dorothy blinked at Ulrich's prone figure on the ground, her lip curling at the smell of his blood as it spread around their feet. 'Bastard.'

Marguerite looked away. The life had already gone out of him and she couldn't stand the sight of another death. She shouted her thanks to the American soldier, who'd already retreated to the cover of the lime trees, and then turned to Dorothy. 'How did you know where to find me?'

'You were looking for your priest. His church seemed the obvious place.' She pulled a crumpled sheet of paper from the pocket of her Oxford bags and handed it to Marguerite. 'I found this note on the front door step an hour ago. I thought it might be important.'

Marguerite's hands trembled as she unfolded the paper, her eyes squinting in the glare of the morning sun as she read the pencilled message.

Meet me in the park.

She didn't recognise the handwriting and whoever had written it hadn't bothered to sign it. It might be a trap, or it might be from someone who could lead her to Etienne. Who else knew the park was the place they'd first met?

Dorothy pushed her gun into the waistband of her Oxford bags. 'I'd better get back to Catherine. She'll be wondering where I am. I can't risk leaving her alone for too long while the Huns are on the run.'

Marguerite looked up from the note to thank her, but Dorothy had already disappeared, as swiftly and silently as she'd arrived, whisked away on a magic carpet for all she knew.

Finding herself alone, Marguerite collected her bicycle and slipped out of the square and onto one of the quieter streets. She hadn't gone far when she found herself face to face with another maquisard. She recognised him as one of the men who'd been playing poker in the bar on the Rue de la Cigale. Her only hope was that he remembered her, and that her association with Pascal would be enough to save her.

'What are you doing here? Don't you know the streets aren't safe?'

Even as he said the words, another Allied plane flew over, almost low enough to take off their heads.

'I'm searching for Etienne Valade, the priest. Do you know where he is?' she shouted over the roar of the engine, the fumes from the aeroplane fuel metallic on her tongue.

312

The maquisard spat on the ground. 'No, but when we find him, we'll kill him.'

'He's not what you think.'

'We'll shoot him anyway for welcoming the Nazis into his church. You can tell him that when you find him, if he's not already dead.' He waved his gun to dismiss her. 'Go, before I change my mind. And don't tell anyone I saw you, Marguerite. There's blood against your name and the people in this town have long memories.'

She cycled as fast as she could. There was no saying how long ago the note had been delivered. Whoever had summoned her to the park might be gone by now, but she had to find out.

Chapter 53

The Allied tanks were arriving. She could feel their rumble beneath her feet, the rhythmic stamp of the soldiers' boots as they marched into the town. The tension had been pushed to breaking point and the street battles were beginning; the rooftop snipers, poised on the parapets and determined as crows, no longer held back. With the Allied advance, the German retreat was inevitable.

Things were changing by the minute as the push began to drive the enemy back, forcing them into the hills and the beautiful places beyond. The war wasn't over, it was just moving into a new phase.

Every now and then, an American tank trundled past, draped in the wilting flowers thrown at them by grateful women as they advanced from the beaches. Just off the coast, the Allied ships bobbed on the horizon in a grim parody of every luxury yacht that had ever laid its anchor in the many harbours and coves. Barrage balloons hovered above the beaches like bloated sardines, too large and too unruly for the local fishermen's nets to contain, staking their claim to the land as surely as if the Americans had planted their own flag.

Marguerite had almost reached the centre of town when she noticed the commotion. It wasn't bartering for food, but something harsher and more chaotic. She jumped off her bicycle and pushed it into the main square, staying close to the edge where she was less likely to be noticed. Despite the heat, her skin turned cold at the sight of what was happening.

A dozen women accused of sleeping with German soldiers had been dragged from their homes and rounded up like cattle. Having been beaten and spat upon, they were now having their heads shaved. Already their clothes had been torn from their backs and swastikas painted on their naked breasts.

They stood, vulnerable as children, surrounded by a group of local people, their feet shuffling through the shanks of discarded hair on the pavement and in the gutter. She spotted familiar faces in the crowd: the doctor's wife and the local hairdresser, the café owner who'd employed Jeanne and who might or might not have been the one to denounce her, each one unconscious of the shame they brought on themselves rather than on their victims.

A group of American soldiers, straight off the boat, looked on as if it were a local custom put on for their entertainment. Marguerite felt the sting of betrayal on behalf of every woman in the town as fathers and brothers, husbands and sons stood beside the foreign soldiers and watched the debasing of their women.

Most were old enough to take care of themselves, but when Marguerite spotted Nancy being dragged forward to have her head shaved, her pretty poplin blouse already torn from her back, she had to step in.

'She's just a child. Can't you leave her alone?'

'You'll stay out of it if you know what's good for you.'

The voice came from the back of the crowd. Whoever had spoken up was willing to shout, but not show his face.

'If it wasn't for that murdering thief, Pascal, warning us off, we'd be doing the same to you. Don't think we don't know you're the whore of that German-loving priest.'

The words were spat from the mouth of a woman notorious for trading on the black market. The German cigarettes she negotiated from the occupying soldiers had been one of her main forms of currency, but memories were selective and the list of unforgivable misdemeanours had been cherry-picked to suit the conscience of the majority.

Nancy held her head high as the same woman fought her way to the front of the crowd and took up the scissors. Marguerite bit back her rage as she thought about Yves Musel, who'd sacrificed his life working as an agent alongside the British to protect the people of the town. This was how they repaid him, by abusing and terrorising his daughter who'd risked her own safety to assist him.

The woman grabbed Nancy's long plait and held it at arm's length, lining up the scissors close to her head. Marguerite begged her to stop, but Nancy proved braver.

'Please don't, Marguerite. You'll only make things worse for me.'

Marguerite obeyed Nancy's command. There was a reward of ten thousand francs for anyone who shot a collaborator. If she didn't let the town serve this punishment on her, the alternative could be much worse.

A murmur of *Nazi whore* passed through the crowd like a bad smell carried on the warm breeze. There was no getting away from it. If they were to stay in the town, both Nancy and Marguerite would have to live with this scorn for the rest of their lives without anyone ever acknowledging the bravery they'd shown and the risks they'd taken. Defending themselves, explaining the truth to a crowd hungry for blood and retribution, would only make matters worse. Nobody was interested in finding out the truth behind the accusations. People had suffered and they wanted revenge. It was easiest to take it out on the weakest members of society.

It was the atmosphere of anger that shocked Marguerite more than anything. It thickened the air, just as the smoke and the fires from the Allied bombing had done, night after night. The survivors needed to punish someone for their humiliation and the easiest targets were those closest to them.

How would Nancy build a future for herself with this blight on her character? Horizontal collaborators, that's what they called women like her – mattresses for the Boche. Few could imagine why they'd been driven to do it or what it had cost them. Nancy was a heroine; she'd fought her war, just as the men of the town had, and by doing so, she'd had her innocence and her childhood stolen from her. Eventually, the boys would be honoured for it, but Nancy would only be degraded.

'We'll be coming for you next, Marguerite. Don't think you'll get away with what you've done. Pascal won't be able to protect you forever and then you'll be dead.'

The words were whispered in her ear by Madame Damas, who'd refused to sell her any bread, whose daughter had condemned Armand to death when she denounced him to the Germans for shooting the enemy soldier in the bar. They'd never know if he was guilty or not, but he'd died for it anyway, a man who'd only tried to do the best for his country and fought for it the only way he was able.

'You should beware of making too many enemies, Madame Damas. People here have long memories.'

The look of shock on Madame Damas's face proved she hadn't expected Marguerite to answer back, but Marguerite was beyond living in fear of a bitter old woman. Her only fear was for Etienne. If he'd encountered a mob such as this one, he might be dead already. And if he was still out there, she had to find him before they did.

The heat dripped steadily through the afternoon as Marguerite cycled along the outskirts of the town to the park, her hands slippery with perspiration where she gripped the handlebars, each turn of the pedal taking her nearer to Etienne. Already in her mind she'd built herself up for the prospect of a reunion. Why else would she have been summoned?

The park was quiet when she arrived and Marguerite found herself alone among the pine trees, wandering the gravel paths, staying in plain sight in the hope that whoever had summoned her might have had the patience to wait.

All around, the street battles were continuing in fits and bursts. It wasn't safe to be out when a stray bullet could be the end of everything. After half an hour, Marguerite forced herself to admit she'd been sent on a fool's errand. She left through the main gate, lingering a moment or two on the pavement, making her presence felt in case whoever had sent the note was watching, but there wasn't a soul in sight. After so much searching, she'd missed her rendezvous.

Just as she was about to leave, an American jeep thundered past, the soldiers whooping and jeering, as if a Frenchwoman was something rare and exotic. She gripped the handlebars of her bicycle, instinctively using it as a barricade. The invasion of more foreign troops was the only way to free France of its German oppressors and so for now, they had to put up with it. They couldn't win the battle alone.

As she climbed onto her bicycle, Madame Damas appeared around the corner, her ample form thundering towards her.

'There she is.'

It was a trap. She'd been a fool to obey the note, to think love would be as easy to rescue as a walk in the park on a sunny afternoon. Suddenly she was facing three maquisards, their guns pointing at her chest.

'She's a Nazi whore. Shoot her. Shoot her now.'

Marguerite risked a glance at Madame Damas, her well-fed face twisted with hatred and spite.

'What have I ever done to you, Madame, that you treat me like this?'

But the woman's expression didn't change. She wasn't interested in a discussion; her prejudice and her fear wouldn't stand up to it.

'Whore.'

The tallest maquisard, a boy of no more than fifteen, his bandana thick with dirt and blood, stepped forward and prepared to shoot.

Marguerite braced herself for the impact. There was no point in running away; they'd only shoot her in the back and that was no way to die. If they were going to kill her, they'd have to look her in the eye while they did it.

The young boy hesitated, his arm trembling as he took aim. Madame Damas, who was quickly losing patience, punched his shoulder with her fist.

'Go on, shoot the whore.'

There was another pause while he steadied himself, then a quiet click as he released the safety catch on his pistol.

'Drop your guns. It's time to start behaving like men, not boys,' someone bellowed from the corner of the street, just behind where Marguerite stood, his voice steady as he broke into a run. In spite of everything, Marguerite's heart lifted. She'd have known his voice anywhere.

Madame Damas screamed. 'Go on, shoot her. Quick.'

This time, all three maquisards raised their guns.

'You take your orders from a fat old woman now? Then don't think you can call yourselves men.'

Marguerite didn't dare move or turn around, but she recognised the smell of him, her heart beating rapidly at his closeness and the safety he offered as he stood beside her and slipped his arm around her shoulders.

'Drop your guns, boys, unless you're prepared to shoot me as well.'

One by one, the young maquisards lowered their guns, their heads dropping in shame as Pascal removed his arm from Marguerite's shoulders and slapped each boy in turn across the face.

'Get out of my sight, all of you.'

Madame Damas turned on him, her eyes full of hate. 'You've made a big mistake protecting that Nazi whore, Pascal. You'll pay for it, if not today then tomorrow, or next year. There'll be people watching and waiting for both of you, and we'll get you when you don't expect it.'

The accusation was too much, coming from a woman who'd grown fat and prosperous from her black-market trading with the Germans, and Marguerite would take no more of it.

'Who do you think it was who procured the maps showing the mines along the coast and on the beaches that allowed the Allies to land safely, Madame? Who do you think risked her life to make sure they reached Allied hands?'

Madame Damas sneered and something inside Marguerite snapped. She slapped her hard across the face, throwing the full weight of her body behind the blow. 'I'm a British agent and don't you ever forget it.'

She'd broken her cover, but she didn't regret it; it had been worth it to see the look of shock on the old woman's face.

Pascal nodded, dismissing Madame Damas. 'Go, before Marguerite gets really annoyed. She has permission to kill. I've seen her do it in cold blood.'

After Madame Damas had gone, Pascal led Marguerite into the park and ordered her to sit down in the shade.

'Why did you walk into their trap?'

'I thought it might lead me to Etienne.'

Pascal lowered himself onto the bench beside her and offered her a slug of brandy from his hipflask. 'Reckless woman. You're still risking your life to get hold of the code?'

She wanted to put her arms around him and thank him for all he'd done. She desperately needed to be held, but he'd think it was an over-reaction, and the ingrained smell of onions that emanated from his hair put her off. She knocked back the brandy, relishing its fire as it burned the back of her throat.

For a fleeting moment, she'd thought it was Etienne coming

320

to her rescue as she'd faced the gunmen. It was wrong to have been disappointed when she'd realised it was Pascal after he'd saved her life.

'How did you know to come and find me?'

'Madame Damas has a big mouth. She couldn't help shouting about her plan to ambush you. Someone made sure word of it reached me. Not everyone here is your enemy.'

The shock began to abate as the alcohol relaxed her muscles and her hands stopped shaking. 'Sometimes, it's hard to believe that.'

'My brother saw what happened outside the church. The woman who shot the German soldier as he held a gun to your head; she's a British agent, as well. Yes?'

She thought about Dorothy's knife-throwing skills, how she'd taught her to shoot and to pick a lock, how she'd appeared under the cover of darkness after being blackmailed by someone threatening to expose her, how it had happened around the same time that Marguerite was recruited by Violet.

'Perhaps she is.'

Pascal looked up, finally meeting her eye. 'You're still determined to find the priest?'

'Do you know where he is?'

'A few days ago, a group of resistance fighters drove out some German soldiers who'd dug themselves into a foxhole somewhere outside the town. Unfortunately, they got away and retreated into the hills. There's a rumour that the same soldiers have since been involved in another gun battle, this time with a priest. I can't tell you if it was Valade or not. After he was shot, he was taken to a convent in one of the hill towns near where they grow the flowers.'

Marguerite was on her feet in an instant. 'Which is the quickest way? By road or over land?'

'Nowhere is safe, Marguerite. You can't go.'

'You can't stop me.'

She climbed on her bicycle, trying to work out the best route in her head.

'It might not be him, Marguerite.'

She nodded, fighting back the tears that could have been hope and could have been fear for what she might find at the convent. 'I know, but I have to find out.'

Chapter 54

It had reached the hottest part of the day by the time Marguerite set off, labouring up the steep roads that led to the hill town twenty kilometres inland. The slug of brandy Pascal had given her sloshed around her empty stomach, making her head swim every time she swerved to avoid the potholes in the bomb-damaged roads and the booby-trapped blockhouses strategically hidden along the way.

Everywhere there was a risk of machine gun and sniper fire, of being shot from above by an Allied or an enemy plane, or from the surrounding land stalked by soldiers, half crazed with hunger and desperation. Ulrich wasn't the only German to have gone rogue. In spite of all the dangers, the main road was still the safest route while the hills and the forests remained seeded with landmines.

No matter the heat and the risk, reaching Etienne as quickly as possible was all that mattered. If he was in a convent, then he'd be taken good care of. If anyone could save him, it would be the sisters.

Military vehicles thundered past her every few minutes, throwing up the dust of the road. She could feel it sticking to her face and coating her tongue as she took deep breaths, pushing on ever upwards, counting down the time until the sun would begin its descent, until she reached the higher land where the breeze would be cooler and more insistent.

'Hey, lady. Pull over, why don't you?'

She'd drifted into the middle of the road just as an American army lorry tried to overtake. Her wheels wobbled as she raised her hand to apologise, a wave of nausea almost overwhelming her and she stopped to let the lorry pass, regretting the loss of her gun as it pulled up alongside her.

'You ok, lady?'

The driver looked at her from beneath his tin helmet, his eyes red-rimmed from the dust, the skin on his face already burned from exposure to too much sun. 'Where you headed?'

'The convent, just over the hill.'

He opened the door to the passenger seat. 'I'm going that way myself. Jump in.'

It seemed too much of a coincidence. Marguerite glanced at the thick ropes of muscle on his forearms where he'd rolled back the sleeves of his uniform. The same density of muscle broadened his neck and shoulders, adding brute strength to his hands. It was unusual for a soldier to be travelling alone and there was no one else for miles around.

'Thank you, but I'll be fine. I have my bicycle.'

'It's another eight miles to the convent. You'll be safer with me rather than taking your chances with the enemy snipers. Don't you know you're in the middle of a war zone?'

He pulled a can of water from under the passenger seat and tossed it into her hands. The water was sweet as it went down, washing the dust from the back of her throat and clearing her head. As she drank, he jumped down from the cab and placed her bicycle on the flatbed of the lorry next to a tarpaulin that had been laid to cover a series of objects that could have been anything from food supplies to ammunition.

She commented on how unusual it was to see a soldier working alone. Risk of ambush meant they always travelled in groups.

'Well, ma'am, I'm not alone, or maybe I am, depending how you look at it.' He lifted the corner of the tarpaulin just enough to reveal the leg of a soldier, his boot polished to a high shine and neatly laced. 'I'm taking three of my best buddies here to the convent. The sisters have kindly allowed us to use their chapel as a collecting point for the boys killed in the fighting along the coast.'

As he spoke, Marguerite spotted the blood dripping from beneath the tarpaulin onto the road. She gripped the side of the lorry to steady herself, mourning the fate of the boys who'd died in a foreign land, thousands of miles from the people who loved them.

He pointed to a hill in the distance. 'See over there? We got German prisoners of war digging graves two feet deep right up close to one another. This is where our boys will end up.'

'There's no sense or meaning to this war. It should never have happened.'

He turned away from her, rubbing his forearm against his eyes as if to rub away the dust of the road that had suddenly made them water. Marguerite gently tugged the tarpaulin, covering up the leg of the dead soldier before the flies appeared. The debt owed to these men was impossible to repay.

The soldier, who told her his name was Frank, didn't ask her any questions as the lorry bumped its way up into the hills. The air was clearer on the higher ground, away from the battleships and the tanks. The German troops were putting up less of a fight in the hill villages than on the coast and there was less sabotage and fewer explosions. Perhaps by the time they'd retreated, they'd realised they were beaten.

Instead of talking about the war, Marguerite told Frank about the life that had gone on before – about the generations of families who'd made their living from the vineyards and the olive groves, about the artists and the writers for whom the landscape was an inspiration and a haven. As they drove higher, the air became thick with the scent of flowers, and she told him about the fields of roses and jasmine cultivated by the perfumiers, and the essential oils they produced which were the foundations of the world's greatest fragrances.

He listened all the way, saying nothing about himself, and she worried that she'd bored him with her stories of the land and the community, until he dropped her at the entrance to the convent and she realised it was exactly what he'd needed to hear.

'It's been a pleasure to meet you, ma'am.' He tipped his finger to his helmet in a soft salute. 'You've helped me to see what it is we're fighting for. Good luck.'

He lifted her bicycle down from the lorry before driving to the back of the convent where a temporary chapel of rest had been hastily constructed among the almond trees by the local villagers. She hadn't told him why she was here and he hadn't asked, because he hadn't needed to. Broken souls were everywhere; they didn't need to be laid bare to be recognised and understood.

Chapter 55

Marguerite wheeled her bicycle along the path that led to the entrance of the convent. The building was as old as the hills; its beauty lay in the rubbed away corners and soft edges of the honeyed stone, brought about by centuries of insistent winds and chill winters. The purple spikes of the lavenders planted on either side of the path shifted in the afternoon breeze when she passed them, releasing their heady scent of camphor as if they'd been put there intentionally to soothe her.

She pulled on the rope beside the door, prompting a chorus of bells to ring throughout the building, their jangle as gentle as songbirds. Silent feet must have come hurrying because the door opened quickly and unexpectedly, the warm smile of a nun greeting her without suspicion, disarming Marguerite with her willingness to welcome her without question.

'I'm looking for Father Etienne Valade. Is he here?'

The warmth in the nun's smile reached up to her eyes as she invited Marguerite to step inside. 'I'm Sister Clara. You must be Marguerite. He's been waiting for you.'

Perhaps it was stepping into the cool relief of the convent, or perhaps it was the news that Etienne was there, that he was alive, that finally caused Marguerite to release the tears she'd been holding back for so long.

'He says your name in his sleep. He's been calling you and you've answered. Such is the power of love.' Sister Clara reached into her pocket and pulled out a folded sheet of paper torn from a notebook. 'He asked me to give you this. He said you'd know what it was for.'

Marguerite unfolded the paper, her eyes scanning the line of numbers neatly written in Etienne's hand. It had to be the combination to Schmidt's safe. Etienne had been true to his word.

'Can I see him?'

'He said to come back when you've done what you have to. He'll be waiting for you.'

Frank's truck was parked outside when Marguerite left the convent, the engine running as if he were ready to make a quick getaway. He tipped his helmet at her and smiled.

'I figured you'd want a lift back into town once you'd finished your visit.'

She lifted her bicycle onto the back of his truck and climbed into his cab. 'Thank you for waiting.'

'I'm glad to have your company, ma'am. Tell me some more about them flowers growing in the fields.'

He didn't question it when she asked him to drop her outside the anonymous building that contained Schmidt's office and she could only assume he didn't know the significance of where he was taking her. They parted after shaking hands, knowing they were unlikely to see each other again. Frank's meeting with Marguerite would become one of the many anecdotes he'd carry back home with him after the war, although he'd never know the significance of her task or the part he'd played in helping her to achieve it.

There was no officer on the desk to question her when she entered the building. Marguerite assumed he was busy elsewhere or had already fled. With no one else around to stop her, she took the lift to the ninth floor, where she soon found herself standing once again in Schmidt's office.

The air still carried the stench of brandy and cigars, just as it had when she'd visited with Etienne to beg for the lives of Biquet and his nine friends, the desk scattered with papers as if whatever was written on them was no longer of any importance.

She scanned the rest of the room, taking in the dented cushions on the leather chairs, the dirty glasses on the low table, the ashtray brimming with cigarette butts. Everything was as it was before, apart from the empty suitcase which sat in the corner, its lid thrown open ready to be packed.

If Schmidt was preparing to flee, he was probably in the building and might walk in on her at any minute. She dashed to the safe and retrieved the combination from her pocket, turning the dial by degrees as the numbers dictated, working steadily and carefully. Now wasn't the time to make a mistake or lose courage.

The dial gave a final click as she turned it to the last number. She pushed down on the handle, relieved when the door swung open. Just as she'd anticipated, the safe was stacked with files. She pulled one out at random and flicked through the first few pages, her eyes scanning the information. Her German was limited, but she didn't need to understand every word to know the documents recorded lists of names and the fates of those rounded up and sent to the prison camps.

There was too much information to photograph. The only option was to take the files themselves. Remembering the suitcase, she grabbed an armful of papers and piled them inside. Working quickly, she reached into the safe to gather up a second batch. And that was when she heard it: the click of the door, the beat of heavy feet on the carpet. Marguerite looked up, her blood turning to ice as she found herself face to face with Otto Schmidt.

His eyes burned into her as she dropped the second set of papers into his suitcase.

'What are you doing?'

'I've come to collect these documents. If you have any sense, you'll let me walk out of here with them.' Now wasn't the time to lose courage. She grabbed the final set of papers from the safe and placed them in the suitcase before closing the lid.

'Please step aside.'

Before she could get any further, he darted across the room to block her way. She took a deep breath, trying to remain calm as she remembered how he'd forced a kiss on her the last time he'd searched the house and her studio.

'You must excuse me. I have to go.'

'You're not leaving with that suitcase.'

She took a deep breath to stop herself shaking. 'You can't stop me.'

'I'm the conqueror. I can do anything I choose.'

'Your time here in France is over. Now get out of my way.'

She felt it before she saw it, the slice of his hand across her face, the force behind it enough to send her crashing to the floor. She staggered to her feet, still gripping the suitcase, and tried once more for the door, stars dancing in front of her eyes from the force of the blow.

'Where is he?'

The words raged from Schmidt, carried across the room on a great arc of spit. It took all the courage she had to look him in the face.

'Where's who?'

'Lance Holmes.'

She pressed the back of her hand gently against her bottom lip, testing it for blood. 'Isn't it your job to know that?'

Goaded by her insolence, he grabbed her arm and threw her across the room, her shoulders bruising as she landed heavily against the wall.

Before she could get to her feet, he leaned over and grabbed her jaw. 'You want to know the truth about Holmes? He came to us, offering to do anything we wanted as long as we turned a blind eye to his trading in degenerate art. In return, he agreed to watch Father Etienne Valade for us. We'd been keeping an eye on him since his brother refused to cooperate with us in Paris. We find resistance runs in families.'

'Father Etienne is a good man, a priest.'

'Holmes told me you've been visiting his villa. What is it about Etienne Valade that you prefer him to me?'

She tried to turn away, but he twisted her head, forcing her to look at him. 'You think I don't know a reluctant kiss when I taste one? He's not even a professional soldier. There's no honour in him.'

'He has enough honour never to hit a woman.'

'But not enough to obey his vow of chastity.'

'You don't want to believe anything Lance tells you. He's a born liar.'

Schmidt tightened his grip on her jaw. 'Where is Lance? No one's seen him lately.'

'He's not my concern.'

Schmidt laughed, loosening his grip on her face just long enough for her to roll away from him. Reeling from the pain, she struggled to her feet, only to be brought down again by the full force of another blow, Schmidt's stout form blocking her way before she could grab the suitcase and crawl to the door.

'I should've had you arrested when we took that friend of yours for buying fish. We could have executed you together.'

Simone wasn't the only death he was responsible for. Jeanne had thrown herself out of a high window rather than endure the torture he'd ordered. He'd killed her and her unborn child, just as he'd killed Biquet and his nine little friends, and countless other innocent people.

'Holmes told me you and the priest are lovers. Don't you worry about him burning in Hell for his sins?'

She crawled on her hands and knees, still gripping the suitcase as he made a lunge for it, but fear made her quick and she darted under his desk, thrusting her foot into his face as he crouched to grab her and sending him flying, his pistol dropping from his hand. She had just enough time to snatch it. When he looked at her again, she was pointing it directly at his forehead.

He laughed as she made him raise his hands and stand against the wall.

'You wouldn't dare to spill my blood.'

'I'll give you a choice. I can shoot you and leave you here to die like a dog, or you can escape to your death through the window, just as Jeanne was forced to do.'

'Don't be ridiculous. We're on the ninth floor.'

She moved to the window and pushed it open. Instantly, the warm breeze blew in, a seagull sending a haunting cry as it passed overhead reminding her of the outside world that was waiting.

She waved the pistol in his face. 'Why don't you jump?'

And jump he did, lunging at her and grabbing her wrists, forcing her to the window and arching her back over the sill as he tried to push her out. She thought it was the end. He was too strong for her. Her head was forced back as far as it would go, her eyes streaming at the brightness of the sun above her until she was blinded by its power and her fear of falling.

He started forcing her out of the window, his hands grappling with her body as he pushed and pushed, but he hadn't taken into account her knee, which she brought up hard between his legs, the pain causing him to loosen his grip on her wrist just long enough for her to turn the pistol on him and shoot him through the heart, not once, but twice.

The force he'd used against her fell away as he dropped to the floor, the same look of disbelief on his face she'd seen on Lance's. She stood over him while she caught her breath, shocked by her own audacity and the strength she didn't know she had until she'd needed it.

She took in the mess of blood and splintered bone, the gore spreading across the rug and spilling off the edges where there

332

was too much of it. She deplored the horror of Schmidt's death, but at least he wouldn't be responsible for any more murders; and as a practising Catholic, it was unlikely he'd rest in peace.

She had to get out before anyone came to investigate the sound of the gunshots. Grabbing the suitcase, she headed for the door, closing it quietly behind her before she made her way along the corridor and into the waiting lift, not allowing herself to breathe until she was out of the building.

A minute later, she was on her way, the suitcase full of incriminating documents strapped to her handlebars, her expression set to deny that she'd been forced to defend herself against a mass murderer, that she was guilty of yet another killing.

Chapter 56

The sun was almost set by the time Marguerite arrived at the convent. This time, there'd been no friendly American soldier to offer her a lift, and she'd struggled to cycle the twenty kilometres with the weight of the suitcase on her handlebars. It never once crossed her mind to stop and rest. Etienne was waiting for her and now she'd completed her mission, returning to him was all that mattered.

Sister Clara must have been watching for her because she stepped outside to greet her before Marguerite had dismounted from her bicycle.

She unstrapped the suitcase from the handlebars, hugging it to her chest as she entered the convent. She'd fought too hard for it to let go of it now.

Sister Clara offered her a glass of water and some bread, but Marguerite could only think of Etienne.

'How is he? Can I see him?'

'Just for a little while. He's very weak.'

She followed her along a series of stone passageways until they came to a simple wooden door.

'Can you tell me what happened?'

'He was shot by a German soldier just outside the convent.'

'It happened here?'

Sister Clara lowered her head and whispered as if in prayer. 'We have an orphanage; just thirty children. They're safe here in our fold. Since the war, Father Etienne has been a great protector of our little community.'

'I imagine not all the children you've taken in are Catholic.'

'No, but they are all God's creatures.'

Etienne had found a haven here for the children he'd been unable to get out of the country during the German Occupation and he'd been determined to keep them safe.

'He came to visit us a few days ago. He wanted to make sure the retreating enemy hadn't disturbed us or looked too closely at the children. When a group of soldiers came to the gate, demanding to search the place, Father Etienne asked them not to enter, to respect the privacy of our female enclave. Of course, it was the children he was thinking of.

'He stood before the gate, offering them food and water in exchange for leaving us in peace. There were only six of them, but they were young and scared. When Father Etienne picked up the basket of bread we'd prepared and stepped forward to hand it over, one of them panicked and raised his gun. He'd shot him before any of us could intervene or beg him to think again.'

'And then what happened?'

'They fled like scared children, which is all they really were.'

'And Father Etienne?'

'Three of us carried him inside and tended to him as swiftly as we could.'

'Is he alright?'

'We removed the bullet and did our best to stem the wound, but he lost a lot of blood.' Sister Clara quietly opened the door to the sick room. 'He'll be glad to see you.'

The room was bare, except for a single iron bed, the white distemper on the rough plastered walls bleaching the place of colour, but for the last of the evening sunlight, spilling in from the window like liquid amber.

Etienne lay on his back, his eyes closed in sleep or in prayer; it was impossible to know which. Apart from the paleness of his complexion, the dark shadows beneath his eyes, it would be easy to pretend there was nothing wrong with him, but the wound was deep. The bullet had gone straight through his ribs and glanced his heart.

His lips were cool as she bent to kiss him. He opened his eyes and a gentle spark ignited them when he realised it was Marguerite.

'You found me.'

'You're not an easy man to track down.'

He clutched her hand, his fingers cold to the touch. 'Were you able to help Catherine?'

'She's safe and being well looked after.'

'Did you get the documents incriminating Schmidt and his associates?'

'I did, and it was all thanks to you. Schmidt has already been killed, but the rest will be made to stand trial for their war crimes.' She stroked his hair and kissed his forehead, unable to take in enough of him. 'Are you warm enough?'

She slipped off her shoes and climbed onto the bed, gently embracing him, feeling the love and the reassurance of every part of him against her. Marguerite was home. She was beside Etienne and nothing else mattered.

'Tell me what happened after Schmidt found you in his office and suspected you of searching his desk drawer?'

He spoke in whispers, pausing to snatch a breath after every few words. 'He didn't detain me, so I returned to the presbytery straight away. I'd planned to write down the combination and to give it to Madame Mercier to pass it on to you, but the Gestapo was at the door before I had time to do it. I tried to get away, but I was arrested as soon as I left the presbytery.

'I'd memorised the combination to Schmidt's safe, so they had no proof I was lying when I said I'd simply been helping myself to Schmidt's brandy when he found me in his office. I'd shared a drink with him often enough to know he always kept a bottle in his desk drawer.

'They also questioned me about the disappearance of one of their agents, but there was no evidence I'd been involved.'

The missing agent had to be Lance. Marguerite had killed him and Etienne had been the one to pay the price for it. If she admitted it, would he ever forgive her for it?

'The Gestapo had nothing to prove I'd been working against them, and so they left me to sweat in a cell and locked the door while they decided what to do with me.

'Solitary confinement is no hardship for a priest. It gave me time to examine my soul. My faith was in crisis. I'd broken every vow I'd ever made to God for you. Your love was the greatest happiness of my life, but it had left me tormented. I was struggling to work out my relationship with God. What I wanted it to be. What He wanted from me.

'That night, the Allies began dropping bombs close to the prison. There were fires raging on all sides and missiles screeching overhead. The German soldier who'd been left to guard me panicked and unlocked my cell door, begging me to save his soul for his mother's sake. With his eternal life in question, he didn't take much convincing to release not only me, but all the other prisoners too.

'By now, my own battle had been lost and won. However powerful my love for God, my love for you was stronger. You'd won my soul, Marguerite, as well as my heart and it made me the happiest man alive. I was coming back to you, just as you said I would when I left you, but first I needed to check the children in the convent were safe. The hills were overrun with retreating soldiers; many of them were desperate and crazed, and willing to kill anyone who got in their way.

'As soon as I arrived, I knew I had to stay and protect the children; and still here I am. I knew it was important to get the combination for Schmidt's safe to you, but I had to put the lives of the children first. From the moment I was shot, I prayed you'd find me and you did, just as you'd promised.'

Marguerite kissed his hand, never wanting to let go. 'There's nothing to keep us apart now, Etienne. Lance was killed. We're free to marry, if you'll have me.'

Etienne smiled, raising her hand to his lips. 'Then there's a happy ending for us, after all.'

She lay with him all night, refusing sleep, savouring every precious moment with him, just as she'd done after they'd made love in the Villa Christelle. He was gone by the time the sun came up, but still she clung to him, drawing the last of the warmth from his body as his blood cooled, taking in his final breath and holding on to it. Etienne hadn't really left her. He'd buried himself deep in her heart and that was where he'd always remain.

Sister Clara was outside the sick room, keeping vigil on a wooden chair. She stood up and lowered her head when Marguerite appeared.

Marguerite sniffed back a tear, pressing her shoulder against the wall to stop herself from falling.

'He's gone.'

'He'd been waiting for you. He muttered over and over that he wanted one more night with you. He needed to say goodbye before he could let go.'

One more night. It was all she'd asked when he'd visited her in the garden. One more night to carry her through the rest of her life and he'd held on just long enough to grant it.

Armed with the suitcase of documents, she walked out of the convent into the brightness of a new morning, his spirit fortifying her, giving her the strength to endure the first stab of grief. Already the sun was warming the air, the mild breeze bringing with it the scent of a thousand flowers. She took a deep breath, filling herself up with all the perfume the land could offer. The sky was still, but for the birds, and the guns were silent. The enemy had been driven back and the air was clear enough for Marguerite to see the path in front of her, uneven to begin with, but growing firmer beneath her feet as Etienne took her hand and led her towards the new day, one step at a time.

A Letter from Theresa Howes

Stories form over time and in all sorts of ways. It was my love of early twentieth-century art and my interest in the lives of the artists and writers who made their homes in the South of France that initially inspired the location for *The Secrets We Keep*. Like so many visitors who went before me, I was seduced by the landscape and the weather; not only the blue summer skies and the nurturing heat, but the springtime snow and the relentless winds. Whatever you think about the Cote d'Azur, it will always surprise you.

The more I explored the small coastal towns, the more I began to wonder about the history that isn't so obvious today. Think of the South of France and you probably think of Picasso and Matisse, Brigitte Bardot and the Cannes Film Festival. But what else is there? The war memorial in Nice, carved into the rock face, overlooking the sea, dedicated to the people lost in both world wars made me consider the darker history that lay beneath the sunshine and the glamour.

Whenever I imagined the German Occupation of France during the Second World War, I tended to think of Paris. It wasn't until I started digging deeper into the history of the places I visited in the south that I learned the Cote d'Azur had also suffered under enemy oppression. This started me thinking about the challenges faced by the people living in a place known for its natural beauty, culture and high life, who were suddenly forced to endure the daily cruelties of war. It wasn't the rich and famous who concerned me, because many of those had the means to escape. It was the ordinary people, living ordinary lives who interested me; the ones who had no choice but to dig in and fight, using whatever means they could.

This was the starting point for my story; people like you and me, battling to survive dire circumstances. Slowly, the character of Marguerite began to emerge; an unknown artist escaping her past and living a quiet life, employing whatever skills she had to fight the war. And then came Etienne, a priest; his life dictated by his duty to God, welcoming the enemy into his church, because it wasn't his place to refuse them.

It was the secrets these characters kept hidden that caught my imagination; the subterfuges they would be driven to employ, not only to survive but to defeat the enemy. When no one is who they seem, who can you trust? And is it possible to find happiness in the midst of the terror? What would my characters be prepared to do to protect those they loved? What risks were they prepared to take? And what would they sacrifice to win the war? It was the answers to these questions, inspired by the impossible choices real people were forced to make, that gave me the inspiration for Marguerite and Etienne's story.

Ultimately, this work is a tribute to the people who stood up to tyranny during the Second World War and to the sacrifices they made. I am in awe of their courage and grateful for the following decades of peace and stability that was their enduring gift to us.

If you enjoyed *The Secrets We Keep* and would like to recommend it to others, please consider leaving a review. It's a great way to help bring the novel to the attention of other readers who might also enjoy it.

If you'd like to be the first to hear about my next novel, find out what I'm currently reading, or check out pictures of Claude the impossible cat, you can find me on Twitter @Howes_Theresa, or visit my website: www.theresahowes.co.uk. Drop by and say hello. I look forward to seeing you there.

Acknowledgements

I'm so honoured to be represented by Mushens Entertainment and to be able to call myself part of Team Mushens. Thank you to foreign rights whiz and giver of great notes, Liza DeBlock and to Kiya Evans for your super efficiency. My greatest thanks go to Juliet Mushens, agent, mentor and guiding star. Your thoughtful notes, encouragement and support are helping me to become the writer I've always dreamed of being.

Thank you to all the people at HQ Digital who have worked tirelessly behind the scenes to bring *The Secrets We Keep* to life, especially my editor, Abigail Fenton, whose sensitive and insightful thoughts helped me to hone the characters and the story. Abi, you shared my vision for the novel from the very first moment and have made the work we've done together an absolute pleasure.

Thanks also to Audrey Linton in editorial, freelancers Dushi Horti and Michelle Bullock, to Flo Shepherd in contracts, and Sarah Goodey and Tom Han in Publishing Operations. Thank you to Anna Sikorska and Kate Oakley in Design and to Tom Keane, Halema Begum and Angie Dobbs in Production. In Sales, I'd like to thank Hannah Lismore, Fliss Porter, Georgina Green, Harriet Williams, Angela Thomson, Sara Eusebi and Lauren Trabucchi, and in Finance, Kelly Spells, Conor Anderson and Ashlee Cox.

Thank you to Alliya Bouyis, Lucy Richardson and Sophie Calder in Publicity and to Jo Kite in Marketing. Without all your talent and hard work, *The Secrets We Keep* would be so much less than it is.

Credit also has to go to my writers' group: Julia Armfield, Lisa Berry, Kate Bulpitt, Sarah Drinkwater, Tim Glencross, Kate Hamer, James Hannah, Stephen Jones, Julie Nuernberg, Ivan Salcedo, Emily Simpson and Annabelle Thorpe. It's a joy to share each and every one of your writers' journeys and I treasure your support and your laughter.

I'm forever grateful to my dad, Brian Wood, for having so much faith in me, and to my mum, Janet, who instilled in me a love of books at an early age; also my grandmother, Clara, whose name I've borrowed for one of my characters. I'm sorry you're not here to see your name in print, but I hope this novel would have made you proud.

Thanks to Claude, the impossible cat, for posing for all those pictures I've posted on Twitter. No doubt there will be more to come. Lastly, and most of all, thank you to Bill, for your love and for always being there. I couldn't have done this without you. x

Dear Reader,

We hope you enjoyed reading this book. If you did, we'd be so appreciative if you left a review. It really helps us and the author to bring more books like this to you.

Here at HQ Digital we are dedicated to publishing fiction that will keep you turning the pages into the early hours. Don't want to miss a thing? To find out more about our books, promotions, discover exclusive content and enter competitions you can keep in touch in the following ways:

JOIN OUR COMMUNITY:

Sign up to our new email newsletter:
http://smarturl.it/SignUpHQ

Read our new blog www.hqstories.co.uk

🐦 : https://twitter.com/HQStories

📘 : www.facebook.com/HQStories

BUDDING WRITER?

We're also looking for authors to join the HQ Digital family!
Find out more here:

https://www.hqstories.co.uk/want-to-write-for-us/

Thanks for reading, from the HQ Digital team